CRAZY LITTLE THING CALLED LOVE

Center Point
Large Print

Also by Beth K. Vogt and available from
Center Point Large Print:

Somebody Like You

**This Large Print Book carries the
Seal of Approval of N.A.V.H.**

CRAZY
LITTLE THING
CALLED
LOVE

BETH K. VOGT

CENTER POINT LARGE PRINT
THORNDIKE, MAINE

This Center Point Large Print edition
is published in the year 2015 by arrangement with
Howard Books, a division of Simon & Schuster, Inc.

Scripture taken from The Holy Bible, New International
Version®. Copyright © 1973, 1978, 1984 International Bible
Society. Used by permission of Zondervan. All rights reserved.

This book is a work of fiction. Any references to historical
events, real people, or real places are used fictitiously. Other
names, characters, places, and events are products of the
author's imagination, and any resemblance to actual events or
places or persons, living or dead, is entirely coincidental.

The text of this Large Print edition is unabridged.
In other aspects, this book may vary from the original edition.
Printed in the United States of America
on permanent paper.
Set in 16-point Times New Roman type.

ISBN: 978-1-62899-690-6

Library of Congress Cataloging-in-Publication Data

Vogt, Beth K.
 Crazy little thing called love : a destination wedding novel / Beth K.
Vogt. — Center Point Large Print edition.
 pages cm
 Summary: "Vanessa runs into her ex-husband from her what-was-she-
thinking teenage elopement while planning her destination wedding in
Destin, Florida. Unexpected feelings arise and force her to reconsider
what she thought was her biggest mistake and the possibility that God
has other plans for her"—Provided by publisher.
 ISBN 978-1-62899-690-6 (library binding : alk. paper)
 1. Large type books. I. Title.
 PS3622.O362C73 2015b
 813'.6—dc23
                                                    2015020459

For Sonia, Shari, and Mary,
my Preferred Readers:
Writing novels is easier
knowing the three of you have my back.
Just remember: I called "dibs" first!

Friends . . . they cherish one another's hopes. They are kind to one another's dreams.

—HENRY DAVID THOREAU (1817–1862), AMERICAN AUTHOR

ONE

What we once enjoyed we can never lose.
All that we love deeply becomes a part of us.
—HELEN KELLER (1880–1968),
AMERICAN AUTHOR

Thousands—even millions—of women had routine choose-a-church, select-a-dress, plan-a-reception kinds of weddings.

For some unknown reason, she was not one of those women.

Vanessa scanned the brochures spread out across the scarred top of her mission-style coffee table, her plate of Chinese beef and broccoli shoved to one corner. Photographs of white sandy beaches curving around sparkling oceans presented an enticing mirage for a destination wedding. And then she reread the list of medical workshops her husband-to-be would be attending two days after they exchanged *I do*'s.

TIAs AND STROKES: STATE OF THE ART APPROACH

ADVANCED AIRWAY ENDOSCOPY COURSE

HOT TOPICS IN PEDIATRIC EMERGENCIES

Not the typical themes for a honeymoon following a romantic destination wedding. She'd be lounging on a tropical beach, sipping a refreshing drink flavored with pineapple and coconut, adorned with a tiny paper umbrella. Meanwhile, Ted would be safe from the sun's rays, watching PowerPoint presentations, and earning Continuing Medical Education credits.

Ted leaned forward, shuffling through the pamphlets, his brow furrowed behind his silver wire-rim glasses, his dark hair flopping onto his forehead. With a well-practiced motion, he smoothed it back with the palm of his hand.

"Where's the one I'm looking for? Bahamas . . . Hawaii . . . Aha! Florida." He opened the trifold paper, laying it on top of all the other brochures with a flourish, as if he were presenting some previously undiscovered medical cure. "There. I know it's not as exotic as the other locations, but it offers the best selection of workshops for CMEs."

Vanessa took a sip of her soda, her glass of Coke flavored with a squeeze of real lemon carrying the punch of caffeine she needed. The "Knife and Gun Club" had been out in full force last night, and she'd seen familiar faces for the full twelve hours of her paramedic shift. Some of the same instigators who'd been at the bar brawl she'd reported to at the beginning of the evening also showed up at the subsequent knife fight in an alley and again at the shooting at one of the seedier Denver apartment complexes. After more than five years as a paramedic, she shouldn't be surprised by anything. And, most days, she wasn't.

She needed to concentrate, which was a challenge when all she wanted was to give in to her body's demand for sleep. Picking a destination-wedding site based on what medical conference to attend cued discordant background music in her mind—an off-key version of "Isn't It Romantic?" Vanessa understood the need to multitask, but was it necessary to coordinate their wedding with the needs of Ted's medical career?

"Can't we just stick with the original plan?" She indulged in a morsel of her seasoned beef before continuing. "Get married in our church here in Denver like we talked about? Keep things simple?"

"Don't you see how perfect this is?" Ted waved his chopsticks at the brochure, somehow managing to not drop any sauce on his chinos. "I'm always behind on my education credits. It's almost October, and look how I'm scrambling to get some before the end of the year."

"Well, yes." Vanessa resisted the urge to say, *Tell me something I don't know*. Both their schedules wreaked havoc on their romance. "But won't a destination wedding cost more than a local one?"

"I'm going to have to travel to a conference anyway, right? We'll kill two birds with one stone . . ."

Vanessa rubbed her temples, a few more notes of "Isn't It Romantic?" interrupting Ted's logic as his words lobbed a verbal rock at her wedding plans.

". . . combining the cost of the travel for the wedding and the conference. What's our projected guest list? About one hundred thirty people? Destination weddings are expected to be much smaller—even as few as thirty guests. And we don't pay their travel costs." Ted settled back on the couch, a smile spreading across his face. "What do you think, Nessa?"

This was one of the things she loved about Ted: he was practical. But sometimes maybe a little too practical. She leaned one elbow on the table, running her fingers through her hair, which she'd released from its customary braid. She stopped when the still-unfamiliar engagement ring snagged in the strands and twisted around her finger. The classic-cut round diamond set off on either side with six smaller diamonds was just a half-size too large. When would she find time to get it resized? She was either on the clock for four days straight, or off—and recovering. Trying to sleep or catch up on paying bills, maybe clean her apartment, while checking her in-box to see if she'd received any response to her applications to physician assistant school.

And now she was planning a wedding. Or rather, replanning a wedding.

"I guess it makes sense—"

"Of course it does." Ted reached for his water, draining the last of the liquid from the bottle. "Our schedules are crazy, and I don't want to be behind on CME next year, too. By planning the wedding for the April conference, I'm getting a jump start on credits."

Brilliant. A bit lacking in the relationship category, but she hadn't fallen in love with Ted because of the way he'd swept her off her feet with flowers and chocolates and Hallmark cards. Unlike their adrenaline-fueled jobs, the pace of their romance had been slow, Ted's patience enabling their friendship to ease into a love that would last through whatever the future held for them.

"So where in Florida is this meeting?"

"It's in the Panhandle, I think." Ted flipped the colored flyer over. "Let's see . . . oh, that's right. Destin. We'd fly from Denver into Atlanta and then—"

Destin?

No.

Vanessa stiffened as if she were in the middle of a childhood game of freeze tag. Ted's verbal "touch" dragged her into the past and turned her into an ice sculpture. She needed to tell Ted no . . . and no . . . and no. But she needed to be able to breathe to form words.

As if in slow motion, she curled her fingers into fists. Forced one inhale. One exhale. Her gaze landed on the potted philodendron, wilted from neglect, which sat on her dining room table. What had the well-meaning ER nurse said when she'd handed Vanessa the plant for her birthday months ago? *"Everyone needs a plant or two in their home—and it's almost impossible to kill a philodendron."* Imagine that—she'd performed the impossible.

Vanessa twisted around to face Ted where he sat on the couch, popping a piece of spicy shrimp into his mouth.

"We need to pick another medical conference. Another location."

"But this is the best one."

Vanessa tapped her fist against her mouth. She was only going to say this once. Once would be enough. "Ted, I was married before, remember? In Florida? And Destin is near where I lived— where I was married." Vanessa moved aside the top brochure and studied the others. Ted would understand. He always did. Maybe they could plan a nice destination wedding on a beach overshadowed by a dormant volcano? "Let's find another conference location for our destination wedding—"

"Is that all that's bothering you?" Ted interrupted her, reaching down to pull her away from the coffee table and up onto the couch with him, ignoring how the pamphlets scattered onto the floor. "Nessa, that was years ago. You're not that impulsive teenager anymore. You're a grown woman, in love with me. You don't have to be afraid of your past."

"I'm not *afraid* of my past." She maintained eye

contact. Kept her voice level. See? She was calm. "I just prefer not to have a second wedding in Florida."

"Babe, you haven't told me a lot about what happened, but I know it was some kind of shotgun wedding—"

Vanessa pushed away from him. "Not *shotgun*. I wasn't pregnant!"

"Sorry. Wrong word choice. I meant *whirlwind*. Crazy. Look, I don't care about your first marriage. We're having a real wedding this time." Tugging her back into his arms, he kissed the top of her head. "Don't you see how even more perfect this will be? You go back to Florida and have the wedding you always wanted. We'll go down a few days early with the wedding party and a few close friends and family and do some fun things. Snorkel. Parasail. Whatever you want. Have a one-of-a-kind wedding—our wedding."

Vanessa settled against Ted's shoulder, snuggling closer as his arm wrapped around her waist, and inhaled the faint musky scent of his aftershave. Listening to Ted, she could just begin to imagine going back to Destin. To get married. Again.

"I haven't been to Florida in years—not since I left for college, really. Well, except for my brother's high school graduation. And occasional holidays." But how could she explain to him that she'd never made time to drive over the Mid-Bay Bridge, to walk along the beach in Destin? That yes, she was afraid of ghosts. Specifically, of one particular ghost she might see when she strolled along the shore.

Could she do it?

"Trust me, Nessa."

Wasn't that exactly why she was marrying Ted? Because she trusted him enough to say yes when he proposed?

"Maybe you're right." She picked the medical brochure up off the floor and gazed at the tranquil photo of white sandy beaches again. "*Where* we marry isn't the most important thing—it's *who* we marry. And who we are when we get married."

"Exactly."

But could she do it?

She'd been an immature eighteen-year-old girl reacting to circumstances the first time she said, "I do." Now? She was twenty-eight. She knew who she was. What she wanted. Why she was getting married—and whom she was marrying.

There was nothing rash about marrying Ted. Nothing at all.

"And if I get in a few CME credit hours, all the better." Ted sounded as if it were all decided. "I won't be in classes all day. We can walk along the beach, ride Jet Skis, eat at some nice restaurants. Destin will be a great place to honeymoon."

Vanessa chose to focus on the "it'll be a great place to honeymoon" part of Ted's comment. "When's the conference?"

"The first week in April."

A little more than six months from now. Absolutely doable. "We'll have to cut down the guest list."

"Saving money, remember?"

Vanessa swallowed her groan, chasing it with a gulp of her lemony cola. Ted wasn't turning their wedding into a low-budget bridal event. She'd already gone that route once—her first wedding had cost less than a hundred dollars, including the motel room. She was all for practicality, but her parents had provided them a generous budget. They could afford a few splurges.

"Ted, I'm agreeing to combine the wedding with your conference. But, like you said, this is my chance—our chance—to have the wedding we want. So, yes, it will be small. Probably no more than thirty or forty guests. But I want our wedding to be beautiful. Elegant."

"Absolutely, babe. I want you to be happy. I'll handle the conference registration, but before I do, why don't you call the hotel—" He circled the phone number with ink. "—and make certain they can accommodate a small wedding? Wait a minute . . ."

"What? What are you thinking?"

Ted tapped the end of the pen against his chin. "Don't you have a vacation week coming up?"

"Ye-es. I have the week after next off. To relax. *R-e-l-a-x.*"

"This is perfect. You can fly down to Destin and talk to the wedding coordinator face-to-face. Check out florists . . ."

Of course his plan sounded perfect to him—he'd be back here triaging emergencies in the ER while she hopped on a plane and handled the wedding details on her own, all the while dodging her past.

"I'll think about it." She forced a smile, hoping she looked like a happy bride-to-be, eager to plan their wedding. "Let's keep making a list. What else?"

"Invitations—and maybe those things they do nowadays . . ."

Vanessa scrawled a numbered list on the back of the take-out receipt from the Chinese restaurant. "Save-the-date announcements?"

"Yes, those."

Vanessa wrote down the number three and circled it. "I also want to do engagement photos."

"Engagement photos? How expensive are those?"

"Ted, you cannot ask 'How much?' every time we talk about wedding details. Most photographers have wedding packages, and engagement photos are included. I'll look into it. And—" She held up her hand, fending off his next question. "—I'll outline a basic budget, okay?"

"I was going to ask if you think the photographer would come to the hospital and take photos of us there."

Vanessa dropped the list, pushing away from

Ted, gathering up their plates and disposable chopsticks. "Not funny."

"Who said I was kidding?" Once in the kitchen, Ted leaned against the white tile counter while she rinsed the dishes under scalding hot water and loaded them into the stainless steel dishwasher. "I'm not saying we have to wear scrubs. But you've got to admit the hospital is our life. We could get a picture by the ambulance or the nurses' station. It'd be fun."

Proof that she needed to let go of the idea of a normal wedding. Again. But was this worth fighting about? Probably not. After all, marriage was about compromise, right? Planning the wedding was giving her plenty of opportunity to practice. Creative engagement photos, check. "I'll see what I can do."

Ted bent to open the cabinet beneath the sink, talking over his shoulder. "So, with a small wedding, we'll both have just one person in the wedding party, right? I'll have a best man, and you'll have a maid of honor."

"Sure." Even the simplest of weddings were complicated—not that she hadn't learned that inescapable truth years ago. Now to figure out who could be her bridal attendant. Somebody. *Anybody.*

Nobody.

She retrieved another can of soda and a slice of precut lemon from her container in the fridge, along with a bottle of water for Ted. "Why don't we skip the whole best-man-for-you, maid-of-honor-for-me tradition?"

"Really?" Ted looked up from loading soap into the dishwasher. "I should ask my brother to be my best man. Tradition, right?"

"Oh." Right. Tradition. Vanessa shrugged. "I'm sure I can think of someone."

Because, somehow, some way, getting married for the second time would be easier than the first. It had to be—even if she had to hire someone to be her maid of honor.

TWO

We cannot change our past. We cannot change the fact that people act a certain way. We cannot change the inevitable. The only thing we can do is play on the one string we have, and that is our attitude.
—CHARLES R. SWINDOLL (1934–),
PASTOR AND AUTHOR

Vanessa should call Ted. Insist the whole Florida-destination-wedding-and-medical-conference idea wasn't going to happen. She hadn't even packed for the trip—the one he'd talked her into that sacrificed her time off—and her flight to Florida left in less than twelve hours. All hopes for a relaxing week of vacation vanished the moment she told Ted yes. Yes, she'd go to Destin and plan their wedding.

Back to her past to plan her future.

God knew she didn't go backward. Life was all about moving on to the next thing in front of her. No looking back. Because what was the use of that? It seemed as if by saying yes to Ted's "Will you marry me?" her life had spun out of control.

The first thing she needed to do was laundry. She needed clean uniforms waiting for her when she got back to Denver and had to go to work. Then she needed to pack for her six a.m. flight. And she should probably toss a little water on the philodendron. Pray it survived until she got back. Even if she asked Ted to water it while she was gone, he wouldn't remember.

The hours to sleep between now and her departure were getting fewer.

Vanessa could have skipped going to see the Ackermans. But then she would have worried about them all week. Wondered if Anna had any money to buy groceries or if her husband had spent his paycheck on beer and cigarettes and lottery tickets and who knew what else. And if they didn't have groceries, then the baby wouldn't have diapers. And with no family living nearby, who was going to help them?

Of course, some might say the Ackermans weren't her concern. Yes, Vanessa had been working a year ago when Anna called 911 because her then-thirteen-month-old son was in respiratory distress from a croup attack, but that didn't mean Vanessa had to worry about them now.

But she did.

Something about the woman reminded Vanessa of herself. Maybe it was because Anna was new in town. No family. No friends.

She wasn't Anna's friend. Not exactly. She was only checking in.

Besides, while she shopped for groceries earlier tonight and then sat in Anna's small apartment with its few pieces of rented furniture, she didn't think about arriving in Florida . . . crossing the Mid-Bay Bridge . . . seeing Destin again, much less fine-tuning the details of her destination wedding. All of that had taken a backseat while she made a little boy laugh.

But now she had to make up for lost time. Vanessa sidestepped the laundry hamper in her walk-in closet. If she wasn't careful, she'd trip. Break an ankle. And miss her flight. No, she was not going to inflict bodily harm on herself to avoid this trip. But how had she let Ted convince her to take her week's vacation—her chance to do nothing—and fly to Florida to meet with a wedding coordinator? Florists. Caterers.

And the ghost of a wedding past.

No matter how many times she assured Ted that all the particulars could be managed long-distance, he vetoed her idea.

"You said it yourself, Vanessa. You want a beautiful, elegant wedding. And I want you to have all that—and more." He gave her one of his reserved kisses—the kind that created a slight warmth in her heart without demanding she lower the barrier she'd erected there years ago. "And while you're gone, I'll have your ring resized. It'll be waiting for you when you get back home."

Backed into a corner by her own proclamation —and a caring, considerate fiancé.

She found her glass of Coke chased with a liberal

squeeze of lemon sitting on the top shelf in her closet, diluted by melted ice. What was this, her third or fourth jolt of caffeine?

Just what she needed to spike both her stress and sugar levels. Between the soda overload and the lack of sleep, she'd be a jittery wreck when she went through security. The TSA agents would pull her out of line so fast . . .

But just in case she *did* make it all the way to Florida, she needed to pack. Vanessa rubbed her hands along the bottom of her I'M A PARAMEDIC. WHAT'S YOUR SUPERPOWER? T-shirt. At least she didn't have to pack any uniforms. Vacations were times to wear "real" clothes.

Boots first.

She'd need two—no, three—pairs. Her well-worn low-cut blue pair with a dusting of gold, and then her old reliable brown burnished-leather boots with harness-ring accents, and another pair of tan low boots with lacy accents.

Time to turn her back on the rest of her boot collection or she'd be hauling an entire suitcase full of her addiction.

Within thirty minutes she'd scrounged together two pairs of boot-cut jeans, a red-striped pullover, a coral sleeveless tank, her brown eyelet dress, and her Pemberley-style blouse, along with the needed underwear and socks and her comfortable pair of red Merrell tennis shoes.

She stared at the pile of clothes on the floor of her closet. She needed a suitcase . . . a Windbreaker . . . and at least one pair of shorts. Her Teva sandals. She was going to the beach, right? Yes, she was. It was still warm in Destin in early October. And even if she had to walk along the shore from dawn to dusk, she would put her past to rest so she could embrace everything waiting for her.

When she pulled her rolling suitcase from the top shelf of her closet it hit the floor with a thud, barely missing her bare toes.

"Okay, I don't really want to go back to the hospital anytime soon . . ."

Now, where were her Tevas? Probably in the hall closet with her Windbreaker.

She grabbed her glass of watery Coke. She could refresh her drink and pass by the hall closet on the way back to her room. If she kept up this level of efficiency, she'd be packed before midnight.

Vanessa dumped the liquid down the sink, stretching and twisting as she walked to the fridge. Aha! Her iPhone lay on the kitchen counter— probably forgotten after she'd texted Ted while getting more ice and soda. Had he replied?

No text—but there were three missed calls from her mother.

Why would her mother call her multiple times in one night?

As she hit redial, Vanessa popped open a can of soda, the cool liquid easing her dry throat.

"Vanessa?" Her mother's voice came across the phone like a zing of electricity.

"Hey, Mom. Sorry I missed your phone calls—"

"Vanessa, where were you? I've tried and tried to call you!"

"I'm sorry." Vanessa's fingers tightened around the soda can. "I was in my closet—my bedroom—packing for a trip. What's going on? What's wrong?"

"Your father . . . he had a heart attack . . ."

Vanessa closed her eyes, the words rooting her bare feet to the floor. She needed to stay calm. Assess the situation. Ask the most important question. "What's his condition now? Is he—"

"He's alive. He's in the cardiac-care unit at Benefis Hospital."

She leaned back against the kitchen counter, easing her grip on the can. "What happened?"

"We went out to dinner—your father wanted steak and a baked potato—"

"Mom, I don't want a rundown on what Dad ate."

"I'm sorry." A shaky inhale interrupted her mother's words. "He started having some indigestion—he's complained of heartburn a lot lately. I gave him some antacids. It didn't help, so we were going to head home. But then he said this was worse than any heartburn he had before. And his left arm started hurting. So I told him I'd take him to the hospital."

"Mother! Why didn't you call nine-one-one?"

"I didn't think your father was actually having a heart attack, Vanessa! He's had heartburn for years." Now her mother sounded like her normal self. "But as soon as we got to the ER, they took him right back—so I guess they were concerned."

Of course they were.

"After that . . . well, I can't even remember everything that happened. The cardiologist showed up within thirty minutes, and they wheeled your father away on a stretcher—to have a heart catheterization done."

"Okay, Mom." Vanessa closed her eyes, pressing the cold metal of the Coke can against her forehead. "What's going on right now?"

"I'm outside your father's room in the cardiac-care unit. He's sleeping—it's not surprising, since they sedated him. The doctor said they were able to open the artery back up and get blood flow back to the heart muscle. But apparently that causes other problems—I didn't understand everything . . ."

"Sometimes reperfusing the heart—I mean, restoring blood flow to the heart muscle—can cause it to have more irregular heartbeats."

"The cardiologist is going to come talk with me more in the morning. I'm going to stay tonight—there's a recliner I can sleep in."

"Have you talked to Rylan?"

"No, not yet. It's the middle of the night in Germany."

"That doesn't matter. He's going to want to

know about Dad. I'll call him." Vanessa paced the kitchen. "Okay. Let me think. I have a flight out of DIA tomorrow to Destin. I'll work on getting that switched—"

"Destin? Why are you flying to Destin?"

Even in the midst of a medical crisis, her mother didn't miss a thing.

"I, uh, I had some vacation time. I'm going to see Mindy—you remember her, right? We were friends in high school and college."

There. She hadn't lied to her mother. She was going to see Mindy—she just needed to call Mindy and say, *Surprise! I'm coming to town.* Announce she was getting married. And then ask Mindy to be her matron of honor.

That was going to be an easy conversation.

"Mom, it's not important what I was doing—I'll change my flight and get to Montana as soon as I can."

"Vanessa, why don't we wait? Let me call you after I talk to the cardiologist in the morning."

"No, Mom. This is not the time to wait." Vanessa headed for her bedroom. She'd need to add a few more clothes to her suitcase. "You go get some rest. I'll call Rylan. Then I'll work on changing my flight. I'll see you tomorrow—as soon as I can get there."

If she didn't keep walking, she'd collapse on her parents' couch right there in the immaculate living room and sleep for the next twenty-four hours.

The cuckoo clock, the one her father took hours selecting one Saturday afternoon in Germany, sounded the half hour. The notes of "It's a Small World" were familiar. Comforting. If Vanessa closed her eyes, she could imagine the little figure of a man chopping wood . . . the cuckoo bird that would appear at the top of every hour . . .

Had she dozed off standing up?

"All things considered, a good day, Mom." Vanessa opened her eyes and realized she stood at the foot of the stairs leading to the upstairs bedrooms. "The nurses I talked to say Dad's cardiologist is one of the best. Very knowledgeable and compassionate."

"I like him." Her mother hung her navy blue coat up in the hall closet.

"I wouldn't say that's all that matters, but it's nice to know the other medical staff respect him, too." Vanessa pulled her suitcase behind her, causing it to bump against her heels as she ascended each carpeted step. "First bedroom on the right at the top of the stairs, correct?"

"Yes. I'm sorry I didn't have a chance to change the sheets." Her mother followed behind her.

"Not important." She probably wouldn't even pull the bedspread back. Just fall across the mattress, still fully clothed. And sleep.

But the gallery of family photos lining the wall on her right caused her to stop on the landing. The

Hollister family, caught in dozens of photographic freeze frames. School photos where she and Rylan smiled for the unknown man behind the camera, growing up year-after-picture-perfect-year. Her father's air force promotion photos—another reason to assemble the family in their best clothes and best smiles. Family vacation montages interspersed with artwork from around the world, compliments of Uncle Sam's decision to move them every two to three years.

"Do you need anything?"

Vanessa startled at the sound of her mother's voice right behind her. "No. Once I manage to get up these stairs I'm going to drag myself to bed."

"I'll get you some towels—"

"It's okay, Mom. It can wait until tomorrow."

But in typical she'd-do-what-needed-to-be-done-no-matter-what fashion, her mother bustled past her. She headed straight to the linen closet, which was organized with baskets and plastic bins, leaving behind the faint scent of her rich floral perfume. White Diamonds. Her father bought her a bottle every Christmas.

Thank you, God, that he'll be here to carry on the tradition this year, too.

The guest bedroom was painted a soft Wedgwood blue, the queen bed covered in a Mariner's Compass quilt in rich blues and white. How did her mother have the patience to craft such stunning hand-stitched works of art? The bed in each of the four bedrooms boasted a handmade quilt—and who knew how many her mother had given as wedding gifts? Most likely her mother had started working on one the minute she found out Vanessa and Ted were engaged.

Vanessa set her suitcase just inside the door beside the antique white dresser cluttered with . . . two medium-sized packing boxes?

Why were the cardboard boxes in here, reflecting in the oval mirror? Her mother didn't do disorder, and brown boxes were hardly part of the room's décor.

"Here you go." Her mother bustled into the room like the hostess at a bed-and-breakfast. "Fresh towels—and I brought you a spare robe, just in case you didn't pack one."

"Thanks." Vanessa motioned to the boxes. "Um, do you want me to move these?"

"Hmmm?" Her mother stopped pulling back the quilt. "Move what? Oh, no. Those are yours."

"The boxes are mine?" Vanessa ran her hand over the surface of one of the boxes, the packing tape rough beneath her fingers. "What do you mean?"

"Just what I said. Your father and I were going through things stored in the basement, and we found those. They have your name on them. Since you're here, I thought I'd ask you what you want me to do with them."

Since she was here—because her father had a

heart attack. Turning the box around, Vanessa read VANESSA HOLLISTER, 2004 scrawled in black marker across the side.

How had she forgotten about these?

"You're not going to open those now, are you?" Her mother was plumping the pillows. "It's late, and you have to go pick Rylan up at the airport at nine tomorrow—"

Did she want to play the part of some modern-day Pandora, opening not one, but two boxes best left alone? Vanessa closed her eyes, imagining the contents, realizing that knowing what was inside them wouldn't diminish the pain when—*if*—she looked at the contents.

"No. No, I won't open the boxes tonight. You're right. We both need to get some sleep."

But an hour later, Vanessa sat cross-legged on the bed. Wide awake. Both boxes set in front of her on top of the quilt like unwanted birthday gifts— socks, maybe, or hand-me-downs that you knew weren't your size or style.

Vanessa braided her hair, threading her fingers in and out of the wet strands. She shouldn't have indulged in a hot shower. Yes, it had rinsed away the tension of her flight and the few hours she'd spent at the hospital. Watching her father sleep. Evaluating his skin color. His heartbeat. His respiration. Talking to his cardiologist. But now she was awake, and the contents of the boxes demanded her attention like an open bag of potato chips.

Vanessa's faint laugh slipped into the silence of the room as she pulled the larger box closer. It was nice to know she still had some sense of humor, because there was nothing funny about opening either of the cartons. Doing so would only unleash the power of her past . . .

And now she was being ridiculous.

Nothing . . . absolutely nothing . . . had that kind of hold on her. The past couldn't hurt her anymore. And she'd prove that truth to herself by dealing with the boxes. Then she'd go to Florida two days from now and march up and down the shoreline of Destin until she made it so. And the next time she set foot on the white sands of the Emerald Coast she'd be walking toward Ted, prepared to say, "I do."

Besides her name, one simple word identified the contents: FIGURINES.

"Logan . . ."

So many questions wrapped around his name, stained with tears and laughter. Years ago, she'd thought it best not to ask them. Or maybe she thought she knew all the answers. And then she'd abandoned everything. Walked away from both the questions left unanswered and the ones that were answered all wrong.

What had he been thinking, starting her a collection of delicate figurines? He knew she didn't collect things. Too many moves had taught her it was better to stick to the essentials. Clothes.

Shoes. Even books by her favorite authors could be checked out of the library and returned.

The worn packing tape tore easily, the top of the box lifting back to reveal a layer of crumpled white tissue paper. Vanessa pressed her fingers into the softness, probing for . . . there! Her fingers touched the sculpted outline of a figurine. But which one? Unwrapping several more layers of paper, she revealed a graceful lady with ginger curls in a green gown and black gloves, seeming to sway in a half-curtsy. A birthday gift from Logan. Next, she uncovered a woman dressed all in white, except for the red ribbons tying her bonnet. The very first Royal Doulton figurine Logan had given her—and which had once belonged to his grandmother.

Enough.

Vanessa rewrapped the two statuettes. Four more remained in the box, each just as delicate, as lovely. Each a gift from Logan.

She closed the box, moving it aside. Her mother could mail this box back to her, and Vanessa would pay her for shipping and insurance.

On to box number two.

The flaps weren't even taped together, merely folded in on one another. What had she cared so little about that she hadn't even sealed the box . . . ?

A shimmer of purple covered the top layer.

Her homecoming dress.

"I'll get my dad's car—no riding the motorcycle that night."

Her fingertips grazed the simple bodice of the gown, Logan's voice whispering through the room.

Underneath lay a white T-shirt emblazoned with the words CLASS OF 2004 and the still-vivid air-brushed image of a sunset over Pensacola Beach.

Spring break.

Her Niceville High School yearbook and maroon graduation cap, the gold tassel still in place.

A framed photo of her, sitting astride Logan's silver and red motorcycle, a ridiculous grin on her face, her helmet tucked in the crook of her arm, taken the first day she'd mastered the controls and succeeded in driving around the school parking lot.

Oh, how her parents had lectured her about being all kinds of reckless when they'd found out about her motorcycle lessons.

What else?

Her journal.

She pressed the brown leather book to her heart. Had she really forgotten about that? How she used to scribble her thoughts . . . hopes . . . dreams? She hadn't journaled a single word in years. No longer browsed the store aisles trying to find just the right notebook to use, examining covers and pages. Selecting the perfect pens.

Setting the journal aside, Vanessa found a small cherrywood box underneath everything else. She knew what she'd see once she released the latch. Two rings: Logan's larger class ring—white gold with a ruby-colored stone—resting next to the plain white-gold band he'd bought for her a few days after they were married.

She held up the class ring, twisting it around in the light, noticing again how Logan's initials— LH—were etched inside in basic block print.

The trill of her iPhone shattered the silence, causing her to jump and drop the box and rings onto the bed. She scrambled, reaching for her phone where it lay on the bedside table.

"Hello?"

"Hey, babe." Ted matched her whisper. "Did I wake you?"

She collapsed against the pillows, her hand seeking and finding the rings. "No, no—I'm awake. Having a hard time unwinding."

"That's what I figured—so I thought I'd call. Check in on you. How's your father?"

"Overall, doing well. He's sleeping, so I convinced my mother to come home with me and rest in her bed tonight. Rylan flies in tomorrow. I'll stay another day or two and then head to Destin. I won't have a whole week to plan for the wedding."

"Why not? You've got at least two months of untouched vacation. Talk to Gary. Ask him for more time off."

"I don't know—"

"Vanessa, you're not the only paramedic in Denver. This is our wedding. Beautiful and elegant, remember?"

Was Ted going to make her regret speaking those words out loud?

"Fine." She stared at the ceiling, shifting against the pillows. "I'll talk to Gary tomorrow and see if I can extend my time off."

"I miss you, babe."

Vanessa unclenched her fist, allowing the rings to fall onto the quilt. "I miss you, too."

"Listen, I know you're exhausted. Try to get some sleep. When you get to Florida, take some time to lie out on the beach and relax—don't make it all about the wedding, okay?"

"Ted, the whole reason I'm going down there is to plan our wedding—"

"You know what I mean. Have some fun. Go get a pedicure or something with Mindy—"

"Right."

"Go out to eat. What's that fish you mentioned—the one you can only get down there?"

"Amberjack?" Vanessa thought of asking Ted where he was in his apartment. Sitting on the couch, maybe? Or in bed?

No. She couldn't imagine Ted in anything more—or less—than his scrubs and a white medical jacket. At work.

"That's it. Go out to eat and order amberjack. Got it?"

Vanessa nodded. "Yessir."

"And eat some hush puppies for me."

She couldn't hold back a laugh. "Absolutely."

"Now get some sleep. I love you."

"Love you, too. G'night."

Vanessa scrolled through the camera roll on her iPhone, the various photos of Ted causing her lips to curve into a smile. He was a good man—a competent ER doc, an avid Broncos football fan like she was, a man who understood her introvert's need for space.

Why was she sifting through this box from her past when so much good waited for her in the future—waited for her now?

Time to get some sleep.

But first . . .

Vanessa gathered up the homecoming dress, the T-shirt, the framed photo, and the graduation cap and tassel. A quick trip to her parents' garage to toss them in the trash can and . . . done. She had no need for them. Why had she ever thought she would?

She wiped her hands on her flannel pajama top as she walked back upstairs and made a mental list.

She'd mail the figurines herself on the way to pick up her brother at the airport. Her mother had enough to do—and she'd avoid any questions. Not that she had to explain herself to her mother anymore.

The rest of it—the yearbook, the journal—were easy enough to toss into her carry-on bag. She might want to show her kids her high school yearbook one day. And she couldn't convince herself to throw away her old journal, even if she never read it again. There was something wrong about throwing away handwritten memories.

But she couldn't leave Logan's class ring here, and she couldn't ask her mother to deal with it. Throwing the ring away seemed wrong somehow. Even though Logan had never asked her to return it, the ring still belonged to him.

Vanessa reopened the box containing the figurines, slipping Logan's class ring and her wedding band into the folds of the tissue paper. She'd figure out what to do with both of the rings later.

THREE

True friendship is a plant of slow growth.
—GEORGE WASHINGTON (1732–1799),
FIRST PRESIDENT OF THE UNITED STATES

The Florida air mugged Vanessa in an unwelcome hug as she exited the Fort Walton Beach airport terminal and made her way to the waiting rental car. Even as the days eased into the first week of October and the temperature hovered in the low seventies, humidity refused to release its grip on the Panhandle.

Vanessa stowed her brilliant green, hard-sided suitcase in the trunk and placed her laptop satchel and teal leather purse in the front passenger seat. Then she settled behind the steering wheel, cranking up the air-conditioning and tuning the radio station but leaving the car in park.

Time to point her car east and head toward Destin.

Or . . . first she could call Ted and let him know she'd arrived. He was working, but he'd be checking his phone for a voice mail or text. She wasn't truly stalling if she was calling her fiancé, right?

When the phone rolled to his voice mail, as she expected, Vanessa adjusted the seat as she spoke.

"Hi . . . Ted." She rolled her eyes at herself in the rearview mirror. Why wasn't she one of those women who did nicknames? She couldn't imagine herself calling Ted "honey" or "sweetheart" or some other syrupy term of affection. Ted called her "babe," which was . . . fine. But she just didn't do pet names. "I'm in Florida. The flight was fine. Uneventful. I even got a full can of soda. So, yeah. I'll call you later once I'm all settled at the hotel. Love you."

And that had taken less than one minute.

It was too early to call her mother or brother to ask for an update on her father. She'd hugged Rylan goodbye less than four hours ago. Vanessa stared at the keypad of her cell phone, thinking of the folded sheet of yellow legal-sized paper in her laptop case labeled "Wedding To-Do List." One item near the top was "CALL MINDY."

"I can do that."

Her casual assurance to Ted that she'd ask Mindy to be her matron of honor came back to mock her.

Ted was right, of course. He should ask his brother to be his best man. Which meant she needed a maid—or matron—of honor. But her "I can do that" statement implied she had a friend to ask, when all she really had were business colleagues. Church acquaintances.

And Mindy.

Mindy, the closest thing she had to a friend—if they both overlooked Vanessa's abysmal ability to maintain a relationship. Yes, they were friends during their senior year of high school only because Mindy pursued her as a friend. And because they roomed together in college, because, well, that's how it worked out. And because Mindy sent Christmas cards, ignoring the fact that Vanessa didn't do Christmas cards. Or birthday cards. Or Facebook. Or phone calls.

Yes, Mindy was her friend. But Vanessa could never say she was Mindy's friend without stumbling over the word.

Still, she was here to plan her destination wedding, and she needed help making that happen. Mindy had always been there for her. And, knowing Mindy, she'd be there for her again on the other side of the yawning chasm of silence that had become their relationship since college.

Please, God, let this wedding come together without too much drama. And please help me convince Mindy to be my matron of honor a lot faster than I've been able to convince myself to call her and ask her.

Maybe she and Mindy could manage a pedicure, too. Something normal girlfriends did together. Something relaxing.

All she had to do was make a phone call.

Mindy answered the phone before the second ring ended, as if she'd been expecting Vanessa's call for the past eight years.

"Hello?"

"Hey, Mindy—it's Vanessa. Vanessa Hollister." Vanessa fisted her hand against the steering wheel, staring at the palm trees surrounding the parking lot that didn't quite hide the view of construction along the road outside the airport.

"Vanessa? Oh, my gosh! I can't believe you're calling me! How are you?"

"Good. I mean . . . I'm good." Vanessa cranked up the air-conditioning a bit more, adjusting the vents. "And surprise! I happen to be in Florida—at the airport in Fort Walton, to be exact."

"You're here?" Mindy's voice pitched higher.

"Yes. I'm sorry I didn't call sooner. I was supposed to be here last week." Not that she'd have called Mindy before then, either. "But then my dad had a heart attack—"

"What? Vanessa—is he okay?"

"Yes. I mean, it was bad, but he's recovering. He's home now, and my brother is in Montana with my mom."

"Isn't Rylan stationed overseas?"

"Yes—Germany. How'd you know that?"

"Facebook is an amazing thing—that and Google Plus. And Rylan posts lots of photos on Instagram."

Imagine that. She really ought to get online more often.

"Anyway, I had some vacation time and decided to come to Destin." Vanessa stared straight ahead, watching a mother and father, loaded down with

43

luggage, herd their three backpack-toting young children and make their way to a rental van. "I got a little delayed, but now that my dad's doing better, my boss okayed another week off, so here I am. I thought maybe we could meet for lunch."

"I would love to! How about you come to my house?"

"Oh, Mindy, I don't want to put you out. I could treat you to lunch—"

"Absolutely not. This is so much easier. How about tomorrow? Is that too soon? Eleven o'clock?"

Vanessa considered her day. She was seeing the hotel wedding coordinator in the morning, so lunch should work. "That's great. Remind me where you and—" Her mind went blank. She couldn't remember Mindy's husband's name. Oh, this was awful!

"Jett."

"Sorry. Jett. Tell me where you live, and I'll be there at eleven."

After confirming the information, she tossed her cell phone into her purse, sliding her seat belt into place.

Now to conquer the Mid-Bay Bridge. Pay a toll. Cross a bridge. Check into her hotel. And then decide if she wanted to go for a walk along the beach.

A purely optional activity.

Deep breath. She had one more chance to ease

into the past with a slow drive through Niceville.

The town had changed. Of course it had. Nothing and no one stayed the same. She managed to keep her eyes on the road instead of looking left and right, noticing all the new restaurants that had appeared but how the Dairy Queen still anchored the center of town. How so many grocery stores and retail stores—even a Publix—had been built in the years since the Mid-Bay Bridge opened, and residents no longer had to take the circuitous, forty-five-minute drive to the Gulf beaches in Fort Walton.

The bridge.

Vanessa pressed two fingertips against her left temple. The traces of a dream she'd had the night before she flew to Montana fluttered at the edge of her mind like a tattered curtain in the window of an abandoned house.

What was it? She'd been . . . walking across the Mid-Bay Bridge. No cars traveling in either direction. It was dark . . . the middle of the night, maybe? . . . and the far end of the bridge was shrouded in fog.

And then what?

She'd been sitting on the edge of the bridge . . . looking down at the Choctawhatchee Bay, trying to see the water . . . someone yelled, "Jump, Vanessa!"

And then the bridge started to crumble beneath her . . .

She shook her head, scattering the memory. It was just a dream . . . just a dream.

She could do this. Brave the bridge again . . . cross over the expanse of sparkling waters. Park the car and leave her shoes near one of the dunes. Walk along the sand, just close enough for the waves to play tag with her toes.

Yes, this trip conjured up memories she'd tried her best to leave behind. Would an invisible companion walk alongside her, reminding her that this was his favorite place to be, wanting to discuss past choices, past mistakes? Well, she had a week to confront him and then leave him behind for good.

Vanessa blinked her eyes against the sunlight streaming into the car. How had she forgotten to put on her sunglasses? With one hand on the steering wheel, she used the other to dig around in her purse, finding them between her wallet and her change purse, slipping them on so that the world faded to a calmer hue.

This was how she needed to get through this week. Surrounded by a protective layer that prevented her heart from getting scorched. Focus on the wedding—her future—and keep the memories of the past from overwhelming her.

As dusk settled over the Emerald Coast of Florida, shadows stretched out across the white sand that formed into dunes topped by feathery sea oats, muting the vibrant colors of the water that transitioned from a pale blue to turquoise to deep green.

"You ever get tired of coming here?"

Brady's question interrupted Logan's musings—unwanted conversation when what he liked to do best was walk along the shore and *not* talk. Just because they'd been together since Logan had first brainstormed about forming a storm-chasing team didn't mean Brady had to dog his heels when Logan walked the beach in search of some elusive serenity.

"I mean, you grew up here—"

"That doesn't make me love it any less." After graduating from college, he came back to Destin every October like a pilgrim on a journey to a seaside mecca. No better way to shake off months of storm chasing. "We all love what we do, but eating fast food and sleeping in motels while we wait on storms and try to gather data gets old."

And the near-disaster that marred this past season on the run in Tornado Alley still scraped his emotions raw. The reality that they had all survived did nothing to appease the memories that woke him up too many nights—and kept him pacing his apartment until his alarm sounded on his cell phone.

Logan scraped the palm of his hand down his face. When he was awake, he knew Max was alive, rehabbing his way back to normal. When he fell asleep, too often his mind subjected him to instant replays. He hadn't battled nightmares in years—not since high school—but now he found excuses to stay up late.

"Of course, I'm not complaining about sun and surf and all the seafood Max can eat." Brady's nudge sent Logan closer to the waves, the warmth of the water still bearing the hint of the summer just past.

"You got that right. And Julie's managed to work on a tan, so she's happy."

"And then it's back to Oklahoma—processing data, looking at grants for next season."

If they still had grants for their work. Not that Brady needed to know about the emails and phone calls he'd been fending off for the last few months. Logan shoved his hands in the pockets of his cargo shorts. "Same old, same old."

"You don't sound excited, boss."

Logan scanned the sky as it darkened to purple, the sun dipping along the horizon. Now was not the time to talk about the future—and what the future held for them in Oklahoma. That was a conversation for the whole team.

The waves nipped at his feet as he continued along the shore. He also couldn't explain how, while he came here to relax, all of this reminded him of a loss he regretted no matter how many years distanced him from then and now.

And yet he came back, year after year, willing to taste the bitter for just a sip of the sweet.

The sand, still warm from the day's sunshine, squelched beneath his bare feet. Only a few people remained on the beach. A family shored up the sides of an elaborate sand castle, their laughter mingling with the cries of seagulls. An older couple walked hand in hand wearing wide-brimmed hats. And a lone woman farther down the beach, her long-legged stride putting even more space between them, her brown hair teased by the breeze.

The woman stopped near a trio of drenched teenagers stumbling out of the Gulf. Arms flailing, they pointed back toward the water. She seemed to listen for a few brief seconds. Her head swiveled left, then right, as if she were searching for something. Then in one swift beat of a heart she kicked her feet, sending her shoes catapulting into the air behind her, and pulled off her white long-sleeve sweatshirt to reveal a dark camisole underneath. As she knotted the sweatshirt around her waist, she dashed into the surf, the waves splashing against her legs.

"What?" Brady stood beside him, watching the scene unfold. "Why is she running into the water like that?"

Diving beneath the rolling waves tinted by the setting sun, the woman disappeared from sight for a few seconds, then appeared again, her arms moving in smooth, even strokes.

Faint broken cries directed Logan's attention . . . *there!* Someone fought against the choppy breakers, going under and surfacing in the inky water again—and just as quickly vanishing.

"Call nine-one-one—now!" Tossing Brady his wallet and keys before pulling off his long-sleeve T-shirt, Logan raced down the beach, churning up the sand beneath his feet. He trained his eyes on the woman, following her path toward the drowning person before he, too, plunged into the surf. The waves seemed to push him back toward the shore, but Logan powered forward. For all he knew, there was more than one person out there, near drowning, possibly caught in a riptide.

A riptide. All of them could end up drowning. *God, help us.*

The salt water burned his eyes, even as it weighed down his cargo shorts. He kicked harder, willing his breathing to even, spewing water out of his mouth. He raised his head above the swells as he kept swimming. How far out from shore was he? Where were the woman and the person—or persons—she was trying to rescue?

Vanessa shoved the teen away, treading water and gathering the soaked cotton material of her sweatshirt back in her hands. She spit out the gulp of salty water she'd inhaled when he'd grabbed her, pulling both of them beneath the water.

"Relax!" Her voice rasped against her throat. "Relax!"

If the kid didn't calm down he was going to drown them both.

She fought to stay above the water, kicking harder and tilting her head back, her long hair an unwelcome burden. What was the rescue routine she'd memorized so many years ago?

Call 911.

Well, she had told his friends on the beach to do that.

Reach. Throw. Row. Go.

She couldn't reach the boy from the shore. There was nothing to row out to rescue him. And when she threw the length of water-soaked material toward him the first time and yelled, "Grab this!" he ignored it, arms thrashing, eyes wide, and disappeared underneath the water.

Releasing her sweatshirt, Vanessa held her breath and dove beneath the surface, searching the murky darkness for anything—an arm, a leg—as she tried to position herself behind the boy and pull him back up.

Come on, God. Help me find him. Please. I'm not going back to shore without him—and he's going to be alive.

There!

With both hands, she grabbed the light material of his T-shirt that billowed away from his body, straining and kicking to pull him up to the surface, all the while trying to avoid any of the boy's blind strikes from his arms and legs.

She broke the surface and sucked in welcome air. She spoke through gritted teeth. "Come on, kid! Let me . . . help . . ."

As she tried to maneuver her arm underneath both of his to anchor him on his back on the surface of the water, he twisted around, gasping for air, grabbing for her again. She didn't want to slap the kid, but if that's what it took to save him—and herself . . .

Once again she tried to turn him over, only to be shoved aside, losing her grip on the teen, water splashing her face and stinging her eyes.

What?

Another swimmer, who'd appeared off to her left side, grabbed the boy, flipping him over onto his back. Then a muscular arm slipped under both the boy's arms so he couldn't struggle. The boy's eyes widened in his pale face.

"It's okay . . . okay." Vanessa treaded water, raking the strands of hair out of her face. As the unknown man towed the teen toward the shore, she swam beside them. "Not going . . . to let you drown."

The boy's eyes darted back and forth, his skin pale, his hands clawing at the other swimmer's arm. Vanessa used one arm to swim, grabbing the boy's hand with her free hand. Out of the corner of her eye she could just see the man's head bobbing in the water against the night sky, his hair slicked back as he swam toward shore.

"It's okay." She kicked harder so the guy wouldn't have to pull both of them in.

The moment her toes touched sand, Vanessa stumbled to her feet, fighting the invisible pull of the tide against her trembling legs. The man lifted the teen into his arms and trudged through the surf, water rolling off his bare shoulders. The lights of several emergency vehicles flashed red and white in the parking lot, and three emergency personnel came toward them with a stretcher.

Vanessa swiped at the water streaming down her face, her hair heavy against her neck and shoulders. Her camisole clung to her torso, her jean shorts were congealed against her thighs. Her sweatshirt was lost in the Gulf. The night air cooled the skin on her arms and legs, the sand gritty between her toes. With the arrival of the paramedics and EMTs, there was nothing more for her to do. Still, she waited, bent over at the waist, gasping, watching them stabilize the teen before transporting him to the hospital. Their familiar actions anchored her back to reality.

"What were those kids thinking?" The other rescuer, who had shown up at just the right time, stood off to the side, hands on his hips.

"I don't know—" As she caught sight of the shadowed profile in the glare of the emergency vehicle's headlights, the rest of her reply died on her lips. "Logan?"

The sound of his name caused the man to look away from the crowd gathered around the teen. Shadows hid his face.

She had to be mistaken. The man standing a few feet from her wasn't her ex-husband. He couldn't be.

"Vanessa?" He took a half step toward her, stopping when Vanessa stumbled backward. "What are you doing here?"

"I—I heard somebody yelling . . . and I went to help." She hadn't answered his question.

"But why are you *here*—in Destin?"

She hadn't seen Logan Hollister in eight years, and all she could do was stand there, the water dripping off her body onto the sand, and give him half answers. "I'm visiting Mindy."

Someone came up behind her and wrapped a blanket around her shoulders, a flimsy shield against the humidity-laden air. "How are you feeling? That's amazing what you did, saving that kid."

Vanessa gripped the soft edges of the blanket, a shiver coursing through her body. "I didn't do it alone."

Logan waved away the offer of a blanket. Before she could say anything else—and really, what would she say?—another man pointed a handheld video camera at them.

"I got it all on tape! You guys are heroes! My wife's calling the local news station—they're gonna want to see this!"

"I just helped." Logan's voice pitched low as he motioned to Vanessa. "But she got to the kid before I did."

The ambulance lights glinted off Logan's wet hair—cut so much shorter than he used to wear it—and outlined his muscular build.

Vanessa couldn't seem to speak above much more than a whisper. "I only did what anyone else would have done."

The man pointed his camera at her. "What's your name?"

"It doesn't matter—"

"Oh, come on! What you did was amazing."

Vanessa clutched the blanket closer. "Vanessa. Vanessa Hollister."

"Do you live here?"

"No." She kept her eyes averted, knowing Logan watched her. "I don't live here."

"How do you feel—"

"I'm wet. And tired. And you're not a reporter." She rubbed the soft cotton of the blanket across her face and bit her bottom lip. "I'm sorry. I didn't mean to snap like that."

"I understand. You've got to be exhausted." The man stepped back, one hand held up, the video camera still pointed at her face. "No problem."

As the man turned his attention on Logan,

Vanessa saw her chance to escape. Besides, did she really want to hear the whole *Wow, you both have the same last name—how funny is that?* reaction?

There was no reason for her to wait around to see if a professional reporter showed up. She'd done her job—just in a different state. She'd pray the teen would be okay and could watch the news for that information. Hope he would be smart enough not to go swimming in the Gulf again after drinking too many beers just because his friends dared him.

She'd learned the hard way how foolish it was to take stupid risks. How you could lose your life—*yourself*—if you weren't careful.

FOUR

A wise girl knows her limits, a smart girl
knows that she has none.
—MARILYN MONROE (1926–1962), ACTRESS

Sanctuary.

Vanessa retreated to her hotel room—the
stillness a buffer from all that she could have said
to her ex-husband. The activity of the paramedics.
The growing crowd of gawkers—and the arriving
news team. Only when her sand-covered feet
made contact with the cool of the lobby tile did
she realize she'd left her sandals behind somewhere. She ignored the stare of the front desk
clerk, holding her head high as she walked past,
avoiding the elevator and climbing the stairs to her
room.

Thank God the plastic key card to her room had
somehow remained in the pocket of her shorts,
not ending up in the Gulf with her sweatshirt. The
air-conditioning blew a frigid kiss against her
chapped lips, threading unseen fingers through her
hair where it lay against her neck.

If she wasn't soaking wet . . . if her legs weren't
shaking as if she'd just swum an Olympic trial . . .
if her eyes weren't stinging from salt water . . .
she'd book the first flight back to Colorado and

insist Ted go back to their original plan to get married in their home church.

Tomorrow.

Not in April.

As another shiver shook her body, Vanessa turned off the air-conditioning. Then she opened the off-white vertical blinds and yanked open the glass door to the balcony, the sound of metal scraping against the cement going right up her spine. Dropping to the carpet the damp blanket the onlooker had draped around her shoulders, she turned back to her bed, pulled back the bedspread, and removed the blanket underneath. Her journal fell to the floor.

It was as if daring to read a few entries earlier had conjured Logan Hollister out of the past and onto the beach—just as she'd feared.

She picked the book up from where it lay facedown, pages splayed open against the muted blue carpeting. Her handwriting skimmed across the pages, a silent dare to face the past scrawled across the pages. Sentences. Paragraphs. Words and more words that lured her into memories best forgotten.

Funny. I put the rings away, but I look down at my hand and I still expect to see them. Of course, I've only been divorced for twenty-four hours. I need to give it some time. I was Vanessa Hollister before I married Logan—and I'm still Vanessa Hollister. No one needs to know that there are actually two different versions of the same woman.

Logan and I didn't even say goodbye to each other.

It was all done so quietly and nicely via mail. Sign here, convenient little yellow sticky arrows pointing to the appropriate lines for our signatures.

But then, would I know how to say goodbye to Logan—the girl who's always been so good at goodbyes? What do you say when a divorce is finalized? Thank you for the good memories? Thanks for asking me to marry you . . . and thank you for turning in all the paperwork on time so this didn't drag out?

Yeah. So you say nothing. Your signature speaks for you. We're done. There's no longer an "us" standing in the way of what you want to do with your life.

Vanessa flung the journal onto the bed. How appropriate. Skip to the ending.

She searched the hotel fridge, reaching past the six-pack of Coke she'd purchased to grab one of the "complimentary" bottles of water. Let 'em charge her for it.

Wrapped in the comfort of the dry blanket, she

hid in the darkness of the balcony. She huddled in the white plastic deck chair, her arms hugging her knees. With the chair pulled forward, the Gulf breeze caressed her face. The beach looked normal again. Safe. No more rescue crews. No more reporters. No more crowds.

No ex-husband.

She pressed her forehead to her knees, her eyes squeezed shut.

Why, God, why?

She was being brave, coming here. Crossing the bridge that led to her past.

And then she decided to walk the beach—the same stretch of beach she and Logan had strolled so many evenings, watching sunsets. Or had sat on a blanket and watched lightning storms rage across the night sky. The same beach where he'd coaxed her from the security of the shore out into the water and onto a surfboard for the first time.

The same beach where Logan had first said he loved her.

Tonight, she walked alone.

No ghost.

Not a whisper of Logan's voice.

And then someone needed help—and what was she supposed to do? Ignore the pleas of the boy's friends? Of course not. But why, God, why did she have to come face-to-face with Logan . . . so close she could have touched him.

"Vanessa? What are you doing here?"

"I'm getting married, Logan." Her voice wavered. Cracked.

Vanessa twisted the cap off the bottle of water, tipped it back, and drank, the cool liquid burning her lips even as it soothed her parched throat.

Coming here was a mistake.

She couldn't start a new life with Ted by having their wedding in the same place where she'd fallen in love with her first husband.

What was that saying again? *A wise girl knows her limits.*

Between her undergrad degree and all her training to be a paramedic, she considered herself intelligent and street-smart. When it came to what she could and could not do, she was wise enough to know marrying Ted Topliff in Destin was beyond her limits.

If Ted was determined to attach their ceremony to a medical conference, then he'd have to choose one in another locale.

That was it, plain and simple.

Ted was a reasonable man—and she wasn't asking for much other than a change in venue.

For now, she was going to take a long, hot shower. Order room service, without looking at the prices. And then find a ridiculous movie—something that would make her laugh until she cried.

AUGUST 2003

It was bad enough her parents had moved the family—again. But why couldn't they have figured out a way to cross the Florida state line before school started?

Vanessa lifted her chin, staring at the high school's double doors leading outside—where she could exhale, stop smiling, and stop saying hello to everyone. Stop pretending that remembering dozens of names and faces really was as easy as she made it look. Other students flowed past her, while some stood around the lockers lining the hallways. A few called her name—evidence of how well she pulled off the new student role—snippets of conversations and laughter swirling together.

She'd survived the first day at another new school. Proven that she knew how to be the perfect new girl, even if it meant walking into Niceville High School two weeks after classes started. One day she should count up how many times the phrase "new student" had been attached to her name. When she went to college—wherever she went—she would stay there from the first day of freshman orientation until the day she walked across the stage and received her diploma.

As she left home that morning to walk to school, she'd straightened the worn HOME IS WHERE THE AIR FORCE SENDS YOU tole-painted wooden plaque hanging in the foyer. As Hollister family tradition dictated, it was one of the first things Mom put up in the new house. As far as Vanessa was concerned, home was where the military dragged you kicking and screaming, not bothering to ask if you wanted to move. If you were ready to say goodbye again. If you wanted to make new friends . . . not knowing how long you'd be in town . . . or if what they offered you was true friendship.

Vanessa pulled on the curved metal handle of the door, the blast of air-conditioning shoving back the humidity that greeted her. In August, temperatures in the Florida Panhandle were set and locked on "swelter and sweat" from nine in the morning past ten at night against a backdrop of overgrown underbrush and the nonstop noise of crickets and frogs. By the time she walked home, her short-sleeve T-shirt would cling to her back, her bangs wilted against her forehead.

"Hey, Vanessa! Vanessa Hollister! Wait up!"

She paused halfway down the concrete stairs. Who, among all these unfamiliar faces, wanted to talk to her? And why?

A thin girl with a riot of red curls piled on top of her head jogged down the stairs, a grin splitting her face, which was splattered with freckles. "Glad I found you. I didn't know where your locker was. I'm Mindy Adams—we're in Honors English together."

"Hey."

"So, you're new here."

Vanessa swallowed back the snarky comment that sprang to mind. "Yeah."

"Your father military?"

"Yeah." When Vanessa moved down the stairs, Mindy kept pace with her, pink flip-flops slapping against the concrete.

"I've lived here all my life." Mindy set her backpack at the bottom of the stairs. "Must be cool to travel."

"Sure." *Whatever.* People had no idea what it was like to be in a military family, moving whenever Uncle Sam said to pack up.

"So . . . I just wanted to say, if you need anything . . . have any questions about school or anything, you could call me." Mindy held out a torn piece of notebook paper, folded in half. "Here's my phone number. I ride the bus. You?"

"No. I walk home. I don't live far from here."

"Too bad. I thought we could sit together and talk—if we were on the same bus." She lifted her hand, waving the torn piece of notebook paper again.

"Yeah. Too bad." Vanessa took the paper—not that she'd call Mindy. Acquaintances were fine. Friendships . . . well, that only led to people getting hurt. "Thanks."

"Sure. I gotta run before my bus leaves. See ya tomorrow!"

Vanessa waved. Of course she'd see Mindy tomorrow. In class. Probably pass her in the hallways. Casual. She tucked the paper into the back pocket of her jeans, adjusting her backpack on her shoulders, a trickle of sweat slipping down her back. Time to get home, see how many boxes Mom had unpacked and how many were waiting in her bedroom. Maybe her mom was ready to talk about what color Vanessa wanted to paint her room this time.

Vanessa kept her head down, weaving through the moving pack of students heading to their cars or the line of yellow school buses along the perimeter of the parking lot. Some, like her, were walking home solo or in small groups. Being alone was fine with her. Easier. As Vanessa made her way around a group of kids, her shoulder collided with something—or someone—and she stumbled forward, almost falling to her knees on the sidewalk before a pair of strong hands reached out and steadied her.

"You okay?"

The guy's voice held the hint of a laugh.

"I'm fine." She pulled away, her gaze colliding with a pair of blue eyes, the laughter adding a bit of sparkle to them. Her *Watch where you're going* lodged in her throat.

"Sorry about that." The boy brushed his long blond hair off his forehead, smiling at her again as if sharing a joke. "My sister says I'm a klutz."

"It's okay. No big deal." She shifted her backpack to her other shoulder. "Well, I gotta go."

"Me, too." He motioned to a silver and red motorcycle parked behind him. "Don't want to show up to work late."

Vanessa nodded and moved past him, aware of the half grin on his sunburned face. How tall he was. The sun seemed to up its intensity, and she resisted the urge to hold her hair up off her neck—and the even stronger desire to turn around. To look back. Was he watching her with his intense blue eyes? A minute later, she gave in and glanced over her shoulder. Stumbled again. And sure enough, he sat astride his motorcycle, watching her. He lifted his hand and waved, offering her another glimpse of his grin. With a groan, Vanessa waved back and faced forward again.

She should have kept walking. Never turned around. He must think she was a bumbling idiot.

But he did have a cute smile. Worth a second glance.

Logan exited the school a few seconds after Vanessa, careful to keep some distance and a few other students between them. After waiting in the school parking lot and watching her walk home for the past week and a half, he was beginning to feel a little bit like a stalker. Usually he sat on his motorcycle while Vanessa walked past him, and then he headed to work mowing lawns. If she looked his way, he waved hello. Some days she ignored him, but he got the feeling she knew he was there, watching her. Today he decided to mix it up a bit—only now he had to hang back and wait while she and Mindy talked on the steps.

Vanessa Hollister. What were the odds that the new girl in school would have the same last name as he did? And that they'd have the same math and science classes? Not that sitting near her meant anything. She was friendly enough—said hi to everybody, including the teachers, seemed to know a lot of kids' names already. But after watching her—and hoping no one else noticed—he could almost see a barrier surrounding her marked "This far and no farther." The way she held her backpack on one shoulder, so that it half shielded one side of her body. The way she'd keep walking even as she said hello to the other kids in school. A nod. A wave. The briefest of smiles—and moving on. And how she volunteered in the office during lunch—avoiding the whole *Who do I sit with?* dilemma.

Her elusiveness made him want to get to know Vanessa Hollister better. To figure out how to earn more than a "Hi, Logan," from her—to move past those two words where she barely even looked in his eyes. But what was he supposed to do? Wait at her locker and ask her if she knew that day's math assignment?

Lame.

So far he'd avoided being late to work despite his new habit. Waiting on his motorcycle for a few minutes didn't delay him that much. It helped that Vanessa had a routine.

Walk outside with Mindy. Talk for a few minutes until Mindy headed for the bus. Then head the opposite way, through the parking lot, walking home. By herself. Every single day.

That was his in.

All he had to do was wait for her. Ask the right question. And hope she said yes.

FIVE

No one is brave alone . . .
the bravest among us do not stand alone.
—ANNIE F. DOWNS (1980–),
AUTHOR AND SPEAKER

Logan gripped the opposite ends of the metal lat pull-down bar, closed his eyes, and exhaled. The machine was loaded with extra pounds. Maybe a ramped-up workout would overcome last night's memories still lurking in his brain.

And yet it was impossible to focus on his reps when his teammates crowded into the too-small hotel workout room. Brady was the only one of them even attempting to exercise. He'd commandeered a treadmill over in the corner where the TV was tuned to the local news. Max, his leg still encased in a long black brace from his ankle past his knee, leaned against the wall nearest the door, while Julie stood guard nearby.

"So, how's it feel to be a hero, boss?" Julie's question broke his concentration—again.

After Brady told them during breakfast about Logan going into the water to help rescue someone, Jules couldn't seem to stop talking about the teen's near-drowning. This was one year Logan wished he'd left the team back in Oklahoma when he came to Florida.

He wished he hadn't come back to Destin at all.

"Enough already." He pulled the bar behind his back, slow and smooth. Paused. Raised it back to the starting position. "I'm not a hero."

Brady, who had embellished the story in the retelling, hit pause on the treadmill and pointed to the television mounted on the wall, the sound turned off. "You watching this? That guy's video is on the news *again*. And from the way the witnesses described it, you were the one who saved that kid."

"Vanessa—" He would not say "my ex-wife." Just because they all knew who she was didn't mean he had to say it. "—went into the water first. I just hauled him back to shore."

Brady wiped at the sheen of sweat on his forehead with one end of the towel resting on his shoulders. "From the video on the news last night, it looked like you hauled her back in, too."

Logan performed a few more reps before replying. "Knock it off. Vanessa kept the kid calm and swam in herself." Logan closed his eyes. Mere inches from his wife, who he hadn't been able to forget about for eight years, and he hadn't realized the woman swimming next to him, one hand clasping the teen's to help calm him down, was Vanessa.

Julie helped Max get settled in a chair, leaning

his crutches against the wall. "You saw the updated newscast, right?"

Logan repeated another round of reps. "I've been avoiding watching it—no thanks to the three of you."

"Well, *you* know Vanessa is your ex-wife. And *we* all know she's your ex-wife. But while the reporter didn't know it last night—he does now."

Logan released the lat bar, the weights clunking against one another. "Meaning?"

"You know reporters—they have to go looking into everyone's background." Julie shrugged, her smile lopsided. "And it didn't take him long to figure out you and Vanessa were married—'former high school sweethearts,' he said."

"Wonderful." Logan stood, staring at the TV. "Why'd that guy have to be running around with his video camera?"

"Everyone wants their five minutes of fame—" Now it was Max's turn to chime in. "—even if it means videotaping someone else's five minutes."

"It's sad but true. Think about all the people who we've encountered trying to chase after tornadoes who have no right being out there in the middle of a storm." Julie, her straight dark blond hair pulled into a high ponytail, nudged Max's shoulder. "You ready to head to the pool yet? It'll do your leg good."

"You're right, Mom." Max tugged the end of Julie's ponytail, causing her to swat his hand away.

"I'm not your mom. Call me that again, and I'll push you into the deep end of the pool."

He forced himself to his feet again, reaching for his crutches and ducking. The glass door closed on the sound of their laughter-filled banter.

Brady, who had abandoned the treadmill, sat beside Logan on a weight bench, running the towel across his shaved head. "You know, if you play this right we could get some free publicity for the team."

"That kid almost *drowned*. Yes, it was thanks to his own stupidity—but I'm not going to use him to trump up attention for the Stormmeisters."

Logan tilted up his water bottle, swallowing a gulp of water and the bitter taste of secrets. He needed to come clean. Tell the team his decision about next year. After all they'd been through, he owed Brady and Max and Julie honesty. Draining the plastic water bottle, he threw it in the trash, rubbing his hands against the material of his workout shorts, as if he could still feel Max's blood on them. "You about done here?"

"You're the gym rat, not me."

Logan paused as a special news bulletin scrolled across the bottom of the TV screen. "What did that say?"

Brady crossed the room and turned the TV to face them more directly.

A HURRICANE WATCH HAS BEEN ISSUED FROM PENSACOLA TO PANAMA CITY. LAND-

FALL LIKELY TO BE WEST OF PANAMA CITY AND INTO LOUISIANA. FURTHER DETAILS AT NOON OR ON OUR WEBSITE.

"Huh." Brady watched the words scroll past again. "Is that why I've been hearing jets all morning?"

"I hadn't thought about it until now, but you're right. The U.S. Air Force doesn't wait until the last minute before evacuating the fighter jets from the military base. During Hurricane Opal back in '95, they flew the jets to a base in Oklahoma—Tinker, I think." Logan stood with his hands on his hips. "We'll watch the Weather Channel updates. You know as well as I do how unpredictable these things are. It'll probably stall out. We'll be fine."

"Not in the mood to chase a hurricane around Florida?"

Logan led the way to the elevators. "We chase storms for our day jobs. I'm on vacation." The thought of getting in a car, buckling in, and going after a storm caused his stomach to tighten and roll, as if he were standing on a ship that had encountered a sudden squall and pitched to the side. He clenched his fists and then eased his hands open again, shaking them at his sides.

Relax. Any bad weather headed for the Panhandle wasn't his problem.

In high school, Mindy had always talked about envying all the different places Vanessa had lived.

73

She'd daydreamed about stuffing some clothes in a backpack and trekking across Europe or going on a year-long mission trip to the Philippines or even South America.

But instead she'd met Jett during their sophomore year of college. Married him the week after graduation. And then come back to Niceville, renovating a fixer-upper like a star member of a flip-this-house TV team.

Mindy's landscaped yard set off a classic wraparound porch. Inside, the refurbished wood floors gleamed with a high polish, and walls had been removed to allow for an open-concept living area.

Mindy's interior design degree had obviously allowed her to pour all of her know-how and talent into the ranch-style home on a quiet cul-de-sac off John Sims Parkway. The rich colors on the walls flowed from room to room—deep greens, a New England blue, a weathered gray, and muted yellow. Each piece of furniture, understated lines and simple patterns, was arranged just so, while avoiding the artificial appearance of a showroom. Vanessa relaxed, knowing there were no bills waiting to be paid—none that she needed to worry about, anyway. No laundry she needed to wash. No plants dying of thirst.

But there were puppies.

Six rambunctious, yipping, brown, gold, black, and white puppies that romped and rolled through the house nonstop.

"They'll tire out eventually, I promise you." Mindy stepped over two of the puppies as they played tug-of-war with a rope dog toy, holding two plates laden with carrot cake high above her head. "We've been fostering rescue puppies for a couple of years now. Jett and I never know how many we may be asked to keep. I have to admit half a dozen is a handful."

"How long will you keep them?" Vanessa accepted the dessert, the aroma of cinnamon and nutmeg blending with cream cheese icing as she cut a bite with the side of her fork.

"Until they're eight weeks old at least—and then they're taken to a pet adoption fair to find their families—we hope." She set her cake aside, reaching for one of the golden brown puppies, its four paws adorned with white socks. Mindy scooped it into her arms before coming to sit beside Vanessa on the couch. "So, I was watching the morning news—did you know there's a hurricane watch for the Panhandle?"

"The front desk clerk mentioned it when I left the hotel this morning." Vanessa moved her braid so that it fell behind her back. "And I noticed the wind has picked up a bit out on the island. Did they say anything else I should know about?"

"No, just to watch for updates." Mindy cleared her throat, looking as if she were fighting to hold back a smile. "I also saw the video of you and *Logan* on the news this morning. Several times."

Vanessa forced herself to swallow the bite of carrot cake, which suddenly seemed dry. Stale. "Oh. That."

"Yes—that. Honestly, Vanessa, you and Logan rescuing a teenager from drowning? I thought you weren't even talking to him—"

"I'm not. Up until last night, I hadn't seen Logan in eight years."

"You're kidding me."

"Mindy, as crazy as it sounds, it was a complete accident—an insane coincidence—that Logan and I were on the beach at the same time. I didn't even know he was in Destin."

"But we don't believe in coincidences, remember?" Mindy's smile, set in her still-freckled face, her now-wavy red hair pulled back by a black headband, reminded Vanessa of when they were eighteen-year-olds. When they believed anything was possible. And that God was in charge of the world. That he cared about even the small details of their lives.

"There'd be no reason for me to contact Logan because . . . I'm getting married again."

There. Now she had Mindy's attention.

"What?" With a small yip, the sleeping puppy in her friend's arms jerked awake. "Really?"

"Yes, really." Vanessa mimicked her friend's little shriek of surprise before stealing the puppy from her. "That's the reason why I wanted to see you today."

"What do you mean?"

"Well, Ted and I— Ted Topliff is my fiancé. He's an ER doctor in Denver. Ted and I are planning a destination wedding. And, despite the marital mishap in my past, Ted thinks Destin is a great location. I actually met with a wedding coordinator before I came over here today. And I'm here to ask you to be my matron of honor."

"Are you kidding me?" Mindy bounced up on her knees. "I would love to! I was always sorry I missed your first wedding—" She stopped, clapping her hand over her mouth. "I am so sorry. That was totally inappropriate of me."

"I understand." Vanessa stroked the puppy's soft ears. "And believe me, at first I tried to talk Ted into some other location for our wedding. Getting married for the second time, you'd think I could manage to select a different location, right?"

"Obviously you lost that argument."

"It wasn't an argument . . . well, not much of one. Ted's too laid-back for that kind of thing."

"So you two are one of those we-never-argue kind of couples."

She hadn't ever thought of it that way, but it was true. "That's a good thing—we know how to talk things out. And Ted helped me see that coming back here to get married isn't a problem. I'm not that girl anymore."

"Meaning you're not eighteen anymore?"

"Exactly."

"So why is Destin so important to your fiancé?"

Of course Mindy had to ask. And Vanessa would tell her the truth. If she didn't now, it would come out sometime later. "We're mixing a bit of wedding pleasure with medical business."

Mindy tilted her head, her hair framing her face. "And what does that mean exactly?"

"Ted's attending a medical conference at the hotel the week after our wedding." Vanessa focused on the puppy's sweet face. "He's a very practical kind of guy—and he's always scrambling for time to go to medical conferences. And a destination wedding will be smaller than the one we were planning in Colorado, so it will cost less. See? Practical."

"Makes sense."

And once again, Mindy came through for her.

"So, let's get some details down." Mindy reached for her cake again. "The most important thing first, of course. When is the wedding?"

"Next April."

Mindy slumped back against the couch. "April? When in April?"

"The first week. Why?" Vanessa's hand stilled on the puppy's fur. "Is that a problem?"

"Kind of." Mindy pressed a hand against her abdomen. "I'm pregnant."

But I'm desperate. Vanessa pressed her lips together to keep from speaking the insensitive thought out loud.

"How pregnant are you . . . I mean, when are you due?"

"The middle of March."

"The middle of . . ."

It looked as if Mindy's pregnancy trumped her need for a matron of honor after all.

"Wait a minute . . . if you really want me to be your matron of honor—"

"I do, Mindy. You're my . . . best friend. But I didn't know you were pregnant." How could she, when she'd been so unavailable? And how to explain to Mindy that it wasn't because she didn't want to be friends—real friends? She just didn't know how to do the whole "friends forever" thing.

She didn't believe in it.

And Vanessa couldn't tell Mindy that she was the only person she could ask. But her friend probably knew the truth.

Mindy licked frosting off her fork. "My mom always delivered early—four kids, and each one of us at least a week early. And my sister Ginger— you remember her? She had a baby two years ago. And he was born two whole weeks before her due date. So, the odds are I'll go early—maybe even the first week of March. No problem."

No problem. Right. More like no other option.

"Mindy, I don't want to pressure you like this—"

"Are you kidding me? You're getting married again. And I get to be in the wedding. Do you think

I'm going to miss this? I can always ask my doctor to induce me early. And you've heard of Spanx, right? I'll fit in whatever dress you pick out for me."

"You're an amazing friend." Vanessa pulled Mindy to her in a half hug, still cradling the now-sleeping puppy. "And you're *pregnant!*"

"I know . . . how crazy is that? Jett keeps telling me if we can manage puppies, we'll do fine with a baby."

"You're going to be a mom. I'm getting married again. Look at us—all sorts of dreams are coming true."

"So what do your parents think? They're happy for you, right?"

"Yes. Absolutely." Vanessa released the squirming puppy and got comfortable on the couch again.

"You *have* told them, right?"

"Of course. There are no surprises with this wedding, believe me."

"So what did your mother say?"

"She wanted to know why I wasn't getting married in Montana—as if that was home or something. Just because my parents retired there doesn't require me to have my wedding in Great Falls."

"True." Mindy motioned to the dessert sitting on the coffee table. "Eat your cake, but keep talking. So what did she think of your Florida destination wedding?"

Traces of their conversation the night before she left Montana intruded on the conversation.

"You're getting married again? In Destin?" Her mother paused, her hand suspended above the latest quilt she was working on. "Ted knows about your first . . . wedding?"

"Well, we both know that wasn't a real ceremony." Vanessa would say it before her mother. Beat her to the verbal punch. "And Logan and I were married in Alabama, not Destin."

The past, which Vanessa tried so hard to keep behind her, hung between them.

Her mother was the first to step away from the simmering tension. "Well, fine, then. Maybe you know what you're doing."

Not exactly a vote of confidence. Was Vanessa going to be forever branded by what had happened ten years ago?

"Hey, where'd you go?" Mindy snapped her fingers in front of Vanessa's face.

"What? Sorry . . . My mom's a bit preoccupied with my dad's recovery right now. I promised to keep her updated on the wedding details."

"Details—which brings us back to me being your matron of honor. Do we have time to go shopping for dresses while you're here?"

"You mean a dress for you? I guess so."

"For me—and you, too. What else are you doing?"

"I have a list in my purse."

"Hand it over, girlfriend." Vanessa giggled at Mindy's elaborate hand gesture. Back in high school, Mindy's friendliness had somehow slipped past Vanessa's protective barrier. For some reason, the girl wanted to be her friend back then—and still wanted to be her friend now all these years later. "Your matron of honor needs to have a look-see."

Mindy was the next-best thing to a fairy god-mother stepping out of a children's book and into her life.

Now that Vanessa knew Mindy's secret super-power was organization, Vanessa could have her talk to the hotel wedding coordinator and the florist. She'd nibbled on another sliver of carrot cake while her friend powered up her laptop and transferred the wedding to-do's to an Excel spreadsheet, fine-tuning it with an online wedding checklist—and one for the matron of honor—creating a shared Dropbox folder labeled HOLLISTER-TOPLIFF WEDDING.

They discussed flower options. Clothing options for Ted and his best man. Dress styles for her and Mindy, even pinning a few options on a Pinterest board. Decided on a late afternoon wedding—

despite Mindy's pleadings for a sunset ceremony on the beach. But no matter how much Mindy begged, Vanessa vetoed the idea of walking toward Ted as he stood against the backdrop of a brilliant sun setting into the horizon.

She couldn't bring herself to explain to Mindy that a decade ago, she and Logan had daydreamed about a second wedding ceremony—this time with family and friends celebrating with them—saying their vows on the beach just as the blaze of the sun seemed to extinguish itself in the Gulf.

So even though Mindy had tempted her by showing her the Henderson Park Inn's website, Vanessa resisted. Still, her newly appointed matron of honor scrolled through the different wedding packages, the photos, all the while suggesting Vanessa and Ted consider the Destin bed-and-breakfast for their wedding site. The thought of privacy—no medical colleagues, no conference sponsor booths—did appeal to Vanessa. All she had to do was convince her much-too-practical fiancé to change his mind about a two-for-the-price-of-one wedding venue.

With yet another slice of carrot cake stored in a disposable container—and declining the offer of a puppy—Vanessa hugged Mindy goodbye and headed back toward Destin.

It wasn't until she turned the rental car off John Sims Parkway onto Edgewater Drive that Vanessa admitted she'd intended to drive past her old home all along.

"Another way of saying goodbye." She nodded at her reflection in the rearview mirror. "Drive by the house, see how it's changed."

Cruising along the quiet street, she slowed the car to almost a complete stop but allowed it to roll past the long driveway leading to the house, which was hidden by a tangle of old magnolia trees and wild underbrush. Putting the car in park, Vanessa stared straight ahead.

What was she going to do? Trespass?

Maybe no one was home. She could walk part of the way up the driveway—far enough to see the house. And then she'd leave. One more door closed on that part of her life. It wasn't as if the house were significant to her. She'd lived in it less than a year. And with all the moves her family had made, she wasn't one to return to those places in her past for any reason, much less sentimental ones.

Even with the cooler fall weather, humidity still crowded the air, accompanied by the familiar ongoing hum of insects. A smile curved her lips. How Rylan used to love to capture the green lizards that lived outside their house—much to their mother's horror. And when one managed to find its way into the shower, they all came running at their mother's screams, only to stop outside her locked bedroom door. And laugh.

Vanessa took the driveway as if security cameras were wired in every tree branch. She was being ridiculous. She wasn't stealing anything—except a look at the house she'd lived in when she was eighteen.

In the distance, a boat roared across the bayou, probably towing a die-hard water-skier. The scent of grilled fish floated on the breeze. Good. Maybe the home owners were out back, enjoying an early dinner on the porch that ran the length of the house, not sitting in the living room, watching for someone to come skulking up the driveway.

A few more steps and the house came into view, now painted a soft moss-green so that it blended into the surroundings, off-white shutters bracketing the windows, the front porch painted white with coordinating green trim.

See? The house didn't even look the same anymore.

But if she stood still for just a moment or two and closed her eyes, inhaled the moist air laden with the scent of grass and grilled fish and the faint sounds of someone laughing . . .

She remembered all the times Logan had brought her home from school . . . sitting on the porch, her daddy in one of the rockers, while she chose the other, and her father talking about the latest history book he'd read . . . how her mother would come to the door and say dinner was ready, sometimes inviting Logan to join them

. . . and after dinner Rylan would ask Logan for a ride on his motor-cycle . . .

And then all of that was ruined.

"Worst mistake you ever made."

All these years later, the echo of her mother's words could still reduce Vanessa to an uncertain eighteen-year-old newlywed.

Fine. After all this time, she was not going to change her mother's mind about what had happened. But she'd made her choice for a reason . . . for reasons. Good ones.

Even if in the end she'd had to agree with her mother that she'd made a mistake.

Enough of this. She was ruining a good day by standing here staring at a house that meant nothing, nothing at all, to her. She returned to the car without a single backward glance, her half boots scuffing on the cement.

But once she was at the car, her hand stayed on the door handle.

Was she really going to be this close—and drive off without saying hello to the two people who had made Niceville seem a little like home?

The Wrights had lived two houses down from her parents and had become adopted grand-parents to Vanessa and Rylan. Between glasses of lemonade and homemade cookies—and Mr. Wright's outrageous white cockatiel named Mr. Chips—her parents had a challenge keeping Vanessa and Rylan from dumping their schoolbooks and heading straight for the Wrights' every day—and Logan liked to join them, too.

Leaving the rental car, Vanessa walked the short distance to the Wrights' home, listening for the familiar barks of Mrs. Wright's two beloved papillons. Only the peal of the doorbell broke the silence.

Was she being foolish? Most likely the couple who had provided just a bit of what she'd longed for—lemonade on their back porch and the welcoming love of proxy-grandparents—never even thought of her anymore. Or maybe they'd moved.

But when the door swung open, Mrs. Wright stood before her—older, of course, her white hair a mere wisp of a cloud framing her face, her once-sparkling gray eyes dimmed.

"Yes?"

"Mrs. Wright? It's me, Vanessa Hollister—from down the street?"

"Who?"

"Vanessa?" See—this was what happened when you moved away—people forgot you. How could Vanessa jog Mrs. Wright's memory? "I used to walk Mollie and Maggie for you."

"Vanessa!" Mrs. Wright pulled the door wide open, her eyes lighting. "Well, my word! Look at you! Come in, girl. Come in!"

As Vanessa stepped over the threshold into the dark foyer, Mrs. Wright hugged her, thin arms pulling her close. Within seconds the fragrance of rose and orange blossom wrapped around her, the elderly woman's signature scent. Vanessa had begged her mother to help her buy Mrs. Wright a small bottle of Red Door perfume for Christmas, promising to clean the minivan every month for a year to pay her back.

"How are you, Mrs. Wright?"

"I'm just fine. Come on in here and say hello to Mr. Wright. We were just finishing up a late lunch." The woman's white slippers scuffed along the wood floor. "You want some lemonade?"

Vanessa had grown up learning just how quickly things could change. But Mrs. Wright's offer of lemonade brought an unexpected rush of tears to her eyes. How many glasses of the tart, cold drink had she consumed on their back porch? "Yes, please. That sounds delicious."

Mrs. Wright's oil paintings still decorated the walls leading to the kitchen. It, too, was unchanged, decorated in cheery yellow, the windows hung with blue and white gingham curtains.

"We're out on the enclosed porch today. Mr. Wright likes it out there."

Out of habit, Vanessa braced herself for the yips of two little dogs as they came bounding to greet her, but only Mr. Wright was in the screened-in room.

His tall, lanky frame sat slumped in a chair, a wooden TV tray to one side, a plate of food left untouched, the chicken patty and green beans cut into pieces. A Miami Dolphins ball cap covered his head, and he wore his slippers in a one-on, one-off fashion.

"Sweetheart, look who came to visit—Vanessa from up the street."

"Who?" The elderly man lifted his chin, his gaze fixed on his wife's face.

"Vanessa. You know, the girl who used to walk Maggie and Mollie."

Mr. Wright tilted his head back, struggling to find Vanessa, and then a grin lit up his face. "Vanessa-girl! Where you been?"

Vanessa grasped his hand, the skin dry and cracked. "I'm sorry it's been so long. I've been busy—"

"Is Logan with you? I want him to give me a ride on that snazzy motorcycle of his while you walk those puppies!"

Vanessa's grip tightened around his thin hand. "What?"

"Is he mowing lawns today?"

Mrs. Wright, who was clearing up the lunch dishes, just nodded, offering a small smile.

"Y-yes, Logan's working today." Vanessa blinked away the moisture blurring her vision. "I'm sorry. Maybe he'll come by tomorrow."

"Well, I hope so. I'm going to convince that boy to let me on that motorcycle one of these days."

"Vanessa, will you grab those glasses for me?" Mrs. Wright motioned toward the kitchen, then turned back to her husband. "Now you just rest, and I'll bring you some cookies."

"Not the sugar-free ones. I don't like 'em."

"Of course not, dear."

Once in the kitchen, Mrs. Wright stored the leftover food in a plastic container. "He might want it later. I'm so glad you came by, Vanessa. He's having a good day. He even let Christina, the home health care woman, dress him and bring him downstairs."

This was a good day?

"Has he been sick, Mrs. Wright?"

"Well, he hasn't really been sick, but his memory isn't what it used to be."

"Are you okay? You know the news is talking about a hurricane watch, right? I could get you some groceries if you need anything."

"Yes, dear. I watch the news in the morning and at night, too. It's nice to have the TV on. I like to watch the old movies, you know—although Mr. Wright doesn't care for the musicals." The older woman closed the fridge, finished storing the leftovers. "And our daughter, Ruth, in Tuscaloosa checks on us. It's just a little rain and wind. No need to get upset. We'll be fine."

Vanessa knew the answer to her next question, but she had to ask. "And the dogs . . . ?"

"I lost the girls a few years ago now. And it's for

the best. I spend all my time taking care of Mr. Wright."

No Maggie, no Mollie—and in a sense, no husband. How did Mrs. Wright stand it, day in and day out?

Plates clinked against the dishwasher spokes. "So, what brings you to town?"

"I'm here to plan my wedding." Vanessa filled the glasses halfway with lemonade. "I'm . . . well, I'm getting married again."

"You and Logan are getting remarried?" Mrs. Wright closed the dishwasher with a soft click. "But why would you do that?"

Yellow liquid sloshed over the edge of the pitcher and onto the countertop. "No, no—not me and Logan. We divorced eight years ago." Vanessa searched the kitchen for a roll of paper towels. "I'm living in Denver now. I'm a paramedic, and I've been dating an ER doctor. We're getting married—having a destination wedding in Destin."

"Really?" Mrs. Wright opened a package of molasses cookies. "Does Logan know?"

"No." A jerk of her hand caused Vanessa to pull too many paper towels off the roll she found hanging on the side of the fridge. "Why would Logan need to know?"

"Because he's your husband. What if he wants to do the *I object!* part?"

Maybe Mrs. Wright wasn't as alert as Vanessa first thought.

"Logan is my *ex*-husband. That's not going to happen." Vanessa mopped up the spill with the wad of paper towels. "Our relationship ended years ago."

Mrs. Wright stopped arranging cookies on a small plate decorated with blue flowers, reaching over to pat Vanessa's hand. "Just because you and Logan divorced, that doesn't mean you and he are over."

Vanessa was about to argue, but Mrs. Wright interrupted her when the doorbell rang. "Oh, that must be Christina, back for the second home health care shift. Would you take these to Mr. Wright while I go get the door?"

Mr. Wright had dozed off. After introducing Vanessa, Mrs. Wright got caught up talking about the day with the home health care representative. Vanessa made her exit once Mrs. Wright returned, her lemonade untouched, promising to come back again before she left for Denver.

"You better. Mr. Wright won't remember you've been here to miss seeing you—but I will!"

SIX

You can't base your life on
other people's expectations.
—STEVIE WONDER (1950–), MUSICIAN

"You can't go home again."

How many times had Logan proven that statement true?

While they'd lived in Niceville all his life, his parents seemed to make a habit of moving to a newer, bigger house every few years. Or renovating a room or two in the home they were living in. Changing the landscape so the yard looked completely different.

This time, the landscape remained the same, but his sister warned him that they'd expanded and retiled the sunroom, adding space for his mother's plants.

More than a casual dinner waited for him behind the large wooden door with smoky glass panels on either side guarding the front of the house.

"Let's go this way." Logan motioned for Brady, Max, and Julie to follow, knowing Max would be able to navigate the well-manicured lawn even on his crutches. He sidetracked to the back, where an in-ground pool covered half the yard, screened in and surrounded by an assortment of low-growing bushes. The gate was unlocked, and from the pool area he entered the updated sunroom, decorated with an assortment of new white wicker furniture. How did his mother manage all of the foliage?

No family in sight, but the faint hum of voices and the rich aroma of his mother's beef brisket led them to the kitchen—and his mother and sister, Caron. She stood in front of Alex, who towered over her, his arm around her waist. Visual proof to back up his mother's report that Caron and Alex were dating. Had they caved to parental pressure—decades' worth of not-so-subtle hints from both sets of parents that they were perfect for each other—or was there real potential for a long-term relationship between them?

"Logan!" Caron slipped away from Alex and dashed, barefoot, across the kitchen, pulling him into a tight embrace. "How are you, big brother?"

He squeezed her in return, enjoying her laughing protest. "Good to see you again, Caro." Over her shoulder, he nodded at Alex. "Nice to see you, too."

"Logan."

His mother added onions and shiitake mushrooms into the Crock-Pot on the kitchen counter and replaced the glass lid. "Now I'm a happy mother. Both of you are home."

Logan opened his arms and pulled her in next to his sister, both of whom barely came up to his shoulder, completing the tradition they'd repeated hundreds of times through the years. Would he ever outgrow these double hugs? The jasmine scent of his mother's perfume, the soft chime of his sister's giggle—*this* was coming home for Logan. He'd ignore how his mother's hair was more gray than blond now, how a few more fine wrinkles bracketed her wide smile. Yes, his mother was getting older—but she never aged.

"Mom and Caron, you both remember the team, but I'll do introductions for Alex. So, Max is the one on crutches, Brady's our resident bald guy—" Logan talked over Brady's groan. "And Jules brings class to our motley crew."

As he talked, his mom hugged each team member, and then insisted they all get comfortable in the family room while she finished with dinner.

"Caron made a baked crab dip, so why don't you relax a little bit longer and enjoy that?" His mother pointed to the room just off the kitchen. "Logan, help them get settled, will you? And find out what they want to drink."

"Sure thing, Mom."

Once the trio was settled with dip and veggies and tall glasses of iced tea, he excused himself and headed back to the kitchen.

"Where's Dad?"

"Oh, you know how he always has just a few more things left over from work." His mother patted his back, standing on tiptoe to place another kiss on his cheek, and then moving to retrieve a spinach salad from the side-by-side fridge. "Even with Caron working there now, he hasn't slowed down a bit."

"Enjoying being a Realtor, sis?"

"Absolutely." Caron rejoined Alex, who seemed more than happy to stay by her side. "You know it's been my plan since I was in high school."

"I know. And thanks to you, I don't have to go near that corporate ladder to success."

"No—you always wanted to go drag real ladders from the garage and use them to climb up on the roof. And then jump off. I'm happy to rescue you from the life of planning open houses and negotiating contracts." His sister leaned back into Alex's embrace. She'd cut her hair shoulder-length and dyed it a soft blond. His father must have requested she have a normal hair color if she was going to be a part of Hollister Realty. "So, we're still trying to convince Dad to finally take that cruise down the Danube he and Mom have always talked about—'we' being Mom, me, Alex, and his parents. Who knows, maybe next year he'll relax enough and book it."

Leaning down from his height of six-foot-six, Alex pressed a kiss on her lips. "You're doing a marvelous job, sweetheart."

"Thanks for the vote of confidence." Caron stood on her tiptoes and returned his kiss, brushing his brown hair back off his forehead. "It's nice to know someone believes in me."

"I always have." Alex stole another kiss. "You're beautiful and talented."

"Yeah, yeah. Just see if you can talk up the Danube over dinner."

Just how serious was this thing between his sister and Alex? So long as the guy treated her right, then Logan was good with this. It was nice to see his sister laughing. Content. An air of wounded uncertainty had lingered after her last breakup—but that was gone now.

"So what's the latest on the hurricane?" Logan noticed the small TV mounted under one of the rows of kitchen cabinets. A new addition—convenient for his mom while she cooked.

"Alex and I checked the news about ten minutes ago. It's still only a hurricane watch."

"Okay, then. Are you and Dad still planning on throwing a block party and riding it out here if it actually turns into the real thing?"

"Logan—we do not throw a block party." Even as she reprimanded him, his mother laughed. "We just let the neighbors know they're welcome to stay here if they want."

"Well, Dad built this house like a fortress."

"And that's why we won't have to evacuate—ever. You know you and the team can come here if the hurricane shows up, right?"

"Yes—but I'm not worried about it. And really, I wouldn't want to interrupt the party."

"Enough." His mother pulled a bottle of her

homemade creamy bacon salad dressing from the fridge. "Go tell your dad dinner is ready in five, will you?"

"Sure thing, Mom." He nodded toward the family room. "Caro, will you and Alex check on Julie and the guys?"

He grabbed a bottle of water for his father and a Coke for himself, noting his mother had a small dish of sliced lemons waiting on the shelf. "Thanks for remembering."

"How could I forget? You've been guzzling that stuff since middle school. I don't understand it, but I'm your mother and I like to spoil you when I can."

"I'm not spoiled."

"Shoo!" She snapped the towel at his backside, reminding him of all the times she'd sent him scurrying from the kitchen in the same way. His mother knew how to wield a kitchen towel like a guy in a high school locker room.

He paused in the kitchen doorway before heading to his father's office at the back of the house. "Dad still on the health kick like last year?"

"It's no 'kick.'" His mother shrugged and held up her hands. "He's lost twenty-five pounds. And he has me juicing every morning and going to the gym three times a week."

Amazing.

Being told his father had lost weight and then seeing the new and improved thinner version of his father were two very different things. As his father paced his office talking on the phone about a new property for sale, Logan set the bottle of water on his desk and waited. Gone was the paunch that used to rest above his father's belt, the bit of jowl that had added a *Godfather* look to his face.

Phone call done, his father settled back behind his dark wood desk, motioning Logan to sit down in the black leather club chair set off to one side. A wall of inset bookshelves lined with the classic books he'd collected through the years provided a perfect backdrop to his father's office.

"How are you, son?" His father nodded a brief thanks for the water.

"Good. Enjoying the beach."

"I don't know why you don't stay at the house. We have plenty of room here."

Logan gulped back the soda, cold, and with the zing of lemon he relished. They had this same discussion every time Logan came back to Florida. Maybe one year his father would understand he needed space. That staying at the hotel in Destin was a personal preference, not a snub. He liked waking up and having the Gulf just outside his door—well, just outside the hotel's door. "I come to Destin for the beach. And the team is with me—"

"Yes." His father opened the desk's top drawer and tossed several magazines onto his desk. "How did it feel, having your team make the national news?"

With only a brief scan of the covers, Logan knew what each magazine article detailed. The first two highlighted the killer tornado that had ripped through Kansas last July. The third lasered in on the Stormmeisters, the all-too-familiar photograph of his battered chase car overturned in a ditch. Mud-splattered. The windshield shattered. If he stared at the image long enough, he could hear Max's screams . . .

"Back up . . . back up . . . Logan, the tornado's right in front of us!"

They said a picture was worth a thousand words. Sometimes those words hung suspended in one long scream . . . and silence so loud a man couldn't sleep at night for fear of what he'd see again when he closed his eyes.

His father waved his hand over the magazines. "Is this why you called me a few months back?"

Logan stood and bridged the gap between them, turning the magazines facedown. "Yes."

"You're finally ready to give up storm chasing?"

"I think it's time."

"Well, it's probably best to do it now before someone does get killed."

Exactly. Or before the team lost all its funding. Logan swallowed, his throat suddenly parched. Even if—when—he walked away from the team, how long would it take to forget that day? To forgive himself?

He cleared his throat. "Max is recovering well. I thank God for that."

"I don't know if it's right to thank God because your—what did that one news anchor say?—'error in judgment' only put your teammate in the hospital with a broken arm and a broken leg and didn't kill him."

Logan shifted his weight from one foot to the other, forcing himself to maintain eye contact with his father. Not to blink. Back down. Leave the room. It was as if he'd been called into his father's office to explain he'd flunked out of high school. Not that he'd ever dared to do that. No, his father could never complain about his grades.

Logan had failed at his dream—one his father had never understood. Was he making another mistake? "I didn't come here to talk about what happened this summer, Dad. It doesn't change anything."

"Well, if you're finally ready to grow up and quit storm chasing, I'm ready to offer you a real job."

And of course his father would bring it all back to that.

He gripped the can of soda with both hands. "Let me make one thing perfectly clear, Dad. I *have* a real job, with stellar credentials. I'm a meteorologist, and I've led the Stormmeisters—successfully—since I was in college."

"You know I've never supported your decision to be a storm chaser. You've had ten years to pursue this. Fine. Now you're quitting—and that's a decision I can support." His father tossed the magazines into the trash can. "I'm offering you the chance to come work for me at Hollister Realty."

"Dad, you've already got Caron working for you. From what I hear, she's doing a great job—"

"Of course she is. I wouldn't hire her if she weren't capable. But there's room for both of my children in the company." Resting his elbows on the arms of his chair, his father dusted his hands off and then steepled his fingers against one another. "She's dating Alex now. Couldn't make your mother and me—and Alex's parents—happier. If this relationship goes the way I think it will, her priorities will be changing."

"Dad, selling real estate—providing homes for families—that's always been your passion. And I respect that. But real estate—that's not for me. I've seen how storms destroy people's homes. Don't you remember what happened to Pop Pop and Mom Mom?"

"Of course I remember! I grew up in that house—"

"Exactly!" Logan paced in front of his father's desk. "And all it took was the hand swipe of one tornado to destroy everything—photographs, heirlooms, even Mom Mom's wedding dress. And to . . . to . . ."

"To kill your grandmother."

Even all these years later, Logan's vision blurred with tears as he remembered how the tornado took his grandmother's life. How could his father sit there and show no emotion?

"I saw how heartbroken Pop Pop was when he realized Mom Mom had gotten caught in the tornado coming back from town. I walked their property with him . . . sifted through the rubble days later. Looking for remnants of their life together. That's why I'm a storm chaser. If I can help figure out a way to predict tornadoes . . . maybe help save lives that way . . ."

"But you said you're done with that." His father leaned forward. "I'm offering you a good job."

"I have other opportunities I'm investigating—jobs that will keep me connected with the storm-chasing community."

"So you're still refusing to grow up and see what I'm offering you?"

"No, Dad." Logan closed his eyes, pressing his thumb and forefinger against the bridge of his nose. They always came to this point. "You're still refusing to accept that we can have different dreams."

An invisible barrier seemed to separate him from his father. Would they ever be able to find any kind of common ground between them?

His dad shoved his chair back from his desk,

the squeaking of the wheels causing Logan to look up. "Does your team know yet?"

"No. I wanted a relaxing vacation for all of us. I'm going to talk to them when we get back to Oklahoma. That's soon enough."

"I was hoping we could tell the family tonight at dinner that you've come to your senses."

Logan shrugged off the insult. "No, not tonight. Brady and Max and Julie are here, too, remember? They deserve to hear my decision from me first—not announced during dessert. Once they know, then we can tell the family."

"But your mind's made up? At least you're finished with this foolishness of chasing tornadoes?"

Logan nodded, swallowing back the words burning on his tongue. What was that proverb he'd read this morning? Something about harsh words stirring up anger. He wanted to have a pleasant dinner with his family and his friends—not destroy what his mother had worked so hard to prepare. No more arguing.

All too soon he'd walk away from everything he'd pursued since he was sixteen.

But he couldn't lead the Stormmeisters like this—second-guessing himself, dreading the thought of getting back behind the wheel of a chase car . . .

He crushed the soda can, tossing it into the metal trash can, where it landed on top of the magazines with a dull thud, liquid splashing across the pages.

It was time to walk away. All he had to do was replace a car and help cover Max's medical bills—although he would have to fight his friend to do that. Keep lobbying for grants for next summer.

"I'm proud of you, son. I have to admit, it was hard seeing the family's name displayed in the national news like that." His father stood, giving Logan a swift pat on the shoulder as he walked past. "Let's go have dinner, shall we?"

The sound of his father's whistle drifted down the hallway as Logan sat back down in the chair facing his father's desk. *Now* his father was proud of him—when Logan abandoned everything he'd worked so hard for? Where were the words of comfort or encouragement? Why couldn't his father tell him that he could overcome this? That he believed in him?

Logan leaned forward, his elbows on his knees, head down. Ridiculous thought. When had his father ever said that?

A strangled prayer fought for release, caught in the tangles of self-accusation. What right did someone as reckless as he was have to ask God for help?

A little help here, God. I know I don't deserve it. But for Brady and Max and Julie . . . help me do the right thing. To walk away.

"Dinner's ready, brother-mine."

His sister's announcement yanked him upright.

"Alex, perfect man that he is, is helping Mom get

the food on the table. She knows how you love her brisket." Caron infused a lighthearted tone into her announcement, standing in the doorway of their father's office.

Logan pushed himself up from the chair, pasting a smile on his face, as he joined his sister in the hall, draping an arm around her shoulders. "Thanks, Caro."

"It's great to see you and your team. Jules knows how to keep those guys in line. I can understand why you love working with them."

Her words seared a bit, as if she'd spilled a bit of acid on his skin. "Yeah, they're the best."

"So you and Dad okay? What was the powwow all about?"

"Just catching up, that's all." He hated not being honest with his sister—but she knew how he and their father had wrangled over Logan's job for years. "How goes it, working for him?"

Caron slowed her steps, her bare feet with toenails painted a brilliant blue silent on the carpeted hallway. "Most days, it's fine. I love my job. In fact, Alex took me out for a celebratory dinner when I passed the real estate exam. And I think Dad appreciates what I do—even if I'm not you."

Logan pulled his sister to a stop, resting his chin on her head. "I'm sorry—"

"Hey, it's not your problem that Dad's old-fashioned. 'Need my boy to carry on the family

106

business, you know. My daughter will be staying home and having babies.' " Caron's gruff imitation of their dad was lousy. "Too bad you're the one who went off to Oklahoma chasing storms and I was the one who only wanted to chase a business degree."

Was his decision going to make things more difficult for his sister? "Are you happy dating Alex?"

His sister narrowed her eyes. "What kind of question is that? From real estate to my love life? Not that it's any of your business, but yes, I am."

"The last I heard you were dating some other guy—what was his name? And it's just . . . odd to see you and Alex together, you know?"

"No, I don't know." Now his sister's eyes glinted a dark blue, like the Gulf when a storm was approaching. "I dated Kade for half a year. It was nothing. And just because we all grew up listening to that silly joke about our parents betrothing us at birth, well, that doesn't mean Alex and I couldn't actually fall in love. We've known each other forever. I trust him. I'm safe with him."

Logan held up his hands. "Okay, okay. I just asked a question. I am your big brother, after all. Come on, you always swore you'd never date— much less marry—Alex. Said you'd become a nun or run away and join the circus before you'd do that. If you're happy, I'm good."

"I'm happy—and we're just dating. But you never know." She nudged his shoulder. "Don't worry about me. I know what I'm doing."

"Then I'm good. And I'm hungry, too."

"Food's this way."

"Lead on, little sister. Lead on."

EARLY SEPTEMBER 2003

Logan stashed his books in his locker, shutting the door with a metallic click and then giving the lock a quick spin before heading straight to his motorcycle. No chance of Vanessa getting by him just because this might be the day she broke her after-school routine and didn't stop to talk to Mindy on the steps outside the high school.

But just like the last two weeks, she exited the school's double doors, side by side with Mindy. Stood on the steps and talked with the other girl, smiling and sharing a hug. Waved goodbye as Mindy ran for her bus, her curls bouncing against her shoulders. And then Vanessa shouldered her backpack again and moved toward the parking lot—his way—at last.

Logan leaned against his bike, arms crossed over his chest, the afternoon sun warm on his back. Wait. Wait. No need to jump the gun and holler at her across the empty parking spaces, the cars, the other students, attracting unwanted attention.

"Hey, Hollister." He kept his voice low. Casual.

She stopped, her head turning right, then left, until he raised his hand.

"Can I give you a ride home?"

She gripped the strap of her backpack with one hand, chewing on her thumbnail, seeming to debate his offer.

How could he convince her to say yes? Let her know he was a good guy? Logan shifted to one side and tapped the spare red helmet hooked on the back of the motorcycle next to his black helmet.

"I've got an extra helmet—see? One for me, one for you. I like speed, but I'm not gonna hit the asphalt with my head if some driver doesn't see me. When you ride with me, you'll be safe."

Vanessa tilted her head to the side, her gaze going from him to the helmet and back again. "Sure." Her smile, which lit up her brown eyes, was the reward for all the waiting. "Sounds fun."

Logan hooked her backpack onto his bike with a pair of worn bungee cords and then helped her with the tricky helmet buckle, aware of how close they stood to each other. Vanessa smelled of something floral. Sweet.

"This thing going to stay on?" Vanessa's voice had a breathless quality. She kept her arms crossed over her waist, her sandaled foot tapping the asphalt.

"My sister wears it all the time."

"Your sister?"

"Yeah—Caron. She's a sophomore."

"You don't give her a ride home from school?"

"No, usually I have to be at work right after school. But I'm good today."

And if Vanessa Hollister wanted a ride home from school from here on out, he'd talk to his boss about changing his hours. Today he had already asked another worker to cover his shift—just in case Vanessa said yes.

He backed up, rapping his knuckles twice on the helmet, unable to hold back a grin at the glint of another smile in her eyes behind the visor. "You're all set. I'll climb on first and hold the bike steady while you climb on behind me."

Vanessa nodded, and a few moments after he straddled the bike it shifted beneath her weight. She didn't touch him, leaving plenty of space between their bodies. And without looking back, he'd bet she was gripping the sides of the seat, too. He couldn't blame her. They knew each other's names. Shared a couple of classes together. But if he handled things right, maybe things would change. All he had to do was give her a good, safe ride home so she'd say yes when he offered her a ride again tomorrow.

He wouldn't confess to gunning it just a bit when he pulled out of the parking lot. But Vanessa slid closer, her hands gripping his waist. Once again, since he was facing forward, his face covered by his helmet, she couldn't see him smiling.

• • •

Vanessa shifted the small stack of books in her arms, following Mindy to their Honors English class.

"What did you think of last night's assignment?"

"I'm not crazy about Shakespeare, but—" Mindy clutched her arm. "Here comes Logan Hollister!"

"So?" Vanessa shook off Mindy's hand, wishing her friend would lower her voice. That she'd calm down. It was just Logan. He'd say hi. She'd say hi. No big deal.

He wore jeans and his black boots, a gray T-shirt that revealed his strong, tanned arms.

"Hey, Mindy." He nodded to the other girl and then gave Vanessa a smile that made her want to stop right there in the hallway and just watch him walk the rest of the way down the hall. Or maybe skip class and go wherever he was going. "Hey, Vanessa. See you after school, right?"

"Yes. Sure."

And then he was gone, disappearing into the crowd. And Mindy was grabbing her arm again. And giggling. She could only hope Logan didn't hear how ridiculous her friend sounded.

"Stop it!" Vanessa double-timed it down the hallway.

"Oh, my gosh! Logan Hollister likes you!"

"We're just friends, Mindy."

Her comment only made Mindy laugh harder.

"Sure you are. Have you seen Logan giving any other girl a ride home on his motorcycle?"

No. No, she hadn't. And that realization made her slow her steps.

"You want to date him, don't you?"

Did she want to date him?

"Maybe."

"Maybe? Vanessa, are you out of your mind? Do you know how many girls want to date Logan Hollister? I mean, look at him! That whole leather jacket, long hair, bad boy look—and yet, he's nice."

"He is, isn't he?" Vanessa tucked a strand of hair behind her ear. "I mean, I've never dated a guy with long hair before—not that there's anything wrong with that. It's just that I was on the swim team before, and I went out with one of the guys on the team. They tend to keep their hair short, if not completely shaved."

Okay, now she was babbling—and that had to stop because the bell was ringing and they'd just made it to class.

By afternoon, the questions began again— because Vanessa hadn't figured on Logan giving her a ride home from school becoming an after-school routine.

But she liked it—more and more every day.

As he started the motorcycle, Vanessa slid in closer, wrapping her arms around his waist. He glanced over his shoulder. "All set?"

She nodded, knowing the helmet muffled her words. "Yep. I'm ready."

She could tell by the way his eyes narrowed that he was smiling at her, and he gave her hand a quick squeeze before easing the bike out of the parking space. He kept his speed low as he watched for students walking to their cars. Once they got to John Sims Parkway, he'd gun the motor just a bit, an unspoken signal for her to hold on, to rest her head against his back and enjoy the too-short ride home.

Vanessa needed to admit it to somebody—if only to herself—that she was getting used to Logan Hollister waiting by her locker every day after school. It had only been a week, but still, she liked seeing him leaning up against the wall, wearing his jeans torn at the knees, his black boots, his hair skimming his shoulders.

The first few days she tried to convince herself that his "Hey, Hollister, have a good day?" was enough. Just Logan being friendly to the new girl. But every day he asked her if she wanted a ride home. And every day she said yes, ignoring the little voice warning her that her parents wouldn't like her hopping on the back of Logan's motor-cycle. But her parents' disapproval was no reason to tell Logan no. Her mom was picking up her little brother from middle school, and her dad? Well, he never got home from work before seven.

And what would her father say? She wouldn't

date Logan just to annoy her father, would she? That would be mean . . . and Logan had been awfully nice, taking her home from school.

She liked having a friend—well, two friends, if she counted Mindy. And she did. In the past she'd be in the pool every afternoon, hanging with all the girls on the swim team. No real conversations, since she spent most of the time in the water, swimming laps. But the thought of coming in as the new girl to an established team . . . no, thank you.

This wasn't the senior year she'd imagined—or the one she'd been promised.

Make the best of it, her mother said. So far, Logan Hollister was the best thing to happen to her since she rode into town with her mom, right behind the U-Haul van.

SEVEN

The most called-upon prerequisite
of a friend is an accessible ear.
—MAYA ANGELOU (1928–2014),
AUTHOR AND POET

She was a coward.

Vanessa gripped the balcony railing, inhaling the morning breeze that brushed her hair away from her face. Golden sunlight dappled the waves along the beach. Dozens of sandpipers ran back and forth along the sand, while an occasional jogger ran past the couples out for an early morning stroll.

And here she stood, on the balcony of her hotel room, acting as if she was afraid Logan might appear on the beach again.

Because he might.

Vanessa ran her palm along the smooth metal edge of the railing. Which one of the hotels bordering the beach was Logan staying at? What if they were at the same hotel? What if she went down to the lobby for breakfast and ran into her ex-husband again? But if she stayed in her room, then she was tempted to keep reading her journal—and doing that only pulled her into the past. Their past.

She banged her fist on the railing. Maybe she

should call the airport and book a ticket on the first flight back to Denver.

But that would only prove she was a quitter. She'd leave Florida with nothing done for the wedding except having secured Mindy as matron of honor—and handing the wedding to-do list over to her. Seeing Logan for less than five minutes was not going to stop her from marrying Ted.

Vanessa turned her back on the view of the beach, returning to her room and retrieving her cell phone. Nine o'clock here, which meant it was eight in Montana—but surely Rylan was awake. She'd check on her father, then change out of her pajamas, brave the hotel's breakfast area, and force herself to walk the shoreline. She was not going to live her life afraid of Logan Hollister. She hadn't done so for the past eight years. She wasn't going to start now.

"Hey, Rylan, I hope I didn't wake you. I wanted to check on Dad."

"No, I've been up for a couple of hours—already had my run. Sitting here having coffee with Mom and Dad." Her brother sounded cheerful—too cheerful. "Say good morning to them."

"Hello, Vanessa." Her mother's voice was calm—no surprise there. "How are the wedding plans coming along?"

"Just fine, Mom, but I called to see how Dad was."

"Everything is just fine here. Don't worry

about us. Rylan leaves tomorrow to head back to Germany, and then we'll settle back into our routine."

"Good. How's Dad feeling?"

"Oh, you know your father. He doesn't like change. Doesn't like the way I'm cooking his food now. Says it's bland. Let me have him talk to you."

Vanessa waited as her mother handed the phone off to her father. It sounded as if he grumbled about talking to her before he took the phone.

"Hello, Vanessa." Her father's voice sounded flat. Monotone.

"Good morning, Dad. How are you feeling?"

"I'm fine. I wish everyone would stop fussing."

"Dad, you did just have a heart attack."

"I'm fine." But even his protest was weak at best.

"Are you taking your medicine?"

"Of course I'm taking my medicine—don't need it, but I'm taking it. And your mother is making me walk back and forth to the mailbox twice a day, too."

"Well, good for you." Vanessa paused for a moment. Had anyone spoken to her parents about depression following a heart attack? "Dad, I really didn't get to see you very much when I came out after your heart attack. Would it be okay if I adjusted my trip and came back by? I have lots of unused vacation—"

"No need to do that. We'll see you for the holidays—or the wedding."

"Are you sure? I don't mind—"

"No use wasting your vacation to come see me." Her father cleared his throat. "I'm going to finish my breakfast now—although I don't know why. Your mother is feeding me oatmeal. Here's your brother."

Vanessa choked back a laugh. "Okay, Dad. Love you."

Rylan's voice replied, "Love you, too, Vanessa."

"Sure you do." Vanessa paced the room from the bathroom back to the sliding glass doors. "Can you tell me what's going on? I mean, besides Dad not wanting to eat oatmeal?"

"Yeah. I'm in the living room. Dad's fine physically. I mean, he's tired. But he just seems down. He sleeps a lot. When he's awake, he watches TV. Reruns of *Bonanza*."

"He's probably depressed, Rylan."

"Dad? Are you kidding me?"

"A heart attack is a scary thing. And while he's recovering physically, I don't know if his doctor has talked to him and Mom about the emotional and mental recovery."

"I hadn't thought about that."

"I'm not sure what we can do. He's not going to let his kids talk to him about how he's feeling. I mean, he's the dad, right?"

"Right." There was a few seconds of silence on

the phone. "He's not supposed to see the doctor for another month. I head back to Germany tomorrow, but I'm here now. I'll see what I can do. I mean, maybe I can figure out a way to talk to him about how he's feeling."

When had her little brother grown up—and what was he doing, being so mature? So brave?

"Will you let me know how things go?"

"Sure."

"Thanks, Rylan."

"No problem. We're family, even if we are spread out all over the world right now. Talk to you later."

That settled it. If Rylan could dare to talk to their father about his feelings, she could stop acting like a recluse and go eat breakfast. And then walk on the beach. She'd work her way up to it by showering and getting dressed. And she'd call Mindy, too—see if she wanted to talk about the wedding. But first . . . she removed her old journal from the bedside table, pulled her suitcase out of the closet, and tossed the leather-bound book inside, zipping it shut.

There. Out of sight, out of mind.

"Mindy, what have I done?" Vanessa buried her face in her arms, which were crossed over the glass-topped table positioned on the porch of the Henderson Park Inn.

"You just planned your destination wedding!"

Mindy clapped her hands, laughter in her voice. "Why are you upset? This is fantastic!"

"Because this is not the wedding Ted and I agreed upon!" Vanessa peered up at her friend. "He wants the ceremony at the same hotel as the medical conference, remember? You're my matron of honor. You're supposed to be helping me—not encouraging me to do something this . . . this . . ."

"This spectacular?" Mindy shook her head, all the while grasping Vanessa by the shoulders and pushing her back into a sitting position.

"Don't act like this. You're the bride-to-be. *Be happy.*" Mindy caught a piece of paper as it fluttered in the strong breeze coming from the beach. The incoming storm was stirring up the waves, and rain was predicted for later. "Here. Tuck the receipt into the folder the coordinator gave you."

Vanessa took another look at the total. "I put down a deposit, Mindy. A deposit on the inn—and Ted doesn't even know."

Mindy waved aside her concern. "Will you relax? It's refundable. Remember how horrified the wedding planner looked when you said, 'Could you pencil me in until I talk to my fiancé?' Of course the first week in April is the beginning of their busy season. This way you've got dibs on the inn. If Ted vetoes the idea when you get back home, then you call and cancel. No problem. But he won't. Not once you show him the brochure. And the website. And the videos."

Mindy's calm self-assurance backed Vanessa away from the edge of hysteria. She was right—nothing was undoable. And oh, how she wanted to have her beautiful, elegant destination wedding here.

She could imagine the beachfront wedding ceremony she and Ted could have here, come April. If he agreed. The green-roofed inn nestled right up against the white sands, and they had an idyllic view of the Gulf of Mexico from their vantage point on the inn's porch. Maybe before they left, she and Mindy could walk down to the beach and relax in the freestanding white wooden swing.

"It was fun daydreaming out loud with the assistant wedding coordinator. I can't believe we talked for over an hour."

Mindy ticked items off on her fingers. "Menus. Wedding cakes. Decorations."

"But I didn't plan on handing over my credit card—"

"No one twisted your arm, bride-to-be." Mindy's grin was infectious. "But if there's even the slightest chance you want to get married here next April, you were smart to put down that deposit."

"I need to talk to Ted face-to-face. That's the only way I'm going to convince him that we have to get married here. And so, matron of honor, you now have another responsibility on your to-do list."

"O-kay. And that would be?"

"Help me figure out how to persuade Ted that we absolutely must have the wedding here!"

"I told you—didn't I? Isn't it perfect?"

"Oh, Mindy, it's . . . stunning. Absolutely everything I could ever want for a wedding!" Vanessa lowered her voice to a whisper, as if she might break some sort of magic spell surrounding them.

"That's what you tell Ted—with exactly that look on your face."

Vanessa swallowed the last of the sweet iced tea in her glass, the ice cubes clinking together. Almost as good as a jolt of caffeinated Coke with a spritz of lemon. "What else?"

"Tell him how romantic and private and . . . and . . . perfect the inn is."

"It is perfect." Vanessa rested her chin on her hands. "The other hotel will be overflowing with conference attendees and their families and medical vendors and workshops presenters. I'll spend most of my time poolside—alone."

"You could still end up alone—"

"Maybe. But I'll be alone *here.*"

"True. Tell him about the catering package. The flowers—not that he'll care about Gerbera daisies. Do you think Ted will like the steel drums?"

"He may opt for the DJ."

"You can always switch—but you love the idea of the drums, don't you?"

"Well, a DJ is traditional, but wouldn't a steel drummer or harpist be lovely?"

"Will Ted want to help decide about the cake?"

"Maybe the flavor—but I don't think he'll care too much about the design." Vanessa opened the folder again. "I liked the inn's Gold Catering option. Appetizers, salads, entrées, and side dishes. My mouth started watering just reading over the list of crab cakes, kung pao shrimp, a classic Caesar salad, Mediterranean chicken—"

"Stop! You are talking to a pregnant woman here!"

"You don't want me to mention pasta Alfredo or the roasted vegetable platter—"

Mindy clasped Vanessa's hand across the table. "You did a whole lot of daydreaming today. The assistant walked away with a filled-in list, you know. It was fun, admit it."

"Yes, thanks to you." Vanessa knew her grin was taking on goofy proportions. "But this is the first time I've really gotten excited."

"How can Ted say no?" Mindy pushed her windblown hair back from her face. "Any more thought about what color you want me to wear?"

"After sitting here, looking out at the water, yes. All I can think about is how stunning it is—the blues and the greens. What would you think of wearing turquoise?"

"That's a favorite color of mine. Just don't tell me that you want me to go strapless—not when I've just had a baby."

"You take it from turquoise, Mindy. Didn't you mention an Empire waist would be better than form-fitting the first time we got together at your house?"

"Even with an Empire-waist dress, I'm going to be wearing pantyhose and Spanx, you know that, right?"

"Mindy, it's a beach wedding. Casual."

"And I'll just have had a baby. Spanx it is. So, turquoise for me—but what about you? Do you have a dress yet?"

"No. No dress."

"Six months to go—you've still got a reasonable amount of time, but you don't want to cut it too close. Do you want to look while you're here?"

"I don't know—shouldn't I shop for a dress in Denver?"

"That makes sense, especially if you need alterations. But we could stop by a bridal shop today and just have fun. Try on different styles. I've got time. Do you have any idea what you want?"

Vanessa shook her head. "Not at all. Something for a beach wedding. Long. Or short. White. Or ivory. Sleeveless. Or short sleeves. See? I don't know. I've never shopped for a wedding dress before . . ."

Her voice trailed off.

She'd never shopped for a wedding dress.

When she and Logan got married, she'd worn a yellow flowery sundress she'd packed for spring break—something she'd brought along in case they had a chance for a romantic dinner together one night, without the rest of the group. She hadn't imagined it would be her wedding dress.

"What happened, Vanessa?" Mindy's quiet question interrupted the memory.

"What do you mean?" Vanessa couldn't quite meet her friend's eyes.

"What happened between you and Logan? I never asked, because, well, I figured it was none of my business." Mindy twirled her straw in her water glass. "One weekend you're married, all excited to go surprise him at college in Oklahoma—to see about turning your marriage into a non-long-distance one. And when you come back, you say you're getting a divorce."

"Nothing happened." Vanessa scanned the horizon and then met her friend's gaze. "And that was the problem. Logan and I got married—and nothing happened. He liked his life in Oklahoma more than he liked being married. I was in the way of what he wanted."

"You two loved each other—"

"We never should have gotten married. It was an immature thing to do. Logan felt sorry for me and I . . . I thought I was in love with him. But I wasn't." She rested her head against the back of the chair. "Want to hear something funny?"

"What?"

"When I went to see my father after his heart attack, my mother had two boxes waiting for me."

"Two boxes? Of what?"

"High school stuff. My yearbook. My cap and gown." Vanessa shook her head. "Mostly junk. But I also found Logan's class ring."

"Oh, my gosh! What did you do with it?"

Vanessa ran her fingers through her bangs. "I didn't know what to do with it. I mean, it's not my ring—even if Logan gave it to me. But I don't know where Logan is—or at least I didn't. And even seeing him on the beach for a couple of minutes doesn't mean I know where he lives now."

"So where's the ring?"

"I mailed it back to my apartment along with some other things. I didn't know what else to do."

Mindy stared at her, her lips pursed. "Hmmm. I'll think on this. I mean, his family still lives here. Even his sister Caron works in town—I ran into her when Jett and I were house shopping. Maybe I could contact her—"

"It should probably be you, rather than me. I'm not sure Caron would want to talk with me." She pushed her chair away from the table. "Enough talking about the past. If we're going to look at wedding dresses, then we need to stop sitting around here."

"Oh, we're definitely shopping for dresses, girlfriend. I want to have fun trying them on before I'm showing."

"Good point."

"I thought so." Mindy linked their arms together. "But then, I am your matron of honor. Thanks for asking me, Vanessa."

Vanessa shared a half-hug with her friend. "No—thank you for saying yes, Mindy. Having you as part of the wedding is perfect."

"Because I led you to the inn, right?"

"No. Because every bride wants her best friend there when she gets married."

EIGHT

Life is a challenge. Meet it.
—MOTHER TERESA (1910–1997),
FOUNDER OF THE
MISSIONARIES OF CHARITY

The Gulf waves clamored against the shore, as if warning anyone walking along the beach of the incoming hurricane. Surfers created a staggered chorus line. Some paddled out toward the building waves while others faced shoreward, balancing on their surfboards, intent on conquering the challenge of balance, force, and motion.

"So, are you ready to go home?"

Julie's question tugged Logan's attention away from the surfers. If only he was wearing a pair of boardshorts and had hauled his board out of his parents' garage. He'd join the locals—take on the challenge. As one surfer wiped out, he acknowledged Julie's question.

"Do you mean am I packed?"

"Not exactly—although, sure, we all need to be packed before our flight tomorrow." She moved closer to the waves, so that the water reached above her ankles. "But I was wondering how you were doing after seeing Vanessa."

"Oh. That."

"Yes. *That*." Julie turned her back on the waves,

hands on her hips. "Logan, why aren't you two still married?"

"Because we're divorced—"

"But why? It's obvious you still love her."

"Julie, why are we having this conversation now?"

"I remember what you were like right after the divorce—the look on your face." Julie stopped walking, anchoring her feet in the sand beneath the water. "You looked lost. I haven't seen that look in years . . . until now."

Maybe Max wasn't so far off when he called Jules "Mom." She saw too much. "We couldn't make our relationship work. Too much pressure. Not enough time together. I thought we were managing the long-distance relationship okay, but we had a fight and we couldn't figure out a way to forgive each other. To get past it. All of it."

"Have you ever thought that maybe seeing Vanessa again is your second chance?"

"If this was some sort of chick flick, sure. But it's not." Over Julie's shoulder, one of the surfers caught a wave for just a moment—perfect—and then tumbled into the Gulf. "One random meeting doesn't bridge eight years of silence. And it wasn't like we even had a real conversation the other night. She ran off."

Again. Vanessa had run off *again*.

Brady splashed through the waves alongside them. "Don't mean to interrupt, but I think Max is about done with all the sand and surf." He pointed to where Max had settled onto the sand, his crutches lying next to him. "Let's have a little mercy on the guy, huh?"

"I can go sit with Max if you two want to hang a little longer." Julie ran out of the water and onto the beach, sending droplets of water onto Logan and Brady.

"That's okay." Logan turned to follow her. "I'm about done here."

"Last time I checked, our flight was still good to go for tomorrow." Brady's footsteps kicked up bits of sand behind him. "I'll double-check again in the morning."

"It'll be fine. We're probably looking at some wind and rain, but we'll be out of here before anything serious happens—if it does." Logan moved back up onto the beach, the salt-scented air cooling his sunburned neck. "Yeah, they've upgraded the storm to a weak hurricane, but it's not supposed to make landfall until the day after tomorrow—maybe as a Category 1. By then we'll be back in Oklahoma. I'm not worried."

"Just keeping you posted, boss. It's what I do."

"Thanks."

She had not requested a wake-up call.

Vanessa lifted her head off the pillow, shoving her hair out of her face, squinting into the darkness of the hotel room. The second sharp ring of the bedside phone had her grabbing for the receiver. Who was calling this early in the morning?

"Hello?" Her tone of voice should broadcast how little she appreciated this unplanned phone call.

"Ms. Hollister, this is the front desk. I'm sorry to disturb you, but we're evacuating the hotel—"

Vanessa scrambled upright, pulling the phone off the bedside table with a crash. "What?"

"We're evacuating the hotel. Hurricane Cressida increased speed overnight and is now expected to make landfall later today. Destin is under mandatory evacuation."

"Thank you." She hung up, stumbling to her feet, turning on the lamp, and righting the phone.

Mandatory evacuation. She needed to pack. To leave. But where was she supposed to go?

She found the remote control and hit on, clicking the channel selector and surfing for the local news station. When she pulled back the blinds shielding the sliding glass door to the balcony, the scene on the beach matched the ones on the TV. Winds whipped the Gulf into a frenzy, the sky dark, rain pummeling the sands of the deserted beach. In the background, a newscaster reiterated what the front desk person had already told her.

". . . Cressida gained strength overnight and is expected to make landfall as a Category 3 hurricane . . ."

No, she wasn't *having* a bad dream—she was wide awake in the middle of one.

She needed to stop alternating between staring at the TV and the view outside her hotel room. She needed to pack. But first she was going to shower—even if she only got two minutes of hot water, she was going to wash her hair and put on clean clothes. After she figured out where she was going, she didn't know how long she'd be there and when she'd have access to hot water again.

Once in the shower, Vanessa resisted the temptation to close her eyes and savor the steamy water sluicing over her skin. Pretend everything was calm outside. Two minutes, that was it. As she toweled off, her cell phone rang. Mindy started talking even as Vanessa said hello.

"Vanessa, are you okay? Are you off the island?"

"I'm not even dressed yet. The front desk guy woke me up ten minutes ago to tell me that they're evacuating the hotel."

"The hotel? The entire island is evacuating. This hurricane caught everyone off guard!"

"I don't have any intention of staying here, Mindy."

"Come to my house. Jett's been boarding up windows since yesterday when they declared a voluntary evacuation."

Somehow she had missed that information. "Why don't you go to the shelter?"

"Well, we could—the shelters take animals— dogs and cats. But six not-quite-housebroken puppies in an arena with two thousand people?

We're just going to ride it out here. We'll be fine. Jett bought a generator a few years ago."

"Okay, let me pack. I'll call you when I'm on my way. Or text. The phone lines are going to be a mess."

"The phone lines? Have you seen *the roads?*"

Vanessa could imagine what Highway 85, the main road heading out of Niceville, looked like. "I'm hanging up now. Don't worry about me."

"Of course I'll worry—but only until you get here. Then we'll play board games."

"I'll be fine. See you soon."

Vanessa started a small pot of coffee in the hotel pot. It wouldn't be a perfect cup of coffee—but it would be caffeine. She surveyed the leftover seafood scampi in the hotel fridge. Nope. That wasn't going with her. Two cans of Coke. A couple of slices of lemon. Those were a yes.

She hauled her suitcase onto the bed and opened all the dresser drawers, first selecting a pair of jeans and a sleeveless top to wear, along with her burnished leather boots with harness-ring accents—sturdy and casual. She needed to get dressed first, and then finish packing.

The strong aroma of coffee filled the room, and the ongoing commentary of the TV news the background music as she transitioned her clothes from the dresser to her suitcase, hiding her journal under a mound of clothes. She tossed her bottles of shampoo and conditioner and face wash into her kit, not even taking the time to dry them off from the shower.

"Go to Florida, he says." She checked the drawers one more time. The shower. Underneath the bed. The closet. "Have fun planning our destination wedding, he says. Relax, he says."

What part of going to Destin to plan their destination wedding, running into her ex-husband, and then having to evacuate because of a hurricane would Ted consider *relaxing?*

She did a quick three-sixty of the room. All ready to go. It was too early to call her parents to tell them she was fine. She would call Ted later, too, but for now she'd just text her parents and her fiancé.

Evacuating because of hurricane. I'm fine. Going to stay with Mindy. Will call soon. Love you.

It was only once she was checked out of the hotel, on her way toward the bridge, a bitter cup of hot coffee in the car's cup holder, that she thought of the Wrights. Were they okay? Surely they wouldn't stay in their house—not with a Category 3 hurricane headed for the Panhandle. What did Cat 3 winds max out at? Somewhere around 125 miles per hour.

But Cressida had surprised everyone—coming in faster and stronger than expected.

Most likely the Wrights were sound asleep, unaware of what was happening—just like she'd been an hour ago.

NINE

God does not remove us from all harm;
He uses harm to move us close to Him.
—DILLON BURROUGHS (1967–), AUTHOR

Thank God they were going back to Oklahoma later today.

Logan rolled over on his side, twisting the rumpled sheets and the dark geometric-design bedcover even more, and checked the time on the bedside clock. Four-twenty. Still too early to get up.

He shoved aside the blankets, sitting up against the pillows. Who was he kidding? A nightmare had awoken him hours ago, and when he'd fallen back asleep, it had started again, right where it had left off.

Thanks to unreality woven with just enough truth to make his heart ache and slick his skin with sweat, he'd been awake for the past two hours, staring into the dark. Not wanting to think about Vanessa. About what waited for him in Oklahoma.

He'd lost his wife because of his involvement with the Stormmeisters. And now he was walking away from the team. What would Vanessa say if she knew that?

He huffed out a short laugh, scratching at the roughness of his jaw. She wouldn't even talk to him—disappearing while some guy with a video camera acted like he was employed by *NBC Nightly News* and asked him a string of questions about rescuing that teenager. When he'd finally managed to get away from the wannabe reporter, Vanessa was gone. In eight years, he hears nothing from her—and then he gets, what, a minute with her? Two minutes?

She probably thought he was "living the dream"—chasing storms and loving his life—unaware of how many nights he was jarred awake by nightmares or how often he reached for the warmth of her, only to find emptiness on the other side of the bed.

The terror had been worse tonight. He'd been caught in a chase car, tumbling over and over, the tornado a merciless adversary . . . and someone else was in the car with him . . . screaming . . .

But it wasn't Max.

This time it was Vanessa.

Logan switched on the lamp, twisting the cap off the bottle of water he'd left on the table and draining it to ease the dryness in his throat as he paced the hotel room. Outside, the storm winds rattled the glass-paned door to the balcony. In years past, he would have stood outside, let the rain drench him. Laughed, even.

Known God was in the storm.

God was with him when he chased storms.

But something happened when Vanessa walked out of his life. Like a broken compass, something had spun out of control. Gone off-kilter. She said he didn't need her . . . but she couldn't have been more wrong. Vanessa was his ballast—helping him stay balanced . . . not capsize.

"God, why couldn't I have my dream and Vanessa, too?"

His question, spoken out loud, marred the stillness inside the room. Not that he expected an answer. He knew God wasn't listening.

How many times had he thought of trying to find her—only to feel as if God had blocked that path, said no to that desire? And yet there'd been no one else besides Vanessa—no matter how many times Julie fixed him up with a friend, or Brady suggested online dating, or Max told him to take another look at the women in the church's singles group. Dating dulled the isolation for a few hours, but he'd rather be alone—and lonely—than imagine pursuing a serious relationship with someone else.

Just like his grandfather, he'd found the woman he loved early in life. But he'd lost her.

And he had no one to blame but himself.

And his pursuit of tornadoes.

Well, he'd be finished with that in a week or so—but too late to save his marriage.

A sharp rap on his door interrupted his musings.

A distorted view of Brady through the peephole had Logan opening the door.

"Do you know what time it is? Are Julie and Max okay—"

Brady held up his hands for silence. "Logan, the island's being evacuated."

"What are you talking about?"

"The hurricane sped up and is making landfall *today*—not tomorrow. We're not going any-where—except to a hurricane shelter, boss."

Logan barreled the rental car through the toll lane, the booth empty of anyone waiting for drivers to pay the customary fee. Brady sat in the front passenger seat, hanging on to the handle of the door.

"Nice of them to not ask us to pay a toll." Brady saluted the vacant booths.

Logan gripped the steering wheel so hard his hands ached. "No toll when they've evacuated Destin, buddy. It's all about getting off the island—fast."

He glanced in the rearview mirror. Julie and Max sat next to each other in the backseat. Max watched news updates on his iPhone while Jules stared out the window at the rain and wind buffeting the trees lining the road.

As they traversed the bridge, the bay below tossed and turned like an unruly beast seeking release from the confines of the shoreline. High winds heralded the oncoming hurricane, lashing rain across their windshield. Logan ratcheted the speed of the car's wipers as high as they would go. The branches of trees along the side of the road tangled together, a few broken limbs skittering across the roadway.

When Julie leaned forward and touched his shoulder, Logan met her gaze in the rearview mirror.

"So where we headed?"

"The evacuation shelter—Raider Athletic Arena at Northwest Florida State College." Only fifteen minutes or so—in good weather. He could do this. He would get them all there safe and sound. "I tried to reach my parents, but the cell towers are already jammed. I'm sure they've invited all of their neighbors over. My parents' home can handle a decent hurricane."

Logan trained his eyes on the road, keeping a safe distance from the car in front of him, even as he resisted pressing down on the gas pedal. He was not getting into an accident—or causing one.

"I'm surprised you didn't want to hang around the island—" Brady talked fast, his voice pitched higher, just like he did when they chased a tornado. "—maybe hook up with a weather crew."

Logan shook his head, forcing a laugh. There was no way Brady could hear the pounding of his heart. Or the second-guesses that had circled his self-confidence for months. "Not my turf.

We'll let someone else handle this one, right?"

"That doesn't sound like the Logan Hollister I know. What happened to the guy who would go after any thing, any time?"

What happened to him? Did Brady even have to ask? They'd all been there in Kansas. Hadn't the sight of Max's bloodied body, his leg twisted at a bizarre angle, affected him at all?

"I'm still here." Logan kept his eyes focused straight ahead. Forced a grin. He could only hope Brady didn't see past his bluff. "I'm just on vacation."

"Oh. Got it." Brady lowered his voice, the rain pelting the roof of the car muffling his words even more. "You do know Max doesn't hold you responsible—"

Did Brady think he really wanted to discuss this now? While one very early, very angry hurricane chased them out of Destin? And with Max sitting a few feet behind him?

"I *am* responsible!" He whispered the bitter truth through clenched teeth. "I am responsible for Max . . . and you . . . and Jules. I'm the team leader. And that night I blew it. There's no getting around that."

"We're all a part of the Stormmeisters by choice, Logan. No one forces us to chase storms. We all love the life—the adventure—as much as you do. And anyone else could have made that mistake—"

"But you didn't. *I did.*"

Rain obscured the windshield, the wiper blades fighting against the watery onslaught. Logan's breath came in short puffs, as if he'd been running rather than driving through a torrential downpour, a hurricane at his back.

He unclenched his hands. Huffed out a breath. "Let's drop it, okay?"

"Sure. Whatever you say."

"Thanks."

Brady lowered his voice. "I'm sorry—"

"Let me just concentrate on driving."

With a quick nod, Brady settled back in the seat.

Good. No more conversation. Because really, if anyone should be apologizing, it should be him. To Max. To Brady. To Julie.

But he'd wait until after the storm passed. And then he'd declare his repentance. Tell them that he was done. That he was disbanding the Stormmeisters. Of course, the team could choose to go on without him—if they had the funding. They were all adults, free to make their own decisions.

He just hoped they would respect his decision . . . and he would respect theirs.

Why weren't the Wrights answering the door? Had they left during the earlier voluntary evacuation phase? Or had their daughter come and picked them up last night just in case the storm got worse?

Vanessa pounded on the wooden door again,

pressing the doorbell at the same time, the wind blowing the rain against her back, further soaking her hair and jeans. Her Windbreaker was little protection against the storm's onslaught—and she'd been standing on the doorstep for more than five minutes.

As she peered through the tempered glass oval in the middle of the door, it swung open, Mrs. Wright framed in the middle of the doorway wearing a coral bathrobe and her slippers.

"Vanessa." The woman's smile was as welcoming as always. "How nice of you to come and visit again so soon."

Vanessa wrapped her arms around the smaller woman, inhaling the comfort of her familiar perfume. "Oh, Mrs. Wright, I'm so glad you're okay."

"Well, why wouldn't I be?" The older woman patted her back, ignoring the fact that Vanessa was dripping wet. "I'm just making breakfast for Mr. Wright. He's still sleeping upstairs. He's not an early riser."

Not good.

"Have you been watching the weather reports?" Why did she even ask the question? It didn't matter. "The hurricane is coming in faster and stronger than expected. We've got to get to the evacuation shelter."

"Oh, Christina said something about that when she called this morning and said she wouldn't be coming to work. But we've always stayed home before—"

Why hadn't the home care provider insisted the Wrights go to the shelter? Or asked a neighbor to help them? "Mrs. Wright, this hurricane is bad—a Category 3, last I checked—maybe worse." The salty aroma of bacon wafted from the direction of the kitchen. "Why don't you go wake up Mr. Wright and start getting yourselves dressed? I'll turn off the stove and get some food supplies for both of you. You'll need to pack clothes and whatever medicines you both need—"

"But Mr. Wright doesn't like to be away from home for long—"

"We don't have a choice. I'll help as much as I can. Do you have any sleeping bags or cots or anything?" Vanessa removed her wet Windbreaker and left it in the hall, next to her leather boots.

"We used to camp all the time. There might be some things in the garage . . . I really don't know."

The smell of burning bacon drifted down the hall. "Don't worry about it. Your only concern is your husband. I'll take care of everything else."

"I can drive, you know—"

There was no way Mrs. Wright was driving in this torrential downpour. Should the older woman even have a driver's license? "There's no need to take two cars. The roads are jammed with traffic. I'll drive."

"I guess that's best." Instead of going upstairs, Mrs. Wright followed Vanessa to the kitchen. "Are you sure we don't have time for breakfast? Mr. Wright is very particular."

Vanessa eyed the charred bacon in the pan, the two eggs waiting to be cracked into the skillet. "I'll see what I can do. You go on upstairs and get dressed. Then wake up Mr. Wright. I'll be there in just a few."

After putting the pan of charred bacon on the back burner, she rummaged through the fridge. Most likely the shelter had food supplies, but it would be wise to take some food for the older man's finicky taste buds. She soon had a small selection of containers on the counter: cooked chicken breasts, slices of steak, a baked potato, and some rice. She could only hope Mr. Wright would eat some of the leftovers. Then she grabbed some bread and a few apples and oranges from a basket on the table in the breakfast nook. Foraging through the pantry produced half a dozen cans of Ensure and a handful of straws, as well as a box of graham crackers. She added a dozen water bottles to the pile and, spying a half dozen Hershey bars, threw them in, too. One of the Wrights had a sweet tooth.

Just as she entered the garage, her cell phone buzzed. Of course Ted was smart enough to text instead of trying to call.

Watching the news. Where are you?

She typed a quick reply: *Preparing to head to the evacuation shelter. Safe. More later.*

After texting Ted, she took the time to text Mindy about her detour and her decision to go to the shelter with the Wrights. A hurricane, two elderly people, and puppies didn't go together.

She ignored the phone when it buzzed again, tucking it in the back pocket of her jeans. Right now Ted was not her priority—and she didn't have time to argue by text with Mindy. She had to get the Wrights to safety.

A well-kept black Cadillac sedan sat on one side of the two-car garage. Shelves lined one wall—so nicely organized Vanessa could have shouted an "Amen!" She piled two sleeping bags by the garage door, along with two camp chairs.

Upstairs, Mrs. Wright had her husband sitting on the edge of the bed, his wispy white hair in disarray, a white T-shirt and gray sweatpants serving as pajamas.

"He's cranky in the morning." Mrs. Wright smiled an apology.

"Good morning, Mr. Wright. It's Vanessa." She leaned in, resting a hand on his shoulder, the bone sharp beneath the cotton material of his shirt. "I'm sorry to wake you up so early, but a hurricane's coming and we need to get to a shelter."

"Haven't had my breakfast yet."

"If you get dressed, I'll go downstairs and get that ready for you."

"Eggs and bacon?"

Vanessa mentally calculated microwave cooking time. "Yes. I can make that happen."

"I like scrambled eggs."

"How about you let Mrs. Wright help you get dressed, and I'll see what I can do?"

Vanessa turned to the older woman. "Where's your luggage? You need to pack a suitcase—one for the both of you should be fine."

"There should be one in the closet—or there's a larger one in the garage."

"That will work fine."

While Mrs. Wright cajoled her husband into getting out of bed, Vanessa ran downstairs and put some whisked eggs in the microwave, as well as several slices of bacon. Then she ran back upstairs and ransacked their dresser, tossing basic items into the suitcase she'd found in the garage. Underwear, T-shirts, and socks for Mr. Wright, as well as a few pairs of sweatpants and button-down shirts.

After helping Mrs. Wright walk her husband downstairs and get him comfortable in the recliner in the living room, she stood just inside the kitchen.

"Go back upstairs and get dressed and add what you need to the suitcase. Don't forget your medicines—for both you and Mr. Wright." Vanessa surveyed the Wrights' mementos. Carnival glass displayed in the dining room hutch. Photos of their daughter's family arrayed on the piano. "If there's anything you want to bring with you—something small—a wedding photo, maybe—pack that, too. And I packed some food. Add a few things to that, especially if there are certain things Mr. Wright will eat."

"And then what?"

"And then we pack the car and head to the arena at the college."

"But first—"

But first, what? What had she forgotten? "Yes?"

As the rain pounded on the roof, Mrs. Wright clasped Vanessa's hand in hers. "But first we pray and ask God to protect us. To turn this storm away from us, if that's his will."

For the first time that morning, Vanessa could take a deep breath. "Let's do that right now. Would you pray, please?"

"Absolutely. I've been praying all this time. I learned a long time ago God doesn't mind if we pray with our eyes wide open."

SEPTEMBER 2003

Logan's shoulders tensed beneath Vanessa's embrace as he guided the motorcycle up her driveway. Was something wrong? She lifted her head and peeked over his shoulder, her arms still wrapped around his waist, scant inches separating them. A sigh collapsed her shoulders, and she scooted back on the seat.

Caught. She shouldn't be surprised. But she'd expected her mom to be waiting for them one of these afternoons when Logan brought her home— not her father. It was barely four o'clock, and yet for some reason, her father stood on the front porch.

Nothing else to do but deal with the wrath of Dad now—and the wrath of Mom later.

She'd hop off the motorcycle, hand Logan her helmet, grab her backpack, and say goodbye.

But Logan had other plans. He cut the engine, pulled off his helmet, and ran his fingers through his messy hair. "I'd like to meet your dad if it's okay."

What? Was he crazy?

"Logan, you don't have to—"

"Vanessa, it's okay." His smile seemed to offer comfort, even as it hinted that he found the whole father-waiting-for-them scenario amusing.

Well, he hadn't met her father before.

Her dad stood there, his gaze hidden behind the brown lenses of his gold-rimmed aviator sun-glasses. Logan following so close behind her that she could hear his breathing, Vanessa slowed her steps, knowing how this would go. Her father would grill Logan like a military drill sergeant intent on breaking a new recruit. But before her father said a word, Logan moved around her, walked up the steps of the porch, and stuck out his hand.

"Good afternoon, sir. I'm Logan Hollister. Nice to meet you."

"Logan . . . Hollister, is it?" Not a hint of amusement over the same last name. "I take it you're a friend of my daughter's, although she hasn't mentioned you."

"Yes, sir. Vanessa and I are both seniors. We have some of the same classes together." Logan tapped his helmet against his thigh. "I hope it's okay that I've been bringing Vanessa home from school."

"Little late to be asking that, isn't it?"

Vanessa chewed her bottom lip, refusing to look at Logan or her father.

"You're right, sir. I apologize." Logan kept his eyes trained on Vanessa's father, accepting all the guilt for Vanessa's rebellious oversight. "I do hope I can continue to give Vanessa a ride home from school."

"Is that all you want to do with my daughter?"

Heat flushed Vanessa's face as she hissed a breath through her teeth. Why, why, why did her dad have to ask that? Logan and she were friends. And now, thanks to her father, he'd never speak to her again. Never offer her a ride home from school again. Not that her dad would allow it, anyway.

Logan choked back a cough. "To be honest, sir, I'd like to date your daughter."

Vanessa forced herself to stand still, staring at

the potted plant her mother had hung in the corner of the porch, its long green vines trailing over the sides of the planter.

"I see." Her father seemed to notice her for the first time. "Vanessa, why don't you go get this young man some iced tea. I'll take a glass, too. We'll sit out here and talk."

"Sure thing, Dad. But I think Logan has to get to work soon."

"Is that true, Logan? Don't want to make you late."

"I've got about half an hour, sir."

"Fine." Her father settled into one of the Jefferson woven-back rocking chairs, motioning for Logan to sit beside him. "This won't take long. Vanessa? Weren't you going to get the drinks?"

"Yessir."

Vanessa slipped inside the house, aware that her father had begun questioning Logan about school and work—even what he hoped to do after graduation. As she shut the door to keep the heat outside, Logan looked up from where he sat in the other rocking chair and gave her a quick wink when her dad wasn't looking.

Seeing Vanessa at the top of the stairs made running the virtual gauntlet with her parents— her father a few days ago and her mother tonight— all worth it. She wore a pair of jeans that hugged her long legs and a sleeveless cotton top the soft yellow color of sea oats. Her brown hair, illuminated with blond highlights, skimmed her shoulders, pulled off her forehead with a barrette. When she offered him a smile, he couldn't help but wonder if Vanessa Hollister believed in kissing a guy good night on the first date.

"So, what are you two doing tonight, Logan?"

Mrs. Hollister's question caused heat to streak up his neck.

"Um . . . I thought I'd take Vanessa to the Crab Trap, one of my favorite restaurants in Fort Walton Beach, and then maybe go see a movie, if she's interested."

Rylan, her younger brother, sidled up beside Logan. "Did you ride your motorcycle?"

"Sure did."

"Can I see it?"

"If it's okay with your mom."

Mrs. Hollister hesitated, but gave in when Rylan said, "Please, Mom? Just for a minute?"

Before leading her brother outside, Logan acknowledged Vanessa waiting at the bottom of the stairs. "Is it okay if I show your brother my bike real quick?"

"Sure. I don't mind."

Vanessa followed them outside, humoring her little brother's interruption.

"Can I sit on it?" Rylan circled the motorcycle, eyes wide.

"Sure." Logan paused. "I mean, if your parents

say it's okay. I could even give you a short ride—"

"Really? That would be so cool! Could we, Vanessa?"

Her laughter filled the air with a light bit of music. "Let me go ask Dad. You know Mom's gonna say no."

Within minutes, Rylan was seated behind him, the helmet cinched tight beneath his chin, his arms locked tight around Logan's waist. Both Mr. and Mrs. Hollister stood on the porch. Vanessa stepped close, speaking to her little brother.

"Remember what Dad said, Rylan. Logan's staying on this street—just up and down one time. Okay? And he's not going fast. Got it?"

Looking over his shoulder, Logan chuckled when Vanessa tapped the top of the helmet Rylan was wearing, imitating Logan's one-two action.

"All set?"

Rylan nodded and Vanessa moved away, brushing her hand across his shoulders, causing a warmth to settle in his chest. He understood the "first this, then us" message.

Once they were finally out to dinner and on their own, Logan realized there were all sorts of reasons he liked being on a date with Vanessa. It was fun to learn she dipped her french fries in ranch dressing and ketchup. To watch her drink Coke flavored with a squeeze of fresh lemon for the first time and decide that maybe, just maybe, she might try it again. To convince her to try fried calamari.

But the best part of being on a real date with Vanessa Hollister was having time with her—more than the thirty minutes that ticked away too quickly when he took her home after school. He could watch her face as they talked. See how her brown eyes lit up when she reminisced about how she had been on swim team since she was five years old—and loved to swim backstroke. Hear how her laughter had music hidden in it.

He talked about his grandparents, about going to the beach and watching lightning storms, and how he was saving to buy a bigger motorcycle. She even agreed with his suggestion to skip the movie and go for a walk along the beach instead.

Logan pulled the motorcycle into the beach-front parking lot. Cut the engine, set the kickstand, bracing the bike while Vanessa clambered off the back. By the time he turned to face her, she'd removed her helmet and was running her fingers through her hair to untangle it.

"You sure you don't want to go see the movie?" He reached over and tucked a lock of hair behind her ear, the strands silky against his fingertips.

"Absolutely. A walk along the beach sounds like fun."

Logan locked their helmets onto the bike, and then he clasped her hand and guided her onto the wooden walkway leading to the sand.

"This is one of my favorite places to come to." He twined his fingers through hers, tugging her closer. "Sometimes I even get up early and ride out here before school starts."

"You're kidding! That early?"

"Yeah. If I . . . have something on my mind, I come here to think." He hesitated to say *and pray*. They hadn't talked about God yet. He stopped, sitting down at a small sand dune, and unlaced his boots, tugging them off and then taking off his socks and tucking them inside. "Let me help you."

He knelt in front of Vanessa, pulling off her dark brown boots, setting them side by side. "Cowboy boots, huh? These new?"

"Uh-huh."

There was something soft, hesitant in her reply. "Good protection, since you're riding on the motorcycle with me."

He caught the sound of her soft exhale, saw her shoulders relax as she tugged off her socks. "Yeah . . . that's what I thought, too."

"Ready to walk?" He stood, offering his hand.

"Yes."

Their hands intertwined again. Easy. Silence fell between them. There were a million more things he wanted to tell her. To ask her. But for now it was good just to walk, to watch the waters of the Gulf darken as the sun dipped below the horizon, the sky changing from pinks to purples to the grays and blacks of a charcoal sketch.

"You live here all your life?"

Her question invaded the quietness.

"Yep. I'm a Niceville native."

"Ever thought of going anywhere else?"

"Sure, I have. But I wasn't in any rush—I figure that's what college is for. In a few months I'll be packing up my bedroom and living in a dorm somewhere."

"Have you applied to a lot of schools?"

"Well, I applied to Florida State, which is where I'll go, most likely. And a couple of out-of-state schools—but my dad says why pay out-of-state tuition when there are perfectly good colleges in Florida?" He wrapped his arm around her shoulders, pulling her closer so she rested against his side. Inhaled the faint scent of her perfume mingling with the salty air.

"Do you know what you want to study?"

"Weather."

"Weather? Like to be a weatherman?"

"Nah. I don't want to sit in a TV station and point at a green screen and tell people to carry an umbrella. I want to . . . I dunno. Report on storms. Or work for *National Geographic*. Something exciting."

He'd never spoken his dream out loud to anyone else . . . well, not since he'd tried to and his father had shut him down.

"That's a pretty unusual dream, Logan."

"I know it sounds crazy, but I lived through a tornado that hit my grandparents' farm in

Nebraska." He paused as the all-too-familiar threat of tears built behind his eyes.

"Oh, my gosh! I can't even imagine—"

"It was . . . awful. My grandmother was coming back from town when it hit. And she—she was killed."

"Oh, Logan." Vanessa stopped walking, turning to face him. The wind tossed her hair across her face. "I'm so sorry—"

"Thanks." Logan had to look away, out at the endless expanse of water, if he wanted to hold back the tears. "My grandfather got my sister and me to the storm shelter. I didn't want to come inside. I mean, it was pretty scary . . . but exciting, too, ya know?"

Vanessa stood beside him, leaning to rest her head on his shoulder. Listening.

"And then when we found out about my grandmother—we called her Mom Mom—well, it just about broke my grandfather's heart. Tornadoes fascinated me . . . but I hated 'em, too. I've been reading everything I can get my hands on about them ever since then."

"Because of what happened."

"Yes. And when I'm here, sometimes when there's a hurricane out there, miles offshore—it whips up the waves. The wildness of it reminds me of a tornado. I love to come down and surf then."

"You're kidding. Isn't it dangerous?"

"Sure—but that makes it more fun." He risked a

glance at Vanessa. Would she think he was crazy? Stupid? But something akin to admiration glinted in her eyes. "Do you know how to surf?"

"No. I'm a swimmer—but no, I don't know how to surf."

"I could teach you."

"I'd like that."

"What about you? Are you planning on going to college?"

"That's always been the plan." Vanessa shrugged. "The expectation, I guess."

"So why didn't you join the Niceville swim team?"

Her sigh mingled with the soft whisper of the waves. "I didn't want to join a new team again. I've done it too many times."

"So what about college? What do you want to study?"

"Kinesiology, maybe? Or sports medicine." A brief note of her laugh sounded between them. "I've heard most college freshmen change their majors, anyway, so I'm keeping my options open."

"So you're beautiful *and* smart, huh?" Another breeze caused strands of Vanessa's hair to tangle in front of her face, and Logan brushed them back with his fingers. Traced the outline of her jaw before he dipped his head and kissed her.

The faint taste of salt tinged their lips, and he forgot all about being careful, taking it slow. He pulled her to him, pressing his body against hers, even as her arms wrapped around his waist and then slipped up over his back, pulling him closer. Vanessa seemed as ready for the kiss as he was, and only when the cool, wet surf splashed against their ankles did he pull away from her, resting his forehead against hers.

"So, homecoming's in October."

"Yeah." Her voice softened.

"Would you go with me?"

"Yes." She finally looked up at him, a smile parting her lips. "I'd love that."

"I'll get my dad's car—no riding the motorcycle that night."

The wind caught their laughter, tossed it out onto the water, bringing it back to them again like a virtual wave that wrapped around his heart.

Oh, how he liked being with Vanessa Hollister.

TEN

One word described the college athletic arena: chaos.

Logan would like to be generous and say "controlled chaos," but at first glance he couldn't figure out who, if anyone, was in charge. The parking lot was a treacherous moving maze, requiring him to navigate through cars parked in clearly marked spaces—and anywhere else people decided would work.

"This is more dangerous than chasing a tornado." Max's joke caused Brady and Julie to laugh, but Logan found no humor in it.

"I'll get as close as I can to the gym entrance, Max—then Julie and Brady can help you get into the building. I'll haul the stuff in."

Brady already had his seat belt unbuckled. "I can take some of the stuff, too, boss."

"Max is the priority—"

"I can walk. I'm slow, but I can walk." Logan stiffened as Max clasped his shoulder. "Stop doing penance for what happened last July. I didn't

159

die. My leg is healing. Yeah, I may end up with a limp. But Julie tells me the ladies think that makes a guy mysterious."

Brady shook his head, motioning to the backseat. "And we know this guy needs all the help he can get with the ladies."

Even in the middle of a hurricane, his team kept joking. They always did.

"Enough already. Get out of my car, will you?" Logan swiped the back of his hand against his forehead, making eye contact with Max in the rearview mirror. "Thanks."

"No problem. We good?"

"Sure. We're good."

Brady hauled a couple of their suitcases from the trunk and then banged on the hood of the car as he passed by, signaling Logan to go in search of one of the quickly disappearing parking spaces.

Once outside the car, Logan braced his legs against the hurricane's assault. He grabbed the remaining suitcases. Julie had carried in the sleeping bags—something he'd resisted buying at first but then decided was a smart idea. After they used them, they could donate them to the Red Cross—which was probably running the shelter. And with Hurricane Cressida barreling in at up to 129 miles per hour, who knew how long they'd be roughing it? The arena might be fairly new, built in 2008, according to one of the reporters providing "color" stories with interesting details and facts about the area and other past hurricanes, but sleeping on a gym floor was still sleeping on a floor.

He passed other evacuees, just as soaked as he was, trudging to the arena. Parents herding their children—some carrying babies, some pushing strollers containing both children and grocery bags filled with food, as well as diaper bags. Children carried their own little backpacks, most hugging a stuffed animal or toy or carrying a book. Some people carried metal lawn chairs while others lugged camp cots. Even more surprising, some families had made a fast-food run on their way to the shelter and hefted bags of burgers and fries or chicken and super-sized sodas.

"Everyone prepares for a hurricane in their own way." Logan muttered the words to himself as he scanned the crowd inside the gym. Where had his team staked a claim?

No . . . no . . . no . . . there! To his immediate right, setting up at the base of one of the sections of fixed red stadium seats, Julie and Brady spread out a blanket and arranged two of the suitcases on one end while Max leaned against the retaining wall.

"I see the accommodations aren't quite ready." Logan added his suitcase to the line. "Should I call the front desk and complain?"

Julie, always cheerful and ready for a laugh, picked up on his banter. "If you can find anything that remotely resembles a front desk, I will turn down your bed for you tonight and put chocolate on your pillow."

"Okay, then. I'll see if I can find out who's in charge."

"Don't know if you got the lowdown from the Red Cross rep when you came in, but we all need to check in. Name, address, that sort of thing." Max pointed out where the organization had set up a check-in point. "They like to know who's staying in their shelter."

"Got it. I don't suppose we can give you all of our driver's licenses and let you handle that?"

"Worth a try."

"Good." Logan ran his hand through his wet hair. "I just realized I forgot the bags with the flashlights and batteries and radio we purchased on the way in. I'm gonna make a run for the car again."

"Going back out in the storm can't be any more dangerous than going into the store and trying to buy those supplies." Brady saluted him. "See you soon, boss."

"Yeah, yeah."

As he made his way through the ever-growing crowd back to the exit, two women stumbled in just ahead of a family. One clung to the arm of the other, bent over, her face hidden by a wide-brimmed rain hat. Logan stepped over and put his hand out, steadying the women.

"Thank you . . ." As the taller woman spoke, she looked up, her words fading.

Vanessa.

The thought of trying to pull off a fancy-meeting-you-here with his ex-wife lasted for all of five seconds. Instead, he nodded, transferring his attention to the other woman, who was removing her hat, water dripping onto the floor that was already dotted with puddles.

Recognition jolted through him a second time, along with the urge to hug the diminutive older woman. "Mrs. Wright . . . how are you?"

She peered at him through hazy gray eyes. "Logan?" She reached out and pulled him close, apparently not caring that both of them were wet through. "It's so good to see you."

"Where's Mr. Wright?" Had he asked the wrong question? The last time he'd seen the man he seemed as old as Santa Claus—maybe older.

"Vanessa left him in the car—it's parked right outside. She said she'd get me inside first and then go help him. He's having a little trouble getting out of the car. Doesn't want to use his walker."

His walker?

"How about if I go help him—maybe bring in your luggage?"

Vanessa, who'd stood quiet while he talked with Mrs. Wright, gave him a quick nod. "Let me get Mrs. Wright settled, and I'll come help you—"

"I've got this, Vanessa." He waved off her protest. "Help Mrs. Wright get dry."

It wasn't hard to find the rental car idling by the entrance. Logan rapped on the front passenger window and then opened the door, squatting down so he was eye-level with Mr. Wright.

"Good morning, Mr. Wright. It's Logan Hollister. I don't know if you remember me—"

"Logan!" The older man peered at him from beneath the brim of a Seminoles baseball cap. "I told Vanessa I wanted a ride on your motorcycle, but I don't think this is such a good day for it, do you?"

Logan swallowed. Adjusted his response. "No, sir, I don't think so, either. I don't like to ride in the rain. Not safe. Can I help you get inside?"

"Well, now, son, I dunno. Why don't we wait and see if this lets up soon?"

Logan's shoes and socks were soaked, as were the bottom of his jeans. Meanwhile, Cressida dumped more water down on his head. How was he going to convince Mr. Wright the hurricane had no intention of "letting up" anytime soon?

"Need some help?" Vanessa's voice sounded just over his shoulder. Why wasn't he surprised she hadn't listened to him? "Mrs. Wright insisted I pack a wheelchair and a walker—both of which he refuses to use. Now, I like independence as much as anyone, but I would prefer to have him inside before the hurricane makes landfall."

"Agreed." When Logan looked at her, cold rain pelted his face. "He, um, wants to see if it'll *let up*."

The way her eyes widened and her mouth dropped open caused a renegade chuckle to slip past his lips. Within seconds she giggled, and then they both gave way to laughter, the sound almost blocking out the storm.

Vanessa came to her senses first. "Okay . . . this is no time to be standing around laughing. Be serious."

"Right." Logan stood and swiped the moisture off his face to hide his smile. "My bad."

"Let me have another try—"

"Vanessa, go back inside. I'll do this."

"Well, let me at least get the luggage."

He gripped her wrist, holding her still. "My team's in there—the guy with a brace on his leg is Max. And then there's Brady—you remember him . . ."

"Yes." Vanessa tensed at the mention of Brady's name.

"Have him help you—and then tell him that he needs to go get the radio and flashlights."

"I can do this—"

"Just tell him, okay?" He couldn't blame her for not being thrilled about being here with his team—especially Brady. But he couldn't worry about that now. "We've been here all of fifteen minutes, and he's already bored. A bored Brady is a bad, bad thing."

Man, he'd forgotten how he loved to make Vanessa smile—and he'd managed it twice in less than thirty seconds.

"Go on. I've got a stubborn gentleman to deal with here."

He squatted down beside the passenger door again. "Hey, Mr. Wright, I don't think it's going to stop raining anytime soon. How about I help you get inside?"

The old man shook his head. "Not as spry as I used to be."

"Well, that's okay. We can take it as slow as you need to—or I can give you a piggyback ride."

The older man stared at him for a moment, and then a rusty laugh rumbled up from deep in his chest. "A piggyback ride. Now, wouldn't that be a sight for my wife? I haven't had a piggyback ride since I was a little tyke. But if it's all the same to you, I think I'll walk."

It'd been worth a try, and Logan knew he would have gotten a full-fledged laugh out of Vanessa if he'd carried Mr. Wright into the gym on his back. But he could at least tell her about the offer— maybe see another one of her smiles.

Life was never dull when Logan Hollister was around—not that he was responsible for the hurricane arriving twenty-four hours sooner than expected.

No. Logan usually brought the storm with him.

Vanessa found a hair tie in her jeans pocket and secured the end of her braid, tossing it behind her shoulder. For eight years, she hadn't talked to Logan. Hadn't seen him—except for when he showed up in the national news, usually standing tall in the midst of the devastation left behind by a tornado. And then she comes to Destin and immediately runs into him again in the middle of the Gulf—when they're both rescuing a drowning teenager.

And now she comes across him again during the mandatory evacuation for a Category 3 hurricane. Why was Logan at the shelter and not at his parents' house? Was Mindy wrong about his parents still living in Niceville?

Vanessa's gaze kept wandering to the double doors, but Brady made it back inside with two plastic grocery bags before Logan and Mr. Wright did.

"They're fine. Slow but steady progress. The old guy—"

"Mr. Wright."

"Yeah, sorry. Mr. Wright is going to need some dry clothes by the time he gets in here."

"I hadn't thought of that. Thanks, Brady."

"No problem. Logan mentioned it. He said he'd handle it once they make it inside, but I thought you might want to have stuff ready."

As another group of people entered, Vanessa backed away from the doors leading into the building. There was no sense in standing around wondering when Logan and Mr. Wright would make it from the car to the building. Logan would get them inside as fast as he could.

Mrs. Wright sat in one of the canvas camp chairs, chatting with a woman who'd commandeered the other camp chair. Logan's teammate had set their luggage nearby, along with the cots. She could at least put some order to all of this, after she found some dry clothes for Mr. Wright.

"Excuse me, Mrs. Wright? Your husband's clothes are going to be soaked. What will he want to change into?"

Putting her hand on the other woman's arm, Mrs. Wright focused on Vanessa. "Oh, well, he's going to want a nap when he gets in here."

"Understood. But we'll have to get him into dry clothes first. So why don't we select those now and have them all ready for him?"

"You're right. Let me look in the suitcase. You don't have to do everything."

Vanessa moved the suitcase closer to where the older woman sat, taking a moment to acknowledge the younger woman. "Hello. I'm Vanessa Hollister."

"Yes, I know. I'm Julie Cabot, one of Logan's teammates."

She knew? What did that mean? What did she know *exactly*?

"Oh. Well, it's nice to meet you." She sounded as

if they were having high tea. "If you don't mind helping Mrs. Wright, I'll go wait for Logan . . . I mean, for Mr. Wright."

Julie stopped her with a hand on her arm. "If you give me your driver's license, I'll take that and Mrs. Wright's over and check you both in at the Red Cross station. They want everyone in the shelter to check in."

"Thank you."

"And we have some beach towels, if you want to use those."

"Thanks . . . again."

Grabbing two multicolored beach towels from the pile of supplies, Vanessa returned to her post by the doors just as Logan shepherded Mr. Wright out of the storm. Once Logan helped Mr. Wright out of his drenched overcoat, Vanessa wrapped a striped blue and yellow beach towel around his shoulders. The old man's body trembled, but whether from cold or exhaustion, Vanessa didn't know.

"Here—" Vanessa held up the other towel."—I brought one for you, too."

"Don't worry about me." Logan ran his fingers through his hair, pushing it out of his face. "I won't melt."

His smile held the hint of years past, and before she even realized what she was doing, Vanessa reached up and wiped away the trickles of water from of his forehead. In less than a second Logan's smile vanished, his hand slipping over hers so that their fingers grazed one another.

Vanessa stilled. "Thank you for helping with Mr. Wright."

"I'm glad to do it."

"I know."

"I—I met Julie. She's helping with Mrs. Wright. If I can get her husband's driver's license, I'll go over and give that to her." She dropped her hand away from his face, fingers curling into a fist. "You should probably—"

"Go help him get into some dry clothes. You're right."

She backed away, fighting against a feeling of breathlessness. "And then I'll find out who's in charge and let them know I'm a paramedic. It's probably unnecessary, but it's always nice to go say hello."

"Good idea. And I should text my parents, let them know where I am."

So his family *was* still in town. Then why was he here?

"Right." She fingered the damp ends of her braided hair. "I should do the same . . . text my parents, I mean. And Ted. My fiancé. I'm sure they're watching the news."

Logan's face paled, his jaw tight. He cleared his throat—the tenuous connection between them lost. "Yes. I'm sure they're all worried."

"Exactly." They stood, staring at each other, as if

there was more to say. But there wasn't. "Okay, then. I'll check in with you—"

"After I get Mr. Wright into dry clothes."

"Thanks again."

"No thanks needed." No smile. His blue eyes seemed to be icing over. "He was always nice to me—and I know how much you love both of them."

"I did. I do."

Logan was the first to move, prompting Vanessa to go find her iPhone.

She needed to text Ted. Now.

OCTOBER 2003

The sand was cool beneath her feet as Vanessa held up the hem of her long purple dress with one hand. Her strappy high heels dangled at her side from her other hand. Beside her, Logan carried an oversized beach blanket, the cuffs of his black pants rolled up around his ankles.

"You okay with leaving the homecoming dance early?"

"Yes." Slow dancing with Logan had been wonderful—the strength of his arms around her, listening to him sing along to the music, song after song. But when he'd kissed her during Celine Dion's "The Power of Love," and said, "You ready to get out of here?" she hadn't hesitated to agree. On the drive down in his father's sedan, he'd

171

kissed her at every red light. How did Logan know how to kiss like that?

He spread the faded blanket in the slight valley between two sand dunes. They sat side by side, the sound of the waves caressing the shore with the hush of a lullaby.

"I can never decide if I like the beach better at night or in the morning." Logan stared straight ahead, his elbows resting on his bent knees, his hands linked together. He'd taken off his dress jacket and tie, leaving them both in the car. "I love watching sunrises and sunsets—it's when I feel closest to God."

Vanessa rested her head against his shoulder, trying to feel whatever it was that Logan experienced sitting here. "You believe in God?"

"Yeah." His answer was so low it was almost lost in the soft murmur of the waves. "Sometimes it's easier to believe in God here than when I'm sitting in church, you know?" He took her hand, intertwined their fingers, his thumb tracing a gentle circle on the palm of her hand. "I'm not a God-is-in-nature kind of person. I know God made all of this—the world, you, me—but when I'm here I sense his power. Or sometimes when I watch lightning zigzagging across the sky and listen to the rumble of thunder . . . that's when I know God is real."

Vanessa sat quiet, trying to absorb Logan's belief. His assurance in God.

"I know I mentioned my grandfather to you, right?"

"Yes."

"He . . . he was this giant of a man. Tall—six-foot-four. He knew what he believed, and it seemed like he never doubted himself—or God. He married my grandmother when he was eighteen and she was sixteen—"

"You're kidding me!"

"He saw her in Sunday school when he was fifteen and said he fell in love with her then. Felt like waiting three years was long enough. They were married for sixty-two years."

For a few moments Logan sat silent, watching the waves. "After that tornado came through that I told you about—the day before my grandmother's funeral—my grandfather and I walked the land, looking at what was left. Not that there was anything. While we were walking, Pop Pop said, 'God is in this, Logan.'"

Vanessa pulled away from him. "What?"

"Let me finish. He said, 'God is in this, Logan. Not in the destruction. Not in the loss. But you catch a glimpse of how powerful God is when you see the fury of a tornado—only God is powerfully merciful. He comes to give us life, not death. And you'll see him in the way people respond to this— the way they choose to help one another even as they grieve.'"

"Your grandfather sounds wonderful."

"He was. I want to be like him."

"You *are* like him, Logan."

He turned and traced the outline of her face with the lightest touch. "When I'm with you, Vanessa, I believe I can be the kind of man my grandfather was. I believe my dreams can come true."

"They will, Logan."

"When you say it, I believe it."

His gaze held her hostage, and then he kissed her with an intensity that stole her breath and seemed to scorch her heart—an unseen mark that made her his.

His kiss seemed to ignite something that caught both of them off guard. When he pressed her back against the blanket she didn't resist . . . didn't want to resist.

The warmth of his body against hers, the enticement of his kisses, both lured and lulled her. It seemed only seconds before his shirt was unbuttoned, her dress twisted . . .

"I love you, Vanessa . . ." His words rasped against her ear.

"Logan . . ."

Vanessa knew they were going somewhere dangerous . . .

And then Logan shoved himself away from her. Sat up. Turned, so that all she saw was his back. His shoulders shook. Vanessa lay on the blanket, looking up at the canopy of stars scattered across the sky, the skirt of her new gown caught around her knees, the night air cool against her shoulders.

What had she done wrong?

After a few moments she sat up, adjusting her dress, fumbling with the thin straps, the zipper, trying to breathe as tears dripped off her face onto the twisted bodice.

What was he doing?

Logan knew what he wanted. He wanted to turn back around, not think about where they were or how they would feel about . . . everything after it was over. Not think about whether what they did was wrong . . .

He wanted to tell Vanessa it was right. It was good. That he meant it when he said he loved her.

And he did.

But somehow his grandfather's voice intruded on his thoughts, interrupting what he wanted. Reminding Logan of something he'd told him the summer Logan was fourteen. The last time he'd seen his grandfather.

"There'll come a time, son, when you're gonna want to make love to a gal. You're gonna even tell her you love her—and she'll believe you. But the question is, will you love her enough to stop before you both do something you'll regret?"

He reached behind him and tried to find his shirt, but his fingers found only the soft weave of the blanket.

"Here." Vanessa nudged his arm with her hand, offering him his shirt.

His whispered "Thank you" disappeared into silence.

How was he supposed to face her?

His hands shook as he buttoned his shirt, the breeze off the Gulf blowing the strands of his hair into his face.

Vanessa was never going to want to see him again.

And then he heard a faint sniff . . . a shuddery inhale . . . and his guilt welled up and strangled him.

He turned, scrambling on his knees, reaching for her, only to stop when she raised a hand to fend him off.

"Vanessa . . . this is my fault. I'm sorry . . ."

She shook her head, the curls of her updo tumbling around her face, as if discounting his words.

"No—what? What are you saying no to?" Logan fisted his hands on his legs. "Are you saying it's not my fault? It is. I shouldn't have brought you here. I was a jerk."

She looked at him then, her lips trembling and tears evident in the moonlight. "What did I . . . do wrong?"

With a groan, he hauled her into his arms, the curves of her body sparking heat through him again. But he gritted his teeth. He would do the right thing—for both of them.

"You didn't do anything wrong. This is on me." He brushed the hair back from her face, resisting the urge to kiss her. He was not going there again. "I meant what I said, Vanessa. I love you. And I want to do this right. Which means I am not going to do this here . . . on an old blanket covered with sand. You deserve better than that."

She touched his face, her fingertips soft on his skin. "But what if—"

"No what-ifs." God help him, she needed to stop trying to talk him into it. "I don't want either of us regretting something tomorrow, okay? I don't want you avoiding me in school on Monday because you're sorry about tonight."

"What am I going to do with you, Logan Hollister?"

"I hope you're going to forgive me. And then I'm going to drive you home, kiss you good night on the doorstep—and hope your mom isn't watching from the living room—" That comment earned him the ghost of a laugh."—and then I'm going to call you in the morning and ask you out to a movie tomorrow night."

ELEVEN

Looking back, I have this to regret . . .
that too often when I loved, I did not say so.
—DAVID GRAYSON (1870–1946),
AMERICAN JOURNALIST

The concrete wall pressed against Logan's back, causing the still-damp material of his cotton shirt to stick to his skin. He'd peeled off his soggy shoes and socks, but the soaked material of his jeans clung to his ankles and lower legs.

He needed to get up off the arena floor. Grab some dry clothes from his suitcase. Go change in one of the men's bathrooms. And he would—as soon as he felt like he hadn't been knocked flat on his back.

Vanessa was engaged. To some guy named Ted.

The entire time he'd helped Mr. Wright out of his wet clothes and into a dry sweatshirt and sweatpants, he kept hearing Vanessa's voice again: *"I should do the same . . . text my parents, I mean. And Ted. My fiancé."*

Vanessa was getting married again.

The thought hit him like the first sighting of a funnel cloud—the times when his rational mind told him to run but he always overruled himself and drove straight toward the danger.

178

What if he and Vanessa had made it? What if they'd figured out a way to make their long-distance marriage work? What if he'd chosen differently—or she'd chosen differently? Would she and Julie be friends? Would she have become part of the team—inviting them over to their house for cookouts on the weekends? Sitting outside on their porch swing, talking and laughing with him and Brady and Max and Julie?

What if Vanessa wasn't planning a wedding with some new fiancé . . . because they were still married?

Logan pressed a fist against the pressure building in his chest. Ted, whoever he was, was getting the woman Logan still loved. Ted would be the man to fulfill the dreams Logan had destroyed. The man to restore Vanessa's broken heart.

He'd given her his class ring and a night in an Alabama motel. Their "Till death do us part" vow ended less than two years later with the signing of divorce papers.

His grandfather would be ashamed of his actions.

"Hey, Logan!" Max's voice brought his attention back to the board game in front of him. "It's your turn."

LIFE.

Logan stared at the game board, complete with the white plastic spinner with numbers against a rainbow-colored background. How did he get talked into playing LIFE with Max and Brady and a trio of teens?

How ironic.

There was no way a classic family board game, where the spin of a wheel determined if you went to college or started a career before you cruised around in plastic mini-cars waiting to be outfitted with tiny "parents" and "children," could prepare anyone for *real life*.

Real-life choices you made.

Long-term consequences.

And sometimes you won . . . or lost . . . and watched as someone dumped the pieces of your life in the trash and walked away.

Game over.

In the midst of two thousand people, Vanessa found a small corner of normal.

Yes, she was wearing jeans and a sleeveless tank beneath her jean jacket instead of the familiar uniform. But she was standing around talking with people she understood. Paramedics. EMTs. Inhaling a bit of adrenaline through conversation.

"So what's going on?"

"We've had a couple of people with anxiety symptoms—" Paul, the team leader, drained his cup of coffee. "—but that's not surprising, when Cressida decides to show up sooner than expected."

One of the EMTs joined the conversation.

"Another guy forgot his meds, so we had to escort him back home. That was pretty soon after they opened the shelter."

Vanessa accepted a cup of coffee from a slender blond paramedic, nodding her thanks. "Understandable."

The other female team member offered creamer, which Vanessa declined. "We've got several pregnant women here, too. We just checked on them to see how they're doing. One woman's due date is tomorrow, so we're about to transport her to the hospital in Fort Walton. Twin Cities Hospital doesn't do deliveries."

Paul motioned behind him. "Other than that, the only thing going on is a twelve-year-old boy brought over by his mom. He's been throwing up since early this morning. The family had a flu bug last week, so we're monitoring him."

Vanessa wrapped her hands around the warmth radiating through the insulated cup. "Best to keep him quarantined."

"Yeah. It's odd, though. He was the first one in the family to be hit with the bug a week ago. He got better—and now it's come around and taken him down again."

"That is odd. Poor kid."

A tall, lanky guy about her age with deep-set eyes and thinning black hair approached. "Didn't you go to Niceville High School?"

"Yes. I graduated in 2004."

"I thought I remembered you." He stuck out his hand. "I'm Grant Franklin. We were in the same math class."

"Grant." Vanessa scrambled to recall the name and face. "Sure. I remember you."

"I'd heard you'd moved out of town—Oklahoma or Colorado or somewhere, I thought. What brings you back to Niceville?"

"I'm visiting Mindy—Mindy Adams from back in high school."

"So then I was right—you and Logan don't live here anymore?" The guy grinned. "You two will probably win a prize at our class reunion for being the class's 'Old Married Couple.'"

Vanessa sucked in a breath. "Um, no. Logan and I got divorced eight years ago. I live in Denver now."

Grant's face flushed. "Sorry. I didn't know."

"There's no way you could have known."

"But didn't you two just come in the shelter together? What's up with that?"

"We're just here—at the same place, at the same time. It's complicated. Weird."

"I saw you on TV—"

Was saving that teen going to be an unexpected topic of conversation the entire time she was in Florida? "Yeah. That was another random, same-place, same-time thing."

"Really?" Grant shrugged his shoulders. "If you say so."

Vanessa forced a shrug and stepped away.

She needed to get out of town. Fast. And hope she avoided any more accidental run-ins with old classmates.

Vanessa had never been good at waiting—and she was playing a huge wait-and-see game with a couple of thousand other people—and Logan—all trying to find a way to be calm and comfortable in a college sports arena.

She continued another lap around the perimeter of the gym, the sound of her boot heels muffled by the nonstop swirl of conversation and laughter and the cries of fussy babies and even a rough, hoarse snore from a man sprawled out in a lawn chair, ball cap pulled low on his face. The odor of too many perfumes mingled with the occasional whiff of cigarette smoke clinging to someone's clothes. Here and there unlit cigarettes dangled from people's lips, but so far no one had crossed the no-smoking ban put forth by the shelter team.

When she neared the corner occupied by the Wrights and Logan and his team, she almost turned around. Walked the other way. Ridiculous. Logan hadn't acknowledged her once since she'd started her circuit around the gym.

He'd acted as if she were nonexistent ever since he brought Mr. Wright back after helping him change into warm, dry clothes. He'd double-checked the cot Brady and Max had put up for the older man—and ignored her. Chatted with the couple, regaling them with stories of his team's storm-chasing adventures, causing Mrs. Wright to warn them all to be careful. And ignored her. Gone off and played a board game with Brady and Max and some teens who thought storm chasing was totally cool. Still ignored her.

And that was fine.

If this hurricane hadn't disrupted her life—well, everyone's lives—she'd be packing to leave for Colorado. Thankful to say goodbye to the humidity. And the memories. Maybe not so excited to say goodbye to Mindy, who was proving to be a godsend when it came to pulling off this destination wedding.

"Mind if I walk with you for a lap or two?" Julie came alongside her, matching her pace.

"No. I'd love the company."

"Mr. Wright finally fell asleep."

"It's been a rough morning for him."

"My grandfather has early-onset dementia. Changes in his routine unsettle him, too."

"I'm sorry to hear that."

"I could wax philosophical about it, but the truth is, it's hard." Julie's steps slowed. "I've taken my grandmother's approach to handling it."

"And what's that?"

"You know how people say God will never give us more than we can handle?"

"Yes—I've heard that all my life from my mother."

"My grandmother says that's not true. That we do face things we can't handle—and that's when we're supposed to realize how much we need God—his strength, his peace, his wisdom. So, when my grandfather started getting ill, my grand-mother told me, 'No pretending I can do this, Julie. I can't. But I wake up every morning and ask God to help me love my husband— whatever he needs from me.' "

Vanessa was silent for a few moments. "I think that must be how Mrs. Wright handles it, too— taking it one day at a time and trusting God to help her. I'm not so certain I'd be that kind of wife."

"Well, I'm not even close to being married. I can't even get Max to ask me out on a date, the big goof—"

"Oh, really?"

"Yeah. Pathetic, I know." Julie stepped around a dog crate, where a medium-sized retriever lay snoozing. "Anyway, I'm not married, but isn't that what the whole for-better-or-for-worse part of the ceremony is about?"

"Yes, of course it is." Vanessa couldn't help wondering if there was a hidden agenda in Julie's conversation. "You know what I wish?"

"What?"

"I wish that, when I was a teenager, someone had told me, *'The choices you make today will affect you five years from now. Some will affect you for the rest of your life.'"*

"You think you would have listened?"

"I don't know. I thought I was so smart when I was eighteen."

"Didn't we all? I know I sometimes look back and wonder, *Why did I do that?* or think, *If only I had made a different choice.* Everyone asks those questions—everyone." Julie's laughter returned. "I've learned you can only spend so much time looking back before the future runs you over."

As they passed the medical station, Vanessa paused. "Do you mind? I think I'll stop in and just see how things are going here."

"Not a problem." Julie leaned forward and hugged her. "I know my way back."

TWELVE

Fear of danger is ten thousand times
more terrifying than danger itself.
—DANIEL DEFOE (CA. 1660–1731), AUTHOR,
*FROM THE LIFE AND ADVENTURES OF
ROBINSON CRUSOE*

Logan's neck spasmed—and his back responded with an echoing wince.

And why did his hotel room smell like a school cafeteria?

"I don't think he's awake." Julie's semi-whisper nudged Logan further from sleep.

"It amazes me how that guy can sleep anywhere." Brady didn't even bother to lower his voice. "I've seen him sprawled out in the back of our chase car, dead asleep, in the middle of a storm."

The melody of Vanessa's laugh had Logan rolling onto his back, staring up at the trio—and Max, leaning on his crutches—standing above him. He wasn't in a hotel room—he was in the hurricane shelter. He rubbed his hand down his face, scraping against the early arrival of a five o'clock shadow.

"You all have nothing better to do than watch a man sleep?"

"We weren't sure you were asleep, boss." Max looked anything but apologetic.

"I was."

Brady nodded toward Vanessa. "The lady needs to talk to you."

Logan pushed himself to a sitting position, twisting his neck from left to right. Not much better.

"Can we talk—in private?" Vanessa twisted the end of her braid as she stepped away from the group.

Julie lifted her hands, palms up, and shook her head, mouthing, *Got me,* as Logan stood and followed Vanessa.

A constant hum of conversation competed with the sound of rain and wind buffeting the building. Various styles of music blended together from people's MP3 players, while others chose to read. The barking of dogs and meowing of cats added a whole other level of racket to the shelter. Nearby, a mom sat cross-legged on a blanket, reading one of the *Little House on the Prairie* books to her son and two daughters, who sprawled in front of her. The staff must have prepared lunch while he dozed, because the scent of pizza and burgers and fries lingered in the air.

Once they were a few feet away from everyone else, Vanessa turned and faced him. "Logan, I need your help."

"Sure." Logan stifled a yawn with his hand. He

could be a nice guy. "Need me to do something else for the Wrights? I mean, I still have to say no if Mr. Wright wants a motorcycle ride—"

His comment earned only a brief smile before Vanessa turned serious.

"This sick kid came into the shelter earlier—the paramedics have been watching him. They thought it was a recurrence of the flu he had last week." She glanced over her shoulder toward where the medical team was set up. "But he's complaining of right lower quadrant pain and a fever. And he's throwing up."

"That doesn't sound good."

"They've been talking to the ER doc at Twin Cities, and she thinks this kid has appendicitis—and he may be becoming septic. His pulse is high, and he's more lethargic than we would expect—"

Logan tried to follow what she was saying, but he wasn't a medic. "So what do you need from me, Vanessa?"

"The kid probably needs surgery. The paramedics are dealing with stuff here. I told them about you—that you're a storm chaser and have experience driving in difficult weather conditions." A brief laugh followed her statement. "That you go looking for the bad stuff, even. And I said you could take the mom and her son to Twin Cities Hospital."

Vanessa's announcement felt as if she'd hauled him back outside into the middle of the hurricane's raging wind and rain. Okay. He was wide awake now. "What? No. They have plenty of paramedics or EMTs here—"

"Logan, this boy just needs to be transported two miles to Twin Cities—that's all. They've already got an IV in him. I told them that I'd ride along with you to supervise, check the IV, reassure the mom—"

The wail of a baby interrupted Vanessa's words, rasping across Logan's frayed nerves like the howl of the ambulance siren that came to the rescue when he and Max had been tossed around by the twister.

"No. There's got to be someone else."

She stepped closer, resting her hand on his arm, warmth seeping through the fabric of his sleeve. "I'm scared for this boy." Her words reached into his heart and lodged there like some sort of verbal thorn. "He could get septic—infected—at this point pretty quickly. Worst case, he could die. No one wants to make a big deal in front of his mom and dad. They've got two other younger kids to take care of. Please, help me help this family."

Vanessa might as well have backed him into a corner. Being this close to her again tangled his senses. He knew he needed to listen to what she was saying—a young boy was dangerously ill— but found himself noticing the flecks of gold in her eyes. Realizing she wore the same perfume he remembered from high school. Wondering why she'd let her hair grow so long and if she ever released it from the confines of the braid.

Even as he battled the physical attraction, her words tore at his heart. And yet the thought of driving this sick kid—and the mother and Vanessa—through a hurricane threatened to buckle his knees. Vanessa was thinking of what he was capable of doing—but Logan knew he wasn't invincible. And yet he wanted to help . . . to figure out a way to say yes. To help Vanessa.

Fine. He would do it—but he was going to do it his way.

"I'll take them—but I'm taking them *by myself*. I know how to get to the hospital from here."

"I'm not going as your navigator, Logan, just to give you directions." Vanessa stared him down, her brown eyes darkening to the color of jasper.

"What are you talking about?"

"Well, we're not taking an ambulance, but still, if things go bad—and they could, even in a five-minute ride to the hospital—there are some things I can do because of my medical training."

"Send another paramedic."

"I volunteered both of us—you driving, and me to ride along and monitor the boy. I've talked to the mom already, and she's comfortable with me and with this plan." She held up her hand when he opened his mouth to continue arguing with her. "We're done negotiating, Logan. There's simply no time. I'm going to go tell the team it's all settled. We need to leave in fifteen minutes—or less."

Logan wanted to grab Vanessa by the shoulders. Stop her. Shake her. Try to talk sense into her—but she turned her back on him and walked away.

JANUARY 2004

Vanessa had hoped to avoid a standoff with her parents. Wishful thinking.

"Why Florida State?" Her father leaned against the kitchen counter. "I'm not sure you'll be qualifying as a Florida resident yet, which means you'll be paying out-of-state tuition costs."

Vanessa clutched the acceptance letter to her chest, as if her father might tear it from her hands and throw it in the trash. "Only for the first semester. After that, I'll qualify for in-state tuition."

Her mother turned from the stove, steam rising from the pot of boiling water waiting for the spaghetti noodles. "Did you even apply to any other colleges like your father and I recommended?"

Great—now it was two against one. Couldn't just one of her parents be on her side? Should she give her mother the answer she wanted or be honest? "I thought about it—but I don't want to move around anymore. I want to stay in Florida."

Her mother's sigh seemed to press onto Vanessa's

shoulders. "You'll have to move anyway to go to Tallahassee, Vanessa."

"It's a three-hour drive. That's not the same thing as going across country again."

"It's because of that boy, isn't it?"

That boy. She and Logan had been dating since early October—almost three months—and her mother still called him "that boy."

"FSU has really grown since 2001, Mom. Mindy's been telling me all about it. They've renovated their dorms and built a lot of new buildings. It's a great college, whether Logan goes there or not."

"Logan Hollister is a nice young man, Angie." At least her father defended Logan to her mother. "But where *he* goes to college isn't our concern. It's still not too late to apply to other colleges."

Applying to other colleges was a waste of time and money—that's what Vanessa wanted to say to her parents—because it was all settled. She and Mindy—and Logan—were going to Florida State in the fall.

College. A chance at four years in one place— and nothing changing even if the military made her parents move again. At last she would be in charge of her own life. Free to make her own decisions. To stay. No worrying about whether she was moving or not moving.

Never again.

She could make real friends, not who-knows-how-long-we-can-be-friends friends. And Logan would be on campus with her. They would have time to figure out . . . everything.

Later that evening her mother came and stood in the doorway of the bathroom. Vanessa watched her through the mirror, as she scrubbed her face with a warm, wet washcloth.

"I hadn't mentioned this yet because nothing's definite—but your father may be deploying for a year."

"What?"

"And if he does, I'm planning on going back to Colorado to be near family."

That didn't make any sense. "Just for a year?"

"We can rent out this house, and you and Rylan and I can get an apartment in Colorado. It will be easier." She waited until Vanessa finished washing her skin. "We'll come back here after your father's deployment, when Rylan starts high school. I want you to go with us."

The wet washcloth dropped into the sink. "No."

"Vanessa, your father and I have discussed this, and we think it's the best choice for the family."

"And I'm eighteen. I can make my own decisions. You can't make me move back to Colorado."

"Are you forgetting who pays your tuition?"

Vanessa turned on the hot water, rinsing the washcloth again and again so that her hands were scalded red. Her parents wouldn't hold her tuition money hostage . . . would they?

Her long-awaited dream of independence seemed to slip a bit, move just out of her reach.

"I—I can always pay my own way through college."

"I suppose you could. Or you could come to Colorado for one year—just one year—and then, if you still want to . . . you can transfer to Florida State after your freshman year is over."

But so many things could change in a year. She'd learned that the hard, heartbreaking way. People didn't wait for you, even if they promised.

Logan loved her now . . . but would he love her a year from now?

Since homecoming, he'd made sure they never came close to making that . . . almost-mistake . . . again. He'd continued to say, "I love you," but the words remained lodged in her throat, even though she knew Logan wanted to hear her say them back.

And she did love him. She did. She just couldn't say it out loud.

Going to college together would give them time to figure out their relationship. She'd never even come close to forever with anyone before. But maybe, just maybe, Logan was the one. Maybe she'd be one of those girls who married her high school sweetheart.

And Mindy had applied to Florida State, too. If she got in, she'd already said they'd be roommates. Imagine that—heading to college with her boyfriend and a roommate.

Why couldn't her parents understand that not everyone liked packing up their belongings every couple of years? That some people wanted another type of life? That she wanted something different? Stability.

"Well?"

"I'll think about it, Mom."

"I thought so."

Vanessa shut the bathroom door. Slumped to the floor, her back pressed to the wall.

Thinking about it didn't mean she'd change her mind.

THIRTEEN

Adversity introduces a man to himself.
—H. L. MENCKEN (1880–1956),
AMERICAN JOURNALIST AND SATIRIST

If he were alone in the rental car, maybe he'd find the words to pray. Out loud. If not the words, maybe that groan that the Holy Spirit knew how to interpret when you didn't know what to pray.

At this point, Logan had nothing.

He unclenched his fists, wiping his damp palms on the front of his jeans. He wasn't going into the storm—not exactly. Not the way the Stormmeisters did when they traversed miles and miles of Tornado Alley, hunting down every possibility of a storm. Playing what some people thought was a reckless game of hide-and-seek as they sought the monsters that could wipe out entire towns within minutes.

And he wouldn't be doing anything more than he needed to—just what Vanessa asked of him. Drive to Twin Cities Hospital and back. No need to push the edge. To think, *Maybe just another half mile, another minute longer*—and then regret that decision for months. He was helping someone—not harming them.

He needed to focus. To pray. But with the way

he'd initially refused to transport a dangerously ill boy to the hospital and even now fought against the urge to go back into the arena, surely God wasn't listening.

The prayer of a righteous man. He stared straight ahead into the storm. Right now he didn't come close to qualifying.

"Thank you." The tear-soaked voice of the woman sitting in the passenger seat next to him yanked Logan's attention from his internal struggle. "I'm so worried about my son . . ."

"Of course you are, ma'am." Logan forced himself to make eye contact with her, hoping she didn't discern how he wanted to turn the car off, pocket the keys, and return to the evacuation shelter. "Any mother would be."

His mom would walk to the hospital in a storm if that's what it took to get him or Caron the medical help they needed. And his dad—even though he didn't understand Logan's passion for tornadoes— he wouldn't let his son die in a hurricane shelter.

"I'm Logan Hollister, by the way."

"I'm Tonya—my son is Christian." She wore a red raincoat, her brown hair plastered against her scalp even though Logan had pulled his rental car up to the entrance of the arena.

She stopped talking as Vanessa and another paramedic exited the building, supporting Christian between them. The boy was hunched over, his eyes half open, his steps slow. Vanessa fought to hold an umbrella over him, even as Hurricane Cressida tried to pull it from her hands.

"Wait here."

The wind-driven rain battered Logan the minute he stepped outside the car to open the back door. The other paramedic handed him a bucket with an apologetic, "He's probably gonna need this."

Well, it wasn't as if he'd expected a pleasant afternoon drive around town.

Logan stood back while Vanessa and the other paramedic helped the boy into the backseat, water soaking his hair and wetting his face and neck, shutting the door once Vanessa said, "We're all good back here."

The other man patted him on his shoulder with a hasty "Good luck," and disappeared inside the building.

Nothing left to do except get in the car and drive.

God help them all.

Logan slid behind the steering wheel. Stared straight ahead at the storm raging outside. He needed more than luck—he needed someone to pray for them, even if they were "only" going to Twin Cities Hospital. He looked into the rearview mirror, his gaze catching Vanessa's unwavering one. And when her hand rested on his shoulder, he knew she was interceding for them. For him. He reached back and, for just a moment, rested his hand on top of hers.

For those few seconds, it was as if only the two of them were in the car. Her touch somehow anchored and steadied his heartbeat.

It had always been that way.

A quick memory returned of the evening he'd shown up at Vanessa's house, spewing words against his father because he wanted Logan to major in business, not meteorology.

"I'm riding out to the beach. I need to walk. To think. Will you go with me?"

"No."

Her refusal brought him up short. "What?"

"I'm not getting on your motorcycle with you when you're upset like this, Logan."

"I know how to drive—"

"Have you been listening to yourself? Because I have. You're angry—and I don't blame you." She tugged his helmet out of his hand, wrapping her fingers around his wrist. "I will walk with you. And listen— all night if you want. But you're not getting on that motorcycle when you're this mad. You told me I'd always be safe when I rode with you—"

Her words, her touch, had been enough to calm him. To begin to diffuse the turmoil fueling his actions.

The slight pressure of Vanessa's hand pulled him back. He would do this. He cranked the defroster higher. With four wet people in the car, he'd be battling to keep the windows from fogging up, even as he navigated his way through whatever Cressida threw at him.

As he wheeled out of the parking lot, Christian groaned in the backseat, and Logan eased back on the gas pedal. Vanessa murmured something to the boy, even as she squeezed Logan's shoulder before shifting away.

"So, you're a storm chaser?" Tonya twisted around to face the front again, raising her voice to be heard above the pelting rain and the wind.

Was she making conversation just to distract herself? Probably. But he would prefer to drive in silence.

"Yes, ma'am. I've driven in all sorts of bad weather—usually because I chose to be out in it." A dismembered tree branch fell into the road, causing Logan to swerve. Christian cried out again. "We'll get through this okay. The hospital is only about two miles from here. Normally about a five-minute drive."

Logan stopped talking, battling with limited visibility—maybe fifteen feet ahead of him. Every bump and jostle, every time he drove over a smaller downed tree limb thrown in front of the car, seemed to distress Christian. And then came the sounds of the poor kid retching into the bucket. *Please, let him be puking into the bucket and not all over the backseat of the rental car.* An acidic, sour smell filled the thick air.

"Sorry—" Vanessa's voice was small, tight.

He met her eyes for just a moment in the rear-view mirror again. "Don't worry about us. We're good."

When Christian's mother went to unbuckle her seat belt, as if to turn and assist her son, Logan stopped her, placing a hand on her arm. "I need you to stay sitting down." He patted her hand once, then gripped the steering wheel again. "Everyone needs to stay seat-belted. We'll be there as soon as possible. Pray—if you believe in that."

"I do."

"Then let Vanessa take care of Christian. Let me drive. You pray."

"You have to do *something*—"

"I'm sorry. We can't help you." The doctor overseeing the hospital shook his head, not swayed by Vanessa's pleading. "Our generators were hit when a chunk of our roof blew off. We only have enough power to keep up basic utilities—our operating rooms aren't functioning."

Vanessa pressed both of her fists to her mouth, turning to face the glass sliding doors leading outside. An ER physician knelt half in, half out of the rental car, examining Christian, seemingly oblivious to the rain soaking the lower part of her scrub pants and her shoes.

"We've been in contact with Eglin Air Force Base Hospital, which is a larger facility than we are." The doctor spoke behind her. "It's also a hurricane shelter—and it's fully operational."

Vanessa spun back around. "Remind me how far that is from here?"

"Just under ten miles—less than fifteen minutes in good weather—if you go by Eglin Parkway. You don't want to go through town and risk crossing the bridge in Valparaiso."

In good weather.

The ER doctor came in, slipping out of the raincoat someone had handed her and joining Vanessa and the other doctor.

"I thought we could stabilize him here with pain meds and antibiotics." Her forehead furrowed over her glasses, which were splattered with raindrops. "He's diffusely tender—I'm afraid his appendix may have perforated. You need to get antibiotics on board now."

Vanessa hadn't expected to hear anything different.

"I'll radio Eglin you're on the way." The other doctor headed for the nurses' station.

"And I'll go get the piggyback antibiotics for you to run while you're on the way there."

Vanessa backed toward the door. "And I need to

go tell the mom—and my driver—that we're not stopping here."

She tapped on the driver's-side window, motioning to Logan.

Logan started asking questions before he was fully out of the car. "Do you want me to help Christian? Or is someone else coming—"

"We have to go on to Eglin Air Force Base Hospital."

He stared at her as if she'd told him he had to perform surgery on Christian. "What?"

"The ORs are down—the generators are out . . ."

"They can still handle him here."

"No, Logan, they can't."

Logan looked around as if he wanted to hit something, clenching and unclenching his fists, his lips pressed together in a tight line. "I agreed to transport him here, Vanessa. Let someone else take Christian to Eglin in one of their ambulances—"

"They're already swamped transporting urgent cases. The ER doc examined him. She thinks he needs surgery—that his appendix may have perforated and that he's developing peritonitis."

"Vanessa—*English*."

"His appendix may have ruptured, and he's developing a spreading infection in his abdomen. It could kill him."

The glass doors slid open as the ER doctor came out carrying a clear IV bag and some tubing.

"Here are your antibiotics. Get 'em on board as

soon as possible. We've already told Eglin you're on the way."

Vanessa nodded and turned back to Logan. "Let's go."

When Logan stopped her, opening his mouth to say something, she shook off his hand and pushed past him.

"I need to get these antibiotics running. *Now.* Unless you're praying, there's nothing more to say. And you can pray while you're driving."

MARCH 2004

The first day of spring break, and all she could do was cry. Logan was going to wish she'd stayed home.

At least he'd listened to her—finally—and gone out with everyone else for lunch and to hang out on the beach. Vanessa had kept repeating, "I just have a bad headache, that's all. I'll take a nap and feel better," pushing Logan out the door. Asking him to bring her back some Coke had done the trick.

How was she going to tell him that her parents were insisting she go to Colorado while her father was deployed overseas for a year? For the past few months, she'd refused to tell Logan, thinking her parents would change their minds. But no matter how many times she said she wouldn't leave Florida, her mother replied, "We'll do what's best for the family," and walked away.

First they moved during her senior year of high school—although she had met Logan because of that—and now they were making her move again. Right before they left for Pensacola, her mother handed her applications for several colleges in Colorado. She couldn't think of any way to win the argument except to keep saying, "I'm going to Florida State."

Stalemate.

A knock on the motel room door halted the fresh flow of tears. Who was that? Everyone had left less than an hour ago.

She peered through the little glass viewer, unlocking the door when she realized Logan stood in the hallway outside her room.

"What are you doing here?"

He held up a two-liter bottle of Coke and a plastic lemon filled with lemon juice. "I brought you some soda—and this will have to do for lemon."

"I meant for you to bring it to me after lunch."

He shrugged. "And I decided to bring it to you now. Hey—" He traced the tear stains along her cheek with the pad of his thumb. "—how bad is your headache?"

When Vanessa threw herself into his arms, Logan dropped the plastic bottle of soda onto the floor and held her.

"What's going on, Vanessa? Come on, you're scaring me. Did somebody die or something?"

She shook her head, forcing herself to take a deep breath. "My parents are . . . are forcing me to go to Colorado in the fall."

"What? They can't do that." Logan gripped her tighter. "You've been accepted to FSU—we're both going. It's all planned out."

"My mom keeps saying it's only for a year—she wants the family together while my dad's deployed."

"Your dad's deploying?"

"Yes. I'm sorry. I haven't told you that yet." She twisted out of his arms and sat on the edge of the bed. "I don't get it. Why does my mom have to go back to Colorado? And why do I have to go with her?"

"But, Vanessa—you're eighteen. They can't make you do anything anymore."

"Oh, Logan, that doesn't matter to my parents. They're paying my college tuition, so I have to do what they say."

Logan paced back and forth in front of her, not even bothering to pick up the soda bottle that had rolled next to the window. "You don't want to move, do you?"

Vanessa shoved her hair out of her face. "You know I don't."

"And you want to go to Florida State, right?"

"Logan . . . why are you asking me this?" She buried her face in her hands.

He came and sat down next to her on the bed. "Vanessa, you know I love you—"

She didn't hesitate to answer his question. "I do, Logan. I do."

"And you . . . you love me, too?"

Heat flushed up her neck and across her face. Logan had never asked her that straight out. And she'd never said she loved him, either—no matter how many times he told her. It wasn't that she didn't love him . . . she just held the words so close to her heart, as fragile as the china figurine he'd given her for Christmas. Once she admitted how she felt, once the words were out there, she couldn't take them back.

She traced the outline of his face, taking a deep breath. "Yes, I do. . . . I—I do."

Her answer caused him just a moment's hesitation, and then he said, "Then marry me."

"What?"

"Marry me." He leapt to his feet again, resuming his pacing. "It's the perfect solution—the only solution. If we're married, then your parents can't tell us what to do."

She fisted the bedspread. "You're serious."

"I am. Remember I told you that my grandpa was eighteen when he married my grandmother—and remember how long they were married!" He grabbed her hands, pulled her up, and spun her around the room. "Come on, Vanessa, I just proposed! Say yes!"

Logan's words and actions tilted Vanessa's world—and yet she wanted to lean into everything he offered her. Himself. A future together. Them becoming a family. Stability. Marrying Logan meant so much more than going to FSU. . . . For a few moments, she allowed herself to be caught up in Logan's embrace, their laughter silenced by a kiss that stole her breath away.

And then the weight of reality pulled Vanessa back to earth. Married. To Logan. But that meant her parents wouldn't pay for college.

"Logan, what about my tuition?"

"We'll apply for loans. Lots of kids do." Logan held on to her hands, his smile unwavering. "Look, the gang's all at lunch, and then they're going to the beach. Let's do this! We can get on my motorcycle and drive over the state line to Alabama and find a justice of the peace or whatever to marry us."

"But don't we need a license or something before we get married?"

"I don't know . . ." His ran his fingers through his long hair. "All right. Let me do some checking around. It may take me a day to figure this out— and we might have to at least tell Mindy what we're up to. One way or the other, we're getting married this week—and then we're going to college together in the fall. Say yes, Vanessa. Please?"

Vanessa stared into Logan's electric-blue eyes. He seemed so sure. He was offering her the chance to own her life. The two of them becoming *the*

Hollisters—no parents having a say in what they did or didn't do. To stop moving around at the whim of the military.

And Logan did love her.

And just because she couldn't say the words "I love you" yet, that didn't mean she didn't really love him, too. She was just being cautious.

"Yes, Logan. Yes."

Logan stopped Vanessa from opening the door to the ground-floor motel room in Alabama.

"What are you doing, Logan?"

"Hey, we've only been married three hours, but I do know the tradition." Before she could stop him, he picked her up in his arms, kicked the door open, and carried her into the room. Then he deposited her in the center of the room, giving her a swift kiss—the realization that his action was a prelude of what the night held for them causing his heart to thud faster in his chest.

"What was that?" Vanessa couldn't stop laughing as she slid the strap of her sundress back in place.

"I carried you over the threshold. It's tradition when you're just married."

"Well, now you have to go back out and get the suitcase."

"No problem, Mrs. Hollister." He saluted her as he exited through the door.

"Why, thank you, Mr. Hollister."

After he placed the suitcase on the bed, Vanessa

rummaged through it, pulling out the T-shirt with an airbrushed design of a beach sunset he'd bought her the day before.

"I, um, think I'll take a quick shower. Is that okay?"

A shower? They'd been here less than five minutes. What was he supposed to do while she took a shower? Watch TV? "Sure. Go ahead. It's been a long—and adventure-filled—day."

With the soft click of the bathroom door, Logan was left alone.

He was a married man. Vanessa Hollister was his wife.

He twisted Vanessa's class ring around the pinkie finger on his left hand, a short huff of air escaping between his pursed lips. He'd managed to get a marriage license—but forgotten they'd need wedding rings. Vanessa had improvised, not hesitating for a moment when he slipped his class ring on her finger, a giggle escaping as she moved it to her thumb, where it was still a bit too large. And now he wore her class ring, but only after promising to buy her a proper wedding band once they got home.

And now . . . it was their wedding night. How could he ensure he handled that right?

The motel room was old. Brown. No other way to describe it. The walls were painted a beige-brown. The curtains were a faded tan, and the bedspread was dark brown threaded through with lackluster gold. Well, he couldn't change that now. He couldn't afford anything else. But he'd make it up to Vanessa—someday. Maybe on their first anniversary he'd find a way to surprise her and take her to a nicer hotel in Destin.

He paced the confines of the room. Why was he daydreaming about next year? He needed to figure out what he was supposed to do tonight.

Vanessa was taking a shower. Just how long was she going to be in there, anyway? Should he get in bed . . . be waiting for her when she came out? Or would that seem a bit presumptuous, like he was thinking, *What took you so long?*

After all this time, he wouldn't have to stop, wouldn't have to tell himself, *Don't go there . . . don't think about Vanessa like that . . .*

He was waiting in a motel room while Vanessa . . . his wife . . . was on the other side of the closed bathroom door, taking a shower.

Hey.

A shower sounded kind of nice.

He sat on the bed, pulled off his worn tennis shoes, stuffing the socks inside. A prayer stuttered across his mind, seeming to keep pace with the pounding of his heart.

God, we did the right thing . . . I mean, Vanessa and I waited until we got married for this. And yeah, maybe we got married a little sooner than expected . . . but we're eighteen. Adults.

What had his grandfather said? "You either get

married young—and you grow up together. Or you get married when you're older—and you still grow up together."

And we didn't do anything illegal, although I know our parents aren't going to like it.

The prayer stalled.

Now was not the time to think about their parents. Somehow he'd stopped praying and started defending their actions.

Just help me, God, please? I don't want to mess this up.

He knocked on the door.

"Logan?" Vanessa's voice was muffled. "Is everything okay?"

"Yeah." He eased the door open. Stepped inside the bathroom, the steam scented with Vanessa's floral shampoo enticing him closer. "I, uh, just thought a shower sounded like a good idea."

He held his breath, waiting for Vanessa to protest . . . to tell him she wanted to enjoy her shower in peace.

"Well, don't let the cold air in."

"Whatever you say, Mrs. Hollister."

Her laughter from behind the plastic curtain eased the tightness in his chest. They'd figure out tonight . . . and tomorrow and the next day . . . together.

FOURTEEN

Don't judge each day by the harvest you reap
but by the seeds that you plant.
—ROBERT LOUIS STEVENSON (1850–1894),
SCOTTISH NOVELIST

Just moments ago Cressida had shaken the car like an invisible woman bent on preventing them from getting Christian to safety. Now the air stilled, wrapping them in an eerie calmness. Trees lining the highway had been caught in an hours-long wrestling match with an unseen, mighty foe. Some stood straight and tall, victors in the battle, while others bent, broken, stripped of branches and leaves.

"Is it over?" Tonya spoke in a whisper, as if afraid she might summon the hurricane again by speaking too loud.

"No." Logan eased his grip on the steering wheel, flexing his fingers. "We're in the eye of the storm."

"What does that mean?"

Logan swallowed a quick gulp of coffee, setting the Styrofoam cup back in the holder in the dash. Hot and strong—perfect. "This your first hurricane?"

"My husband's military. Air force. We moved here in August from Washington, D.C."

"The eye is the calm part of the storm. It could last five minutes or twenty-five minutes, depending on where we're located in the storm and how fast it's moving."

"In other words, enjoy it while it lasts."

"Exactly." Logan tossed her a quick smile. "And I need to make good time while I have a chance."

Darkness was falling, but they were the only ones on the road at this point. They had a dangerously ill boy in the backseat—and picking up speed would get them to the hospital sooner. Breathing a prayer, Logan accelerated.

Less than half a mile down the road, he slammed on the brakes, causing the car to fishtail on the wet road. Tonya screamed, grabbing the dash with both hands. Christian groaned. Only Vanessa stayed silent.

"No, no, no." Logan fought for control, turning the steering wheel in the opposite direction of the skid and slowing the car down.

"What was that?" Vanessa's voice was low.

"That." Logan motioned to the battered upper part of a tree that lay a couple of feet in front of the car.

Tonya patted his arm. "We missed it. *You* missed it."

"Yep." The one word masked the energy coursing through his body and how he couldn't release his grip on the steering wheel.

Calm down. They were all safe.

"What now?"

"I need to get out and move that thing. Be right back."

Every second gave Cressida more of a chance to gain on them. A stupid tree part wasn't going to delay them—he wasn't going to stay out here any longer than needed.

The slam of a car door sounded behind him, but he focused on grasping the trunk of the tree, branches scraping his skin, and pulling it, inch by inch, out of the way.

"Need some help?"

Vanessa appeared beside him, reaching down and grabbing another section of the tree.

Logan gritted his teeth. "Get back . . . in the car."

"I will not." She tugged the tree in the same direction he did, her shoulder bumping against his. "Couldn't we just go around the stupid thing by driving over the median?"

"And risk getting stuck?" Logan inhaled, the strong scent of rain-soaked air a refreshing relief after being locked in the car. "It's been raining for hours now. That ground is nothing more than a bog."

"You're right." She tried to mimic Logan's movements. "Wouldn't this work better . . . if we counted one, two, three?"

"It would work better . . . if you let me . . . do it." Logan took another deep breath and prepared to haul the tree farther. "Go take care of Christian."

"His mom is with him. And the most important thing . . . is to get him to the hospital as soon as possible." Vanessa stopped. Rested a hand on his. "Let me help you."

Logan closed his eyes. Swallowed against the longing building inside. He was trying to outrun a hurricane, and he still couldn't handle Vanessa's touch? "We don't have to haul it all the way out of the road—just far enough out of the way so the car can get by."

"Got it."

"On three."

"Count it out."

A few moments later, they had moved the tree enough to clear the road. As they approached the car, Logan pulled a red bandanna out of his back pocket and put his hand on Vanessa's shoulder, causing her to stop. He wiped a long streak of mud off her face.

"Sorry, you got a little dirty."

"You should see your own face." She brushed her fingers across his forehead.

What was he more afraid of? The hurricane or Vanessa's touch? "What? No."

"Oh, yeah. You're a mess, Mr. Hollister."

He tucked the bandanna back in his pocket. *Mr. Hollister.* Did she even remember how they used to call each other "Mr. Hollister" and "Mrs. Hollister"?

"I'll clean up once we get to the hospital."

The interior of the car reeked. Tonya sat beside her son, holding the bucket, tears streaming down her face. "He threw up again—and he keeps saying he's hot."

"You should have called for me, Tonya."

"You had to help Logan—"

Wind whispered against Logan's neck. An unwelcome *I'm back* from Cressida. "Let's go, ladies. No time to argue about who should have done what."

Logan adjusted his speed, slowing down as the eye passed over them and the hurricane returned. He seemed to be going both forward and backward—watching the scene moving past his window. He realized the military base was on his left and the entrance was only a mile or so away.

But the wind sped up again, throwing driving rain at them, as if taunting them, daring them to try to cross the finish line.

A gust of wind buffeted the car at the same time a flying tree branch hit the windshield. The car swerved as Logan jerked the steering wheel, but then he regained control.

Tonya covered her face with her hands and screamed—high, shrill—and didn't stop.

Out of the corner of his eye, Logan glimpsed Vanessa reaching across from the backseat and gripping the other woman's arm. "We're going to make it, Tonya. We're going to make it."

Logan couldn't risk taking another look at the two women.

He lowered his voice. "Tonya, please, you're scaring your son."

She covered her mouth with her hands, swallowing back her screams.

"It's okay." Vanessa rested one of her hands on Tonya's shoulder. "Logan knows what he's doing. He'll get us there."

"Vanessa—" Logan used the rearview mirror to make eye contact. "—you talked about praying—"

"I have been praying. I am praying."

"I'll pray, too." Tonya's shaky voice was muffled behind her hands.

Logan focused all his attention on navigating the car through the increasing velocity of the storm . . . past the gate at Eglin Air Force Base . . . not seeming to breathe until he pulled the car up underneath the awning protecting the ER entrance.

As people ran out of the hospital to help Christian, he leaned into the driver's seat, his sweat-soaked shirt pressing against his back. After a few seconds, he peeled his hands off the steering wheel. Tonya stumbled from the car, as Christian was assisted into a wheelchair, one of the nurses taking the IV bag of antibiotics from Vanessa as she exited the car. Logan knew she'd tell the hospital staff everything they needed to know. She paused for a moment, glancing back.

Logan nodded for her to go on, her smile the catalyst for a slow burn in his chest.

She's getting married. Remember that.

Logan closed his eyes, resting his forehead on the steering wheel.

A sharp one-two knock on the window jerked him upright.

"Sir, you need to park your car."

The muffled command had his gaze connecting with that of the military policeman standing outside the car.

"No problem."

"Just park it by the ambulances and get in here— the second eyewall of the hurricane has already passed over us."

Adrenaline only lasted so long—and Vanessa was ready to admit her supply was tapped out.

The steamy shower in the hospital call room had rinsed the dirt and grit from her skin, but also left her wanting to do nothing else but crawl into one of the waiting hospital beds. The clean pair of black scrubs she'd been given could easily be a luxurious robe provided by a five-star hotel. She'd washed her hair but was too tired even to braid it, so the damp strands hung around her face and down past her shoulders.

Oh, well. She'd just played chase with a hurricane—she wasn't a beauty pageant contestant.

She wadded her wet clothes up into a ball,

shoving them into a plastic bag, the kind surgical patients used to stow their belongings. She set her brown boots at the foot of the bed, knowing they'd still be wet when she put them on again.

The hospital commander had promised them food, but she needed to text Ted. And her parents. Her phone was loaded down with unanswered messages—including ones from Mindy and her brother.

They'd all be watching the news, getting information about the progress of the hurricane from various updates by reporters paid to stand outside and take on storm surges. She'd texted them hours ago and told them she was evacuating to a shelter—that she was safe. For now, they didn't need to know anything different—the real story in between the first "I'm safe" text and this "I'm still safe" text.

The brief messages were sent with a series of soft *ping*s. Now to slip on her soggy boots and find some food. But the thought of putting her warm, dry feet back into something wet and cold . . . she couldn't do it. No one would notice if she walked the hospital hallways in bare feet, right?

Logan found her twenty minutes later, as she sat in the ER waiting room listening to the storm go one last round outside.

"Hungry?" Removing the magazines on the table beside her, he set down a plastic cafeteria tray loaded with containers obviously filled with food before taking the chair across from her.

"Where did you get all of this?"

"Well, there's only a skeleton staff manning the hospital—but they're eating well." Logan began removing the lids from several plastic containers. "Let's just say the field ration meals in a brown plastic bag—"

"MREs."

"What?"

"They're called MREs—for Meal, Ready to Eat."

"Okay, whatever. They're being ignored."

"Homemade fruit salad . . . fried chicken . . . Oh, my gosh! Biscuits!" Vanessa ignored the paper plates and broke a biscuit in half, taking a bite that caused crumbs to dust the front of her scrub top.

"Almost makes it worth driving through the hurricane, doesn't it?"

"Indeed. I know people like to pour gravy on these, but I think it's sacrilegious. Biscuits, butter, and honey, and I'm happy—"

"Sorry. Just biscuits tonight."

"No complaints." She wiped her fingers on a paper napkin and reached for a piece of chicken.

"Be right back." Logan jogged down the hallway to the ER, returning a few moments later with two plastic bottles of Coke. "Now the meal is perfect, right?"

"Almost. No lemon slices?" Vanessa knew her

smile wavered as she accepted the soda from Logan. It was stupid—he'd handed her a carbonated drink. Nothing more.

"Sorry. Those I couldn't find." He settled into the chair facing her. "You okay?"

"Me? Yes." She twisted off the plastic bottle cap. "I talked to the ER doc before you came. Christian was taken to surgery. Sounds like his appendix ruptured."

"So it's a good thing we brought him here."

"A very good thing." She set her soda aside, reached over, and risked resting her hand on his. "You saved his life, Logan."

Logan turned his hand palm up so his fingers wrapped around her hand. "I couldn't have done it—couldn't have driven through that storm—without you, Vanessa." Logan's mouth twisted. He seemed to fight against the words wanting to be spoken.

"Of course you could have—"

"No . . . you . . . your prayers kept me calm." There was something dark, something unspoken, in his eyes. "You know I didn't want to do that drive."

"Why? You're a storm chaser. I knew you could do it—"

His grip on her hand tightened, almost as if he were clinging to her because he was afraid that if he let go, he'd be lost. "Even storm chasers never forget the power of a storm. And you prayed for me." His eyes reflected questions, as if trying to unravel a mystery. "Knowing that, I knew I could get back in that car and drive as far and as long as I needed to. Today I remembered that we make a good team."

His words lit a spark inside of her. "Logan, I—"

"You're not going to argue with me about that, are you?" His grin tugged a responding smile from her. "You know I'm right."

Vanessa forced herself to tamp down the emotion threatening to flame up inside of her. Eight years of silence—and now she spends less than a day with Logan, racing to save a young boy's life, and her heartbeat falls out of rhythm. "We did some-thing good here tonight. I do know *that*. Thank you for helping Christian."

"There's something I have to know, Vanessa."

"What?"

"If you can pray for me . . . does that mean you've forgiven me . . . for what happened between us?"

The man sitting across from her—the man she'd once been married to—never looked away as she scanned his face. The teenage boy she'd fallen in love with was replaced by an adult, his blue eyes edged with faint wrinkles—or should she call those laugh lines? Logan always liked to laugh. A scar marred his forehead. How had he gotten that?

"It's been eight years. There's no need to talk about what happened—"

"You don't think about us? About me?"

Unfair questions. She couldn't think of him, not when she was marrying Ted. This whole trip to Florida was to plan her wedding and prove life was no longer about Logan Hollister in any way.

What did he want her to say?

Nothing she had the freedom to tell him.

"No. I don't think about you, Logan." And she didn't—she hadn't, not until she'd said yes to Ted. Until she'd made a decision to have a destination wedding in Florida. In Destin. Trying to prove what? That she wasn't that eighteen-year-old girl anymore?

Well, she wasn't. She didn't have to prove anything to anybody.

She wasn't lying to him—or to herself.

One of them had to grow up. Be the adult. Acknowledge that what they had was over. Done with. That the marriage probably never should have happened in the first place.

"We both need to admit getting married at eighteen was a mistake." Why were her words tinged with the salt of unshed tears? "If we're going to talk of forgiveness, then let's forgive ourselves for being immature. For being foolish. And let's be thankful we were able to walk away before we hurt each other any more. Or before we had children. We didn't compound our mistakes— or hurt anyone else when it ended."

There. She hadn't said what he'd asked her to

say. No. But she'd said what they both needed to hear.

But why didn't she feel lighter? More free?

She pulled her hand away. Picked up the plate of homemade food. "I—I think I'll head back to the call room—try to sleep for a bit."

Logan rose to his feet. He didn't ask her any more questions. Didn't try to stop her.

"I'll come knock on the door if there are any developments." Logan's voice was flat.

"Thanks . . . for everything."

"Good night, Vanessa."

" 'Night."

Logan's stare heated her back. It took all her willpower not to turn around. To keep walking away . . . No, not away. Forward. She was walking forward. She had to believe that.

What had he expected?

Did Logan think that something as unexpected, something as . . . as *minor* as a hurricane could push back eight years? Undo all the damage that had been done? Did he really think helping Vanessa transport Christian and his mother to the hospital would somehow heal all the ways he'd broken Vanessa's heart?

Logan shifted onto his side, causing the hospital-issue blankets to twist around his legs. A faint antiseptic smell lingered in the room, probably having leeched into the walls.

Darkness filled the room. And silence.

After making her presence known for hours—assaulting the Panhandle, stripping the trees of branches, causing the waves to surge with the power of the storm, tossing boats up onto the roads and houses out into the Gulf—Cressida took her leave and moved north.

And only the sound of his own breathing disturbed the darkness.

Somewhere in the hospital—how close he didn't know—Vanessa slept in another room.

For months after their divorce, he'd avoided his empty bed, choosing to sleep on the couch, the TV left on, the sound turned low. Yes, they'd had a mostly long-distance marriage. But he'd always known the weeks apart would be spanned by nights when he'd fall asleep with Vanessa in his arms, her long brown hair scented of flowers, soft against his skin.

During those days and nights, the space between them would disappear. Their times together always seemed set on fast-forward. He'd come back to Niceville and be Vanessa's husband again. He never forgot he was married, but for most of their almost two years together, he lived as if he were single, rooming with Brady.

What had he been thinking, allowing the lure of tornadoes to pull him away from his wife? Accepting night after night alone in exchange for too few nights together?

If he listened hard enough . . . held his breath . . . he could almost hear the echo of Vanessa's musical laughter that could ease the ache in his heart when he held her in his arms. The memory of the mingling of their whispers in the middle of the night still caused a sweet longing to build.

Logan shoved away the sheets and escaped his bed, scattering the too-intimate memories.

He'd lost her. And was left with endless nights alone. No reprieve.

She never thought of him?

He deserved that.

Seeing her again seemed to ignite his memories. The colors were bright again. And one image bled into another without any effort.

She was moving on, and he had been drawn into what they'd had . . . what they'd lost.

God help him.

Although she hadn't granted him the absolution he'd sought, Vanessa had helped him realize the precious truth that he should have told his team about his decision sooner. He shouldn't have waited until they went back to Oklahoma.

That whole silence-is-golden belief? It was bogus. Sometimes silence was as corrosive as battery acid. Silence could eat away at a relationship. Destroy the trust between two people. If he and Vanessa had talked things out more—had some out-loud arguments that scared them into a counselor's office—maybe they would have found a way to work things out with each other. Found a way to mean it when they'd said "for better or for worse" as two clueless eighteen-year-olds.

They'd loved each other when they'd eloped during spring break—they just didn't know what loving each other meant.

But the realization didn't do him any good now, coming eight years too late and just a few hours after he discovered his ex-wife was remarrying.

But maybe he could learn something from all of this . . . even if it didn't help him with Vanessa. It was wrong for him to continue stalling with Julie and Brady and Max.

Logan paced the dark room, wrestling with his decision, the internal battle almost as intense as the earlier one waged with Hurricane Cressida.

No. He'd made the choice to wait, and he couldn't undo it now. They'd go back to the shelter tomorrow and have to deal with the aftermath of the storm. Check in with his family. Hassle with arranging new flights out. Now was not the best time to drop the news. And he still didn't know where the team stood with funding—or the lack of it—for next summer.

His grandfather would say something about not being able to change your crop once you planted the seeds.

Yes. He was reaping what he'd sown.

MARCH 2004

Why wouldn't Logan let her talk to her parents by herself?

Of course he was right that they were married—for all of three days. But it was difficult to remember that new reality when they'd only spent one night together before leaving the motel in Alabama and heading back to Pensacola. And then Logan returned to the guys' room at the motel. She went back to the girls' room—sharing a bed with Mindy, who had told the group what Vanessa and Logan were doing once they were on their way to get married. The only outward difference was Logan's school ring, which she'd managed to fit on her ring finger by taping a small, folded piece of paper torn from her journal onto the back.

She didn't regret saying yes to his impulsive "Let's get married." They just hadn't thought about how they were going to tell their parents. Riding home on the back of his motorcycle, her arms wrapped around his waist, the minutes ticked down with every mile marker they passed. And the answer to "What do we say?" eluded her.

And now here they sat, side by side on the plaid couch in the family room, Logan gripping her hand, her class ring that he wore on his pinkie finger pressing into her skin. Her father sat in his recliner, waiting for her mother to come in with a plate of cookies, probably expecting some sort of recounting of their spring break adventures. Surfing. Lying out on the beach. That kind of thing. Certainly not an announcement of, *Surprise! We're married!*

"You two ready to get back to school?" Her father muted the television. "Graduation will be here before you know it."

"Yessir." Logan squeezed her hand. "Vanessa and I wanted to talk to you about—"

Her mother set the plate of peanut butter–chocolate chip cookies on the coffee table in front of them. Logan's favorite—but he ignored the treat. "Logan, your mother and I are already talking about doing some sort of combined graduation party."

"Well, that wasn't exactly what we wanted to talk about—"

"It wasn't?" Her mother deposited a small pile of paper napkins beside the plate of cookies.

Logan sat up straighter. "No, ma'am."

Her mother sat in a chair across from the couch, a large quilting hoop and lamp positioned next to it. "If this is about Vanessa coming to Colorado with me, we've already discussed—"

"Mom, I'm married."

Vanessa's words plunged the room into a black hole of silence for a few moments. Then—

"What did you say?" Her mother gripped the arms of the chair.

231

"I'm married. Logan and I got married three days ago, while we were on spring break." She thought once she told her parents, saying it again would be easier, but her heart seemed to struggle to beat in her chest. The words seemed to ring louder and louder.

"You're pregnant, aren't you?"

Her mother's accusation brought Vanessa to her feet. "No! Why would you think that?"

"What else am I supposed to think, Vanessa? Why else would you get married?"

"I asked Vanessa to marry me, because I love her—" Logan stood, too. Only her father remained seated.

"You're eighteen years old! You two don't know what you're talking about—what you're doing! And how are you going to manage a baby and go to college?"

"I'm not pregnant!"

"I can't believe you've done something so stupid—" Her mother turned toward her father. "Don't you have anything to say?"

"I'm waiting to hear what Logan and Vanessa have to say."

"They've already said it—"

"Sit down, Angie." Her father waited as her mother paced back to her chair. "Now, Logan, do you want to explain yourself?"

Logan's face flushed red. "Well, sir, I asked Vanessa to marry me—"

"Why?"

"Because I love her."

"And you love her so much you had to get married over spring break? You couldn't wait to have a normal wedding ceremony with family and friends?"

"Well, no, sir—"

"Dad, I didn't want to—"

"Vanessa, I am not talking to you at the moment." Her father never looked away from Logan. "I am talking to this young man, who had the common courtesy—the *expected* courtesy—to ask me if he could date you. And yet he did not ask me if he could marry you."

"I'm sorry, sir." Logan's voice diminished with each word he spoke.

"It's a bit late for apologies. Where and when did this wedding take place?"

"Three days ago. In Alabama."

"Ah."

"Is that all you have to say?" Her mother rejoined the conversation. "Our daughter makes the biggest mistake of her life, and you ask where and when?"

"I did not make a mistake—I made a choice." Vanessa moved closer to Logan. "I know this . . . this is sooner than expected, but Logan and I know what we're doing. We've got it all figured out. We'll be going to FSU together in the fall."

Her father was silent for a few moments, looking

233

first at Logan, and then at her. "Am I correct in assuming this . . . marriage was to ensure that Vanessa didn't have to go to Colorado?"

"Logan loves me—"

Her father ignored her outburst. "You checked the state laws regarding marriage licenses?"

"Yes, sir, I did."

"Vanessa, how could you do something so foolish?" Her mother's voice struck out from across the room.

Footsteps pounded down the hallway as her brother ran into the room. "Are Vanessa and Logan back—"

"Go to your room, Rylan." Her mother didn't even look at her younger brother when she spoke.

"But I wanted to ask Logan—"

"To your room. Now."

The four of them stared at each other for a few moments after Rylan left, muttering under his breath. Her mother spoke first.

"What are we going to do, Jerome?"

"There's nothing we *can* do. Logan and Vanessa are married—legally. And it appears they're going to Florida State University in the fall— paying their way themselves." Her father took a measured breath. "And where will you live until then?"

"With my parents, sir." Now Logan's answer sounded overly loud, as if he were relieved to finally have something to say. "They have a small, separate grandmother's apartment behind their house that we can stay in."

"And do they know that you two are married—and that they'll be providing a honeymoon suite?"

"Jerome!"

Logan cleared his throat. "We came to talk to you first—"

"Thank you for that, I suppose."

"Vanessa is going to pack up her things while I go talk to my parents. I'll be back in a couple of hours with my father's car to pick her up."

"Well, then, son, I suggest you go talk to your parents and find out if you do, indeed, have someplace to take my daughter tonight."

Logan carried Vanessa's suitcases into the small stand-alone brick building out behind his parents' house. She followed behind him, not saying a word, her eyes red, her face blotchy.

What could he do to make this right?

"So, this is it." He let the suitcases drop beside the rust-colored floral couch. How long ago had that been banished from his mother's living room? "My parents said we could stay here until we go to FSU."

Vanessa stood just inside the room, her arms wrapped around her waist.

"What did they really say, Logan?"

"I told you what they said. We can stay—"

"No—when you told them that we were married. Did they think I was pregnant, too?"

"No. No. I mean, they were surprised, sure." Logan wasn't going to tell her about how his father had yelled—and his mother had cried. "You know my parents like you."

"Yeah. Sure. But that doesn't mean they wanted you to marry me."

"Vanessa—" He grabbed her hand, tugging her to him until she stopped resisting and came into his arms with a groan. "We knew our parents might be upset. So what? We made this decision—and we're going to be fine because we love each other. Right?"

She buried her face in his shoulder, tears dampening the cotton material of his Pensacola Beach T-shirt, her words muffled.

"Hey—" He nudged her chin up so she had to look at him. "I can't fix this if I don't know what you're saying."

"Oh, Logan . . . did we make a mistake?"

"No." His arms tightened around her. "No. They'll come around when they see how happy we are—how right this is. Is it a little rough right now? Yeah. But that doesn't mean we did anything wrong. Your parents were wrong to try to force you to go to Colorado with them."

"How could my mother think I was pregnant . . . ?"

There was no way he was going to tell Vanessa

his parents had asked him the very same question.

"We know the truth—that we got married because we love each other. Why wait until we were in college or after we graduated?"

She shrugged out of his arms, turning a slow circle in the room.

"So what do we do now?"

"Well, I guess we unpack." He surveyed the area again. "It's not too bad, is it?"

A small living room–dining room area. A kitchenette, with outdated appliances. And straight back, a bedroom with a small bathroom that only had a shower. The carpet was threadbare, but clean.

"I didn't even know this was back here."

"It's nothing fancy. My mom furnished it with stuff she didn't want whenever she redecorated."

"It's great. Really."

He chose to believe her. "I told my parents that we'd pay rent."

"How much?"

"My mom said no, but my dad said if we're old enough to get married, we're old enough to pay rent."

"How much rent?"

"A hundred dollars a month."

Vanessa's eyes widened. "A hundred dollars—Logan, should I get a job?"

"I don't know. Do you want to get a job?"

"My parents always said going to school was my job." Vanessa twisted her hands together. "But now that we're married . . . and paying rent . . . and paying for my tuition . . ."

"We're applying for loans, remember? And let's not worry about that tonight. I'll start bringing my stuff from the house, and you can start unpacking your suitcases. My mom said there are linens in the bathroom—sheets and towels. And then later we'll go buy some groceries."

"Hey, Mr. and Mrs. Hollister!"

His little sister blew into the tiny house, wearing a red bandanna over her double braids and hauling a bucket full of cleaning supplies. Setting it down, she threw her arms around Logan and then repeated the embrace with Vanessa, turning her around in a happy dance. "I couldn't believe it when Mom told me! Are you two really married?"

"Yep." For the first time since telling their parents, a smile crossed Logan's face. "You really think Mom would make up something like that?"

Caron bounced up and down and hugged Vanessa again. "This is so cool! Of course, I wish I'd had the chance to be a bridesmaid or something. I could have thrown you a bridal shower."

"We're good."

"I should say!" She kept an arm around Vanessa. "Did you know Audrey Blake keeps waiting for you and Logan to break up so she can date him?"

"Are you kidding me?" Vanessa's laughter joined Caron's, pushing back the heaviness that had shadowed them from Vanessa's parents' home.

"Oh, yeah. She's wanted to date Logan forever—and then you came along and got him. And now you're *married*. She's gonna die when you two show up at school on Monday wearing—" She lifted Vanessa's left hand. "Where's your ring?"

Vanessa tucked her hand into the pocket of her cutoffs. "We didn't have time . . ."

"What kind of husband are you, Logan?" Caron rounded on him, brandishing a feather duster. "Go get your wife a wedding ring."

His wife.

"I thought we should unpack and get settled here first."

"You can do that anytime."

Vanessa defended him, slipping her hand into his. "It's okay, Caron. We can do it another time—"

"Oh, no, you don't! Get out of here and go shopping." She shooed them toward the door. "I'll start cleaning while you're gone."

His sister was right—what kind of husband was he? He was about to let his wife—*his wife*—walk into school on Monday wearing his class ring as some sort of jury-rigged version of a wedding band.

"Come on, Vanessa. Let's go."

Vanessa hung back. "We don't have to do this—"

"I want to do this. Let's go." He winked at his sister. "Thanks, Caro."

"You're welcome, big brother. Have fun. And welcome to the family, Vanessa."

FIFTEEN

If there is no struggle, there is no progress.
—FREDERICK DOUGLASS (CA. 1818–1895),
LEADER OF THE ABOLITIONIST MOVEMENT

The parking lot at the sports arena was starting to empty out. Logan wove the battered rental car through the stream of people making their way from the building to their cars, pulling into a row of vacant parking spaces.

"People must be eager to get home and find out what kind of damage they're dealing with." Vanessa unbuckled her seat belt. "Can't blame them."

"Most, if not all, of them are probably going home to no electricity for at least the next twenty-four hours." Logan motioned to some people cleaning up shattered glass from blown-out car windows. "And quite a few are going to deal with stuff like that before they go anywhere."

"True. But I'm thinking a lot of people are saying, *We're alive, and that's the most important thing.*"

"Agreed." Stepping out of the car, he ran his hand along the scarred hood. "It's going to be interesting turning this back in to the rental agency in a couple of days."

Vanessa shaded her eyes with her hands as she scanned the parking lot. "Don't remind me. I'll be doing the same thing before I leave—and, no, I didn't purchase the extra insurance."

"You want me to go with you while you take a look?"

"No, thanks. I want to check on the Wrights first. I appreciate your team staying with them, but I never expected to be gone overnight." The air around them was overloaded with humidity. "And I want to report to the medical team, too."

"Sounds like a plan. Let's go find the group, and then while you check in with the medical team, I'll take Brady to check out your car."

"Logan, you don't have to do that."

"You can't take the Wrights home if Cressida blew out your car windows, can you?"

"No."

"Well, you're not the only one who drank lemonade on the Wrights' back porch, you know." Logan ran his fingers through his hair. "Have you forgotten Mr. Wright's crazy bird that used to sit on my head?"

"No—do you remember all the times Mr. Wright laughed and said, 'Nice hat, Logan'?"

"Yeah, and I said, 'Thank you, sir. I got it special-order from Australia.'"

"And he laughed every single time."

"Indeed he did."

Just as they entered the arena, laughter flowing between them, Vanessa's cell phone buzzed.

"Oh, sorry. It must be—" Vanessa checked the phone. "—Ted . . . wanting to know if I'm okay."

"Surprising he got through. You probably want to take that."

"Yes." Vanessa stayed back at the doors.

"Go ahead—I'll find Jules and the guys."

"And the Wrights."

"Yes—them, too."

"Tell them I'll be right there—"

Logan backed away. "Sure thing."

Vanessa covered her ear with one hand as she answered the phone, hoping to shut out the noise all around her. "Hello?"

"Vanessa? Are you okay, babe?"

Ted's voice was a precious bit of normal after twenty-four hours when her life had spun out of control. Vanessa closed her eyes, blocking the sight of Logan disappearing into the crowd milling around the arena floor.

"Yes, yes, I'm fine."

"I'm heading home from the hospital. I've been following the hurricane all night while I've been on call. I know that, despite the earlier forecast, it only came as a Category 2, but still it must have been frightening."

"Especially when you're driving in it—" She covered her mouth with her hand. Why had she said that?

"What? You were out in the storm?"

Vanessa imagined Ted, driving his black BMW sedan he had detailed once a year. She never worried when Ted drove—he maintained the speed limit as meticulously as he maintained the interior and the engine of his car. For him, a hurricane warning would mean seeking shelter, nothing more.

"Yes—transporting a critically ill boy to the hospital so he could have surgery."

"Vanessa—why would you do something like that?"

"It was necessary to save his life. And it's over. And I'm safe."

"But what if something had happened?"

"Well, nothing did—and the boy is recovering." Vanessa climbed the stairs to the first row of stadium seats, lowering her body into the one on the end. Why did she have to defend her actions to Ted? He was a doctor—he understood saving lives. Or he should. "It makes it all worthwhile."

"So what's happening now?"

"Well, you're watching the news, so you probably know more than I do." She leaned her elbows on her knees. All around her, people dismantled cots and rolled up sleeping bags. Industrial-sized trash cans positioned around the arena overflowed with garbage. "I'm just getting back to the shelter. I spent the night at the hospital on Eglin Air Force Base. We had to take the boy there, because Twin Cities Hospital's generators weren't functioning. They're letting people leave the shelter now, so I just need to find out how the rental car survived the storm and then get the Wrights back home."

"The Wrights?"

"Oh. I forgot to mention them." She rubbed her eyes, which were gritty with lack of sleep. "The Wrights are an older couple who were our neighbors when my family lived here. I took them to the shelter with me."

"Vanessa, you are not responsible for everyone in Niceville."

"No. No, I'm not. But the Wrights were like my adopted grandparents. I wasn't going to leave them in their house with a hurricane heading for the Panhandle."

Why was she having to explain this to Ted, too?

"And once you take them home, then what?"

"Well, I imagine the Wrights' daughter will come get her parents and take them to Alabama. And I'll get on my flight home—"

Ted interrupted her. "Not right away, you won't."

"What?"

"According to the news reports, Fort Walton Beach Airport is closed for at least the next twenty-four hours, maybe longer."

Vanessa's shoulders slumped, and she rested her

head on her arms. "I wasn't thinking that far ahead—sleep-deprived, I guess."

"And you won't be able to go back to the island."

Vanessa needed to sit up. And she would—in a minute. "I can only imagine what Destin looks like."

"Some hotels are completely destroyed. And there's all sorts of debris on the beach."

"Of course there is."

She needed to think. To figure out how she was getting back to Colorado. But any residual adrenaline from yesterday's crazy adventure had disappeared. She couldn't get back to Denver—and she had no place to go in Florida. What was she going to do?

"You want me to start calling around to see if I can find a hotel room for you?"

"Good luck with that. Everyone else is going to be doing the same thing. Ugh. Why didn't I think of this sooner?"

"Maybe you could stay at the Wrights'?"

"Maybe—but I really hope Ruth, their daughter, will drive down and get them. One of the first things I want to do is have Mrs. Wright call her. They shouldn't be living on their own. And besides, I doubt they'll have electricity." Vanessa forced herself to sit up. "Maybe Mindy has room for me. It's worth a try."

"You want me to come down there?"

"Oh, Ted, that's sweet—but no. Like you said,

the airport isn't open—and won't be for another day or so. Let me see what I can do. I'll help the Wrights. Talk to Mindy. And I'll call you later."

Vanessa pocketed her phone, standing to her feet and scanning the arena. Within seconds she found Julie and Max, gathering up their supplies as the Wrights sat in the two camp chairs. Logan and Brady were nowhere in sight—probably checking on her rental car—which made it easier for her to go and talk to the Wrights.

Not that she was avoiding Logan.

She plopped back down in the chair.

Yes, she was.

Being around Logan felt like she was running from one end of an emotional teeter-totter to the other. Up. Down. Too close to one side and she was going to crash to the ground . . .

It was like inhaling adrenaline. She'd forgotten how much she enjoyed being with him. She'd forgotten how Logan made scary things—like learning to drive his motorcycle or staying outside when it was raining and lightning—exciting. The way he challenged her—made life more daring, more wide open—all the reasons she'd fallen in love with him.

Although she'd never said the words out loud.

Never once in all the months they'd dated . . . never once in the months they'd been married, had she ever said, *I love you, Logan.*

Had that made walking away from him—from their marriage—easier? Had she somehow protected herself, protected some hidden part of her heart, by not saying *I love you?*

Had Logan even noticed? He'd spoken the words so freely himself. And he never asked her why . . . never said, "I love you," and then waited for her to respond in kind.

She said, "I love you," to Ted, but if she was honest, it almost felt the same as when she said "hello" or "goodbye" to him—casual, everyday phrases used in conversation.

She'd grown up and learned "I love you" was the appropriate response whether you felt the emotion or not.

Vanessa pushed out of the seat again. Stretched her back. Pulled the elastic band free from her ponytail and restyled it, all the while standing still as others packed up their belongings and left the shelter.

God, I don't want to be here.

Not here in Florida.

Here—stuck between my past and my future. Stuck between Logan and Ted. I love Ted. You brought him into my life, right? I know you don't like divorce—but it's not the unforgivable sin. And I'm ready to be married again. It's not as if Logan and I can recapture what we had—whatever that was.

She shook her head. This train of thought—this

prayer—was getting her nowhere—except pulled into dangerous territory. Again.

Time to call Mindy. Make plans for where she was staying tonight and then make sure the Wrights were set for tonight, too—and get as far from Logan Hollister as possible.

Logan followed the spicy aroma of chili as it lured him into his parents' backyard like an invisible, soundless Pied Piper. Unexpected company the day after Hurricane Cressida, which, for all her huffing and puffing, had arrived as a Category 2? Fine. As far as his mother was concerned, she now had a reason to throw an impromptu dinner party for his team.

Of course, thanks to his father's foresight, they weren't struggling with a lack of electricity and food thawing in the freezers. No, the backup generator in the garage ensured the Hollister family continued living in relative comfort. They'd need to clear out a few fallen trees, but none of those trees were near the house, so they didn't need to haul out the chain saws tonight—much to Brady's disappointment.

"Hey, big brother." Caron handed him a cold can of Coke. "Mother told me to deliver this—and yes, I brought you a slice of lemon."

"Thanks." Logan popped the top, just the sound of the metallic click causing his mouth to water. "Just what I needed."

"So, Julie's been regaling me with your hurricane adventure."

"My what?"

"She told me that Vanessa was at the shelter—and that the two of you transported a very sick boy to Eglin Air Force Base Hospital."

"Oh. That." Logan slipped the wedge of lemon into the can before tossing back a gulp of soda.

"Oh. That." Caron mimicked his tone with a grimace and a shake of her head. "Really? You see your ex-wife for the first time in eight years and help her rescue someone from drowning. Then you run into her again during the hurricane—and take a casual drive through the storm. You spend the night together. And that's all you have to say?"

"We did not spend the night together. And yes, that's all I have to say."

Caron positioned herself in front of him, blocking his escape. "So how is my ex-sister-in-law?"

"She's getting married again."

"What?" Caron's blue eyes, so like his own, widened.

"You heard me. She's here planning her destination wedding for next April."

"How do you feel about that?"

"How do I feel—" Logan gulped down another swallow of soda. "What are you, Caro? A shrink?"

"I'm your sister—and I happen to know you're still in love with Vanessa."

"Really? I think you're just a hopeless romantic. Does Alex know your e-reader is loaded with romance novels? That when it comes to movies you prefer Sandra Bullock in *While You Were Sleeping* over *Speed*?"

"I don't see you getting remarried, Logan. As a matter of fact, I don't hear any mention of you dating anyone—ever." Caron poked two fingers into his chest. "Why is that? Wait—I know. It's because you're still in love with your ex-wife."

"It's been eight years, little sister. Eight years. We're done."

"But she's back in Florida—and you're back in Florida—"

"And she's engaged. To be married."

"Fine. Be that way."

"Be what way? Smart?"

"So where's she staying while she's here?" Caron relaxed her stance, but that didn't fool him.

"Why?"

"We were friends, too, you know. I might want to say hello."

"Caro, you haven't talked to Vanessa since she and I divorced."

"That doesn't mean I haven't missed her. Where is she?"

"Where is who?" Julie joined them, carrying a plate of homemade guacamole and chips.

"Vanessa Hollister, Logan's ex-wife."

"Oh, she was going to get the Wrights home and then go stay with her friend Mindy."

Logan shook his head. "And you know this because?"

"Because, unlike you, I asked her what she was going to do when she left the shelter today." Julie shrugged. "She wanted to make certain the Wrights' house was okay. Said she was afraid they might have some downed trees."

"Wouldn't be surprising." Logan swiped one of her chips. "I hope there's no major damage."

"We could go over there tomorrow and check on them."

"Check on who?" Max joined the trio, leaning on a solitary crutch.

"The Wrights. Logan's concerned they might have lost some trees during the hurricane."

"I'm game." Max flexed his arm.

"You are not handling a chain saw." Logan scanned the backyard. "And where is your other crutch?"

"Fine. Someone else can cut stuff down. I can still haul off branches."

"You're on crutches, man."

"I'm managing fine on just one. But to keep you happy, boss, I'll sit and visit with Mr. Wright while you work. We got along great." Max lowered his voice as if whispering a secret. "Do you know he thinks you and Vanessa are still married?"

"Yeah, well, he's a little foggy on the details these days."

Caron interrupted them. "So it's a plan, then?"

"What?" Brady joined them, eating a bowl of chili.

"We'll help my mom and dad some tomorrow morning." Caron rushed in to explain before Logan had a chance to veto the idea. "Then we'll load up a couple of chain saws and go check on the Wrights right after lunch. I'll make sure Alex can come along, too."

"Sounds like a plan."

"Whatever." Logan backed away from the conversation. "I'm going to go get some chili."

Vanessa probably wouldn't be there tomorrow, anyway—she had a wedding to plan.

That thought should be comforting—not searing his heart like a virtual branding.

Vanessa was getting remarried.

She was moving on—and so was he. Dreams were coming true in new ways for her . . . and his was ending. And both were his fault.

This kind of thinking was killing him. He'd just deal with today for now—and the possibility of flying home as soon as possible. They could keep checking their flights back to Oklahoma while they swung by to see if the Wrights needed anything. Even if they wielded chain saws for a few hours, Max could visit with Mr. Wright and keep an eye on the news and the airlines on his cell phone.

He wasn't the only traveler whose plans had been disrupted by Hurricane Cressida. The airlines wanted to get things back to normal even more than he did.

It would all settle out once he and Vanessa retreated to their neutral corners.

APRIL 2004

What had woken her up?

With a few blinks of her eyes, Vanessa remembered she was in Logan's parents' apartment.

Where she and Logan had lived for about a month.

Somehow, she needed to start thinking of this as home now.

The window air conditioner filled the darkness with a soft hum. She shifted onto her side, pulling the sheet up to her shoulder.

Why was Logan's side of the bed empty—the covers tossed back?

They'd spent the evening eating ramen noodles and studying for their tests tomorrow. Had he gotten back up for some late-night cramming?

She wrapped the comforter around herself and padded out to the living room. The light of the table lamp highlighted Logan on the couch, slumped forward over his knees, his hands burrowed in the strands of his long hair.

"Logan, what's wrong?"

His bare shoulders shifted beneath her touch, as if he hadn't realized she was there until she spoke. He scrubbed his palms across his face, but his red-rimmed eyes let her know he'd been crying.

"Are you sick?" She wrapped the blanket around both of them. From the way his body shook, he must be freezing.

"No." Logan's gaze focused on his hands, which were fisted against his pajama-clad thighs. "I had a nightmare."

A nightmare?

She brushed back the hair from his forehead. "I'm so sorry. Why didn't you wake me up?"

"It's just a stupid dream . . . I haven't had one in a long time." His words were guttural. Forced.

She tried to pull him close, and after a few seconds he stopped resisting and leaned into her embrace. His head rested in the curve of her neck and shoulder, his hair soft against her skin. She pressed a kiss to his forehead and then combed her fingers through his hair. He often said how he liked it when she did that.

Should she ask him about the nightmare? Or should she just let him relax?

"I was back on my grandparents' farm." Logan's whisper broke the silence. "The tornado was coming . . . and I couldn't find anyone. I was running around looking for Pop Pop and Mom Mom and Caron . . . and you."

"What?"

His arms tightened around her. "I couldn't find you, Vanessa. I couldn't find you—"

Logan's voice broke.

"I'm right here. I'm safe." Vanessa murmured words of comfort, enduring Logan's crushing embrace. When his breathing evened out and his hold on her eased, she shifted so that the two of them could stretch out on the couch. "Stop thinking about it. It's just a bad dream."

Logan settled against her, an unexpected laugh surprising her. "This old couch isn't really big enough for both of us, you know."

She arranged the blanket over both of them. "We'll manage, Mr. Hollister. We'll manage."

"I'm sorry I woke you up."

"You weren't in bed, so I came looking for you."

"Missed me, didja?" Another chuckle warmed her skin.

"Yes, if you must know." She brushed her hand down his back. "Do you have nightmares often?"

"Not anymore." His shoulders lifted and fell in a sigh that seemed to come from somewhere deep inside him. "I used to have them all the time right after the tornado. Mom insisted I see a counselor for a while. I kept trying to explain that the tornadoes didn't scare me. I was just sad about Mom Mom."

"Would it be so bad to admit you were a little scared, too?"

"Not to you."

"I won't tell anyone."

"I love you, Vanessa."

"I know you do, Logan." Her unspoken words hung between them. She filled the void by pressing a kiss to his lips.

There. Didn't actions speak louder than words?

SIXTEEN

Experience is not what happens to you;
it's what you do with what happens to you.
—ALDOUS HUXLEY (1894–1963),
BRITISH NOVELIST

She would figure this out. She would. She would.

If she kept her eyes shut, and kept repeating those words, Vanessa would convince herself— eventually.

But then she'd open her eyes and see the massive tree that had demolished the Wrights' back porch . . . and she'd have to repeat the eyes-shut-say-the-words process all over again.

"It's pretty bad, isn't it, dear?" Mrs. Wright stood beside her, her face shaded by a straw hat decorated with fake sunflowers.

"Yes, ma'am. It is."

"There was a man here this morning. It wasn't even seven-thirty. Ringing the doorbell, offering to remove the tree for me."

How had she managed to sleep through that? "Oh, no. You didn't sign anything, did you?"

"No. I told him that I couldn't let him do anything because my husband was still sleeping."

Thank you, God, that Mrs. Wright was so concerned about her husband.

Vanessa pulled her hair up in a haphazard ponytail. No time to braid it today. All around the Wrights' backyard, trees lay twisted and fallen to the ground, evidence a hurricane-spawned tornado had stalked through the yard. It wasn't much better out front.

She shouldn't have let the older woman talk her into staying here last night, either. No, she should have ignored Mrs. Wright's request to go look at the house and driven straight to Mindy's, who had offered to put up all three of them.

But she hadn't. And so she'd spent the night at the Wrights', without any electricity, sleeping in their daughter's bedroom because she wasn't abandoning the couple. It was time to speak some truth.

"You can't stay here another night."

"I know." Mrs. Wright followed her around to the front of the house, latching the gate to the fence. "Ruth already called this morning to say she's coming to get us this afternoon—but I hate the thought of leaving the house empty."

"We'll contact the police department and ask them to drive by and make certain everything's okay. Let your neighbors know you're going to Tuscaloosa. Let's go see how the home health care worker is doing with Mr. Wright."

Humidity sullied the air inside the house. The suitcase they had taken to the shelter still sat at the base of the stairs. Vanessa lugged it to the bedroom, where Christina's voice mingled with Mr. Wright's grumble.

"I'm trying to sleep!"

"Mr. Wright, it's time to get up and get dressed."

"Oh, dear." Mrs. Wright paused on the landing. "I need to go in and help her."

"That's fine. I'll come help you pack—"

A loud knock on the front door stalled Vanessa's offer. *That tree guy better not be back offering to "help" with Mrs. Wright's tree.*

"I'll be right back. Let me see who that is."

Her boots clomped on the carpeted stairs, and she yanked open the door. "May I help you— *Logan?*"

"I was actually here to offer the Wrights some help, Vanessa." He stood on the brick doorstep, hands tucked in the back of his torn-at-the-knees jeans, a white V-neck T-shirt showing off his broad chest and strong arms. "Good morning."

"Good morning."

"How are they today?" He slid his sunglasses up onto the top of the ball cap covering his hair, revealing the warmth of his blue eyes.

"Well, let's see. Mr. Wright doesn't want to get out of bed. Mrs. Wright wanted to cook breakfast—without any electricity. And there's a huge tree in their enclosed back porch."

"Looks like we showed up at just the right time."
"We?"

He motioned back down the driveway behind

him. "*We*—Brady, Max, Jules, and me. And Caron and Alex. Caron brought along some food she and my mom made."

Vanessa stepped outside and tried to peer around Logan. "You're kidding me."

"Nope. And the guys and I have a couple of chain saws. The challenge will be keeping Max away from the machinery."

"I can imagine. We'll let him entertain Mr. Wright."

"Fair enough." Logan stepped off the porch. "Want to come say hello?"

"Absolutely."

An older truck and a four-door sedan sat in the driveway next to her rental car. Caron jumped out of the passenger side of the sedan and ran up to her, giving her a hug before she realized what was happening.

"Oh . . . my . . . gosh, Vanessa! It's so good to see you!"

"You, too, Caron." Wisps of blond hair peeked out from underneath a distressed gray flat cap. "Blond?"

"Yeah, I know. I get bored . . . so I play around with my hair color. Right now this hair color works for me."

"And Logan said 'Caron and Alex' as if you two were connected or something . . ."

"You don't miss a thing, do you? Alex and I are dating. I don't know if you remember or not, but his family lived next door to my parents for a number of years when we were growing up."

"Well, it's been a long time . . ."

"True. And back then I didn't like him *at all*."

"No, as I recall you liked a new boy every month."

"True. True. But, hey, that was high school, right? Except for you and Logan—" Caron faltered to a stop. "I am so sorry, Vanessa. I can't believe I just said something so insensitive."

"It's okay." Vanessa pointed to the picnic basket Caron had dropped at her feet. "So, what's in there?"

"My mom and I made sandwiches. Ham and cheese. Turkey. Tuna salad. Packed some chips and cookies, too. Nothing fancy."

"This is wonderful. The Wrights had a tree fall onto their back porch—"

"Hey, Hollister!" Logan's voice rang out across the area.

Without thinking, Vanessa turned and hollered back. "Yeah, Hollister?"

"Can you come show us through the house? I want to get a look at the back porch."

"Be right there." Vanessa stopped at the sound of Caron's giggle. "What?"

"You two. 'Hey, Hollister!' 'Yeah, Hollister?' Made me feel like I was back in high school again."

"Oh. That. Yeah. It was . . . just . . . nothing."

Vanessa motioned toward the house. "You want to come with me?"

"I'll wait for the rest of the crew and catch up with you. Go ahead."

Vanessa took a few steps away.

"Vanessa?"

"Yeah?"

"It's great to see you again."

"You, too, Caron. You, too."

Vanessa led Logan to the Wrights' backyard. The ground was churned up around the fallen tree's bare roots, and the porch was smashed—cleaved in two.

Logan stood with his hands on his hips, his ball cap turned backward on his head, sunglasses shading his eyes.

Vanessa picked her way among the debris and broken branches. "Thank God they weren't home."

"You got that right. They would have been killed."

"I know. I've thought the same thing over and over again."

"Why is it I can still hear that crazy cockatiel Mr. Chips?" Logan huffed out a laugh. "Always called you 'pretty girl, pretty girl.' Smart bird."

"Mr. Wright said he never taught him how to say that."

"That's because he didn't—I did." Logan tossed a smile over his shoulder.

"You did not."

"Yes, I did. Mr. Wright had tried to do it before, but he told me that he gave up. I just tried again—and Mr. Chips learned how to say it. The bird just needed the right enticement."

And she needed to get this conversation back on track.

"So what do we have back here?" Alex walked around the side of the house, Brady following close behind.

The appearance of the two men stalled the conversation while Logan discussed what needed to be done and then Brady and Alex disappeared around front once more. Probably a good thing. Vanessa was off-kilter again—and she and Logan had only been talking for all of five minutes.

"What we have is a destroyed back porch. Nothing we can do about that—except start removing the culprit." Logan paced back and forth. "No electricity, right?"

"Right—not sure when it'll be restored. The Wrights are going to stay with their daughter in Alabama. I'm expecting her sometime later this afternoon."

"And where are the dogs?"

Vanessa blinked away the slight sting in her eyes. Must be overtired. "Mrs. Wright doesn't have them anymore, Logan."

"I guess that's one—or two—less things to worry about. Those two were a handful."

"You liked those dogs, Logan Hollister—I know

you did. I caught you sneaking them pieces of food all the time!"

"Guilty as charged—but Mr. Wright did it all the time, too."

"Both of you ignored Mrs. Wright's strict order not to feed those dogs!" Once again, Logan had her laughing when she shouldn't be.

"And they loved us for it."

"You're impossible."

He winked. "I never said otherwise, love."

Her smile trembled for a moment, and her laughter stopped, his offhand endearment as effective as a noose strangling their easygoing banter.

"Hey, boss, you requested these back here, right?" Brady appeared around the corner of the house hauling a chain saw. Alex followed close behind, carrying the second chain saw.

"You would be correct." Logan pulled a pair of work gloves from where they were tucked in his belt. "Where's Max?"

"Right here." The other man shuffled through the damp grass on his crutches, Julie by his side.

"I told you to stay clear of the chain saws."

"Do you see me carrying a chain saw? Turning on a chain saw? Going after the tree with a chain saw?"

"No—but there's no need for you to be out here around this mess."

Julie shrugged. "That's what I tried to tell him."

Vanessa figured this was her cue. "I'm having some problems with Mr. Wright this morning, Max—"

"I'm not a babysitter—" Max stumbled as Julie pulled away one of his crutches. "Hey!"

Julie pointed the crutch at Max. "Stop talking before you fall flat on your face and embarrass yourself even more. No one's asking you to babysit that wonderful old gentleman. I loved talking with him while we were in the shelter. In fact, he promised to teach me how to play chess—and I'm going to see if he's up to doing that now."

Julie stalked off, disappearing to the front of the house.

Brady made a slicing motion across his throat with his free hand. "Oh, dude, you made the great and powerful Julie angry."

"Yeah—she took off with one of my crutches, too."

"If I were you, I'd hobble on after her and apologize." Logan nodded toward the house. "And let her win a few games of chess."

"You're probably right." Max lifted his crutch a few inches off the ground in a brief wave and then made his way back around to the front of the house.

Vanessa didn't know if she should stay here or follow Max. "Is Julie going to give him his crutch back—without bruising him?"

"Those two will be fine." Brady waved him

away. "Jules knows how to handle Max—and Max likes it."

"Oh. That's how it is."

"Yep." Logan lowered his voice. "Seems like the Stormmeisters have a bit of an 'office romance' going on."

Vanessa shared a smile with Brady and Logan. When would Julie realize Max was interested in her?

For the next few hours, Logan, Brady, and Alex worked on the fallen tree, cutting it down, limb by limb and branch by branch. They assessed the more dangerous parts of the job, leaving it for the professional tree company that Vanessa had called. But by lunchtime they'd removed most of the branches and debris from inside the house and the backyard.

Vanessa and Caron worked on hauling away branches, stacking them in a corner of the yard to be run through a commercial wood chipper, with Julie joining them midmorning. And Max played chess with Mr. Wright—coming out on occasion to complain that the elderly gentleman was faking his mental confusion because he'd won every single chess match.

Despite being sweaty and covered in a fine coating of sawdust, they ate lunch in the Wrights' formal dining room. The walls were decorated with more of Mrs. Wright's oil paintings and pastels and an oval wedding portrait.

"I'm sorry my husband didn't recognize you today, Max." Mrs. Wright passed out starched cloth napkins.

"It's okay."

"He'll be better after he wakes up. Being in the shelter unsettled him. Made him a bit of a grouch."

"Once I mentioned I wanted to play chess, he perked up." Max allowed Julie to help him get settled at the table. "And he wasn't so confused that he couldn't beat me at chess."

"He was the president of the local chess club for years."

"And you're just telling me this now?"

Caron choked back a laugh. "How old were you when you got married, Mrs. Wright?"

"It was back in 1946—after the war. He wanted me to marry him before he left, but I said no. I didn't want to be a widow. After he shipped out, I was sorry I hadn't accepted his proposal—but it was too late." The older woman smiled, seemingly lost in reminiscing. "We got married the week he came home from overseas. I was twenty years old. We've been married sixty-nine years. All the time that he was gone, I kept thinking about how silly it was. I didn't want to be a widow, and then I realized I could have ended up never being his wife. I learned an important lesson."

"And what was that?" Julie sat beside Max and rested her chin in her hand.

"You don't do marriage based on what-ifs. Yes,

I could have imagined all sorts of things that would make me sorry I'd married Mr. Wright before we ever said, 'I do.' Reasons not to have married him. But if I kept thinking like that, I would have quit before I ever accepted the engagement ring." Mrs. Wright's thin laugh deepened the wrinkles around her eyes and mouth.

"But that's not a marriage—imagining what it could be like and making decisions based on that. And if I was going to think about what might happen, why not think about all the wonderful things that could happen? The adventures? The romance? Getting through the tough times? Yes, I had five miscarriages—but we had one beautiful daughter. And the tears of happiness I shed when I held Ruth for the first time . . . oh, my. They outweigh all the tears I cried for the babies I lost."

Caron reached across the table and clasped the older woman's hand. "You're a very wise woman, Mrs. Wright."

"Oh, you live as long as I do, you get smart, whether you want to or not. God and me—we talk a lot. I've learned to listen more and talk less."

"More women need to learn that." Max ducked when Julie tried to punch his arm.

"And for that comment, you get to help me clean up after lunch."

"Who? Me? I'm injured."

"Right." Jules stood, gathering up paper plates.

"Come on. Sometimes I wonder why I hang around you."

"Because I'm cute?"

"You wish. It's probably because I feel sorry for you."

Caron waited until they left the room and then turned to Logan. "How long have those two been dating?"

"They aren't 'dating' yet." Logan did air quotes as he spoke. "But something's going on. They bicker like an old married couple. Pardon me, Mrs. Wright."

"Oh, it's quite all right, Logan. We do bicker, but we know how to make up, too. Mr. Wright will tell you that we never had a fight. He just doesn't remember them anymore."

"Mrs. Wright, you remind me of my grandparents." Caron leaned her elbow on the table, resting her chin in her upturned palm. "They were married for sixty-two years."

Logan pushed his chair back from the table. "She and Mom Mom would have been great friends, don't you think?"

"Yes, I do. And now, it's time to get back to work."

"And I need to make sure the Wrights are packed and ready to go before their daughter gets here." Vanessa drained her glass of tea. "Ruth called about an hour ago to say she'd be here before dinner."

Logan couldn't resist teasing Vanessa. "You just don't want to haul shrubbery around anymore."

Vanessa paused. "You want to pack their stuff?"

"No. I'll stick with the outdoor work."

As the room cleared out, Logan followed Vanessa to the foot of the stairs. He was about to ask a ridiculous question—and get himself shot down in the process. But for some reason, he couldn't stop himself.

"Hey, Vanessa." He slapped his work gloves against his jeans-clad thigh.

She paused three steps up. "You need something, Logan?"

"Just had a crazy thought. After we're done here . . . you want to meet me later at the Rocky Bayou Bridge? Just for old times' sake?"

SEVENTEEN

A whole stack of memories
never equal one little hope.
—CHARLES M. SCHULZ (1922–2000),
CARTOONIST

Logan still couldn't believe Vanessa agreed to meet him at the Rocky Bayou Bridge. Of course, she could always change her mind. Leave him sitting here. Waiting. Would serve him right for even asking her such an off-the-wall question.

She'd covered any hesitation with a smile and a laugh that seemed to say, *Why not?*

There'd be no jumping into the water below—the hurricane had deposited enough debris into the bayou to make doing so foolhardy. Sitting on the cement ledge was one thing. Making a trip to the ER because one of them needed stitches from a gash to their foot or leg or arm . . . yeah, that was no way to end the day.

The slam of a car door, followed by footsteps among the small stones and weeds, signaled Vanessa's approach.

"Logan?"

"Yep—I'm here."

"Sorry I'm late."

"No problem." She didn't need to know he'd arrived early. Had been sitting here for a good half hour, watching the setting sun stretch long fingers out across the water. Hearing the faint echoes of invisible friends' voices from years past in the breeze that moved among the trees along the shoreline. Closing his eyes and almost being able to feel the weight of a wedding band on his ring finger . . .

She slow-stepped her way across the cement ledge and then eased down beside him, careful to leave some space between them. Her loose hair lifted off her shoulders, the scent of flowers teasing him.

Logan knew Vanessa hated it when he asked questions while they were watching a movie. But he was tired of wondering.

"What perfume are you wearing?"

"Beautiful." She whispered the reply without taking her eyes off the small screen of the TV they'd bought and set up in their living room.

"Yeah, I know." Logan leaned closer. "But what's it called?"

Her gaze moved from the movie to him. And then she laughed. "Logan—"

"I'm serious, Mrs. Hollister."

And then he kissed her, and they missed the end of the movie.

"I assume kids still like to jump off here into the water?" Vanessa pulled off her sandals, setting them beside her.

Logan tossed a rock into the water below, breaking the smooth surface, dispersing his thoughts at the same time. "Yes, although no one admits it. And I wouldn't recommend it today, not with all the junk the hurricane mixed up." He offered her a can of Coke.

"Thanks." She nodded. "I hadn't planned on jumping."

"Oh, I dunno. I used to be able to talk you into things in the past."

"That you did." She stared straight ahead. "But let's skip crazy tonight."

"Deal." He opened his soda can, chasing away years' worth of unspoken words with the cool liquid. "We've had plenty of that already, yes?"

"Yes." She left the soda unopened. Clasped her hands together in her lap, focusing on her feet, which swung back and forth over the water. "So, the Wrights are on their way to Alabama."

"That's good."

"Yes, although Mr. Wright couldn't understand why you didn't give him that motorcycle ride."

"That guy never gives up, does he?"

"No. No, he doesn't. Honestly, I think it's part of that generation."

"I think you're right. My grandfather was the same way." Logan leaned back on his hands. "So what did the Wrights' daughter decide about the house?"

"She approved the company that I called to come in and remove the rest of the tree. She appreciated what we did today. Said to say thank you. And then a friend of hers who is a contractor is going to come down from Alabama and do the house repairs."

"Whew! Gonna be pricey. Let's hope they had a good insurance policy."

"Well, Ruth also said they may be putting the house on the market."

"What?"

"Ruth first mentioned it when I talked with her on the phone, and then we talked a bit more when she came down. The reality is, her parents need to live closer to her." Vanessa chewed her bottom lip, sighed, and then seemed to shrug off whatever was weighing on her mind. "So, she'll start working on transitioning them to someplace up there while repairs are being done to the house."

"For the best, I suppose."

"Yes." She glanced at him from the corner of her eye. "So, Caron's a blond . . ."

"My father's just happy it's a normal hair color."

"How are your parents?"

"Good. My dad's on a health kick. He drinks a green, healthy shake every morning."

"No!"

"So my sister says—I haven't been there to witness it. He's lost about twenty pounds. My mom's the same—loves him, loves Caron and me. Wishes I lived closer."

"But your life is in Oklahoma. She understands that."

"Yeah. Storm chasing requires you go where the storms are—or where you think they're going to be."

"Chasing the dream—literally."

"I guess."

"Are you happy, Logan?"

Vanessa's question floated out onto the air and then drifted back to him.

"Most days I go to bed . . . content with my choices. I know why I chase storms—what drives me."

"And what's that?"

"Wanting to help people. Like other storm chasers, it's all about understanding storms. Or figuring out ways to predict them earlier. Or preventing them from being so destructive."

"And on the days you don't go to bed content? What are you thinking about then?"

Logan shifted forward, resting his arms on his knees. Turned, so he could see the woman sitting next to him. The last time they'd sat here, an early fall sky above them, the water below serene, he'd been eighteen years old, working hard to impress Vanessa. Hoping she'd like him. Trying to figure out if what he felt for her was love . . . and what did loving her mean, anyway?

And wondering, if he jumped, would she jump, too?

And now here they sat, ten years later. Somehow, what they'd had together had gotten twisted and tangled up in expectations and misinterpretations. Torn apart by words spoken in anger . . . and too many things left unsaid. Rather than holding hands and reminiscing, he was trying to navigate all the years of silence.

"What do I think about?" The rough side of the bridge pressed into his thighs. "You."

"Logan, don't—"

"You know the saying just as well as I do, Vanessa: don't ask the question if you don't want to hear the answer." He crushed the half-empty aluminum can in his fist. "Sometimes I still lie awake at night and wonder what you're doing. Where you're living. If you're happy. If you're married. If you have kids."

His words hung on the air for a few seconds.

"I work as a paramedic in Denver. Love my job. I'm a bit of an adrenaline junkie. I live in a one-bedroom apartment in the middle of the city. I'm happy." She could only hope her smile backed up her words. "I just applied to physician assistant school—waiting to hear if I've been accepted. I'm getting married the first week in April. No kids. Yet."

This was where he should say he was happy for her. But he couldn't force the words past all the things he wished he'd said years ago: *I'm sorry. What can I do to make this right? Don't leave. I don't want a divorce.*

I still love you.

"What's your fiancé like?"

"Ted?"

"Ted."

"He's an ER doctor. Tall. Very good at what he does. We've dated for a couple of years now. And when he proposed, I said yes, because I realized I was ready for marriage again . . . with him." Her laughter faded almost as soon as it began. "And I love him, of course."

"Of course." Logan forced himself to say the right thing. "Congratulations."

"Thank you. So what about you? Married? A family?"

"No. Julie's tried to play matchmaker a few times through the years. The team even bought me a membership to one of those dating sites for my birthday—"

"Please tell me that was a gag gift."

"Never asked. And I never used it. Don't tell Caron. She'd get online and fill out my profile for me."

"I bet she would."

"So I'm single." He should add the word "happily," but there was no sense in lying.

"I hope you find—"

He couldn't let her say it. Didn't want to hear her say it. "Don't, Vanessa." He rested his hand over hers. "Don't say you hope I find someone else."

For a moment she let her hand remain beneath his. Her skin soft beneath his fingers.

"I'm sorry, Logan."

"I'm sorry, too, Vanessa. More than you know. I've told God. Now I can tell you. And it's okay— I'm not asking you to forgive me. I realize it's enough to tell you that I'm sorry so I know you can hear me—that I'm not just talking to the ceiling."

APRIL 2004

Logan stared at Vanessa's back, her shoulders rigid beneath her bathrobe. He could only hope she wasn't crying. He hated it when she cried.

He picked up the college acceptance letter from where she'd tossed it on the table.

"Vanessa, I don't understand why you're so upset. Can't you see how great this is—"

She whirled around, not a trace of tears on her face, her eyes flashing like lightning over the Gulf at night. "No, it's not great! You're changing the plan, and you didn't even talk to me about it!"

"I forgot I even applied to OU. It was a long shot. And then we got married—"

"Exactly—we got married." She stalked a tight

circle around the room. "And married people talk about decisions like this."

"We are talking about it now. We can still go to school together—we'd just be changing colleges." He held up the letter. "This is an amazing opportunity! Oklahoma is part of Tornado Alley! I can study meteorology and try to hook up with some real storm chasers—"

"We've already got our plan, Logan. We're all set for FSU in the fall. That's why we got married, remember? So I wouldn't have to move back to Colorado with my mom."

Did she even hear what she was saying?

"We got married because we love each other!"

"I know that—don't make it sound like I'm saying something I'm not!" She grabbed the single sheet of paper from his hand. "But this is not what we agreed on. I don't want to move any more—"

"You're not being logical. We have to move to Tallahassee to go to FSU—"

"A couple of hours down the road. No big deal." She waved the letter in the air. "OU is ten or twelve hours away—a different state."

"I can't miss this chance, Vanessa."

"You can study hurricanes here."

"They're offering me a full ride—"

"No, Logan." Vanessa crumpled the letter into a ball and threw it onto the floor. "No. You can't just change the plan like that."

"Who are you to tell me no?" Logan knew he

was yelling, but he didn't care. "You sound like my dad."

She recoiled from his words, as if he'd slapped her. "I can't believe you just said that to me."

Silence, sharp with unspoken words, descended between them. Logan paced the small living space, waiting for Vanessa to say something reasonable. Say she understood. Say she was sorry. That of course she'd go to Oklahoma with him because she knew how important this dream was to him. Say she loved him. Finally . . . finally say the words out loud.

But instead, she ran from the small living area into their bedroom, slamming the door. And then he heard the metallic click of the door locking.

Great, just great.

He'd heard of husbands sleeping on the couch. Seen sitcoms where the poor guy tried to find a comfortable position on a too-short sofa.

And now he was sentenced to a night alone with the TV and remote—and a locked door separating him from his wife.

Yeah. Congratulations, Hollister. Aren't you living the life?

At some point, Vanessa needed to go home.

Go back to the little house behind Logan's parents' home and see if Logan was there, waiting for her. Or if he was gone. Again.

"Mindy, you've been great." She motioned to the

leftovers of the full-blown pity party Mindy had hosted for her in her bedroom. A pile of used tissues next to an empty bag of Hershey's Kisses. Empty cans of Coke and a bowl of squeezed lemon slices. A half-eaten bag of Doritos.

"Feel any better?"

"No." She sniffed. "Sorry."

"You and Logan will figure this out. You love each other. The class even voted you 'Cutest Couple' for the yearbook, remember?"

"Yeah, maybe I should just go home and remind Logan about that, too."

Mindy giggled, her face turning red. "I, uh, heard once you're married, making up is the best part of a fight."

Logan would have to be home for that to happen. And she wasn't going to tell Mindy that for the past week Logan had come home late from work every night, choosing to sleep on the couch, even though she left the bedroom door unlocked—and wide open.

She should never have locked the door on him after their fight that first night.

All seemed quiet in their apartment when she got to the front door. Would she be spending another night alone, waiting for the sound of Logan's arrival sometime in the middle of the night?

But her husband lay stretched out on the couch, the TV on, but the sound muted. She stopped just inside the doorway.

"I didn't know you were here . . ."

Logan clicked off the TV as he sat up. "Finished work. It's been a long week."

"Yeah." She opened the fridge. "Are you hungry? I've got some leftovers—"

"Vanessa."

She jumped, whirling around, surprised he was close behind her, caught between the fridge and his nearness. She needed to remember she was angry . . . hurt . . .

"I'm a jerk." Logan pulled her into his arms, away from the refrigerator.

"Yes, you are." She needed to say that louder.

He pressed a kiss against her neck, the warmth of his lips a balm to the ache in her heart. "Forgive me?"

Yes, yes, she would. But not yet. Not until they talked things out. College. And plans.

"I'm sorry . . ." His kisses replaced her anger with a passion that always pushed reason away. No one had ever kissed her like Logan did— like kissing her was the best thing—the only thing he wanted to do. "I've missed you so much, Vanessa."

He picked her up and carried her into the bedroom, her arms went around his neck, his hair brushing against her face.

"We need to talk."

"Okay . . ." His laughter was low in her ear. "But I thought I was making myself very clear . . ."

"Logan—"

"We'll talk after, okay?"

"Promise?"

"I promise. I love you, Vanessa."

EIGHTEEN

*The way to love anything is to realize
that it may be lost.*
—G. K. CHESTERTON (1874–1936),
ENGLISH THEOLOGIAN

Maybe Mindy was right. She needed a dog.

Vanessa tucked the tiniest puppy into her arms, scratching behind his ears as she watched his brothers and sisters romp in the fenced-off corner of Mindy's living room. Their nonstop acrobatics, accompanied by tiny yips and growls, had both of them laughing all during breakfast. Canine comedic relief.

"You like Minion. Go ahead, admit it." Mindy set two fresh cups of coffee down on the table.

"He's a cutie. But a dog doesn't fit into my life right now. And I don't think you should start married life off with a puppy, an apartment, and two people juggling shift work."

"You're probably right."

"Still . . ." She nuzzled his sleeping face, inhaling the distinct, warm scent of puppy. "They're so cute. Oh, well. Maybe in a year or two."

"Now that we've all survived the hurricane, let's talk about the wedding some more, shall we?" Mindy took a quick bite of her second half of bagel and cream cheese. "We can't go out to the island to go dress shopping again—not with the road torn up, thanks to Cressida. But we can look at dress styles online. There's this one shop that alters used wedding dresses—repurposes them, so to speak."

"I did like that one dress we found—with the long, floaty layers. Remember?"

"Yes. I pinned it to your board on Pinterest. It's perfect for a beach wedding."

"And I also left a message for the wedding coordinator at the hotel where the medical conference is—"

"You're still thinking of having the wedding there?"

"I haven't had a chance to talk to Ted about Henderson Park Inn. The hurricane was a bit of an interruption. It's been more I'm-safe-how-are-you? kinds of conversations or texts."

"True—and then yesterday you were gone all day—and night."

"Not all night."

"Are you going to tell me what you were doing, or are you going to make me ask?"

Vanessa ran her fingers across the puppy's soft fur. "It was no big deal, Mindy."

"Okay, then. Tell me."

"We were helping the Wrights clean up their yard—"

"*We* being your ex-husband and his team. I know

that. And then you went somewhere again last night. That's what I'm curious about."

Vanessa reached for Mindy's laptop. "I thought we were looking at dresses—"

"Vanessa!" Mindy closed the laptop with a snap.

"Fine." The puppy squirmed in her arms, and Vanessa deposited it with the other puppies, knowing the delay was trying her friend's patience. "Logan asked me to meet him at Rocky Bayou Bridge."

"He did? Why?"

"I don't know. Just to . . . talk."

"You went to Rocky Bayou Bridge and—and talked."

"Yes. He asked about what I'm doing now. So I told him. He knows about Ted. There's nothing to worry about."

"I didn't say anything about me being worried about you and Logan. Are *you?*" Mindy focused on her bagel.

"No. Of course not." Especially after last night when her emotions hadn't teetered or tottered. "I think seeing Logan again was a very good thing."

Mindy's gaze locked on hers. "You do? Why?"

"It . . . puts everything in perspective. I came here to plan a wedding. I was afraid of running into ghosts. I even had this crazy dream . . ."

"A dream?"

"Yeah. I was walking on the bridge to Destin. It was foggy, and I couldn't see anything. I heard someone telling me to jump, and then the bridge started crumbling beneath my feet . . ." Vanessa waved away the fragments of the dream. "Something like that."

"Wow. That's kind of telling."

"What do you mean, 'telling'?"

"There's a lot of information out there about dreams and symbolism. Bridges usually have to do with transitions—so you're in a transition time in your life. And fog indicates that you don't know what way to go in life."

"I do know which way to go, Mindy! I'm marrying Ted!" Vanessa held up her hand to display her engagement ring, and then remembered she'd left it back in Colorado to be resized.

"Right. Right."

"That dream was just . . . just me being nervous about coming back to Destin. But I'm here. And I've even seen Logan. And I'm fine."

"Right."

"There's no confusion."

"Right."

"And the only transition I'm having is going from being single to being married again—and I'm marrying Ted."

"Right."

"So let's look at dresses."

"Right."

"And stop saying 'right.'"

"Right—" Mindy covered her mouth with her

hand, her eyes wide. "I mean, okay. Let's do this."

An hour later they'd narrowed down Mindy's matron-of-honor dress to three possibilities.

"I still like the idea of something with an Empire waist." Mindy clicked back to the second dress option. "And I wouldn't mind a one-shoulder-style dress, because it provides more coverage than a halter or a maillot or something with spaghetti straps. I mean, I am going to be a nursing mom most likely . . ."

A knock at the front door interrupted her perusal of the turquoise knee-length dress.

"Look and see if you find anything else. I'll be right back."

A few moments later, Mindy reappeared, followed by Logan Hollister.

"Guess who stopped by?" Mindy's eyebrows were skyrocketing over her eyes.

"Logan?" Vanessa closed the laptop, rising to her feet.

"Good guess."

"Sorry to interrupt." The way he smiled at her, Logan didn't look sorry at all. "I, um, was wondering if you'd like to go for a motorcycle ride."

"A motorcycle ride?"

"Yep." A familiar glint lit his blue eyes. "For old times' sake."

And after all the years of silence . . . of emotional and geographical distance . . . Vanessa's heart still responded to the little bit of I-dare-you in his blue eyes that always pulled her toward him.

Why wasn't she still holding on to the puppy—some sort of furry little barrier between her and Logan?

Completely ineffective.

But she couldn't say yes to Logan anymore. They weren't teenagers. A wedding and a divorce—and so much more, including her engagement and upcoming wedding—separated them.

He stood there, watching her. Not saying a word. And she knew he understood everything she was thinking. And feeling. The *I won't*'s warring with the *I will*'s. Teeter-totter. She'd never been good at saying no to Logan. With him, it had always been about saying yes . . . and her acceptance of his invitation to meet him at the bridge last night had weakened her defenses. And really, what could one short motorcycle ride with Logan hurt?

"Sounds like fun."

His grin lit something long dormant in her heart, but Vanessa tamped it down with a quick shake of her head.

"Is that okay, Mindy?"

"You don't need permission from me—I'm not your mother. Besides, I'm about ready for my mommy-to-be nap, anyway."

And just like that, they stepped into old times' sake.

Standing next to his motorcycle, Vanessa

289

couldn't believe it was the same one he'd bought during their first year of college. "So, it still runs, huh?"

"Yeah. I leave it here year-round in my parents' garage." He handed her a blue helmet. "I think my dad pays someone to keep it tuned up for me."

"Good thing my hair's braided."

"I like how you're wearing it long."

That wasn't a compliment, exactly. More of an observation. "Yeah, well, I don't swim much these days."

"Except when you jump into the Gulf to rescue someone from drowning."

"That was different—and you helped."

"Like I said, we're a good team."

He spoke the words as he reached over to help her adjust the helmet's chin strap, his fingers brushing against hers. She dropped her hands to her sides, her fingers curling tight into her palms. Once the strap was buckled, Logan rapped on the top—once, twice—the sound echoing back to years ago.

"All set?"

"Yes."

When he'd put on his helmet and settled on the bike, he slid forward, steadying the motorcycle with his feet. She climbed on behind him, waiting until she found her balance again. Vanessa stared at Logan's broad back. Where did she place her hands? Did she dare touch Logan again? Wrap her arms around his waist? Lean in like she used to do when they were . . . younger? When she placed her hands where his belt rested just above his hips, he seemed to exhale, bringing the motorcycle to life with a roar and steering it out of the driveway with practiced ease, going slowly until they hit the road in front of the house.

Vanessa closed her eyes. Inhaled, but was unable to smell the morning air rushing by them because of the helmet. Not remembering. Not thinking ahead. Just feeling the power of the motorcycle, how Logan controlled the bike with assurance. Watching his strong hands grip the handlebars, the curve and width of his shoulders beneath his brown leather jacket.

Despite what Logan said, this ride wasn't for old times' sake. The choice to climb up on the bike again and go for a ride with him had nothing to do with the past. She couldn't—wouldn't—remember back to when they were both younger and didn't think before they leapt and mistakenly thought they'd fallen in love forever. No recalling what she and Logan had thought they had . . . because then she'd have to stop and evaluate what they'd lost.

And taking this ride had nothing to do with her future as Ted's wife. She would never do anything this impetuous with Ted. He drove the speed limit. Scheduled his next dental appointment the same day he got his teeth cleaned. Took a multivitamin.

Met with his insurance rep once a year to check his policy.

But she understood his calm, careful approach to life. Appreciated it. Ted faced nonstop drama in the ER, just as she rode the rush of adrenaline whenever she went out on a call.

Being on the motorcycle with Logan—allowing herself to ease just a little closer, to relax, to relish the pull of the wind against her clothes, the subtle sense of speed—was about being in this moment. Nothing more.

The echoes of laughter from the past would fade once he brought her back to Mindy's. She'd forget that being here felt . . . familiar. Comfortable. She ignored the faint whisper in her heart telling her she'd missed this. That she'd missed him.

Because that wasn't possible.

Vanessa opened her eyes. How long had she been sitting here, eyes squeezed shut?

She wasn't surprised Logan headed toward the high school. Not really.

Where else would he go?

Logan had no game plan for what came next. His invitation had been impulsive—and he hadn't expected Vanessa to say yes.

Her agreement nourished something inside his heart. A verbal salve to an invisible wound that ached just a bit less when she climbed on behind him . . . well, not exactly like she had in the past.

She hadn't snuggled up against his back. Hadn't wrapped her arms around his waist. Hadn't run her fingers through the strands of his hair brushing his shoulders.

Because he didn't wear his hair long anymore.

And they weren't that couple anymore. Weren't married anymore.

But he still had to force himself to concentrate on the road. Not think about the woman behind him, her hands warm against his waist. Mere inches separating their bodies. The memories of so many rides together teased him so that he barely noticed the scenery passing by.

He turned the motorcycle into the high school parking lot not because that had been his intention all along. Not because he had anything to say to Vanessa. But because he couldn't think straight.

Logan pulled the helmet off, inhaling a deep breath, raking his fingers through his hair. He twisted to face Vanessa just as she removed her helmet.

"So . . . enjoying the ride?"

"Yes." The one word was quick. Breathless. "I haven't been on a motorcycle since . . . in years."

He steadied the bike as Vanessa dismounted, then set the stand before locking the helmets on the back of the motorcycle and coming to stand beside her.

"How's your family?"

"My parents retired to Montana—where my

dad's from. He . . . he's recovering from a heart attack."

Her statement jolted him a bit—away from his awareness of her. "Is he okay?"

"Yes . . . I mean, he's recovering. It happened right before I came here. He's home now."

"I'm glad to hear that. Your mom okay?"

"You know my mom—she handles everything. Nothing upsets her."

Except her daughter eloping during her senior year of high school. There was that.

"And what about Rylan? Did he ever get his own motorcycle?"

"Yes, he did—once he joined the military."

"Just like your dad."

"Yes. He's in the air force, too—overseas. But he's still single. Makes it easier for him, I think. He likes the travel."

"And you're a paramedic. How'd that come about?"

"I was studying kinesiology in college. After the . . . the divorce, I decided I wanted to get a job to keep busy. I thought about working at a gym, lifeguarding or teaching swim lessons—you know, use my swim-team experience. I needed to get recertified with some of my life-saving certification. And then some of my classmates mentioned they were EMTs. And one thing led to another . . . I found I liked helping people. There's no typical day . . . and there's an emotional rush that's addicting. Yeah, it's kinda outrageous to admit to that."

"So, life looks good. Work. School. A wedding."

"Yes. Ted and I have known each other for a couple of years. It's . . . easy."

"Great."

"And you . . ."

"Like I said last night, I've been doing what I love. Chasing storms. I've had a great time."

No need to tell her all that was ending.

"I saw in the news that there was an accident."

She'd read about that? About him?

"Yes. That's why Max is on crutches. You know how the press is—all about creating headlines—and that means covering the worst stories."

"I'm glad you're okay—you and your team."

"Thanks."

Even with those few words, Vanessa offered him more comfort than his own father had, but then that had always been the case . . . or had been for a few years, at least.

"So when do you head back to Denver?"

"Tomorrow. My boss has let me have a few extra days on top of a few extra days."

"Excuse me?"

"Sorry—that was a bit confusing. I took a couple of extra days to visit my father. Then Cressida added a few more days to my time here, what with closing the airport down. What about you?"

"The team and I fly out tomorrow, too."

The smile she offered him ended with a sigh. "Everyone gets back to normal."

"Exactly."

He scanned the parking lot, which was vacant except for a few cars and what looked like a couple of repair vehicles parked close to the gym.

"Doesn't look like school's back in session yet."

"I heard on the TV this morning that besides the sign damage, the gym roof took a hit from the hurricane. So I think they're delaying school until next week."

"Understandable." He nodded toward the school. "But there's no reason we can't go for a quick walk through the halls—for old times' sake and all that."

"What? No—" Vanessa didn't move.

"Are you going to the reunion next month?"

"No."

"Well, then this is your only chance to walk the hallowed halls of Niceville High School, our alma mater." He tilted his head toward the gym. "Join me?"

He braced himself for her refusal—and so the sound of her laughter, coupled with the way her hand brushed against his as she came alongside him, was an intoxicating and unexpected glimpse of the past.

"Lead on!" Vanessa fell into step with him.

"Just act like we're supposed to be here, and nobody will be any wiser." Logan slung his arm over her shoulders, waving at the workman on top of the gym roof.

She matched her steps to his, the heels of her boots tapping against the asphalt. "We're alumni—of course we belong here."

"That's the spirit. Where to first?"

"The lockers—I want to see my locker." She ran ahead of him. "And then I'm going to all my classrooms."

"You think you can remember your schedule from senior year?"

His question caused her to stop in the middle of the hallway. She closed her eyes, appearing deep in thought. And during those moments, Logan allowed himself to stare at her face—and remember when he had the freedom to touch her thick hair, to kiss her mouth, to watch her brown eyes light up with laughter or soften with the first moments of passion . . .

"I've got it— What?" Vanessa's question interrupted his perusal. "What are you thinking?"

"Nothing." Logan tucked his hands into his jean pockets. "You remember your schedule? Prove it. Take me to each one of the classrooms—in the proper order."

"But we weren't in all the same classes. You won't know if I'm right."

"Vanessa—I knew your schedule senior year. I'll know."

"Oh." A faint tinge of pink stained her cheeks.

"Okay. Here we go: Honors English—I had that with Mindy. And then you and I had math class together . . ."

By the time they recalled both their class schedules and found their lockers, reminiscing about teachers and classmates, the empty hallways echoed with their laughter. Then they found their graduating class photograph framed among all the other graduating classes—their faces side by side.

"My mom had to do some sort of special order to get me senior photos, since we moved two weeks after school started."

He'd never really thought of all the challenges Vanessa faced moving during her senior year.

"Do you ever regret not going out for swim team during senior year?"

"No. You know what teams are like, Logan—you lead one. People get close—they have inside jokes, traditions . . . it was bad enough being the new girl *again*. That seemed to be my role in life. The new girl. I wasn't going to be the outsider on the swim team, too. So, I just decided I wasn't going to swim. It was easier."

"But you loved swimming—"

"Sure. But that's what moving is all about—giving up what you love. Or not getting attached to anything—or anybody." Vanessa moved away from the class photo, the sound of her boot heels echoing in the empty hallway. "Did I ever tell you what happened when I was in middle school?"

"I don't think so."

"We actually lived somewhere for three years. That was like *forever*. Long enough to make friends. Oh, never mind—this was years ago . . ."

"No, tell me. I want to hear."

"I became friends with this girl—Patty. Best friends—we ate lunch together at school and talked about boys and had sleepovers. Yeah, typical girls." Vanessa's laugh was short. Sharp. "And then . . . we had to move. Of course we had to move. But Patty and I swore we'd be best friends forever. And she invited me back to visit for her birthday weekend. I couldn't wait."

"What happened?"

"I should have stayed home. It was four months after we'd moved—and she had a new best friend. I'd been there a whole twenty-four hours when I accidentally overheard her ask her mom, 'Why did you make me invite her?' So I pretended to be sick until it was time for me to get back on the plane and go home."

"She sounds like a real brat."

"No. She taught me an important lesson."

"What's that?"

"That people change. That relationships . . . change. Sometimes I forget that for a moment or two, but not very often."

Vanessa fell silent, and Logan had no response, no challenge to her statement.

The truth was, he'd taught her the same thing.

NINETEEN

Falling in love and having a relationship
are two different things.
—KEANU REEVES (1964–), ACTOR

"Do you have time for a little more 'for old times' sake'?"

Logan's question seemed to whisper on the rush of the wind as he turned the motorcycle onto the tree-lined road leading to the Mid-Bay Bridge. The echo of her yes replayed over and over in Vanessa's head. If she dared, she'd unclip her helmet, yank it off, and let the air rushing by run its fingers through her hair and pull the words out of her mind. Toss them over the side of the bridge so they'd tumble into the water below and drown.

Instead, as Logan increased his speed, she slid forward and wrapped her arms around his waist. Closed her eyes and held on, resting her head against his back.

The asphalt beneath them was solid . . . real. The sky above them was sparkling blue—not a single cloud. She needn't fear falling into the waters of Choctawatchee Bay. Let meaningless dreams of fog and crumbling bridges and jumping into the water below stay where they belonged—in the night.

And she wasn't surprised when Logan parked the motorcycle near the beach they always went to as teenagers. This was what the day was all about, after all.

For old times' sake.

Falling into old habits was easier than she ever realized. Locking the helmets on the back of the bike. Logan's "Ready for a walk?" accompanied with a grin. They couldn't leave their shoes at the base of the weathered steps—not with the debris Cressida had strewn along the beach—so the white sand squelched beneath their feet, but they couldn't feel the coolness against their toes. Still, they were close enough that their arms touched. Their breathing mingled with the sounds of the Gulf . . . the plaintive cries of seagulls as they wheeled back and forth over the water and the sighs of the waves against the shore.

"This has always been my favorite place." Logan settled into an easy pace near the water's edge, but not close enough to give the waves permission to splash up against their shoes.

"That night we rescued the teen?" Vanessa began unbraiding her hair, the wind tugging strands loose. "It was my first time back to Destin in years."

"Really? Why?"

"I finished out at FSU after we divorced—and I came back to Niceville a few times. For holidays. For Rylan's high school graduation." She ran her fingers through her hair, releasing it about her shoulders. "I just could never bring myself to come back here. Too many memories."

"Even with the memories, this was still my favorite place." Logan's hand brushed up against hers. "Because of the memories, too."

"I was afraid I'd run into a ghost coming back here—"

"And then you run into me."

"Yeah."

He grasped her hand, his skin warm against hers, pulling her to a stop. "Are you sorry?"

"No. No, I'm not sorry."

When they fell back into step, it seemed natural—right—to let their hands remain clasped, their fingers intertwined.

"I come here every year after we finish the storm-chasing season. It's my way to relax." Logan's chuckle was low. Brief. "Sometimes my team asks if we can go somewhere else. The mountains, maybe. And every year, I say no, even though I know I'll see you here."

"What?"

"I mean, I thought we might actually run into each other—even though we never did. But more than that, the memories are still here. The good and the bad. And I was willing to have both."

"Logan—why?"

She didn't have to ask anything else. He knew exactly what she was asking.

● ● ●

How could he explain his actions to her?

"If I still loved you, why didn't I come after you?"

"Yes."

"If I say I was stupid, that won't be enough of an answer to erase all the hurt built up between us." He eased her closer, and she allowed him to put his arm around her so she was close against his body. "At first I was angry that you'd even file for divorce, and I let myself stay angry. And I was young—"

"We both were."

"Yes—but getting married young isn't an automatic death sentence, Vanessa."

"I know—like your grandfather said, 'You either get married when you're young and grow up together, or you get married when you're older and you grow up together.'"

"You remember that?"

"Yes."

"I let my youth and my anger and my stupidity become a mixture of stubbornness . . . and rather than figuring out how to work things out, how to stay married—*grow up together*—I let our problems come between us."

"What happened between us—it wasn't all your fault."

"You asked me why I didn't come after you— I'm answering the question. At first, it was easier to blame you. To not say I was wrong. To not ask you to forgive me. But it was more than that." Logan seemed to wrestle with the words. With himself. "You were everything to me, Vanessa. And I kept thinking, what if I came and asked you to try again . . . and you said no? I couldn't face that."

He knew God had granted him this moment. After all, God was a God of redemption. Of reconciliation.

He stopped. Turned to face Vanessa, who remained sheltered in his embrace, his arm angled across her back. Somehow, they'd stepped too close to the water, the waves washing back and forth across their shoes, wetting the hem of his jeans, anchoring them into the sand. A Gulf breeze blew strands of her hair across her face, and he brushed them back, tucking them behind one of her ears, his fingertips trailing along the outline of her jaw.

"If I had it to do again, I'd do it all so differently, love." He cupped her face with both his hands. "But I accept God is not a God of do-overs. I have to face the truth that I won you—and I've lost you. But I have this moment. And I can say I regret not coming after you. Not doing everything I could think of to make our marriage work. Forgive me, please."

"Logan . . . I do . . ." Vanessa's voice trembled over the words, a broken benediction.

His thumb brushed over her full bottom lip, the softness flaming a longing inside of him. His hand slipped along the warm curve of her throat, and he urged her closer, the veil of her eyelids hiding any message her eyes might communicate.

Their kiss held the purity of coming home and the enticement of the forbidden. He'd never forgotten the feel of Vanessa in his arms, the scent of her perfume lingering in her hair, how she accepted his kiss, her lips soft and responsive beneath his.

Sweet torture, when she was marrying someone else.

Surrender.

With every beat of her heart, Vanessa found herself yielding to Logan again. The excuse of "for old times' sake" evaporated, and in its place stood unadulterated desire.

For his touch. His kiss. For him.

Within seconds, restraint gave way to a passion that took her unawares. She'd forgotten how quickly she responded to Logan's touch, his fingers threading through the windswept strands of her hair. The full length of his body pressed against hers until she bent backward, but she knew he wouldn't let her fall . . .

He was right—they couldn't go back. But what about the future? Couldn't they figure out a way to be together again?

No.

No.

Somehow she found the strength to push Logan away, stumbling back a few more steps into the water, the pull of the tide helping her to put even more distance between them. Turn away. Dive underwater. Hold her breath and swim for the horizon. For safety.

"Stop. Don't . . . don't kiss me . . ."

Logan followed her into the surf, splashing water up onto his clothes. "Vanessa, I'm sorry. I was trying to apologize—"

"Stop." She backed up more, the sand shifting beneath her boots. "No more *apologies*."

"I'm sorry. I shouldn't have kissed you."

"You can't kiss me! I'm marrying Ted! You can't kiss me!" He reached for her again, and she dodged his hand. "Don't touch me—"

A wave hit her from behind, throwing her off-balance and tossing her to her knees, soaking her through. Logan grasped her by her wrists and hauled her to her feet.

"I'm sorry."

Gulf water dripped from her clothes and hair. Tears coursed down her face. "Don't . . . kiss me again."

"I won't."

"Take me back . . . to Mindy's. Please."

"You need to dry off."

She shook off his hands and trudged back to

shore, fighting against the rolling waves. "Now. I want . . . to leave now."

During the ride back to Niceville, Vanessa sat on the motorcycle so there was ample space between her and Logan. She shivered inside her sodden clothes as the air rushing by pressed them against her skin. Logan pushed the edge of the speed limit, his knuckles white against the motorcycle handlebars, leaning into the curves so Vanessa clung to the edges of the seat.

Logan barely pulled the motorcycle to a stop in front of Mindy's house before Vanessa clambered off, unbuckling the helmet and yanking it off her head and tossing it at Logan as he anchored the bike before climbing off. It landed on the street with a loud clatter as she turned away.

"Hey!" Logan grabbed her arm. "We need to talk."

"We survived eight years without talking." She pulled against him. Stomped her foot. "Let go of my arm."

"Go ahead and hate me if you want. But I'm saying what I need to say this time." With his hand wrapped around her wrist, Logan forced her to stand still. "That kiss was all wrong, I admit it. You're engaged. I get that. But the truth is, I still love you. I never stopped. If you weren't engaged, I'd do everything in my power to win you back."

She stared up at him. What was she supposed to do? Pretend this was some romantic movie where

307

everything turned out perfectly in the end? The star-crossed young lovers didn't mess things up and die—but somehow ended up married and enjoying happily-ever-after like the Wrights and Logan's grandparents?

Life wasn't like that.

Even Logan's grandmother died.

"We had our chance, Logan." When his grip on her arm loosened, she twisted out of his hold and stepped back. "And we failed."

Footsteps sounded behind her. *Oh, no.* Had Mindy and her husband witnessed what just happened?

Someone rested a hand on her shoulder.

"You okay, babe?"

Ted?

She whirled around and came face-to-face with her fiancé.

"What are you doing here?"

"I flew in early this afternoon. I was worried about you. So I came to check on you and the wedding plans." He motioned back and forth from Logan and Vanessa. "Everything okay here?"

"Yes. Yes, I'm fine. This is my—"

Logan nodded, his wet hair tangled. "I'm an old high school friend of Vanessa's. Stopped by to say hello when I heard she was in town."

"I'm Ted Topliff."

Logan straddled the motorcycle. "You must be her fiancé. You're a lucky man."

He put on his helmet, blocking his face from view and preventing further conversation. When he started up the bike, Vanessa stepped back onto the curb, Ted joining her.

"Why are you all wet, Vanessa?"

"I fell into the Gulf." She stomped toward the house, her sodden boots and clothes squishing with every step. "Time for a shower."

Let Logan drive off. There hadn't been any real goodbyes the first time. Why should she expect one now?

CHRISTMAS 2004

Was this how her mother felt when her father returned home from a long trip?

Vanessa checked her hair in the mirror again, still not quite used to the layers. Would Logan like that she was letting it grow long? Would he like the haircut Mindy had talked her into, the strands framing her face?

She pressed the palms of her hands against her stomach, willing it to settle. This was Logan, her husband, she was waiting for—not some unknown guy coming to pick her up for a blind date. She wouldn't tell him about the couple of classmates she'd had to fend off during the last semester while Logan was in Oklahoma—the ones who somehow didn't see her wedding band. Or didn't care about it.

She resisted sneaking one of the peanut butter chocolate chip cookies she'd baked in the Hollisters' larger kitchen—a treat she'd prepared for Logan. He'd be hungry and tired after a long day on the road from Oklahoma. He'd probably eat half a dozen while he unpacked. And then, who knew? Maybe they'd go have dinner at the Boathouse, or ride the motorcycle over the bridge and walk on the beach. It didn't matter. They'd be together. And after surviving the first semester apart—and Logan not even coming home once for a long weekend at Thanksgiving because he was working on some sort of huge group project—surely he was as tired of their long-distance marriage as she was. Maybe during Christmas break she could convince him to transfer to FSU.

The sound of the door opening had her whirling around, smoothing her hair away from her face.

"Vanessa? You here already?" Logan stepped inside, dropping his bike helmet at his feet.

"Yes—oh, Logan, I'm so glad—" She ran to meet him, throwing her arms around him. Inhaled the scent of his hair, savoring the feel of his arms around her. At last.

"Hey. I've missed you, too." He pressed a kiss to her neck and laughed, low and husky.

And then someone else laughed.

What?

Her eyes flew open, and she stared into an unfamiliar pair of light brown eyes. Startled, she

310

stepped out of Logan's embrace. "Who is this?"

Logan grabbed her hand again, moving her forward. "Vanessa, this is Brady. I met him at school this semester. He's a meteorology major like me. Brady, this is my wife, Vanessa."

Brady nodded, offering her a cockeyed grin and a brief wave. "A lot of us couldn't believe Logan had a wife—especially some of the girls in our classes."

"Hey." Logan lifted his left hand. "I always wore my wedding ring."

"And now I've met the missus, so I can vouch for you."

"Does Brady live in Niceville, too?" Vanessa fought to keep up with the conversation.

"No." Logan refocused on her. "His parents are stationed overseas—and he's stateside for the holidays. So I invited him to come spend the break with us."

His words were a verbal douse of cold water to Vanessa's emotions. "He's staying here?"

"Sure. We've got the bedroom, and I told Brady that he'd have to surf the couch. He's good with that."

Brady took a few steps back. "Let me go get our stuff off the motorcycle."

"Don't worry about it." Logan motioned him inside. "We can do that later."

"Not a problem." Brady disappeared outside.

Vanessa pulled her hand free from Logan's. "You

didn't mention Brady was coming home with you."

"Well, I wasn't sure he was until yesterday. And I knew you wouldn't mind—I mean, you of all people understand being a military kid, right? And what did your mother always say? 'There's always room for one more'?"

"But, Logan, you didn't tell me."

"What was I supposed to do? Leave the guy on campus for Christmas?"

"No, of course not. I'm not saying that." Vanessa rearranged the still-warm cookies into a neater pile. Logan hadn't even noticed them. "I was just excited about seeing you, that's all."

"And you *will* see me." He came up behind her, slipping his arms around her waist and pulling her up against him. "I'm right here for an entire month."

"And so is Brady."

"He's a great guy. It'll be fun."

Fun. Right.

Logan crawled into bed next to Vanessa, who lay on her side, knees pulled up to her chest, her hair spilling across the pillow. Two-thirty in the morning. *Whoa.* He hadn't expected to be out that late with Brady and a few of his high school buddies, playing video games at one guy's house. He couldn't blame her for not waiting up—but why hadn't she come along with them?

He eased closer to his wife, molding his body to the curve of her back, inhaling the familiar scent that lingered in her hair. Beautiful. He hadn't forgotten the enticement of sleeping with Vanessa, but being this close to her caused all his senses to go on heightened alert. He stroked his fingertips along the length of her neck and down her shoulder.

"I'm awake."

Vanessa's words were spoken as a statement—not an invitation. No warmth, not even the hint of *I've been waiting for you. Welcome home.*

"I'm sorry if I woke you up—"

"No. No, I was awake when you came in." She rolled onto her back, shrugging out of his embrace, effectively putting distance between them.

Now he could see the shadowed lines of her face, thanks to the bit of light shining in through the bedroom window. In the semidarkness, he noted the tight lines bracketing her mouth.

"You okay?"

"How can you even ask me that?" The question was a verbal smack, even as she remained motionless in the bed.

"I don't understand—"

She pressed the palm of her hand against her mouth, the sound of her deep inhale—hold—and exhale filling the room with tension so palpable Logan wanted to reach out and shove it away.

"What's wrong, Vanessa?"

"Now you ask me that—what? Four days before I leave for Tallahassee?" She stared at the ceiling. "You go to Oklahoma for college because it's your

313

dream. You don't come home for Thanksgiving because you have homework—"

Logan propped himself up on one elbow. "Hey, we both agreed to that decision!"

"You made up your mind before you ever talked to me about it—don't deny it. And then you come home for Christmas with your buddy—and you spend all your time hanging with him and your high school friends."

"I just want Brady to have a good time. What's wrong with that?"

"Nothing. Nothing at all." She rolled over so he was staring at her back again.

"Vanessa, if you're mad at me, say so."

Silence.

And then, just when he was beginning to think, *What am I supposed to do, sit up all night and make her talk to me?* she bolted upright.

"I am not going to remind you that you're married."

"What are you talking about?"

"And I am not going to beg you to pay attention to me."

"Vanessa—"

"But bringing a—a guy home for Christmas break when it was our first time together since we left for college . . . well, you're the biggest idiot I ever met."

"Hey! I was being a nice guy. What was I supposed to do?"

She rounded on him, holding the blankets up around her chest. "How about talking to me first, so I'm not surprised when some stranger walks into our house?"

"It's my parents' house, Vanessa. They don't mind that Brady's here."

She stared at him openmouthed, and then lay down on the bed, rolling away from him again.

"Don't act like that, Vanessa—"

Her words were flung at him over her shoulder. "Like what? Like my husband prefers his buddies to me? Like I'm 'company' in his parents' house?"

"That's not what I said—"

"Then you weren't listening to yourself, Logan. I heard everything you said—everything."

When he reached for her, she shifted away. "I'm tired. I'm going to sleep."

"Vanessa, we need to talk about this."

"If we had talked about it before you came home, we wouldn't be having this argument now." She pulled the blanket up to her shoulders. "Good night."

He lay on his back, his head resting on his hands. His turn to stare up at the ceiling. How could he make this right? It was too late to redo the holidays—and would he have made a different decision? No. He would never leave Brady alone for Christmas and New Year's. Why couldn't Vanessa understand that?

TWENTY

Coming events cast their shadows before.
—JAMES JOYCE (1882–1941),
NOVELIST, IN *ULYSSES*

"Nessa, who was that guy?"

Ted's question might as well have been a ball and chain, dragging her to a stop halfway to Mindy's front door. Were they going to have this discussion in the front yard? Did they have to talk about "that guy" at all?

"We went to high school together."

Yes, she was hedging. Lying by omission. But she wasn't doing this here, in wet clothes, reeking of the Gulf.

Ted stalked toward her. Always-calm Ted—advancing on her, feet pounding the pavement, looking as if he wanted to shake her.

"Who is he, Vanessa?"

She shook the tangled mess of her hair, the strands stiff with salt water. "Logan Hollister, my ex-husband. Are you satisfied? Can we go inside now? Please?"

She sat on the top porch step in front of Mindy's idyllic home and pulled off her lacy half boots. Ruined. Ted's shadow fell over her.

"What?"

His hair fell forward into his eyes. "You can really ask me that? As if finding you on a motorcycle with your ex-husband is not a problem."

"It's not a problem." She abandoned her soggy boots on the steps and retreated to the house.

The scent of grilled fish and buttery garlic bread lured Vanessa's attention away from Ted—until he slammed the door behind them. Ted, who never raised his voice, even when they watched a football game and the Broncos were losing with the clock counting down the final minute of the game. And now he came into someone else's house and slammed the door.

Mindy appeared in the kitchen doorway, balancing a clear glass bowl brimming with green salad, red tomato slices, and thin rounds of yellow peppers. She must have corralled the puppies in the laundry room off the kitchen, their high-pitched yipping sounding behind her.

"Everything okay out here?" A bogus smile stretched across her face.

"Yes."

Mindy scrunched her nose. "You're . . . wet."

"I know." The sticky-wet strands of her hair clung to her neck. "Don't ask."

"Go ahead. Ask." Ted stood behind her, his voice a near-shout. "She just rode up on a motorcycle with her ex-husband."

There was no missing the way Mindy's eyes

317

widened before Vanessa whipped around to face the man behind her.

"What is wrong with you?"

"What is wrong with me? I come down here to surprise my fiancée—and I find her gallivanting around with the man she was married to ten years ago." He paced circles around her, his voice rising, overriding the barking of the puppies. "Soaking wet because she's fallen in the ocean. And I don't know why she's romping in the ocean with her ex-husband—"

"Ted Topliff!" Vanessa pressed her palm to her forehead, closing her eyes. This was not happening. Not happening. "I am going to get a shower. Then we are going to eat dinner like two rational, civilized people with Mindy and her husband. And then—and only then—will I discuss this with you. Is that clear?"

"And what if I want to discuss it now?"

"Not an option. You're being irrational. I've never seen you act like this."

"I could say the same thing."

Mindy's husband opened the door to the back porch, looking inside, oblivious to the ongoing argument playing out in his living room. "Amberjack will be ready in ten minutes!"

Vanessa backed down the hallway. "As I said, I'm going to grab a quick shower before dinner. We'll talk afterward."

When she returned to the kitchen, her hair pulled

back into a ponytail, wearing dry boot-cut jeans and a favorite Pemberley-style blouse, the house was quiet. Even the puppies dozed.

"Is Ted out back with Jett?"

Mindy leaned against the kitchen counter. She shook her head, her hands twisting together. "He left, Vanessa."

"What do you mean, 'he left'?"

"You went to get a shower, and he walked out."

Vanessa ran to the front door, throwing it open. "Why didn't you come get me?"

"I thought he was just going outside to think. Get some fresh air. I didn't realize he was going to drive off until I heard the car start up." Mindy came to stand beside her. "I thought you said he was this calm kind of guy."

"He is. I don't know what's going on."

"Oh, come on. You rode up with Logan."

"It's nothing . . ."

"And I don't believe that any more than Ted does, girlfriend. You both looked guilty—like two high-schoolers who missed curfew."

Had Mindy watched the whole interaction from her front window? Wonderful. She'd known that smile was fake. Vanessa ignored Mindy's comment. "I don't even know why he's here."

"He said he wanted to surprise you—" Mindy paused, as if debating what to say next. "—and he mentioned something about being asked to be part of the planning committee for the medical conference he's attending after the wedding."

Vanessa had nothing to say. Of course it had to be romance plus something else with Ted.

"Dinner's ready." Jett entered the house, the platter of freshly grilled fish hefted above his head.

"Okay, sweetheart. We'll be right there." Mindy stepped in front of Vanessa, preventing her from walking away. "You don't have to tell me what did or didn't happen with you and Logan—but eventually you have to talk to Ted. And then you have to figure out if you're going to marry the guy."

Vanessa crossed her arms. "Of course I am."

"Really?"

"Yes. I am." Vanessa stared her friend down. "I'm marrying Ted."

"Are you saying that because you want to marry the guy—or because you're trying to convince yourself?"

"Mindy, I appreciate your concern—really, I do. But I asked you to be my matron of honor because I'm marrying Ted next April. I know what I'm doing." Vanessa shut the front door.

"Sure you do."

She took two steps past her friend—and halted. "What did you say?"

"I said let's go eat."

"Sure you did."

• • •

Logan brought the motorcycle to a stop inside his parents' garage. Cut the engine. Stared at the wall in front of him covered with a white pegboard lined with straight rows of tools—hammers, screwdrivers, wrenches.

Why was he sitting here, staring at yet another corner of his father's well-ordered world? He needed to get inside and change out of his wet boots and jeans.

And then he needed to figure out how to place an ad in the *Gazette*. It was time to sell the motorcycle—past time. A nice, brief ad—something like, "UNWANTED MOTORCYCLE FOR SALE. CHEAP. BEST OFFER. SHOULD HAVE BEEN SOLD YEARS AGO."

He shucked his boots off in the air lock, leaving his damp socks lying beside them. His water-logged jeans chafed against his legs.

The kitchen was silent but filled with the aroma of buttery popcorn. Laughter drifted in from the direction of the pool area. Caron and Alex sat in two of the lounge chairs, their hands linked. Julie and Max were at the deep end of the pool, Max's arms encircling Julie.

Well, well, well. Was this the first official sighting of the Stormmeisters' romance?

Caron waved without lifting her head from the chair. "Hey, big brother. Where have you been all day?"

"Out."

"O-kay." Caron sat up at the sharpness of his tone. "Sounds like you had a wonderful day."

"Hey, boss!" Max waved, keeping one arm around Julie, who looked content to stay where she was.

"Where's Brady?"

"I think he's upstairs packing."

"Team meeting in half an hour."

"What?" Julie twisted to face him. "Can't that wait until we get back to Oklahoma?"

"Half an hour." Logan backed out of the room. "I'm going to get a shower, and we'll meet in the family room. Somebody tell Brady."

"Sure thing, boss."

Logan couldn't help but overhear Caron ask, "What's his problem?" as he left the room.

Thirty minutes later Brady, Max, and Julie were all gathered in his parents' family room. Brady stood near the stone fireplace, his hands tucked in his pockets. Julie and Max chose to sit next to one another on the leather couch, Max's arm resting across her shoulders.

Logan finished off his second soda as he stalked into the room. He'd tried praying, tried asking God what to say, how to tell the team of his decision. But the entire time he'd showered, all he could think of was Vanessa. Kissing her again—and the wrongness of his action. The futility of it. And then bringing her back to

Mindy's—straight to her fiancé. The man who had a right to kiss her. To touch her. And all because he'd been stupid. Stubborn. Too afraid to go after his wife. To figure out what he needed to do to make their marriage work.

Well, he was done with being scared. At least facing his mistakes with Vanessa helped him face his mistakes with his team—and do what he needed to do. There was no reason to wait until they got back to Oklahoma.

Straight up was the best option. Then they could all deal with the reality.

Julie offered him a shaky smile. "Hey, I know you want to talk with us. But I wanted to let you know I got our boarding passes for tomorrow—"

Sweet Jules. Always trying to find a way to smooth things over. To keep things working well.

"Thanks. I forgot all about that."

"No problem."

His team. Julie, who worked a camera like it was her third eye. And Max, who might never grow up—but had mad computer skills that let him process incoming storm data while Logan drove. And Brady, who was already dreaming of a storm-chasing team with him during freshman year of college, eager, willing to learn, with the driving skills of a professional race car driver, who manned the second car. Who loved the mystery of weather as much as Logan did.

His decision was going to hurt them as much as it hurt him. Maybe more.

Logan anchored his feet to the ground and faced the three people he trusted most in the world. "So, there are going to be some changes coming up for the team."

"Changes? What kind of changes?" Brady was the first to speak up, crossing his arms over his chest, covering the Stormmeisters logo on his black T-shirt.

"Let me finish, okay? I'll explain the initial change. You three decide what happens after that." Logan scrubbed his hand across his jaw. "I'm leaving the team."

The trio reacted as if he'd lobbed a bomb into the room. Julie gasped, turned white, her hand going to her throat.

"What?" Max struggled to his feet, ignoring his crutches.

"Are you out of your mind?" Brady's voice rose above Max's. "You're the team leader. Our boss."

"I've been thinking about this for a while. We've had a good run—and it's time for me to move on."

"Are you going to another team?"

What kind of question was that? "No. I would never do that."

"Then what are you doing? Just quitting? To do what—go sell cars?" Brady stalked toward him. "You're a storm chaser, man. It's what you do."

"Storm chasing is what I've done. I'm making a

change." Logan stood his ground even as Brady advanced on him. "People do that—they change. I'll stay on while we process this year's research data. After that, I don't know. I've been looking at some other job opportunities."

"This is about Max, isn't it?" Julie's soft question cut through Logan's explanation. "About the accident."

How did he answer that?

"I won't deny the accident shook me up. Got me thinking. But I'm making the decision because it's the right thing to do."

"I'm fine, Logan." Max's steps toward him were slow. Still unsteady. "I'll be off the crutches soon and ready for next season."

"I know. And I thank God for that. Every night." Logan rested his hand on his friend's shoulder. "You're tough."

"Then why are you walking away?" Brady came and stood beside Max. "We all know accidents happen—it's part of the game."

"I don't want to play the game anymore, Brady— okay?" Logan's voice was too loud. "I don't see it as a game. It's life-and-death. I don't want to be responsible for that. This is my decision. I've made it. This isn't open to discussion."

"Perfect. Your decision—and it affects all of us. I like how you worked that." Brady stared at him and then shook his head before walking away— out of the room.

Silence settled for a few minutes. Logan had expected surprise . . . sadness . . . but he hadn't expected hostility.

"Give him some time, boss." Julie, of course, trying to make things okay. "You kinda surprised all of us. What are we supposed to do now?"

"Well, as I said, I've made my decision. What happens to the team now is up to you three. Most of the Stormmeisters remains intact. Maybe you all should look for a new team member. Give him or her a trial run in the next season. I don't know. It's not for me to say."

"But you're staying on long enough to help process the research?" Max accepted his crutches from Julie.

"Absolutely."

"Well, then, we can always try to change your mind."

"Not going to happen, my friend. But I appreciate the sentiment."

"Is the . . . meeting done, then?" Julie stood beside Max. "I need to finish packing."

"Unless one of you has something to say."

"No. Nothing."

"Max?"

"I don't think so, Logan." He adjusted the crutches under his arms. "Lead the way, oh fair Julie."

Alone in the family room, Logan willed his shoulders to relax. His jaw to unclench. He'd done the right thing—and he hadn't waited until they got back to Oklahoma.

Why didn't he feel better?

"Tell me I heard wrong, big brother." Caron stood in the doorway between the family room and the pool. "You did not just quit the Stormmeisters."

"There's nothing wrong with your hearing—and you shouldn't have been listening."

Caron closed the gap between them. "Things got a bit, um, loud. Kinda hard not to hear what was being said, even if I stuck my fingers in my ears. And I wasn't going to do that."

"Of course not."

"What's going on?"

"It was a team meeting, Caron."

"Your quitting the Stormmeisters makes no sense at all."

"Well, your dating Alex doesn't make any sense, either—"

"Hey!" Caron seemed to tear up at his accusation. "What is wrong with me dating Alex?"

"You threatened to disown me when I teased you about our parents betrothing you to him at birth. You barely talked to the guy whenever our families got together for holidays—and when you did speak to each other, you razzed the guy about who he was dating.

"So? I grew up and I noticed Alex—I realized he was a great guy."

"What about Kade?"

His sister hesitated. "What about him? We dated. We broke up."

"Mom told me that you really liked the guy—that you told her that you wanted to marry him."

"I was wrong."

"And how soon after you broke up with Kade did you start dating Alex? Are you sure you're not on the rebound?"

His questions seemed to surprise her, but within seconds she regained her equilibrium. "Back off, Logan. I'm not the one who's divorced."

"No, you're just dating the guy you said you'd never date—"

"And you're still in love with your ex-wife!"

"Everything okay in here?" Alex came up behind Caron, resting his hands on her shoulders.

"Fine. Absolutely fine." Caron crossed her arms over her chest, jutting her chin out. "My brother is quitting the Stormmeisters. And for some reason he thinks we shouldn't be dating . . ."

"Caron—" Logan's voice was a growl.

". . . because he's some sort of *love expert*. He's making one wrong choice after another. I don't know what to do with him."

"That's enough, sweetheart. No more commentary on Logan's life for tonight. It's not your responsibility."

"But he's making a mistake—"

"Leave it be, Caron. Leave it be." Over his sister's shoulder, Alex mouthed, *Sorry*.

"We're not done talking about this, big brother."

"Yes, we are." Logan muttered under his breath as his sister disappeared.

Because tomorrow he was on a plane out of town.

End of conversation.

TWENTY-ONE

There were many ways of breaking a heart.
Stories were full of hearts being broken
by love, but what really broke a heart
was taking away its dream—whatever
that dream might be.
—PEARL BUCK (1892–1973),
AMERICAN NOVELIST

Vanessa was done with wedding planning. Done with natural disasters. She was ready to go home.

Back to Colorado—to Denver—where there was no humidity weighing down the air. No hurricanes roaring into her life and disrupting her plans. No "for old times' sake" pulling her into the past.

She wanted nice, easy normal.

But that wasn't waiting for her in Denver.

Ted hadn't returned a single phone call or text message she'd left him last night or this morning. Not even her "You know we have to talk even if you want to break our engagement" message that she'd left on his phone right before she got in the rental car and headed to the airport had goaded him into a response.

What was going on? She'd been reduced to "goading" Ted? And her bare hand was a vivid reminder she didn't have a ring to return to Ted if the man who had taken two years to propose suddenly decided to break up with her.

She'd returned the car, which took extra time, thanks to the dings and scratches caused by Cressida. Nothing left to do except check in at the airline and clear security, which should be simple enough at such a small airport. And she had a good three hours before her flight. She'd relax at the gate and read the suspense novel Mindy had loaned her. Forget about everything that happened in Niceville and try to avoid thinking about everything waiting for her in Colorado.

Her gate was a short walk through the airport, the floor-to-ceiling windows revealing the runways. Hard to believe the civilian airport shared airspace with Eglin Air Force Base.

The military base.

She could only hope Christian was recovered from his ordeal—back to whatever his normal life was. Hadn't his mother said they were a military family? That they'd just moved to Niceville? She'd pray he'd find friends—true friends. Loyal friends.

If she was going to read the novel Mindy had given her—raving about Patricia Bradley's Logan Point series—she needed something to snack on.

She ignored the overhead announcements of flights preparing to board before hers. Plenty of time to browse the tiny newsstand tucked in a corner. What overpriced, caloric treat did she want to indulge in?

Mixed nuts? No.

M&M's? No.

Twizzlers? No.

Vanessa settled on a bag of candy corn. *Now to find some caffeine.* If she topped off the candy with a bottle of Coke, she'd walk onto the plane with a caffeine-laden sugar rush. She stood in front of the refrigerated drink selection. Water or caffeine and sugar? Decisions, decisions.

"The water's a safer bet."

From behind her, Logan's voice jolted her to attention. She'd hoped she was leaving him in Florida, too. No more conversations. No more con-frontations. No more . . . anything.

She selected a bottle of Coke. Turned to move past him.

"Living dangerously, I see."

"No, just getting what I want."

"Ah. A wise decision."

She ignored him—how good he looked in a pair of gray jeans and a black polo shirt—as he came to stand beside her at the cashier stand. And ignored his comment and its double meaning—if there was one.

"So you're flying back to Colorado?"

Vanessa accepted the change from the cashier. "Thank you." Focused on the exit. "Yes. I'm going home."

"Me, too. The team flies back to Oklahoma in less than an hour."

She stuffed her bag of candy into her purse. "I am not doing small talk with you, Logan. We're done—"

"Good." He stepped in front of her. "I didn't come over here to chitchat with you, either."

"You misunderstood me. I don't want to talk with you *at all*."

He gripped her wrist, his skin warm against hers. "Don't walk away from me. *Please.*"

She would not make a scene by twisting and pulling against his hand. "Let go of me."

"Hear me out, Vanessa." The huskiness in his voice tempted her, coupled with the indigo-blue of his eyes. "And then I'm gone. On a plane to Oklahoma."

"Fine. Say what you want to say. I'm listening."

That made him laugh—a little wild. "No, you're not. I haven't forgotten our arguments, love. You could look straight at me and not hear a word I said."

The next second, he pulled her into the corner of a vacant gate area past rows of empty chairs, turning so she was against the wall, his body blocking her escape.

"But if this is the only chance I get, I'm taking it."

"Stop this—"

"You're listening, remember?" He braced both

hands on the wall on either side of her. "I'm talking."

Now he had her attention. His blue eyes were lit up with a fire she knew from the past, one that kindled a response inside of her . . . slow, heated. The familiar blend of daring and "don't be afraid"—all that had attracted her to Logan from the first day she met him—surrounded her. She should shove his arms away—but she stayed.

"I love you, Vanessa Hollister. Always have. Still do. I know you're getting married. And it's killing me." He closed his eyes for a fraction of a second, but the spell between them . . . the magic . . . didn't waver. "Don't do it. Maybe getting married at eighteen wasn't the smartest decision. But just because it was crazy . . . foolish . . . just because we didn't understand everything behind the *I do*'s . . . it doesn't mean we were wrong. We made mistakes—but marrying you was the best thing I ever did."

He fell silent, but he didn't move away. Didn't release her. He might as well be holding her in his arms, locking her in an embrace that stole her breath.

"Say something." His smile wavered.

Vanessa pressed her back against the wall, establishing as much space between them as possible. "I heard everything you said, Logan . . . but it doesn't change anything. We're still divorced. And I'm getting remarried next April."

The heat drained from his eyes, a muscle working in his jaw. "Vanessa, I've never stopped loving you—"

"This apology and . . . declaration of love is about eight years too late." She stopped, hoping her voice wouldn't tremble when she spoke again. "Did you even think about how I waited to hear all of this back then? How I cried myself to sleep in my dorm room? I wore my wedding band for weeks . . . hoping you'd call me or show up on campus . . ."

"I'm sorry, Vanessa—"

"I think your pride is hurt. You don't want me—but you don't want me to get married again, either. Did you make some sort of bet with your buddies that you could get me to fall in love with you again?"

Even as she hurled the accusations at him, she wanted to take them back. Whose actions were worse tonight? Hers or Logan's?

An announcement sounded overhead—boarding was beginning for a flight to Oklahoma.

"That's my flight." Logan stepped away from her, his arms dropping to his sides.

They stared at one another, Vanessa's every breath labored. Just a few moments more and Logan would be gone—for good.

"This is goodbye, then."

"Yes." The one word scorched her throat.

He reached out, and she stilled as he caressed the

side of her face with the lightest of touches. Her skin heated.

"Be happy, Vanessa."

And then he left her standing in the deserted waiting area—before she could assure him that she would . . . she would be happy without him.

His attempt to reclaim his life had failed.

With a jerk and the muffled roar of the engines, the plane backed away from the terminal, taxiing onto the runway. Logan stared out the window, watching the airport recede—the distance between him and Vanessa widening. Again. Permanently.

The dream of restoring their relationship, their marriage? Destroyed.

The plane came to a halt behind others waiting in line to take off, the flight attendant talking through the emergency flight information.

God promised to work all things for good. *All things*.

He was still waiting to see how God could use his decision to keep going after the tornado last July when he should have turned the car back.

The plane moved forward, the engines surging louder, even as his heart seemed to struggle to find its rhythm again. For just a few seconds, the memory of kissing Vanessa on the beach blindsided him—the sweet temptation swirling inside him like the waves that had pulled against their feet.

He hadn't lost Vanessa again—not really. He'd lost her eight years ago and fooled himself into thinking some sort of all-out-there declaration of love and regret would open her heart to him again.

Wishful thinking slammed up against the reality he'd been living with for years—and crumpled.

TWENTY-TWO

The ache for home lives in all of us.
The safe place where we can go as we are
and not be questioned.
—MAYA ANGELOU (1928–2014),
AMERICAN POET AND AUTHOR

"Home."

Vanessa stood just inside the doorway of her apartment, her suitcase sitting at her feet, the door behind her shutting with a soft click.

"Home." The word rolled into the still-dark rooms.

What was she expecting? Some sort of Disney magic where the sound of the word lit up the apartment with twinkles and sparkles and a sense of belonging that had eluded her for years?

She had an acquaintance on Facebook—one of so, so many she didn't keep up with—who, whenever he came home from a trip, posted the words: *Home. No place I'd rather be.*

There were times she wanted to comment: *Home. How do you find it?*

Vanessa switched on the hall light, grabbing the suitcase handle, determined to make a beeline for her bedroom. A tight, closed-up odor permeated the rooms. She needed to open up a few windows to get fresh air circulating again. She needed to unpack. And tomorrow was a workday.

Everything was back to normal. Or as close to it as she could get until she talked to Ted.

She slowed down, snared by the small mound of mail on her dining room table. The brown, dried-out leaves of the philodendron collapsed against the planter. And the box she'd shipped to herself from Montana.

She released the handle, letting the suitcase drop to the floor with a thud. *Wash laundry* needed to be added to her to-do list, too. But the box . . . how could she have forgotten it? She ran her hand along the top, her name and address written out in precise, neat rows and covered with clear packing tape.

She carried the dead plant to the kitchen and dumped it in the trash. She should have said a firm *Thanks, but no thanks* to the gift—or given the plant to someone who would care for it. Retrieving a knife from a drawer, Vanessa carried the box to her bedroom. With one quick motion, she sliced through the sealed top. She unwrapped the figurines, laying them side by side on the bed. She'd taken all of them, unwilling to leave even one behind. And there, hidden in a corner, was the box containing Logan's class ring and her wedding band.

She slipped the thin white-gold band onto her ring finger. It still fit.

"Dad . . . I'm getting divorced." Vanessa sat on the dock, staring out at the bayou. If she looked right, leaned forward just a bit, she could just see a curve of the bridge spanning Rocky Bayou.

"What happened when you went to see Logan?" Her father stood behind her rinsing the boat off with a hose.

She wouldn't share that nothing happened with Logan. Nothing. That it was clear he had his life in Oklahoma—and that she was holding him back. "It's just that . . . that Logan wants out. And I do, too. We made a mistake."

"I'm not saying I agree with how you and Logan went about getting married—"

"I know that, Dad."

"You and Logan didn't make the best decision, eloping during spring break. Every father dreams of walking his daughter down the aisle." Her father came and sat beside her on the weathered boards of the dock, his legs and bare feet dangling over the water. "But you did get married. And I've always liked Logan Hollister. I knew that young man was going places. He had a future."

Yeah. He was going places—without her. "I'm glad. I hope he's happy."

"You sure you two can't talk this out? Maybe try counseling?"

Vanessa stared out across the bayou. The surface was smooth, the depths hidden. Had he just suggested counseling—the man who believed in keeping family problems within the family? "That's kind of impossible to do with me here in Florida and Logan in Oklahoma."

"Van, nothing's impossible if you want to make your marriage work." He leaned forward, resting his elbows on his knees. "Your mother and I have survived a lot of moves. I don't even know how many TDYs. Every marriage has challenges. You have to figure out how you and Logan are going to make your marriage work—for both of you."

"That's why I went to Oklahoma, Dad. And I—" She couldn't explain to her father that she was tired. Tired of waiting for Logan to come home. Tired of wanting to have a real marriage. Tired of hoping Logan would want to be with her again.

"And what?"

"And . . . I realized Logan doesn't want to be married anymore. He's happy in Oklahoma, pursuing his dream of storm chasing. Being married doesn't fit in his life." She leaned against her father's shoulder. "I'm not going to insist on counseling . . . or anything like that.

Sometimes it's best to let go—say goodbye. I'm good at that."

The echo of that conversation faded. What would her dad say if she told him that Logan had wanted to try again?

And what about her mother? That was a ridiculous question. She knew what her mother would say about giving Logan a second chance: *Why are you repeating your worst mistake, Vanessa?*

Vanessa slipped off the wedding band and placed it back into the box, closing the lid. She placed it in the top drawer of her dresser. It was all a rhetorical question, anyway. She'd told Logan no. She was marrying Ted.

She lined the figurines up along a bookshelf. Two on the top shelf, two on the middle, two on the bottom shelf. The lovely ladies curtsied, swayed, and danced . . . tugging a smile onto her lips. She traced the graceful outlines of one lady's gown with the tip of her forefinger.

When Logan had given her these precious beauties, he'd loved her. Imagined a future with her. He said he'd never stopped loving her. But then why eight years of silence? Surely his love would have conquered his fear.

They'd both grown up. Matured. But that didn't mean they were meant to be together. And she was adult enough to know that. And as beautiful as the figurines were, she knew she couldn't keep them. But she'd deal with that problem another day.

First she needed to talk to Ted.

It had only been a little more than twenty-four hours . . . but still . . .

What had happened to the uncomplicated man she'd dated for two years? The man who was so easy to love? They'd never argued even once until yesterday afternoon—and then he'd stormed out of Mindy and Jett's house and hadn't called her since. It was time to make things right with her fiancé and get back to planning their destination wedding.

First she'd finish hauling her suitcase back to her bedroom. Then she'd fix herself a soda and call Ted.

A sharp rap on the front door caused her to stop in the middle of the living room.

All right, then, first she'd answer the door— although who would be showing up at her door after ten o'clock at night . . . ?

"Ted?"

Was the man going to make a habit of showing up when she least suspected it?

"Hello, Vanessa. May I come in? Of course, I wouldn't blame you if you shut the door in my face—"

"I'm not going to shut the door in your face!" She stepped back, holding the door open wide. "I'm just surprised to see you—"

343

"Well, you did give me your flight information, so I knew you'd probably be home by now." Ted smoothed his hand over his hair. "I'm sorry I didn't call."

"It's okay . . . I'm sorry about what happened in Florida."

"I didn't even know I could be the jealous type until I saw you on that motorcycle with your ex-husband, Nessa." Ted paced the carpeting, still wearing his tan trench coat. "I fly down to surprise you—and get the surprise of my life."

"I'm sorry." How many times did she need to apologize? As many as it took.

"No, *I'm* sorry." He stopped in front of her. "You've never given me a reason not to trust you. I'm sure you had a perfectly good reason for going on a motorcycle ride with Logan."

Silence fell between them. Stretched.

She did have a reason . . . and apparently Ted wanted to hear it.

"It was nothing, really. Just . . . for old times' sake."

Ted's brow furrowed over the rim of his glasses. "For old times' sake?"

"Yes . . . we drove past the high school . . . and went to Destin. That's all."

Ted nodded. "Okay, then. If you say that that's all . . . then fine. I'm sorry I overreacted and didn't give you a chance to explain."

"And I'm sorry I upset you. It won't happen again."

"I know there's nothing going on between you and this guy. It's been ten years."

"Eight. Logan and I have been divorced for eight years."

"Well, I'm not going to argue over a technicality." Ted took her left hand, rubbing his thumb across her fingers. "I trust you."

"Thank you. I'm sorry for all the melodrama."

"I have something for you."

Vanessa stared at their hands. "What?"

He reached into the pocket of his coat and pulled out a small jeweler's box, flicking back the lid. "This."

Her engagement ring nestled against the crimson velvet background. She'd forgotten all about it. "It's resized already?"

"Yes. When I took it in, I asked them to rush the repair, hoping it would be ready before you came back from Florida. It took a little longer than I expected, but thanks to Cressida, well, here it is."

Vanessa couldn't resist admiring the ring. The diamond was set on a thick white-gold band—elegant in its simplicity. She and Ted had visited a few jewelers, allowing her to try on different styles of rings. In the end, he'd surprised her with this one—and she loved it.

"I know I should probably do this with a little more fanfare and probably not in the middle of your living room when you've just gotten back in town—" Ted slipped the ring out of the box and then placed it on her finger again. "—but since we're already engaged . . ."

Vanessa held her breath as the ring slid into place.

"How does it feel now?"

It was . . . perfect.

The weight of the ring on her finger seemed to anchor her heart back into place—back to Ted. To their future.

Seeing Logan again—experiencing a hurricane with him and even helping save not one, but two people's lives with him—didn't mean she'd fallen back in love with him. The lure of what had been and, yes, even the man that he'd become, had confused her.

But only for a moment.

She twisted the ring around her finger. "Yes, it fits."

"Whew." Ted pressed a gentle kiss to her lips. "For a minute there I thought we were going to have to send it back to the jeweler again."

Vanessa turned the ring around and around on her finger. Why did the stone seem so big? Maybe they should have selected a smaller one? "No. Not at all. I'm so glad you brought it to me. I've missed wearing it—I've missed you."

As Ted pulled her close, Vanessa relaxed in the shelter of his arms. This was right where she wanted to be—in a steady relationship. Ted didn't do drama. He wouldn't leave her and go chasing after some uncontrollable dream. She fit in his life—and he fit in hers.

Logan had offered her a marriage of youthful passion that had burned out, fast and furious. Ted offered her reliability and constancy . . . and love, too.

She was an adult now. Passion was a lot like adrenaline—a momentary burst of emotional energy that faded and left you . . . exhausted.

Or worse . . . alone.

TWENTY-THREE

It's a shallow life that
doesn't give a person a few scars.
—GARRISON KEILLOR (1942–),
AMERICAN AUTHOR AND HUMORIST

Someone was in his apartment.

Logan stood with his hand on the front doorknob and hit the light switch, illuminating the short hallway that led into the living room. His keys jangled as he tossed them on the table just inside the door. So much for surprising the unknown intruder.

A few easy steps forward and he was in the living room. "Who's here?"

A shadowed form rose from the couch as Logan flicked on the floor lamp to his right.

Max.

"Hey, man. I thought you were never coming home." The other man wore an old Tim Tebow Broncos jersey and a black pair of cargo shorts.

"The disadvantage of giving you a house key. What are you doing here?"

"Waiting for you." Max tucked his hands in his pockets, jiggling his loose change. "Hadn't planned on waiting quite this long."

"I went to the gym, and then I took a drive."

"Figures. Something on your mind?"

"I'm thirsty."

Max's uneven gait signaled that he'd followed Logan to the kitchen. Logan opened the fridge and grabbed two bottles of water. It was after eleven. A little late for a Coke—even for him. "Why don't you head on home?"

"Are you kidding me? I waited this long. I'm not leaving until I say what I wanted to say."

"Listen, Max, I'm not discussing my decision about the team with you—"

"Yeah—about that." Max stood in the doorway of the galley kitchen, blocking his way. "You were the one who formed the Stormmeisters, remember that? All those times we talked and dreamed and planned about the future?"

Logan gulped back some water. No need to answer Max. That was all in the past.

"We were a team—the whole one-for-all, all-for-one kind of a gig." Max held his ground, balancing on his walking boot. "I've got your back, you've got mine—and everybody has a say."

"What's your point, Max?" Logan twisted the lid off a second water bottle.

"Don't rush me. Apparently you had all sorts of solo in-your-head 'team' discussions that excluded everyone else. So I'm not leaving here until I've had my say. Like I said, if you'd come home earlier we wouldn't be doing this heading on to midnight."

Logan gulped back some water. Fine. Max could talk himself sick—and silent.

"Did you know I was invited to join another storm-chasing team, Logan? But I chose you, because I was a new believer and I knew you believed in God, too." Max leaned against the archway as if they were enjoying a casual discussion about football. "Yeah, I wanted to go after tornadoes—but I thought, if I'm going to do something as outlandish as hunt down tornadoes, I'm gonna do it with somebody who knows he's not in charge of the universe. Someone who knows there's a God who is in control of our world and our lives." Max snorted. "It's hard to remember that when you're staring at what's left of a town after an F4 or F5 tornado has dismantled all the houses. I liked that we prayed before we took off every morning. That we prayed at the end of the day. I wasn't just trusting you—I was trusting you and God. Every day."

Logan wanted to interrupt—to insist his decision wasn't about not trusting God.

"So this choice of yours to leave the team. Let's call it what it really is, okay? You betrayed the team."

Logan stiffened. He wasn't betraying anyone.

"I'm not calling you Benedict Arnold or any-thing, but I mean, come on, man. You don't talk to any of us? We're a team . . . we're friends . . . and you do something like this? Decision made, no discussion?" Max covered his eyes with his hand. Took a breath. "And what is this thing with Vanessa?"

The question came out of nowhere, the words pushing Logan up against the wall. What was going on?

First, Max is confronting me about quitting the Stormmeisters, and now the guy thinks he can talk about Vanessa?

"Hey, my personal life is my business. I haven't asked you about what's going on with you and Julie."

"You could have."

"What?"

"I said *you could have*. It's what friends do. Talk to each other. Ask each other what's going on. And yes, Julie and I are dating. But I'm not here to talk about that."

"How convenient for you."

"Julie isn't engaged to someone else, Logan." Max advanced toward him, the protective boot clunking on the floor. Was he going to take him down this time? "What has gotten into you? I don't know you anymore. You were the one who always talked about doing the right thing. And now you're going after Vanessa. I saw you cornering her at the airport—"

"We were talking—"

"Did you kiss her?"

"That's none of your business."

351

Max shook his head. "And that answer is as good as a yes, man."

"She's *engaged*—not married."

"To some people, being engaged to someone is as good as married. Would you want someone kissing your fiancée?"

"This is none of your business."

"That's a convenient way to shut me down, Logan." Max stared him down. "Am I hitting a little too close to home?"

"I think it's time you went home. It's late, you've had your say—and it doesn't change anything."

"What happened to you, Logan?"

"*Nothing happened to me.* I just want to be happy. I wanted to be with the woman I love—the woman I've always loved. What's so wrong with that?"

No need for him to tell Max that he'd failed at that.

"Have you prayed about any of this? I know for certain you didn't talk to anybody about the decision to quit the team. 'Seek wise counsel' and all that, right?" Max huffed out a laugh without an ounce of humor in it. "You taught me that verse."

"Yeah, well . . . thanks for the late-night visit—and the scripture memory lesson." And if he thought God was listening, he'd have asked forgiveness for being sarcastic. "I've got a job interview tomorrow. So, if you don't mind . . ."

Max knew the way out. No need for Logan to

show him the way to the door. This little con-
frontation had been good. Cleared the air, right?
Let Max have his say. But it didn't change anything. Didn't change his mind. The Stormmeisters
were his past—and despite all his effort, so was
Vanessa.

SPRING 2005

What was that saying? "Desperate times call for
desperate measures" . . . or something like that.
Was she desperate?

She had to be.

Why else would she have purchased a plane
ticket on short notice, packed a fun new red dress,
and flown all the way to Oklahoma to surprise
Logan for the weekend? Sheer desperation.

Vanessa drummed her fingers on the steering
wheel of her rental car in time to Kelly Clarkson
singing "Because of You." No. No, she wasn't
desperate. She was a married woman who
wanted to surprise her husband, that's all. What
had Mindy and Caron said during their girls' night
out?

"Logan misses you as much as you miss him. Go
out for the weekend—guys love to be surprised."

"Yeah—what is wrong with you two? Go have
some fun—" Mindy had waggled her eyebrows
in a way that made Caron collapse against the
restaurant booth in a fit of giggles and Vanessa

cover her face and groan. "—and then talk about how you're going to make this long-distance marriage work. Or maybe how you're going to change it up a bit. You could still switch to OU, you know."

She could transfer. Maybe.

They both needed to talk about their dreams and expectations. Maybe her expectation of finally staying in one place—not moving away from Florida—was getting in the way of Logan's dream. And did she have the right to do that? Did she want to do that? And how realistic was it to expect to stay in one place? She'd moved around so much, moving again should be easy . . .

But that was the whole point. She was tired of moving. Tired of packing up her life and unpacking it all in a new place. And hadn't getting married been all about not moving? And didn't Logan's dream of chasing storms threaten *her* dream?

Dueling dreams. Was that what their relationship came down to?

Maybe they could talk about their hopes for the future—and their marriage—this weekend. And maybe . . . maybe they could have fun, too.

She missed her husband's laugh. Longed for his kiss. His touch. To fall asleep in his arms, to wake up and know he'd still be there—that she hadn't only dreamed about him. And yes, she wanted to hear him say, "Hey, Vanessa . . ." and then suggest something crazy like rock climbing or parachuting or cave exploring.

So, yes, desperation had fueled this trip . . . but so had optimism. And faith. Logan wasn't the only one who believed in God. She just didn't talk about what she believed like he did. Of course, if she let God get a little closer, she might figure out what she did believe.

But when she showed up at his apartment, Logan wasn't there. She had to laugh. Of course her *Surprise! I'm here!* weekend couldn't be easy. The half-asleep guy wearing a *YouTube: Making Idiots Famous Since 2005* T-shirt in the apartment next door seemed to know all about Logan, suggesting she try his favorite hangout, even supplying directions.

Okay—it wasn't *that* difficult.

She found a parking spot right out front of the restaurant. And there was Logan's motorcycle, so she wasn't going to spend the rest of the day chasing down her husband. In just a few seconds she'd walk into the restaurant, up to the booth where he sat, and say hello . . . watch the emotions flit across his face. Surprise. Welcome.

All the planning and expense was going to be worth it.

The burger place was only partially crowded with a pre-dinner crowd. Vanessa stood in the doorway, slipping her sunglasses up onto the top of her head and waiting for her eyes to adjust to the dim lighting. The aroma of grilling meat and onions scented the air, making her mouth water. Logan always liked a good burger. Maybe they could eat dinner first and then—

The sound of his laugh helped her find him.

He sat in a booth with two other guys—Brady and someone else. Who had he mentioned recently? Max? And there was Julie, the freshman who had signed onto the team as a photographer. Logan said she was dating her high school boyfriend. Well, at least she'd have something in common with her.

Vanessa tiptoed over to his booth, holding back a grin. She wasn't going to put her hands over his eyes and pull the whole *Guess who?* stunt. But still, why not surprise him?

". . . I gotta admit, this would be a whole lot easier if I didn't have the stuff with Vanessa weighing me down." Logan leaned forward on the wooden table, a half-eaten cheeseburger on his plate.

Vanessa stumbled to a halt. She was *weighing him down?*

Here she was, coming to surprise him, to tell him how much she missed him . . . that she loved him enough to change things . . . and he . . . he wasn't missing her at all.

She turned away and collided with someone entering the restaurant. Fell back, the force knocking her purse from her hands, the contents spilling onto the floor.

"I'm so sorry." The guy bent to help her.

"My fault. My fault. Don't worry about it." She scrambled to gather everything—her cell phone, lip gloss, Life Savers, loose change—back into her purse.

Get out. Get out.

One quick glance over her shoulder—and yes, Logan was looking right at her—everyone in his booth was.

The smile on his face froze. He half rose. "Vanessa?"

She shook her head and lunged out the door, leaving who-knew-what from her purse still on the floor.

She ran to the rental car and was jamming the key into the lock—*come on!*—when Logan caught up to her.

"Vanessa! What are you doing here?"

How did he manage to infuse just the right amount of surprise . . . and happiness into his question?

"I—I thought I'd surprise you." She stiffened her shoulders. Turned. Somehow found the strength to look into his blue eyes. "I thought we could spend the weekend together."

He reached for her, as if he might pull her close. "Wow—that's fantastic! I never thought—"

She shrugged out of his embrace. "I realize you never thought I'd show up this weekend."

"What?" His eyebrows drew together. "What are

you talking about? I was having dinner with the team—"

"I heard what you said, Logan."

Now he had the decency to avert his eyes, his face flushing red. "Vanessa, you misunderstood."

"'Things would be easier if Vanessa wasn't weighing me down'? That is what you said—although I realize I may not have quoted you exactly."

"There's no reason to be sarcastic."

"Really? Really?" She knew she was raising her voice. That people on the street were staring at them as they walked by. "You're upset that I'm being sarcastic? Logan, you're insulting me to your friends—telling them that you don't want to be married."

"I didn't say that."

"For months now you've been choosing this—Oklahoma, storm chasing, even Max and Brady and Julie—over me. Admit it."

"I'm not standing on a street corner and discussing this with you."

"You won't ever discuss our marriage with me."

"Come back to my apartment. We can talk there."

"No." Vanessa backed up against the car, gripping the door handle.

"What do you mean, 'no'?"

"If I come back to your apartment, I know exactly what will happen—and I'm tired of being sidetracked by . . . by . . . that."

"Come back to the apartment. We'll just talk, okay?"

Hearing the door unlock, she jerked it open, forcing Logan to step away as she dove into the safety of the car. "You're happy here. You don't want to be married . . . fine. I don't want to be, either. I want a divorce."

The word rent the air between them.

"You don't mean that."

She bit her lip to stop the trembling. "I do. I shouldn't have come here . . . but at least I know the truth."

He gripped the side of the door, squatting down beside the car, his face pale. "You are jumping to all sorts of wrong conclusions here, Vanessa."

"Am I?" She stared straight ahead, the rays of the setting sun blinding her.

"I've told you I'm not going to fight about this here. If you won't come back to my apartment, then come on back inside and have dinner with us. Let's cool down."

Of course Logan wasn't going to fight with her—he'd stopping fighting for their marriage months ago. She'd lost him to storm chasing . . . not another woman.

"I need to go—" The word "home" refused to form. "—back to Florida."

Logan spoke through clenched teeth. "Don't do this, Vanessa. Please."

Vanessa swallowed a sob.

"It's obvious now . . . that our marriage has been over for a long time." She cranked the engine to life, shifted into gear. "Don't fight this."

There were people who said they hated surprises —and he'd never understood why. Until today.

Logan stared at his cell phone. "She won't answer her phone."

"Do you know where she's staying?"

Ever-practical Julie, always thinking ahead.

"No!" Logan buried his face in his hand for a moment. "Sorry. Like I said, I didn't even know she was coming out here at all."

"Why didn't she come in? Stay and have dinner?"

"She heard what I said—about how she's weighing me down."

"Oh, no, Logan. That's bad." Julie reached across the table and squeezed his hand. "But you explained you didn't mean it—you were talking about how hard it is to manage a long-distance relationship . . ."

"I know what I was talking about. And you guys know what I was talking about." Logan shoved aside his plate. "But Vanessa knows what she heard. And now she wants a divorce."

"You've got to admit you don't live like a regular married couple, Logan. You're here, and she's there—"

"Thank you for that commentary, Max."

"What are you going to do, boss?"

"Wait for her to call me back. We'll figure this out. We always do."

She'd never know who was more surprised when she used the word "divorce"—Logan or herself. Did she really want a divorce? Or was she overreacting—hoping to finally get his attention? Trying to get him to fight with her, fight for their marriage, even as their relationship disintegrated.

She sat in the rental car outside the first motel she'd found. She needed to go see if there was a vacancy. The silence in the car seemed to seep into her heart, touching the invisible wound that grew with every breath she took.

Yes, they'd grown apart—something more than the geographic distance. But she'd never suspected Logan resented her. That he had stopped loving her. That he wanted his dream more than he wanted their marriage.

He was fine with staying at OU?

Fine with living apart?

Fine.

Then they needed to end their sham of a marriage. He could stop pretending he loved her.

Vanessa inhaled a shuddering breath.

God, this was awful.

She'd stayed.

She'd thought he would come back.

But there was no reason for her to keep waiting for Logan now. To figure her life from Christmas

361

break to spring break to whatever few weeks every summer Logan decided to give her.

How had this happened?

It was all so crazy . . . too crazy to last.

Who gets married at eighteen and stays married—besides Logan's grandparents?

What was that saying about absence making the heart grow fonder?

Ha.

Distance made the heart . . . forget. Not care.

Distance made the heart quit.

TWENTY-FOUR

Just when I think I have learned
the way to live, life changes.
—HUGH PRATHER (1938–2010),
WRITER AND MINISTER

The echo of the poignant lyrics to "All I Ask of You" followed Vanessa out to the lobby of the Buell Theater. Ted sheltered her from the ever-shifting crowd, his arm across her back, the musky scent of his aftershave comforting in its familiarity.

They sought out a quiet corner as lines formed at the two concession stands where vendors sold *Phantom of the Opera* programs, CDs, T-shirts—even musical trinket boxes.

"Enjoying the show?"

Ted's question interrupted the melody replaying in her head. "Yes—you'll have to thank your colleague for giving you the tickets." Vanessa's fringed brown skirt swayed against her embroidered cowboy boots. "It's such a romantic musical."

Ted straightened his striped tie. "If you like being stalked by some deranged guy wearing a mask."

"Ted! The Phantom loves Christine—in a tortured kind of way. And didn't you hear Raoul pledge to love her, to protect her, in the last song?"

"I warned you I wasn't a fan of musicals, Nessa—although the live orchestra is nice."

Before she could reply, Ted's attention caught on someone across the room. "Excuse me, babe. I think I see—yes, it's Dr. Bannister."

"Who?" Vanessa craned her neck, trying to see who had distracted Ted in the swirl of laughing, talking people.

"Dr. Bannister—he's part of the team heading up the medical conference next April. He invited me to help plan the event—"

"Excuse me? Since when did you get involved with planning the conference?"

"I thought I explained that's why I came down to Florida—for a preliminary meeting with the committee."

Vanessa stepped out of the shelter of Ted's arm, bumping into a woman wearing black and a cascade of pearls. "No—you said you flew to Florida because you were concerned about me after the hurricane."

"That, too, of course." Ted was already putting space between them. "I need to go say hello. There's a lot riding on this professionally."

And with that, her fiancé abandoned her in pursuit of some all-important networking opportunity.

By the time he returned, bringing Dr. and Mrs. Bannister with him, Vanessa had purchased a program and a *Phantom of the Opera* CD. She managed an appropriate smile and handshake, murmuring hello when Ted introduced her, and then stood silent as the medical conference hijacked the conversation.

When the lobby lights dimmed, Vanessa excused herself and found her way to their seats in the mezzanine while Ted continued his conversation with the Bannisters—both of whom were physicians. Ted slipped in beside her at the last possible moment, an uncharacteristic grin on his face.

"They invited us out for drinks afterward. Isn't that great?"

"You told them no, right?" Vanessa stopped flipping through the program filled with photos of the musical.

"Of course not. Dr. Bannister is a very influential man in the medical community—"

"And we're on a date."

"We'll finish the show and then meet the Bannisters in the lobby." Ted took her hand in his. "The best of both worlds. This is turning into an excellent evening, don't you think?"

The swell of the orchestra silenced Vanessa's response.

On the drive back to her apartment after a dessert time that stretched through two hours, Ted tugged his tie loose. When he reached over to hold her hand, Vanessa kept a firm grip on the plastic case protecting the CD disc.

"What's that?"

"I bought it during intermission, while you were talking to Dr. Bannister."

"Do you want me to put it in the CD player?"

"No. I'll listen to it when I get home."

"Are you feeling okay, Nessa? You've been quiet."

"You were so busy talking to Dr. Bannister and his wife, I didn't think you even noticed me at all, Ted."

"What kind of remark is that?"

"An honest one." She closed her eyes for a few moments. Did she really want to argue about this? "We were on a date, Ted. Granted, someone gave you those tickets, but still, how often do we get dressed up and go out? And then you turned it into a business meeting!"

"Was I supposed to ignore Dr. Bannister?"

"Yes!"

"Be reasonable."

"Fine. Say hello to the man—but leave it at that." She twisted in the passenger seat to face him. "Does life always have to be about medicine?"

"Medicine is my life, Nessa. You know that. It's your life, too. You spend more time in the hospital than you do at home."

Ted's words reverberated through the silence in the car. He was right.

And so, so wrong.

"But there's more to life, too."

"What? Sorry, I didn't catch what you said." Ted eased the car to a stop at a red light.

Was he even listening to her? "But there's more to life, too. We both have other interests besides medicine . . ."

Even as she spoke, Vanessa couldn't think of anything Ted did that wasn't related somehow to medicine. Even his handball group was made up of other physicians. But when was the last time he'd played a single match with them? And besides reading books—lots and lots of books—what hobbies did she have?

"Sure we do. We'll be starting a family."

That's what he came up with for "other interests"?

"And what if one of our children doesn't want to be a doctor, Ted? Want if *none of them* want to go into medicine? What if they want to be a professional ice skater? Or a stay-at-home mom?"

"Now you're being absurd. Why wouldn't they want to go into medicine? It's an honorable profession."

"But if they didn't—you'd support their decision, right?"

"I don't know. I'd have to talk to them, help them understand all the advantages of a medical career." When the light turned green, Ted accelerated through the intersection. "Talking of advantages, Bannister and I were discussing the April conference."

"Yes?"

"Since I'm on the board now, I'll need to be involved in the conference earlier."

"Meaning?"

"Meaning I'll need to attend a few meetings before the wedding. And a meeting earlier the day after."

"And what did you say to this schedule?"

Silence.

"Ted—"

"This is my career, Vanessa. ER physicians burn out in a dozen years—you know that. I'm thinking of us—our family. I'm giving you the beautiful, elegant wedding you want—and taking care of our future, too. If I leverage this year's conference right, I might get a speaking position next year, which will lead to more opportunities in the future."

"I don't want to be some sort of add-on to your life, Ted. Medicine and, oh, yeah, if I want a family I probably need a wife. A conference and let's add on a wedding, too. Shouldn't we be so crazy in love with each other—so excited about getting married—that it's all we want to do? Not get married *and go to a medical conference.*"

"There's nothing wrong with being practical—"

"Practical is for budgets and buying a house and . . . and . . . anything else but falling in love and planning our wedding! Why do I feel like it's medicine, medicine, medicine for you—and occasionally you'll fit me in?" Vanessa hesitated for a moment before asking the next question. "If

Bannister hadn't invited you to a planning meeting, would you have come down to Florida just to check on me?"

"Of course I would have."

"Nice answer." She leaned back into the passenger seat. "Why don't I believe you?"

Her relationship with Ted used to be easy. Stable.

And yet, for the second time in less than a week, silence stretched between them. No *How's it going, babe?* phone calls. No *What do you want to eat for dinner?* texts.

She missed him—in the same way she missed her most comfortable pair of jeans and her FSU sweatshirt on the first day it snowed in Colorado. Even as she finished another shift that included a roadside delivery of a baby that wasn't willing to wait until Mom got to the hospital, and the aftermath of a high-octane, bar-hopping bachelorette party gone wrong, Vanessa hesitated just inside the ER doors.

Was Ted even working tonight?

As the glass doors swished open, the outside air breathing cool on her face, Ted called her name.

Ignoring the noise of the ER waiting room, Vanessa accepted Ted's brief hug, ready to get things back to normal.

"You're off?" Ted tucked his hands in the pockets of his white lab coat embroidered with DR. TED TOPLIFF.

"Yes. Just finished my shift."

"And I'm on all night." A practiced hand motion and his hair lay in place. "I've got time for a cup of coffee. Care to join me?"

A cup of coffee. An apology. And things would get back to where they belonged. Surely during their time apart Ted had come to understand her point of view.

"Absolutely."

The doctors' lounge was empty, the TV in the corner tuned to a nonstop news channel until someone else came in and switched it to a sports channel. Vanessa retrieved a can of Coke from the fridge while Ted fixed his coffee the way he liked: one cream, two sugars.

When Vanessa settled into one corner of the couch, Ted remained standing.

"Ted, I wanted to—"

"If you don't mind, I want to go first, Nessa."

"That's fine." Vanessa cradled the cold can of soda between her hands.

"I've thought a lot about what you said the other night." He eased onto the couch, setting the Styrofoam cup of coffee aside, untouched. "A lot. About how there's more to life than medicine. And how you feel like an add-on in my life."

"Ted, I—"

"No, that statement in particular stayed with me. And then you said something about being so crazy in love with each other that getting married was all we should be thinking about—or something like that." Ted paused, removing his wire-rim glasses and finally making direct eye contact with her. "And I realized you were right."

At last.

"I have to be honest, Vanessa. I'm more excited about planning this medical conference than planning our destination wedding."

Ouch.

"And I realize that's not fair to you . . . or me."

"Are you saying you don't love me?"

"I do love you—but not in the way I should—or the way you want me to. Not enough to marry you. And I love you enough not to let you marry me, either."

The can of soda almost slipped from her hands. As if in slow motion, Vanessa set it on the coffee table that was covered with an odd assortment of magazines. "You're breaking our engagement—here? Now?"

"Yes, I guess I am." He offered her a half smile. "Ironic, isn't it?"

Was the man actually finding humor in this?

And what was she supposed to do? Argue with him when he was saying she was right—breaking up with her using her very words to do it?

Vanessa twisted the diamond around her finger before slipping it off—the ring that fit so perfectly now that it was resized—and held it out to him.

"I guess this belongs to you."

Ted hesitated. "Do you want to keep it?"

"No. No, it's an *engagement* ring—and there's no longer an engagement, is there?" She covered one hand with the other. At least she and Ted could handle this themselves. No need for lawyers. No need to sign papers.

Ted didn't even look at the ring. "You understand . . ."

"Yes. Of course."

After all, she'd given him all the reasons to break off their engagement.

The door to the lounge opened and a nurse looked inside. "Dr. Topliff, we have an admission —a fifty-five-year-old male with chest pain."

Vanessa stood. No need to draw things out. "You need to go."

"Yes. Looks like it's going to be a busy night." He slipped the ring into the pocket of his dress shirt beneath his lab coat. "Thank you."

"For what?"

"For realizing we both deserve more than what we had with each other."

"Oh. That." She waved his comment aside. "You're welcome."

Vanessa stepped back. A hug seemed out of place. Ted needed to go to work. And she, well, she needed to leave. Go home.

Whatever that meant.

TWENTY-FIVE

I think if I've learned anything about friendship, it's to hang in, stay connected, fight for them, and let them fight for you. Don't walk away, don't be distracted, don't be too busy or tired, don't take them for granted. Friends are part of the glue that holds life and faith together. Powerful stuff.
—JON KATZ (1947–),
AMERICAN JOURNALIST AND AUTHOR

She'd asked Mindy to be her matron of honor. To help her plan a wedding. Was it so wrong to ask her to unplan a wedding, too?

No matter what Mindy said, it was time to make the phone call and begin dismantling her beautiful, elegant Florida destination wedding. As usual, Mindy's exuberance burst past Vanessa's attempt at hello.

"Hey, Vanessa! You calling to tell me you want a puppy?"

At Mindy's question, Vanessa couldn't help but laugh. "Hello to you, too. And no, I do not want a puppy. Besides, haven't Minion and his brothers and sisters found homes yet?"

"Yes, but we've got a new batch now. Only four this time."

"You're going to stop fostering puppies once the baby arrives, right?"

"Yes. This is our last litter." Mindy breathed a sigh of relief. "So, why are you calling? Something to add to the matron-of-honor duty list?"

"Not exactly. I'm, um, calling to take a few things off your plate. A lot of things, actually."

"Vanessa, I told you not to worry about me. Yes, I'm pregnant, but I'm perfectly capable of helping you with this wedding—"

"Ted broke up with me."

Mindy's chatter—so reminiscent of high school—ended. And then came the expected, "What did you say?"

"Ted broke up with me." Vanessa turned her hand so that she could see her bare ring finger. "Soooo . . . you are hereby relieved of all matron-of-honor duties."

It sounded as if Mindy was pacing around her house. "Why would that man not want to marry you?"

"I basically talked him out of it."

"You did not!"

"Yes, I did."

"Vanessa, you're not making any sense. Why would you talk Ted out of marrying you?"

"Well, that wasn't my intent . . . it just happened." Vanessa sat on the couch and tried to gather her thoughts. "Let me save you from having to ask me twenty questions, okay? Ted and I realized we didn't love each other enough to marry each other. He admitted he was more excited about the medical conference than the destination wedding."

"He did *not* say that to you."

"He did."

"My new matron-of-honor duty is to find your ex-fiancé and smack the stupid right out of him."

Again Mindy made her laugh. "It's okay, Mindy. Really. Ted's right—I'm right. We're both right." Vanessa finger-brushed her bangs. "We needed to call off the wedding."

"And how are you doing with all this?"

"I'm fine. Maybe I'm meant to be alone. My first attempt at marriage failed. My second attempt didn't even get me to the altar—which is for the best."

"This question is going to come out of left field, so don't hang up on me, okay?"

"Okay . . ."

"Have you prayed about any of this?"

"Prayed about . . . why are you asking me that, Mindy?"

"Fair enough question. I admit faith didn't figure in my life much during college. Becoming a mom does funny things to you, Vanessa. I've been talking with Jett about what we believe—how do we want to raise our children? And then one of his coworkers invited us to church a few weeks ago."

"And you went?"

"Well, yeah. I mean, I've always believed in God, you know that—just like you. It's just that I kinda got lazy and acted like my faith wasn't that important to me. But now, well, now I want to change that. Trying to figure out motherhood all on my own is kind of scary."

Fine. If Mindy wanted to reconnect with God because she was having a baby, great.

"I know what you're thinking."

"Oh, yeah? Do pregnancy hormones make you a mind reader?"

"No, but I know you. And you think it's fine for me to go back to church—but this has nothing to do with you."

"It doesn't."

"What do you believe about God, anyway?"

"I believe he exists."

"And?"

"And what?"

"You tell me. What else?"

"I believe he . . . he must not love me enough to let me have a lasting relationship." Vanessa covered her mouth with her hand.

Where had those words come from?

"I didn't mean that."

"I think you did."

"Look, Mindy, I was a military brat. We moved a lot. There wasn't any way to have long-term friendships. And then my marriage ended in a

376

divorce—more proof I don't belong in a relationship. And now Ted quits on me before we even finish planning the wedding."

"What about us? We're friends, aren't we?"

"You're my friend—although I don't know why. It's the most lopsided relationship I've ever known. I never call you. I never text. We hardly ever see each other—"

"We're friends, because I like you, Vanessa. And because I want to be your friend. And yes, because I realized you needed a friend—a real friend. And I thought maybe I could be that for you."

"But I've been a lousy friend all these years . . ."

"Yes, you have been." Mindy's laugh lightened her words. "But you know what? I'm okay with that. If that's all you've got to put into this friendship—fine. But if you ever want to change things up a bit—call me, text me, IM with me on Facebook—I'm up for that, too."

"How did we get from my wedding being canceled to talking about God and being better friends?"

"It's what girlfriends do, Vanessa. Just go with it. So listen, about canceling the wedding, what do you want me to do?"

"Would you talk to the hotel wedding coordinator and the florist in Destin—cancel things for me?"

"Sure. Do you want me to contact the Henderson Park Inn, too?"

"No. I'll handle that part since I put down a deposit."

"Have you told your parents already?"

"Yes."

"And?"

"Let's just say my mother handled it better than my elopement with Logan. Compared to my 'worst mistake ever,' a broken engagement is easier to accept. Plus, she's dealing with my dad's recovery right now."

"You aren't going to disappear again on me— now that you don't need a matron of honor? I've liked being back in touch."

Vanessa hesitated, but only for a moment. Maybe she could "change things up a bit," like Mindy said. "I won't disappear. We'll just talk about you having a baby instead of me getting married."

"And who knows? Maybe I'll convince you to take one of these puppies."

TWENTY-SIX

Absence sharpens love,
presence strengthens it.
—THOMAS FULLER (1608–1661),
ENGLISH HISTORIAN

Vanessa should have called to check on the Wrights sooner.

But she'd allowed all of the . . . the commotion with Logan and Ted to distract her. She wasn't going to label it heartbreak—because her heart wasn't broken over Logan. Or Ted. She was stronger than that.

After all those years of moving—helping her parents pack up the house and then unpacking their clothes, their kitchen stuff, watching her mother and father arrange their furniture in a new house, in a new city—she realized something. Something vital and important. She knew how to say hello. How to say goodbye. She just didn't know how to do any of the relationship in between.

Thinking she could marry Ted and make the relationship work, make it last, had been foolish.

It had all been too easy with Ted. Too safe.

And when she'd gone back to Florida and run into Logan again, somehow, some way, she'd gotten caught up in the excitement that surrounded Logan. The façade of "for old times' sake."

But she wouldn't make that mistake again—she was steering clear of both *easy* and *excitement* when it came to men. She'd emailed the wedding coordinator and canceled the "just in case" wedding for next April, requesting her deposit back. So far, her bank account remained the same, but things like that took time. For now, she'd focus on today—not the wedding that wasn't going to happen—and check on Mrs. Wright to make sure the older couple was getting settled in their new home.

Of course, she didn't know where their new home was—or if they were still staying with their daughter. Thankfully, she'd stored Ruth's cell phone number in her iPhone.

"Hello?"

"Ruth? This is Vanessa Hollister. I'm a friend of your parents—we met after Hurricane Cressida . . ."

"Oh, yes. I remember." There was a slight pause. "I'm glad you called. I wasn't sure how to reach you."

Why would the Wrights' daughter want to reach her—and why did her voice sound so tenuous?

"Is everything okay? Is your father doing well?"

"My father's fine." Another pause—longer this time.

A chill snaked its way up Vanessa's spine. "Your mother . . . ?"

A tremulous sigh, choked with unshed tears, preceded Ruth's words. "My mother had a stroke . . . a few days after she came here."

Vanessa's fingers tightened around the phone. "How bad?"

"She went upstairs to rest one afternoon, saying she was tired. I—I didn't think anything about it." The woman's voice wavered. "Mom didn't recover. Her . . . funeral was four days ago."

Vanessa closed her eyes. "No . . ."

"I'm sorry. I didn't have your phone number, so I couldn't reach you—the only thing I knew was that you didn't live in Florida. My mother talked about you quite a bit while she was here. She said you were like a granddaughter to her."

"She and your father were . . . *are* two of the nicest people I know." Vanessa stood, unmoving, in the center of her apartment. Mrs. Wright was gone. *Dead.* "I met them when I was eighteen—the new girl in town. Again."

"I remember hearing about you back then. You moved a lot growing up?"

"In a military family, it's what you do." Vanessa pressed her fingers against her lips, holding back a sob. "I used to drink lemonade on their porch—me and my boyfriend."

"Logan, right? My dad mentions him a lot."

"And the motorcycle, right?"

Finally a hint of laughter tinged the other woman's voice. "Yes."

"Does your father understand . . . understand . . ." Vanessa's voice wavered. Broke.

"Some days I don't think so. And then others . . . yes."

"I'm so sorry."

"I'm trying to remember what my mom always told me."

"What's that?"

"That God knows what he's doing, even when life doesn't make sense to us. It helped her these past few years as she lost my father to the stronghold of dementia." There was silence on the other end of the phone for a few seconds. A sniffle. "I always thought my father would die before my mom. That seemed kinder . . . easier. But it's not the way it worked out. I miss my mother terribly—and I'm only a few days into this. And I'm scared for my father. How long will he live like this? He's only going to get worse."

Vanessa listened. Nothing she could say would ease the other woman's recent loss—or her ongoing one.

"I try to be like my mom. To trust God in all of this. Some mornings I wake up with the smallest bit of trust . . . of hope—nothing more. But it's a start."

"Will you tell your father that Vanessa . . . and Logan send their love?"

"Yes, I will. I know that will make him happy."

When she got off the phone, Vanessa crawled

into her bed, pulling the covers up to her shoulders, trying to get warm.

Could she also trust God about where she was? Alone—again. She hadn't moved . . . but it was as bad as being the new girl in town. No one really knew her. No one cared. She shifted beneath the blankets. Yes, there was Mindy, but she was all the way back in Niceville—with her husband and baby-to-be.

Could she ask God to increase what little faith she had? Could she find some way to believe he would accomplish what concerned her? Her future—even when it made no sense?

Can you see me, God? Can you find me . . . and be enough when I feel so alone?

TWENTY-SEVEN

There is nothing wrong with making mistakes.
Just don't respond with encores.
—AUTHOR UNKNOWN

How ironic that she didn't know Logan's address. Didn't know where he lived in Oklahoma.

She gathered the cardboard box, bubble wrap, the roll of packing tape, and the scissors from her dining room table, carrying them back to her bedroom and dumping it all on top of her bedspread. This was the last thing she needed to do to erase Logan Hollister from her life.

The six Royal Doulton figurines still stood on the bookshelves, as if frozen in time. Lovely ladies, one and all, in long gowns. Some wearing dress gloves. Some with bonnets with bows. All with smiles—knowing or coquettish or shy.

Which statue should she wrap up first?

Why not the lady all in white—the very first figurine Logan had given her for Christmas when they had just started dating?

"What . . . what is this?" Vanessa held the beautiful china lady, tracing the outline of the red ribbons adorning her bonnet.

Logan couldn't stop smiling. "It's a

384

Royal Doulton figurine. My grandmother collected them—and this one was one of her favorites."

"This was your grandmother's?" Vanessa turned the figurine around, studying it from all angles.

"Yes, a few of them somehow survived the tornado. A miracle, my grandfather said. But don't worry. I asked my mother if I could give it to you, and she said yes." His hand rested on hers. "Do you like it?"

"She's beautiful, Logan. Absolutely beautiful."

And the figurine *was* exquisite—too lovely, too valuable for Vanessa to keep. Something irreplaceable like this belonged in Logan's family. And she was no longer a part of that. She should have sent them back to Logan right after their divorce, but she'd forgotten all about the figurines. That oversight wasn't going to continue.

Vanessa wrapped the statue in two layers of bubble wrap, sealing it with tape. She did the same with each of the other five figures. Then she lined the bottom of the box with bubble wrap and placed the statues inside.

Almost done.

The wooden box containing Logan's class ring and her white-gold wedding band went into the box next, nestled among the bubble-wrapped figurines. Then she sealed the box shut with packing tape.

Now all she had to do was to figure out where to send the package.

Mindy to the rescue—again.

But for once, Mindy didn't answer her phone. Of course, the woman deserved a life of her own. She wasn't waiting around to rescue Vanessa whenever she had a problem. She'd leave a voice message and go on with life—normal, everyday life.

"Hey, my friend. It's Vanessa. Would you call me back when you get a moment? I need Logan's sister's address, if you've got it. Or his parents' address—although that would be my last resort. Thanks."

Now all she had to do was wait.

Again.

She placed the box on the top shelf of her closet, shoving it all the way to the back. Until she heard back from Mindy, she wasn't going to trip over the thing.

Logan set his plate of microwave lasagna on the table beside his couch. Not just like his mother made—but he was hungry and this was easy.

He took a couple of quick bites, grimacing when one bite was too hot and another was still cold in the middle. He set the dish aside, powering up his laptop. Time to work on his résumé so he could continue pursuing job options, post-Stormmeisters.

But before he could even open the file, his sister IM'd him.

Logan, are you there?
Yes.
I have something here that belongs to you.
What?
A package came to my condo—but it's
for you.

Logan abandoned Instant Message and dialed his sister's number on his phone.

"Hey, big brother."

"You are not making any sense, Caro."

"Yes, I am. I'm trying to tell you that a package was mailed to me—but it's for you."

He reached for the lasagna again, searching for another heated portion. "See, this is what I mean—"

"I think it's from Vanessa."

The microwave dish slipped in his hand, and he juggled it for a few seconds, balancing it against his knee. "Why do you think that?"

"Well, there's no name on the return address, but it's from someone in Denver, Colorado. I don't know anyone else who lives in Denver except Vanessa. And maybe a couple of friends from college."

"Well, then, it may not be from Vanessa."

"Logan, it's addressed to you *in care of me*." His sister waited in silence for a few moments. "Are you still there?"

"Yes."

"What do you want me to do with the package?" His sister asked a very good question.

"I don't know why Vanessa would be sending me anything." He debated his answer for a moment. "Go ahead and open it."

"Are you sure?"

"Well, it's either that or you mail it out here to me." He chuckled, thankful to be able to find a little humor in the situation. "And then you're going to insist I call you and tell you what she sent me, anyway."

"That's the truth." Caron picked up on his mood change, her voice lightening. "You want to tell me what happened between you two when she was here?"

"No." Logan stood and paced the length of his living room. "Just open the box, Caron Amelia."

"Oh-ho. You never call me Caron Amelia—unless you are ticked off at me."

"Will you open the box, please?"

His sister must have tired of playing with him, because it was silent on her end of the phone. And then Caron announced, "I'm putting the phone on speaker."

The squeaking sound of tape being peeled off plastic bubble wrap had Logan wincing.

"Logan, it's . . . it's one of Mom Mom's figurines."

Logan closed his eyes. She hadn't. He forced

himself to ask the question. "A Royal Doulton lady?"

"Yes. I don't know which one."

"It doesn't matter."

How many had he given to Vanessa while they were dating and married?

"One, two, three . . ." Caron counted out loud. "There are six of them in here."

"That sounds about right."

"Wait a minute. What's this?"

"I can't see you, Caro. You're going to have to tell me." Logan swallowed back the sour taste building in the back of his throat. "I'm sorry. This isn't your mess, even if the box was sent to you."

"It's okay, Logan."

"So what else did you find?"

"It's a little wooden box. Hold on a second."

He didn't have much of a choice.

"Oh, Logan . . ." His sister sounded as if she were trying not to cry. "She sent back your class ring and . . . and . . ."

"What else?"

"Her wedding band."

He deserved it. He deserved it all. The figurines. The class ring. Even the wedding band.

The phone dropped from his hand. Logan leaned forward on the couch, his arms crossed over his knees, and buried his head on his forearms. His blood thundered in his ears as he fought to breathe.

Vanessa had sent back her wedding band. *Her wedding band.*

A few moments later, he realized Caron was yelling at him on the phone. He scrabbled to find his cell phone on the floor and slumped back against the couch cushions.

"I'm here."

"What are you thinking?" His sister's voice was soft. Gentle.

"Why would she send back her wedding band?"

"Logan, you're not married anymore."

His sister's words stopped him cold.

He had no reason to question Vanessa's actions. There was no hope of a future—of a relationship—between them. She was returning his gifts—Christmas, birthday, just because—and her wedding band. She wasn't being cruel by sending back the figurines and the rings. It made sense . . . because she was getting married in just a few months. It was best to get rid of the shards of their broken relationship.

She'd been Vanessa Hollister when he'd met her. And she'd become Vanessa Hollister when they'd married. But once she married Ted, she'd be *his* wife.

They were done.

TWENTY-EIGHT

You never find yourself
until you face the truth.
—PEARL BAILEY (1918–1990),
ACTRESS AND SINGER

"Have a seat, Logan."

After shaking his hand, Frank Morgan, the manager at one of the local television stations, motioned to the chair positioned in front of his desk. As he settled into the swivel chair, Frank picked up a piece of paper and waved it in front of Logan.

"I've got to say, I was surprised to see your résumé come across my desk."

"You do have a job opening, right?"

"Yes, but not for a storm chaser."

"I know what job I applied for, Frank."

"And I know you're not a weatherman, Logan."

"I've got a degree in meteorology." Logan held himself still. "I know storms. Give me some time in front of the green screen, and I think—"

"Are you kidding me?" Frank tossed the paper back on the desk. "What's going on? Your team quit on you or something?"

"I'm not with the Stormmeisters anymore."

"Why?" Frank held up his hand, stalling Logan's

response. "And don't tell me you all of a sudden got a hankering to be an on-air meteorologist."

"You know about last summer's disaster in Kansas—it was all over the news."

"So?"

"My recklessness—my stupidity—almost killed one of my teammates."

"If you're telling me your team axed you, I'm not going to believe that."

"I quit."

"How noble of you."

"What?" Logan had never imagined the job interview careening out of control like this.

"You were being noble, right? Sacrifice yourself because you made a wrong decision—"

"It's not like that—"

"Then explain it to me. Explain to me why you're down here applying for a job at my TV station and not planning for next season."

"If I stayed on the team, there wouldn't be a next season. They were threatening to pull our grants."

Frank leaned forward on his desk. "So you apply for other grants, Logan. You don't run scared. You don't *quit*."

The man's words were an invisible blow, shoving Logan back into his seat. "This is turning into quite a job interview."

"I had no intention of offering you a job, Logan." The man's smile held no hint of an apology. "I invited you here out of curiosity."

"Well, I hope you're satisfied." Logan rose from his seat.

"You have a great reputation among storm chasers, you know that, right? I remember you being interviewed by one of my reporters when you were still in college—starting a storm-chasing team. People thought you were crazy—and you proved 'em wrong."

"I'm not so sure about that."

"I know how the community was rocked by the deaths of Tim Samaras and his son, Paul, and Carl Young back in 2013. It was a heartbreaking tragedy—but you're still here, Logan. Yes, your team took a hit, but it's still here. You need to be safe—every storm chaser balances safety versus seeking answers every day." Frank stood, coming around the desk to face Logan. "I know you're careful when you're out there. If you quit now, you walk away from all the work you've put into trying to understand tornadoes—trying to predict them, to protect people. I don't know what you'll accomplish in this field one day, but we both know what you'll accomplish if you walk away. Nothing."

Logan held out his hand. A handshake and he was out of here. "Well, if that's all—"

"One more thing before you go." Frank picked up his résumé, tapping the line that read "References on request." "All those references? They believe in you. In what you've done.

That's why they're willing to put in a good word for you. You think about that."

Jules arrived at his apartment first, carrying a huge pot of chili fragrant with spices wrapped in a white and blue towel.

Logan held open the door, stepping back when Julie brushed off his offer of help with a shake of her head.

"Max didn't come with you?"

"He dropped me off at the curb and then went to park the car. He'll be here in a sec."

"That guy treating you okay?"

"No complaints." Julie's smile hinted at more than "no complaints." "Actually he's been a perfect gentleman."

"Glad to hear it." Logan moved the stack of crockery bowls to the side of the table to make room for the chili.

Once Julie set the pot in the middle of the table, she offered him a hug, wrapping him in the brisk scent of the coming snowstorm. "It's good to see you again, Logan."

"I've missed you, too, Jules."

"Hey!" Max spoke from the doorway. "You making a move on my girl?"

"My intentions are honorable, I assure you."

"Sure they are."

Logan chose not to comment on Max's brace-free leg and his hop-along pace. It wasn't time to talk about what happened in Kansas—yet.

Brady entered the apartment, his booming, "Am I late to the party?" not quite hiding the way he didn't make full eye contact with Logan.

"Nope—just in time. Julie brought the chili, and I've got the drinks, chips, and all the fixings." Logan motioned toward the small dining room. "Why don't we go ahead and eat?"

He waited until Max and Brady were digging into their second bowls of chili before guiding the conversation away from small talk.

"So, this is great, but I did want to say something to all of you."

Everyone stopped talking, spoons clattering into dishes.

"I want to say I'm sorry—"

Max cut him off. "No more apologies for the accident, okay, Logan?"

"Let me finish." Logan sat forward, taking the time to make eye contact with each of his former teammates. "I'm sorry I didn't talk to you all about how I was feeling after the accident. How much it upset me. And I'm also sorry I made the decision to leave the team without talking it out with all of you. I'm hoping you can forgive me for going all Lone Ranger like that."

Jules spoke up without hesitation. "Of course we can."

Brady spoke next. "Absolutely."

Max sat silent.

"Say something, man." Brady spoke from across the table.

"I'm waiting to see what else Logan has to say."

Of course Max wasn't making this easy for him.

"I wasn't completely honest with you about why I left the team." Logan rubbed the back of his neck. "I was getting calls from some of the people who funded us saying they weren't sure they'd back us again next year because of the accident. We'd wrecked some pretty pricey equipment."

"Not surprising they'd be huffing and puffing about the grants." Brady shrugged off any concern.

"Again, I should have talked it all out with the team." Logan nodded toward Max. "Max reminded me that we've always been 'one for all and all for one.' I forgot that. I'm sorry."

Julie glanced at Max and finally spoke up. "Are you going to say something now?"

"I'm still waiting to hear what else Logan has to say."

"He's apologized, Max. What else do you want?"

"I want him to say he's coming back to the team—what else?"

"Look, I asked you all here for one thing tonight. I needed to clear the air between us and because I wanted to ask you all to forgive me for the way I handled things. It's not my place to say if I'm coming back on the team—to be honest, I haven't thought that far ahead. I'm trying to right some wrongs here, not regain my position with the Stormmeisters."

"I think we should talk about it as a team—" Julie worked her magic with a few soft-spoken words. "—but before that I think we should pray about it. Remember how we used to do that whenever we had a big decision to make—or when we were heading out after some storms?"

"You're right, Jules."

"But before we do—" Max half stood. "—I need to tell you that I'm sorry, boss. I said some things I shouldn't have—"

"No apologies needed, Max. You had every right to say what you did. I'm glad you spoke up. That's what teammates—and friends—are for."

TWENTY-NINE

Faith is deliberate confidence in
the character of God whose ways you
may not understand at the time.
—OSWALD CHAMBERS (1874–1917),
EVANGELIST

Vanessa settled into the corner of the coffee shop, setting her tall cup of caramel macchiato on the table in front of her. The shop was crowded, the buzz of conversation and piped-in music laced with the strong aroma of coffee. The noise and the nonstop activity provided her more of a chance to fade into the background.

To think.

For a woman who didn't like looking back over her shoulder—who was all about the future, not the past—she found herself stalled out.

She was divorced. Still single, the destination wedding destroyed like a sand castle washed away by an onslaught of waves. And she was the new girl again, having left the church she and Ted had attended, because, well, it seemed like the courteous thing to do. She could have opted for the this-church-is-big-enough-for-both-of-us route, but it seemed right to leave. To start over. After all, she was good at that.

Her hopes for attending physician assistant school were still nothing more than hopes.

Yes, she and Mindy talked several times a week now, sometimes even Skyping or FaceTiming, but that was about it in terms of friendships. She attended church services on Sundays, but always slipped out as the last song began. Relationships were best this close—and no closer.

Maybe she'd do better at trying to improve her relationship with God.

Vanessa pulled her purchase out of her purse, trailing her fingers across the cover of the journal. There was nothing special about the red soft cover or the white lined pages waiting to be filled with words. Thoughts.

Prayers.

The last time she'd written in a journal she'd been a naïve eighteen-year-old. Unaware that in a few short months she'd marry the boy with the shoulder-length blond hair and the electric-blue eyes who gave her rides home from school on his motorcycle.

And here she was, ten years later. Alone. Still trying to figure out who she was. Where she fit. How to find home.

Her prayers were stilted. Sometimes she felt as if she were only talking out loud to herself. And then there were the nights she dozed off midsentence, worn out from shift work.

Buying the journal was an act of desperation.

She could only hope God would bless her attempt to draw closer to him.

God,

I don't know how you feel about someone writing to you in a journal—especially a grown woman like me.

But I'm failing at the whole prayer-is-just-talking-to-God endeavor. So I thought maybe I could try writing out my thoughts. I don't mind if you read over my shoulder.

I've always been a keep-moving-forward kind of person (and I apologize for telling you something you already know). I'm not good at relationships—friendships or marriage.

And, to be honest, I blame you for that.

And now that I've written that sentence, I want to scratch it out. Take it back. But you've already read it—and the truth is, you knew it all along.

I got so tired of moving all the time. Of saying hello . . . and goodbye . . . and never having a lasting friendship . . . and not even Logan stayed with me. Couldn't you have given me one person who stayed?

Vanessa dropped her pen onto the open pages of the journal.

This was where she should write the words:

But I know you were with me the whole time, God.

But she needed to be honest. Start where she was. Trust him to be patient with her.

I didn't really think about you much back then—and how knowing you, relying on you, would have made a difference during all the moves. All the changes.

But I'd like to get to know you better now. To understand who you are. What a relationship with you looks like.

You know how bad I am with long-term relationships, but I want to try.

I read somewhere in the Bible that you never leave us or forsake us. I'm going to believe that . . . and I'm going to trust you. Be patient with me, please.

THIRTY

Bad is never good until worse happens.
—DANISH PROVERB

BEGINNING OF MARCH 2015

Another day off. And she'd spent it fighting against being stuck in neutral.

Vanessa continued her slow walk around the lake, hands tucked into the pockets of her coat, one foot in front of the other. Maybe she could fool herself into thinking she was accomplishing something—moving forward—by taking repeated circuits around the lake. The wind, whisking minuscule snowflakes about her face, tugged at the collar of her coat, reminding her that she'd left her scarf and gloves at home.

An overwhelming feeling of "Tell me what's next, God"—tinged with more than a little desperation—had driven her outside. She could have spent the day relaxing. Maybe pulled one of the books from her to-be-read pile. Or she could have decided yes or no on school. And why wasn't that an easy yes? For some reason she couldn't bring herself to send her acceptance email to the school, which made no sense at all.

So she'd opted for a walk. Hoping that as she

braved the cold, the wind, the light snow, she would stop thinking of all she'd lost. Stop wondering what happened next.

She'd pretend she had Mrs. Wright's faith in God—although that kind of strength, of conviction, came with years of choosing to say, "Okay, God, you are who you say you are." Maybe she could pretend to be like Mrs. Wright's daughter. If all she had was the figment of a desire to trust God . . . well, that was a start.

I'm floundering, God, but I'm trusting you. I believe, no matter what, you know what you're doing. You promise to be the stability of my times —no matter how badly life spins out of control.

She'd prayed that prayer over and over since November. Her journal was filled with letters to God. She would trust him, cling to that truth, no matter how confused she felt. How alone.

When her iPhone buzzed, she debated ignoring it. But what if it was work calling to ask her to cover someone's shift? An escape from monotony and sitting on the edge of the Pit of Despair. It was somewhat funny in the movie *The Princess Bride*. In real life? Not at all.

Her phone buzzed again. *Hmmm.* It was the same number that had appeared on her phone several times in the last eight weeks—one she didn't recognize.

"Hello?"

"Ms. Hollister?"

Sounded like a telemarketer. Vanessa positioned her thumb over the end button. "Yes?"

"This is the wedding coordinator at the Henderson Park Inn. I'm calling because we desperately need to finalize your destination wedding plans for next month—"

The iPhone almost slipped from Vanessa's grasp. "W-what did you just say?"

"Your wedding? Scheduled for April third? It's a month away, and I've called and emailed you several times to finalize the details—"

Vanessa stopped in the middle of the path. "I *canceled* the wedding months ago. I sent an email to your assistant. And besides—I really only wanted to be penciled in—"

"Ms. Hollister—"

"Vanessa, please."

"Vanessa, I assure you that we never received an email from you. If we had, you would have received a *phone call* from either my assistant or me explaining that we don't do cancellations via email." The coordinator kept her voice calm— almost soothing. She was good at her job. "Both the Internet and phone service are unreliable on the island—so we prefer to discuss things over the phone. That way if we do get disconnected, we can just redial and continue the conversation. A lost email, well, it's just lost."

Vanessa bent over double, one arm wrapped around her waist. The woman was stating facts—

stating the obvious—and pulling her into a destination-wedding debacle, word by word.

"But I'm not getting married." She stood again, sucking in a deep breath of Colorado winter. "I ended the engagement months ago, back in November."

Silence echoed back to her. Well, the woman had surprised *her*—it was only fair she also had a chance to shock the wedding coordinator.

"I'm so sorry to hear that. I truly am, Vanessa. But—"

Vanessa moved off the path over to a wooden park bench and sat down, staring out at the partially frozen lake. She knew how the rest of the conversation would go. "But . . . that doesn't change anything, does it?"

"No. I'm so sorry, but it doesn't."

"What are you saying, exactly?"

"You put a deposit down on a wedding ceremony for April third at the inn. You even wrote down some basic ideas—what package you wanted. Flowers. Your cake. Music. I contacted vendors based on those details—and those vendors have to be paid in full up front. At this late date, I cannot refund your money—for any of the wedding costs."

Vanessa covered her face with her hand, her fingers cold against her skin. "No . . . please, can't we work something out? Isn't there some other bride and groom who want to get married at the inn?"

"Vanessa, we do one wedding per day at the inn. I'm certain it was explained to you that April through October is prime season for us. We've told everyone who has called that this date is unavailable."

Vanessa inhaled a breath of air that seemed to freeze her lungs.

"I understand." She pressed her hand to her mouth, her fingers chapped. "What happens now?"

"I need to get payment for the balance."

"Fine."

"But it appears that credit card has expired."

Of course it had.

"I'm sorry. I'm not home at the moment—I'm out for a walk. I can be home in less than an hour. I'll call you back. Is that okay?"

"Yes. That's fine."

"I *will* call back."

"Vanessa—it's fine. I believe you. And again, I'm sorry—about everything. I wish there was something I could do to help you."

For all the times she never called Mindy in the past, now she had a definite reason to pick up the phone.

Or she could post something on Facebook.

> Hey, Mindy! Guess what? You know how Logan told me in the airport that he loved me and wanted to remarry me but I turned

406

him down because I was engaged? And then Ted broke up with me and I canceled my destination wedding on the beach? Well, the crazy mess gets crazier. Turns out I didn't cancel the Florida destination wedding. The show will go on—and be paid for—without a bride and groom.

Yeah, it was a little long-winded for a standard Facebook post, but without a doubt, people would click on "read more" . . . and who knew how many comments that post would generate?

Vanessa drained another can of Coke into a glass filled with ice and a slice of lemon and set the can in a line with the other—she stopped to count—one, two, three, four, five, six soda cans. With that much caffeine flowing in her veins she'd be up all night, and probably tomorrow night, too.

At least the barricade of red aluminum cans hid her laptop screen from view—and her charge card statement, complete with the addition of the balance for her wedding. She'd found the emails from the inn's wedding coordinator lurking in her spam folder.

Her wedding.

God, what are you doing here? How is this "being my stability"? My finances just careened into the red zone, crashing through every smart money decision I've ever made!

She bolted upright when her iPhone rang,

toppling the soda cans like dominos as she grabbed it off the coffee table.

"Mindy?"

"Yes—hello to you, too—"

"Mindy—the wedding is still on!"

"You got back with *Ted?*" Mindy sounded as shocked as if Vanessa had told her that she was marrying an alien.

"No—not Ted—"

"Oh, thank God! I knew you and Logan would figure everything out—"

"I'm not marrying Logan, either. I'm not marrying anyone."

"Vanessa, you are talking to a sleep-deprived mother-to-be. I can't see my feet anymore. My back hurts. I think I am truly going to be pregnant forever. *Forever.* Why are you calling and making me crazy?"

Vanessa didn't know whether to laugh or cry. "First off, my friend, you need to have this baby already, because *you called me.* Let me begin again. I got a call from the wedding planner at the Henderson Park Inn. They never got my email canceling the wedding—so they didn't cancel it."

"Nooooo."

"*Yes.* She wanted to finalize plans. And as nice as she was, as sympathetic as she was, the reality is I am paying thousands of dollars for a wedding that no one will be attending. No bride. No groom. No guests . . . nothing."

"Vanessa, come on, surely she could understand—"

"Believe me, I tried having that conversation with her. Need I remind you that I couldn't just have them pencil me in? I paid a deposit. I even talked out ideas with the assistant—you know, just dreaming out loud. They went ahead with those ideas. Vendors have been paid in full. The wedding, so it seems, is going on without me—quite literally."

"What are you going to do?"

"Me? I am going to be paying off my credit card for the next several years. Putting off going back to school, that's for sure."

"What can I do, Vanessa?"

"Pray for me, Mindy. I can't seem to find the strength to pray for myself." Vanessa stopped when her voice cracked. "I keep telling God I trust him. I want to trust him. But why, when it comes to marriage, does God keep messing with me? Why does he keep saying no—and then doing something like this? It's just cruel!"

"God didn't do this—"

"He allowed it!"

"Free will, Vanessa. Free will. Don't go blaming God for—"

Vanessa waited for Mindy to say more, but she'd gone silent on her.

"Go on."

"No, I don't want to do this now—"

"Mindy, you're my best friend. Go ahead. You've earned the right to let me have it."

"All I'm saying is we blame God for hurts we bring on ourselves. Yes, God is sovereign over the world—but he gives us free will. You and Logan made choices back when you were in college—and you broke each other's hearts."

"We did, didn't we?" Why did the admission cause an ache in her heart all these years later? "And then Ted and I made choices—"

"The hard, right thing to do, yes. I've always wished you and Logan could have figured out a way to make things work." Mindy groaned. "Sorry. Just trying to find a comfortable position. You want me to try to talk to the woman at the Henderson Park Inn?"

"No. You're a mama-to-be—and you were relieved of matron-of-honor duty months ago. But thanks for listening."

"I'm sorry."

"I know you are." Vanessa stretched out on her couch. She did not want to talk about her mess of a wedding anymore. "Enough about me. When does the doctor think that baby's going to arrive?"

"Not soon enough—and no matter how often I ask, he won't induce me."

"Mindy, doctors don't induce you just because you want them to."

"I'm miserable . . . which means Jett's miserable . . . it would be a 'mercy induction' . . ."

"Oh, yeah, tell the doctor that."

"It won't change his mind, Vanessa."

"No, but you'll make him laugh—and that would be worth it."

"It's very risky to laugh at a pregnant woman. You don't want to tick us off—and my water could break all over his exam room."

"But that would be a good thing, right?" Once again, talking to Mindy had lightened Vanessa's spirits. "Will you call me when you go into labor?"

"Sure. Anytime?"

"Yes. I want to know."

"All right, Aunt Vanessa. You're on the will-call list."

THIRTY-ONE

To win you have to risk loss.
—JEAN-CLAUDE KILLY (1943–),
FORMER FRENCH ALPINE WORLD CUP SKIER

"I'm awake! I'm awake!"

Logan sat up and almost fell off the couch trying to prove he wasn't asleep. He braced his hands on the edge of the couch, planting his bare feet on the carpeted floor.

What time was it?

Lights were on all over the house. Living room, kitchen, down the hall, and even in the bedroom—where he should have been sleeping. The TV, tuned to the Weather Channel, highlighted rain for the West Coast.

He rubbed his hands over his face. He needed a shave—he needed a shave three days ago.

Wait . . . what had woken him up?

Just then his cell phone rang again, and he lunged across the room, grabbing it off the top of his desk.

"Hello?"

"Logan?"

"Yes. Who's this?"

"It's Mindy—Mindy Williams in Florida. Did I wake you up?"

"As a matter of fact, yes, you did."

"Good."

"Apology accept— What?"

"I said *good*—I'm glad I hauled your backside out of bed." The woman sounded ready to unleash a maniacal laugh. "And it's also a good thing you live in Oklahoma, or I might come over there and knock some sense into you."

Logan looked at the phone screen. "Are you sure this is Mindy—the girl I knew in high school—and not some hired thug?"

"I'm a pregnant woman who isn't sleeping at night—it's almost as bad." Mindy took a deep breath, and Logan braced for another outburst. "Logan Hollister, what is wrong with you?"

"I have a feeling you're going to answer that question for me."

"What gives you the right to break my best friend's heart not once, but twice?"

Mindy's question jolted the last bit of sleep from his system. "Look, I don't know what Vanessa told you, but I admit I got a little out of line when I saw her in Florida—"

"A little out of line? You told her you still loved her!"

Logan braced his forehead on the palm of his hand. "Fine . . . I told her I still loved her—and she stonewalled me, reminding me that she was engaged. I had no right to tell Vanessa how I felt about her when she was marrying that other guy. I was wrong."

"Who told you that?"

"My friend Max. And he was right. It wasn't the honorable thing to do."

"What would you say—what would you do—if I told you that Ted broke their engagement?"

"Why would he do that?"

"Apparently because Vanessa convinced him to."

"Mindy . . ." This conversation was some sort of crazy verbal trapeze act, swinging him back and forth, up and down. Logan forced himself to say the right thing. "Why aren't you calling her and telling her to work things out with Ted?"

"Do you hear yourself, Logan? Is that what you really want?"

No.

"What do you think I should do?"

"Believe it or not, I didn't call you to harass you or to verbally beat you up. I called because I know you love Vanessa—you've loved her since high school."

"I do." The admission came out as half groan. "But fixing this isn't going to be easy."

"Welcome to a relationship, Logan. You think you and Vanessa are different from everyone else? Weren't you listening in English class when we read Shakespeare? *'The course of true love never did run smooth.'* "

"I didn't take Honors English."

"No excuse. You told Vanessa that you never stopped loving her. Even when she told you no, there was a little part of her heart that heard what you said—and believed you. That wanted to say yes. But she was scared—and staying with Ted was safe. Having you come back into her life . . . it was like Vanessa had been set on dim, and then being with you again turned her up to full power."

"And she was the one person who believed in me—and who could calm me down if I was getting reckless." Logan admitted the truth before he realized what he was saying.

"Let's agree you should have handled things differently in October in a lot of ways. Fine." Mindy paused. "There's something else you need to know now."

"What?"

"There's a wedding all set and ready to go in Destin the first week in April. All that's missing is a bride and groom."

Logan shook his head. Was he still asleep? "What are you talking about?"

"When Vanessa was out here, she booked the Henderson Park Inn for a destination wedding. It wasn't what Ted and Vanessa had planned—but it was Vanessa's dream wedding. Somehow wires were crossed, and the wedding ceremony at the inn was never canceled. Make it happen, Logan. Make it happen."

Logan glanced at the clock. Five o'clock in the morning. "I gotta go, Mindy."

"What are you going to do?"

"Trust me." He started to hang up and then stopped. "You still there?"

"Yes."

"Thanks."

"You're welcome."

"And, Mindy?"

"Yes?"

"Hurry up and have that baby, will you? Vanessa's going to need your help—I hope."

"That's always been the plan—but I'm discovering I'm not in charge."

Logan ran his fingers through his hair. Tugged at the collar of his button-down dress shirt. Straightened the front of his coat. Forced himself to exhale, his breath forming a white cloud puff. He shifted his weight from one foot to the other. Stood still.

He was facing a wooden front door—not a firing squad.

True. But behind the door were Vanessa's parents. Once he rang the doorbell, he might have a door slammed in his face or be forced to endure a well-aimed, double-barrel verbal barrage from the Hollisters.

No sense in delaying the inevitable.

The chimes had barely faded before the door swung open. Mr. Hollister, looking thinner and grayer, greeted him with a brief "Hello, Logan" and an outstretched hand.

A handshake—that was better than having a door slammed in his face.

Logan followed his former father-in-law into the living room, bracing himself to meet Vanessa's mother—but he and Mr. Hollister were the only ones there.

"Sit down, Logan." Mr. Hollister motioned to the couch. "Mrs. Hollister won't be joining us tonight."

Logan unbuttoned his coat, mindful that the older man hadn't offered to take it, or to hang it up for him. It appeared he would have only a brief meeting with Mr. Hollister. "I'm sorry I won't have a chance to say hello to her."

"I thought it was best." Vanessa's father settled into a leather recliner, but Logan had no impression that the older man relaxed. "I'm unclear as to why you wanted to talk with us."

"Colonel Hollister, the first thing I want to do is to apologize for hurting your daughter. To tell you that I'm sorry our marriage ended with a divorce." Logan sat straight and tall, maintaining eye contact with his former father-in-law. "I've regretted what happened every day since Vanessa and I walked away from each other."

His apology was met with a tilt of Mr. Hollister's head and a slight raise of his gray eyebrows. Logan would keep talking, then.

"And I also want to say I've never stopped loving Vanessa. I'm not the same man I was eight

417

years ago—I'm not even the same man that I was six months ago. I've come to ask your permission to marry Vanessa again."

His request seemed to plunge into a silence where there was no echo. There was certainly no response from Mr. Hollister. The man didn't even acknowledge he'd heard the last statement.

"I also wanted to apologize to you, sir, and to Mrs. Hollister, if she was here. I know eloping with Vanessa the first time was wrong."

"That's all well and good, Logan. But all of this is history."

Had anything he said met with Vanessa's father's approval? Logan had no idea. But he had to keep going.

"I still love Vanessa. I want to reconcile with her, if she'll still have me. I've never stopped loving her. But before I say anything to her, I wanted to do the right thing this time. I wanted to come and talk to you . . . and to Mrs. Hollister. I'd like your permission to marry your daughter. Again."

Mr. Hollister rose to his feet, coming to stand before Logan, who rose to meet him.

"My daughter's heart was broken when your marriage ended, Logan. I'm not saying you were solely responsible for what happened. But how do I know you won't hurt my daughter again? Why should I believe you're a changed man, Logan?"

"Fair enough, sir." Logan closed his eyes,

imagining standing before God's mercy seat—undeserving of grace, but desiring it all the same. It was the same with this man, the father of the woman he'd walked away from. He didn't deserve mercy—but he needed it.

"When I married Vanessa the first time, I thought I was helping her—but I realize now I was being selfish. Yes, I loved her, but helping her was more about finding a way to get what I wanted." Logan struggled to express everything he'd learned about himself. "I said I was changed . . . but I know I'm not perfect. I don't want to hurt Vanessa ever again. But I'm wise enough to know I will. When we had problems last time, we never asked for help. That won't happen this time. With God's help, your daughter won't suffer a broken heart again because of my words or actions."

The room seemed to pulse with the force of his words. Mr. Hollister's face might as well have been carved in stone. The cuckoo clock began to chime the hour, the faint notes of "Edelweiss" playing in the background. If this was a waiting game, Logan wasn't certain who would win.

"I've always liked you, Logan."

Mr. Hollister's words caused tears to glaze Logan's eyes, so he could no longer clearly see the other man's face. When he had expected anger and judgment—and rightly so—Vanessa's father offered him affirmation?

"I did not like how you and Vanessa married.

But I saw potential in you—and in your marriage. I've followed your career through the years. You've made a name for yourself. Been successful—and I'm not surprised. Put that same kind of effort into your marriage."

Was Mr. Hollister saying—?

"Call me old-fashioned, but I do believe the husband is called to love his wife sacrificially. To live with her in an understanding way. That doesn't happen overnight. I challenge you to think of learning to understand Vanessa as a blessing—not a burden. Forget all those men-are-from-Mars-women-are-from-Venus jokes. We're all made in God's image. Ask him to help you love Vanessa in the right way."

"Yessir."

"So, you want to remarry my daughter?"

"With your blessing, sir."

"You have it, son." Mr. Hollister clasped Logan's hand again in a firm handshake, accompanied by a knowing smile. "Of course, you still have to convince my daughter to say yes."

"I do. I'm flying to Denver tomorrow morning to see Vanessa."

"That confident I'd say yes?"

Logan exhaled. "Hopeful—that's all. Hopeful."

"You realize we need to bring another person into this conversation?"

"Yes, sir."

Mr. Hollister excused himself, leaving Logan

cooling his heels for almost twenty minutes until he reappeared with Vanessa's mother.

Logan rose to his feet again. "Good evening, Mrs. Hollister."

"Hello, Logan."

"I told my wife why you were here, Logan. But I thought you might want to tell her yourself."

Logan waited until Mrs. Hollister took a seat in a smaller chair beside her husband, guarded on one side by a huge quilting loom and a large floor lamp. Was he supposed to say something first, or wait until Vanessa's mom asked him questions?

"So my husband tells me that you want to propose to our daughter . . . again."

"Yes, ma'am, I do." They could probably hear him when he tried to swallow the lump in his throat. "And I would love to have your blessing before I do."

"I'm going to be honest with you."

Logan braced himself. He deserved whatever Mrs. Hollister threw at him.

"I hated it when you and Vanessa eloped—I always considered it a huge mistake. But what you didn't know—" A subtle change came over Mrs. Hollister's voice. "—is that I was also very saddened when you both divorced. As young as you were, as wrong as the elopement was, I wanted your marriage to work."

What was he supposed to say now?

"Before I can give you my blessing, I want to

apologize for not being more supportive, more loving. I'll try to be a better mother-in-law the second time around."

"If Vanessa will have me."

Mr. Hollister rejoined the conversation, a wide grin on his face. "Well, let's pray, shall we? God's in this. We'll ask him to go before you and prepare Vanessa's heart for your proposal."

"I would love to pray with both of you." Logan crossed the room, joining hands with Vanessa's parents.

"Thank you for being brave enough to come talk to us, Logan." Vanessa's father chuckled. "Quite honestly, I'm not sure which requires the greater courage—talking to us or facing our daughter."

THIRTY-TWO

Life's greatest happiness is
to be convinced that we are loved.
—VICTOR HUGO (1802–1885), FRENCH
POET AND NOVELIST, FROM *LES MISÉRABLES*

"What are you doing here?"

The sound of Vanessa's voice jerked Logan awake.

Not good. Not good at all. He forced his eyes open, trying to focus on his ex-wife, who was shadowed by the light in the apartment hallway. He blinked away the grittiness of sleep as a yawn interrupted his attempt to say *hello* or *good evening*—something that sounded coherent.

"Never mind." Vanessa shook her head. "I don't want to know why you're dozing outside my apartment. I don't care."

She turned her back on him, setting down a reusable bag overflowing with a loaf of bread and a bag of potato chips, and fitting her key in the lock with a soft scrape of metal against metal.

Logan hadn't come this far to be brushed off with an "I don't care"—and he hoped Vanessa didn't mean it. He scrambled to his feet, grabbing the bag before Vanessa had a chance to pick it back up.

"Let me get this for you."

"I can manage just fine—"

He moved a few steps closer, nudging the door open with his shoulder. "I insist."

Vanessa had to back up—or go almost nose-to-nose with him.

She backed away.

Vanessa was home, and they were both inside her apartment. But he better talk fast—before she reclaimed her groceries. Repeated that she didn't care. And proved it by shoving him out the door.

"You asked me what I was doing here." He deposited the bag onto the dining room table. "Your father gave me permission to come."

Now he had her attention.

"Excuse me?" She stopped unbuttoning her coat. "When did you talk to my father?"

"Earlier last night, before I flew from Great Falls to Denver."

"You were in *Montana?*"

"Yes." Logan risked moving a few small steps closer to Vanessa. "I had some business to attend to with your father."

She focused on the last two buttons on her coat. "I can't imagine what that would be—"

"I asked him if I could marry you."

"You asked . . ." Her voice trailed off, the coat slipping from her shoulders onto the floor.

"I wanted to do things right this time."

Only a few feet separated them, but Logan held his ground. Vanessa's brown eyes were locked on him, wide with questions, her long hair half hidden beneath a knit cap, the ends loose around her shoulders.

"There is no 'this time,' Logan."

"That's where I hope you're wrong, Vanessa. I fell in love with you when I was eighteen—and I've never stopped loving you. Marrying you was the craziest thing I ever did—and the best decision of my life. And I've regretted losing you every day since the divorce."

His words hung suspended between them as he waited for Vanessa to say something . . . to say she was willing to give them a second chance . . .

"I can't . . ." Her lips twisted, trembling around the words that stalled all of Logan's admissions of love. His dreams for their future. "You're saying everything I wanted to hear years ago . . . and now I'm scared. How can I trust you . . . ?"

"I deserve that—I know I broke your trust." Any hope of a future hinged on being honest with each other. "I asked you to marry me. I told you that I loved you—and then my actions didn't back up my words. Yes, I wanted you—but I wanted to chase storms more."

His words seemed to wound Vanessa, causing her to back away.

"I was wrong . . . immature—I got all caught up in my dream, and I forgot how much you wanted to stay in one place. I didn't listen to you like I should have."

"Stop, Logan. There's no sense in trying to fix our marriage. Let's just admit we got married too young."

Even as she backed away from him, Logan saw the faintest glimmer of longing in her eyes.

"Is that what you really believe, Vanessa? I know I made a lot of mistakes—but marrying you wasn't one of them." He closed the space between them as he spoke. This close to her, when he could just catch a hint of her perfume, desire sparked to life. Didn't she feel the connection between them, too—something that, even after all these years apart, still remained? "We're good together, Vanessa. I don't know how to explain it . . . you temper me. I've been lost without you in my life . . ."

When Vanessa started to protest, Logan wove his fingers through the softness of her hair, pressing his forehead against hers. "Shhh. Don't tell me that you don't heal a part of me that's wounded. I shared my dream with you—and you believed in me. You're the first person to ever listen when I talked about storm chasing. You sat with me on the beach and watched lightning storms . . ."

"I loved those times with you, Logan." Vanessa whispered her admission. "You invited me into your world—I belonged somewhere."

"Tell me you still believe we belong together, Vanessa. Please."

Logan allowed himself the briefest taste of Vanessa's lips, his hands caught in the silky strands of her hair. If she pulled away, he'd stop. But she angled her head, molding her mouth to his, slipping her arms around his neck and pulling him closer.

Logan's kiss was a plea. For forgiveness. For a second chance. His arms embraced her, not in desperation, but with a gentleness that crumbled her defenses. The taste of his mouth familiar, pulling her back to nights together she'd never quite forgotten. No one had ever kissed her like Logan Hollister did.

Vanessa broke away from the sweet enticement of Logan's kiss, hiding her face in the wool material.

"Stop . . . I can't . . . think when you kiss me like that . . ."

Logan found the curve of her neck just below her ear, pressing his lips there so her entire body warmed.

"All I need to know is that you forgive me." Another kiss. "And that you still love me." A third kiss. "And that you'll marry me again."

"Logan, what happened—the divorce—it wasn't all your fault. I'm sorry, too. For not listening to you . . . for being so stubborn. I need your forgiveness, too."

"I know, love. We'll forgive each other. Begin again. Be wiser in how we love each other."

She managed to push him away so she could look in his eyes, which were alight with love—and desire. "You really went to Montana to talk to my father? To ask if you could marry me again? And then flew here?"

"I'm only up for so many questions at a time. I've got a serious case of sleep deprivation. I don't sleep on planes—and you can believe I didn't sleep well the night before I went to see your father."

Vanessa ran her fingers along his face, his jaw scruffy. "Why did you do that, Logan?"

"I've never forgotten what your father said when we told your parents we eloped during spring break."

Vanessa's brow furrowed. "What did he say?"

"He couldn't understand why I had the decency—he said *'the common courtesy, the expected courtesy'*—to ask permission to date you, but I didn't have the same courtesy to ask to marry you." Logan raised her hand to his lips, pressing a soft kiss to her palm that sent tingles along her arm. "This was a chance to right a wrong against your father—and mother."

"What did she say?"

"You are all questions tonight, aren't you?" Logan's words were laced with a chuckle. "Well, she wasn't there at first, but she did join the conversation later—or else I wouldn't be here, I assure you."

"I'm certain that was an interesting conversation between my parents."

"I have both of their blessings—they even prayed with me before I left." A smile curved Logan's lips. "And now, I have a question for you."

"Turnabout is fair play and all that?"

"Not at all." Logan shifted so she was no longer in the warmth of his embrace. "If you'll just stay where you are for one moment, I need to get down on one knee. Although I admit I'm finding it difficult to let you go."

At the words "get down on one knee," Vanessa backed away. "What are you—"

"Have a little patience." He pressed several fingers against her lips, following up with a brief kiss. "I've never done this before—well, in quite this manner."

He stepped back and then lowered himself to one knee, raising her left hand and slipping a ring on her finger, just past the first knuckle. "Vanessa Hollister-Hollister, I knew exactly what I was doing when I asked you to marry me ten years ago—and yet I didn't know how to *stay married*. I'm all in this time. I won't quit. I won't walk away—and if you leave, well, I'll come after you. If I can't figure out how to fix what's wrong, I'll ask for help. Your help. Family and friends' help. God's help. Please, will you trust me enough to marry me again?"

The ring glinted in the overhead light—the oval ruby accented by the two baguette-cut diamonds reminiscent of the faux-ruby in Logan's class ring. Vanessa moved it the rest of the way onto her finger and then knelt down in front of him, pressing her hand against his chest, right where his heart beat.

"Yes, Logan. I want to trust you again. Yes, I'll marry you again."

"When?"

She laughed—pushing away from him. "When?" She'd expected another intoxicating kiss, not another question.

"Yes—when will you marry me? I think the first week in April sounds good—a beach wedding in Destin."

She couldn't hold back another laugh. "Who told you?"

"Mindy did—and before you go thinking I'm proposing so the Henderson Park Inn wedding doesn't go to waste—it's not about that at all."

"I said I trust you, Logan. Do you really want to pick up on the wedding I'd started planning when I was engaged to someone else?"

"I want to marry you—period. If you want to do something else, that's fine. We'll do whatever you want to do, and we'll pay off the bill from that, too."

"To be honest, I never talked to Ted about the Henderson Park Inn. I stopped there one afternoon and thought it would be such a lovely place for a wedding . . . started dreaming out loud with Mindy and the assistant wedding coordinator . . ."

Logan stood, pulling her back into his arms. "Want to know what I think?"

"Yes."

"The inn is perfect for our wedding."

"Why do you say that?"

"Don't you remember talking about re-creating our wedding one day—having a beachside ceremony?"

"We did say that, didn't we?"

"Here's our chance, love."

"Then, Mr. Hollister, it looks like we're getting remarried in a few weeks."

THIRTY-THREE

Forgiveness is the giving,
and so the receiving, of life.
—GEORGE MACDONALD (1824–1905),
SCOTTISH MINISTER AND AUTHOR

How had this evening morphed into a bridal shower?

Vanessa tugged against Caron's hand, coming to a stop in the Hollisters' kitchen.

"I don't feel right about this."

"What's wrong?"

"I mean . . . first your parents host the rehearsal dinner—taking us all out to eat at the Crab Trap in Destin."

"So? Everyone has a rehearsal dinner. And Logan said he took you to the Crab Trap for your first date."

Vanessa closed her eyes, remembering herself at eighteen, so nervous. "That was the first time I tasted fried calamari. I hated it. And Logan kept saying, 'Aren't they good?' But he'd also ordered she-crab soup—and that I did like."

"First dates—aren't they the worst?" Caron grabbed her hand and started pulling her toward the Hollisters' family room. "Now, come on, you're keeping people waiting."

"But I wasn't expecting a . . . a shower."

"We know that." Caron winked at her. "That made it all the more exciting. Logan's out with the guys—nice, clean fun. I think Alex said something about laser tag."

"The guys will love that."

"Come on. Mindy can't stay that late."

"Mindy's here? With the baby?"

Vanessa rushed past Caron into the room, only to stop short again. Her mother and Logan's mother were there. And Julie. And Mindy, with her newborn daughter, Alena. The Wrights' daughter, Ruth, sat next to Vanessa's mother. And somehow they'd found Tonya, Christian's mother. A small group—but that was perfect for Vanessa.

Except for the pile of gifts wrapped in a rainbow of colors matching the flowers in the bouquet of Gerbera daisies she'd carry tomorrow, the room looked the same as it usually did. No streamers or paper wedding bells or BRIDE-TO-BE banner. Vanessa needed to thank someone—probably Caron—for her restraint.

And then she noticed the table with a three-tiered stand of cupcakes, decorated with dollops of creamy white icing and sugar monograms, wrapped in lace cups. Behind the table positioned on an easel was a large framed collage. Photos of Logan and her filled the frame: photos from high school, including their graduation picture and even one of them on the back of Logan's motorcycle.

Photos taken this week while they'd played at Big Kahuna's Water & Adventure Park with their wedding party and guests. While she and Logan clambered onto Jet Skis to go riding in the Gulf. While they walked along the beach, holding hands—and then Logan picked her up and ran into the water with her, laughing. While the two of them sat next to each other in the Hollisters' backyard, enjoying the shrimp boil Logan's parents had hosted earlier that week for friends and family.

"Surprise!" everyone shouted together, causing tears to fill Vanessa's eyes.

"Come on in and sit down. We've been waiting for you!" Mindy patted the cushion next to her, cradling her sleeping daughter in her arms.

"Only if I can hold little Alena."

"Open your presents first." Mindy snuggled the baby closer. "Then you can hold her."

"Deal."

Vanessa leaned close to her friend, lowering her voice to a whisper. "I'm not certain how to do this. I hate being the center of attention. And now everyone's watching me."

"Just consider it practice for tomorrow." Mindy tucked the lavender blanket closer to Alena's body. "For now, just open the presents, look surprised, and say thank you."

"Is that all?"

"Yes. See? Simple."

Her mother and Mrs. Hollister sat on the love seat across from her, both looking as happy as the mother of the bride and the mother of the groom should. Looking like friends. She and Logan had deprived their parents of this opportunity with their first marriage—but she wouldn't think about that now. No. She'd do what Mindy had suggested. She'd say thank you to God for this second chance—for all of them.

As she opened the presents, Vanessa realized Mindy was right about gratefulness being the best thing. And she didn't have to fake that emotion.

Of course, Mindy and Caron made her want to hide under the couch cushions by giving her lingerie. Feminine, yes . . . but still, opening the packages in front of Logan's mother and her own mother had her fumbling with the ribbons and then stuffing both items back into the boxes as she mumbled "Thank you" under her breath.

Ruth presented her with one of Mrs. Wright's paintings—a view of sailboats out on the Gulf. Her thank-you had to be forced past the lump in her throat. Tonya gave her a favorite cookbook, and Julie had bought her a crystal vase, with the instructions that Logan was supposed to keep it filled with flowers at all times. Logan's mother presented her with a delicate blue handkerchief as Vanessa's "something blue," explaining that Logan's grandmother had carried it on her wedding day, as well as a gift certificate to a salon for a massage.

"I don't know if you like massages, Vanessa. But I love them. They're a great way to relieve stress." Logan's mother seemed to be apologizing for her gift.

"I've never had a massage before—but thank you. This sounds wonderful."

Her mother offered her present to Vanessa last— a large box, wrapped as only her mother could do it. The edges sharp and tight. The metallic blue lines matching. Beneath several layers of white tissue paper, Vanessa discovered a quilt.

"Mom . . . this is exquisite."

Vanessa ran the tips of her fingers over the top of the quilt, entranced by the maroons and golds against the snow-white background of the double wedding ring pattern.

"How did you find the time to do this?"

Her mother's eyes shimmered with tears. "I, um, I started the quilt when you and Logan were married the first time. I'm sorry to say I didn't give it the attention it deserved."

Vanessa pressed the folds of the quilt to her face. Her mother had made this for Logan and her back when their marriage was her "worst mistake ever"?

A few moments later, she found her voice. "Thank you for finishing it."

"It's family tradition." Her mother pressed her

hand to her face. "I'm embarrassed to admit that was the only reason I started the quilt. And it gave me something to do while your father was deployed . . . but then I put it away."

"I understand." Vanessa folded the quilt back into the box, imagining how she and Logan could snuggle beneath it—and hoping the heat radiating across her neck and face wasn't a telltale sign of the direction of her thoughts. "I can't wait to show it to Logan."

"I thought it would be fun to use your high school colors. If you want something different . . . a different pattern . . . or colors . . ."

"No. No. This is perfect, Mom. Perfect."

In less than twenty-four hours, she'd become Mrs. Logan Hollister again.

Vanessa Hollister-Hollister-Hollister.

A soft laugh escaped Vanessa's lips. It was a good thing she liked her last name, because she was going to be stuck with it—in triplicate.

"It's late. Are you going to be able to sleep tonight?" Her mother came up behind her, resting a hand on her back as they both looked at the photo collage still positioned in the family room. The sound of laughter and conversation, along with the clink of dishware being washed, floated in from the kitchen where Julie and Caron helped Logan's mom clean up from the surprise bridal shower.

"I need to. It's nice of the Hollisters to let us stay here this week, isn't it?"

"Very nice." Her mother smoothed the sides of her hair, which she'd fashioned into a chignon. "Your father is resting better here than he would in a hotel."

"He looks good, too."

"He's stopped complaining about the new diet. And now that we're walking together, well, he doesn't complain about that too much anymore. We've even talked about getting a tandem bike come summer."

"A tandem bike?" Vanessa tried to imagine her parents riding a two-seater.

"Vanessa, I wanted to say something to you before the wedding—in private." Her mother glanced over her shoulder, as if ensuring they were still alone.

"O-kay." Vanessa chewed her bottom lip. What could her mom want to talk about? She was twenty-eight, too old for "the talk." And besides, her mother hadn't even tried to have that conversation after she and Logan eloped.

"I know it's ten years too late, but I wanted to explain . . . and to apologize."

"Explain what?"

"About why I kept insisting you go back to Colorado with me when your father deployed—the year after you graduated from high school." Her mother seemed to search for words. "This is harder than I expected. I'm not one to discuss family problems—"

Family problems? As far as she knew, her parents never had a fight.

"Quite honestly, by the time we moved to Florida, I was worn out. And the thought of a deployment, so soon after we'd just moved again . . . well, I was angry. The military had promised us a four-year assignment. Your father and I argued about it—a lot. I wanted him to figure out some way to get out of the deployment, and he kept insisting it was his job. His duty. When he went overseas I even threatened that I wasn't sure I'd be waiting when he got home."

"Mom!"

"We never really separated. We managed to talk things out long-distance." Her mother paced a few steps back and forth. "But I was so caught up in my problems I didn't support you—before you were married. Or after." Her mother released a shuddery breath. "And for that I am so, so sorry."

Vanessa searched for something to say, but her mother's confession upended her understanding of who her mother was.

"I wish you'd told me all this back then."

"I was the mom. I took care of the family, Vanessa. I wasn't going to burden you with my problems." Her mother's eyes swam with tears. "I realize we should have talked about the move— all of them—more as a family. Maybe then . . ."

"Maybe then I wouldn't have eloped?"

"I deserve that. But it's not what I'm saying. I'm sorry for not being the mom I should have been before you married Logan—and after you married him. And I am so thankful you and he are getting married again."

What more could her mother say? And hadn't they both made mistakes—and hurt each other in the process?

Vanessa hugged her mother. "I forgive you, Mom. And I'm sorry, too. Tomorrow is about all kinds of new beginnings."

THIRTY-FOUR

The moments of happiness we enjoy
take us by surprise. It is not that we seize
them, but that they seize us.
—ASHLEY MONTAGU (1905–1999),
BRITISH-AMERICAN ANTHROPOLOGIST

Wasn't she supposed to be the one having the meltdown? After all, it was Friday, April third. Her wedding day.

Vanessa wrapped the light cotton robe tighter around her body before rattling the bathroom doorknob again. "Mindy, you cannot lock yourself in the Henderson Park Inn's bathroom. I'm getting married in two hours."

The wooden door muffled her friend's response. Caron and Julie stood nearby. But what were they going to do? Break the door down in their bridesmaid dresses?

"What did she say?" Caron looked ready to find a sledgehammer.

"I don't know." Vanessa pressed her ear against the door. Yes, Mindy was crying again. Or still. "She's probably saying the same thing she's been saying since she put on her matron-of-honor dress: *I am not walking down the aisle. The beach. Whatever. I look horrible.*"

"She looks beautiful." Julie paced the carpeted room, the windows showcasing the Gulf, a glimpse of Vanessa and Logan's upcoming beachfront ceremony. "The color is perfect for her."

"No woman who had a baby two weeks ago feels ready to put on a dress and be in a wedding—even if she's just the matron of honor." Caron pulled Julie to a stop. "Enough pacing."

Vanessa knocked on the door again. "Please, Mindy, just let me in. If you don't want to be in the wedding, fine."

When Mindy opened the door halfway, Vanessa whispered, "Pray," to the other two women and slipped inside.

Mindy had lowered the lid on the toilet and now sat there, still wearing her turquoise dress, her arms wrapped around her waist. All of her makeup—mascara, blush, and foundation—was gone, washed away in a deluge of tears.

Mindy blotted at her face with a wadded-up tissue. "I'm sorry I'm being such a big baby."

"You're not being a big baby." Vanessa knelt on the floor, hugging her friend. "You just *had* a baby."

"And I still look three months pregnant." Mindy choked back a sob.

"No, you don't. That color looks glorious on you. And the style is very flattering." She held up her hand when Mindy started to interrupt. "And I have two options for you to consider for the ceremony."

"What do you mean, two options?"

"Exactly what I said. Options. Choices. As in *take your pick*. This is my wedding day, yes. But I want everyone to be happy—not just me. You've been a wonderful matron of honor. And the truth is, I wouldn't be getting married today if it wasn't for you."

"That's true."

Vanessa brushed the drooping tendrils away from Mindy's face. "So, option number one: if you decide you need to sit out today, that's fine. It's not about the dress. It's about you just having a baby. You're tired. Go ahead and sit with Jett and little Alena. Enjoy the ceremony."

Mindy sniffled, her eyes overflowing with tears again. "Really?"

"Yes. Caron and Julie can manage—"

At last Mindy giggled.

"I know—too funny, right? Look at me—I actually have a wedding party!"

"What's my other option?"

"Option number two: Jett is making an emergency run to pick up another layer of Spanx for you."

Mindy jumped to her feet, causing Vanessa to rock back on her heels. "He is not. That man won't go near a lingerie department—not even for our anniversary."

"He will if the bride asks him to on her wedding day." Vanessa stood. "I told him exactly what to get—pulled a photo up on his cell phone. Brady drove him—after Logan told Brady it was a groomsman's responsibility. They'll be back in half an hour. So which is it? Sitting with your husband and daughter—front row, on the aisle—or slipping on an extra layer of support and being in my wedding?"

"I don't want to miss your wedding—"

"You won't, either way." Vanessa gripped her best friend's shoulders. Lowered her voice. "Think about it. Right now there's a little girl who needs your attention. Sit down, take care of Alena—but come out of the bathroom and nurse her where you can be comfortable. Have some water or some sparkling apple juice. You don't have to make a decision until Jett gets back."

Her mother entered the room designated for the bridal party just as Vanessa and Mindy exited the bathroom.

"Vanessa, you're not in your gown yet."

"There's still time, Mom."

Her ivory gown hung from a padded hanger against one of the windows, backlit by the sun, right where the photographer had hung it earlier to frame it for a photograph. It was one of the gowns she and Mindy had looked at last fall, but she'd left it behind, insisting she'd buy a dress in Denver. Before she broke off her engagement to Ted. And canceled her wedding—without actually canceling it.

And then Caron had found the dress—the exact same dress—on the sale rack in a little boutique in Destin. Another unexpected blessing as they pulled this last-minute wedding together. She'd paid an exorbitant amount to have it cleaned in a rush, but it was worth it. The bodice shimmered with tiny beaded crystals, the same jewels adorning the cap sleeves. The long, layered skirt would flow around her as she walked toward Logan—perfect for a beach wedding.

Her mother touched the loose curls fashioned into a low updo against the nape of Vanessa's neck, a few soft tendrils framing her face. An orange Gerbera daisy was tucked among her curls. "Who did your hair?"

"Julie did." Vanessa nodded toward Logan's teammate. "Do you like it?"

"Yes. You look lovely." Her mother hesitated for a moment. "Your father and I . . . we wanted to give you something for your wedding day."

"Oh, Mom, I wasn't expecting anything else. Not after the quilt . . ."

"Let me finish, Vanessa. Please. Your father and I are happy, very happy, you and Logan are getting married again." Her mother seemed to struggle to find the right words.

As her mother's voice wavered, Vanessa stepped into her embrace. "Thank you, Mom."

"Don't say thank you yet. I haven't given you the gift yet."

"Yes. Yes, you have."

"Well, then . . . here's another gift from your father and me." Her mother handed her a small box wrapped in shiny silver paper and adorned with a small white ribbon.

Vanessa pulled the ribbon and paper away, allowing it to drop to the floor. Inside the small box was a pair of filigree diamond and pearl earrings.

"Mom . . . where . . . ?"

"They were your great-grandmother's—on your father's side."

"Something old . . ."

"Exactly." Her mother held one of the earrings as Vanessa slid the other one on. "You now have something old, something blue—and know the earrings are given with much, much love."

"Thank you, Mom." Once both earrings were in place, she went and looked at herself in the mirror. "I need to go thank Dad."

"He'll know how you feel when he sees you in your gown—when you're ready for him to walk you down the aisle."

Vanessa knew her lips trembled when she smiled at her mother. "I'm so thankful he's here to give me away."

"Me, too, Vanessa. Me, too."

The laughter surprised her.

Vanessa thought she'd stand beside her father and, after seeing Logan waiting for her beneath the wooden arch covered in white fabric that floated in the wind, fight back tears.

But no.

Before she realized what was happening, she laughed—the sound mingling on the Gulf breeze and blending with the notes of the harpist's melody.

"Are you okay?" Her father patted her hand where it lay tucked into the curve of his bent arm.

"I'm fine." Beneath the soft fabric of her gown, her bare toes curled into the still-warm sand. "No. I'm better than that. I'm happier than I ever imagined being."

"It's a perfect evening to get married." Her father kissed her cheek.

"It's a perfect evening to get married . . . to the right man. Again." She hugged her father close. "Thank you for being here, Daddy."

"My pleasure. I'm delighted to walk my daughter down the, um, beach. Now, I'm under strict orders not to keep your groom waiting."

Laughter bubbled forth again. "Who told you that?"

"Logan, of course."

Vanessa knew other brides tried to concentrate on every detail of their weddings. The guests. The music. The surroundings. And yes, all of those things were important. The fact that Brady and Max stood next to Logan, with Rylan acting as best man. How beautiful Julie and Caron looked in their coordinating turquoise dresses, carrying mixed bouquets of pink, yellow, and orange Gerbera daisies, their lacy white shawls flowing around their arms. And how Mindy had gone before her, a smile on her face again, beautiful and confident, thanks to both the extra layer of Spanx and the shawl Jett had thought to purchase all on his own.

But as she walked forward with her father, she only wanted to see one thing—one person. Logan.

He stood facing forward, wearing gray slacks, a gray jacket, the sleeves rolled up, and a brilliant blue tie that matched his eyes. Just like she was, he was barefoot.

When she stood in front of him, Logan leaned forward and whispered, "I thought you'd never get here."

More laughter, this time shared with Logan.

The ceremony was brief, traditional, a repledging of their lives to each other in wholeness and illness, in wealth and poverty, in all God had in store for their lives. Just what she and Logan had planned.

And so, when the minister broke from the script and said, "Logan asked to say a few words," Vanessa couldn't help but interrupt.

"He did?"

Laughter rippled through the thirty-some guests.

"Yes, love. I did." Logan pressed a kiss to her hand, adorned with her engagement ring and wedding band. "I just didn't mention it to you."

Logan could only hope Vanessa forgave him for going off-script with their wedding. While she might think this next part was impromptu, he'd planned and prayed over it for weeks.

He intertwined their fingers. "I love you, Vanessa."

As Max and Rylan crossed the sand and brought the needed items from where they'd hidden them earlier in the day, Logan addressed their friends and family.

"Most of you here know Vanessa and I were married once before when we were eighteen. Yes, I met and fell in love with her when I was a senior in high school. My grandfather, wise man that he was, told me that you either marry when you're young and grow up together. Or you get married when you're older—and you grow up together. I made some mistakes when Vanessa and I got married the first time . . . and I lost her."

"Logan . . ."

He pressed his fingers against her lips, lowering his voice to a whisper so only Vanessa could hear what he said. "Let me do this as your husband, taking accountability for my actions. I know we've talked this all out. We've forgiven each other. And God has forgiven us. But I want to do this. I need to do this."

Max positioned a white wooden chair near Vanessa. Rylan offered her a grin as he set a tall pitcher and basin with a folded towel on the sand and then came and hugged his sister before leading her to the chair.

Once Vanessa was sitting, Logan knelt in front of her. Max stood to one side, holding the microphone so everyone could hear Logan's words. As he spoke, he poured water over Vanessa's bare feet.

"Love is patient. In the past, I was not patient with you. Please forgive me. It is my heart's desire to be patient with you.

"Love is kind. In the past, I was not kind to you. Please forgive me. It is my heart's desire to always treat you and speak to you with kindness.

"Love is not jealous. In the past, I was jealous of other things in your life. Please forgive me. It is my heart's desire to love you freely.

"Love does not brag. In the past I was focused on what I wanted. Please forgive me. It is my desire to celebrate who you are.

"Love is not arrogant. In the past, I was prideful. Please forgive me. It is my desire to be humble and to consider you more important than myself.

"Love does not act unbecoming. My actions toward you have not been a reflection of God's love. Please forgive me. It is my desire to love you in a way that reflects God to the world.

"Love does not seek its own. In the past, I was selfish. Please forgive me. It is my desire to love you in a selfless manner, not seeking my own way.

"Love is not provoked. In the past, I went looking for reasons to be angry. To stay angry. Please forgive me. It is my desire to love you with a merciful heart.

"Love does not take into account a wrong suffered. In the past, I kept an account of my hurts. I held on to grudges. Please forgive me. It is my desire to forgive you—again and again and again. I do forgive you.

"Love does not rejoice in unrighteousness, but rejoices in the truth. It bears all things, believes all things, hopes all things, endures all things. Love never fails.

"I know I will fail you, Vanessa. But I will not quit. I will not walk away.

"I promise to love you as Christ loved the church and gave his life up for her."

As he spoke, Logan bathed Vanessa's feet, washing them clean of the sand that clung to her skin. Then he dried each of her feet with the softness of the white towel, no longer speaking out loud, but praying God would bless them with a new beginning. That God would help him be the husband he longed to be.

When he was finished, he took Vanessa's hands and led her back to stand in front of the minister again.

"Any other surprises?" Even though her words were teasing, he saw how her eyes shimmered with tears.

"No. Not now."

"Logan and Vanessa, you have pledged your lives to each other—again." The minister looked first at Logan and then at Vanessa. "Be wiser this time. Ask for help when times are hard. And they will be. Pray together. Forgive each other. Know God has brought you together—and he will see you through whatever lies ahead."

"He will." Vanessa's affirmation blended with Logan's.

"Logan, you may kiss your bride."

Vanessa turned to face him, the setting sun casting her in a golden glow. Logan cradled her face with his hands, caressing her skin with his thumbs.

"I love you, Vanessa Hollister."

Vanessa covered his hands with hers. "I love you, Logan Hollister—with all my heart, I love you. Thank you for marrying me again."

"Hey!" Brady's voice boomed across the scene. "He said to kiss her—not talk to her!"

Logan leaned his forehead against Vanessa's, who was moving in to meet him. "He did, didn't he?"

"He did, indeed."

Their kiss, woven of love and laughter and renewed promises, was accompanied by applause and cheers and the melody of a harp. The way Vanessa leaned into his embrace, eager to receive him and let the kiss go on, had him tightening his arms around her, drawing her closer.

"Ladies and gentlemen, let me now introduce Mr. and Mrs. Logan and Vanessa Hollister, um, Hollister!"

They broke apart, Vanessa burying her face in his shoulder with a breathless laugh. He caught her up in his arms, twirling her around until she begged him to stop. Then they joined hands and walked down the aisle between the few short rows of seated guests.

"Ready to celebrate, Mrs. Hollister?"

"Absolutely, Mr. Hollister."

THIRTY-FIVE

Love has nothing to do with what you are
expecting to get—only with what you are
expecting to give—which is everything.
—KATHARINE HEPBURN (1907–2003),
ACTRESS

For now, they had Henderson Beach to themselves.

They'd even arrived before the sun made an appearance. As she and Logan walked, they left footprints in the wet sand, not bothering to look back to see the waves erase them. Logan's hand was warm against hers, their fingers intertwined.

He'd woken her with a trio of gentle kisses and a "Come watch the sunrise with me" invitation. Vanessa hadn't hesitated to say yes, slipping into a blue cotton sundress that skimmed her ankles and a light sweater.

"Did you sleep well, Mrs. Hollister?"

A blush heated her skin. "Yes."

He kissed the back of her hand. "I did, too."

She leaned against him, inhaling the fresh scent of the Gulf, watching the sky lighten. "The wedding was beautiful, wasn't it?"

"My favorite part was kissing the bride."

As he swung her in front of him and pulled her

close, she buried her face in the chambray fabric of his shirt. "Logan."

"What?" He nuzzled her neck, his touch sending shivers down her back. "It appeared to me you enjoyed kissing the groom."

"What am I going to do with you?"

"Kiss me again, I hope. That'll keep me happy."

His kiss awoke all of Vanessa's senses, even as she thanked God again for giving them a second chance at loving each other. Logan seemed content with one kiss, settling her close to him, beneath the shelter of his arm, and resuming their morning stroll along the shore. The color of the water was muted, waiting for the sunlight to reveal the vivid greens of the Gulf that earned its title of the Emerald Coast. Vanessa inhaled the scent of salt and surf, savoring the cool touch of the breeze on her face, the strength of Logan's hand on hers.

Logan broke the silence first. "You know, we need to finish talking about a few things."

His words surprised her.

"You sound more serious than I expected for a romantic early morning walk along the beach."

"I admit you're a distraction, Mrs. Hollister—" Logan slipped his arm around her waist. "—but I will force myself to behave for the moment."

"This sounds serious. What's on your mind?"

"The future. Our future."

"I like the sound of that."

"I do, too—but in the midst of our whirlwind

wedding, we haven't really talked about it. Of course, a man can only juggle so many life-changing things at one time."

Vanessa savored the coolness of the waves against her feet. "Logan, we both agreed we're willing to be flexible about what happens next, jobwise. I know you're still trying to decide what comes next with the Stormmeisters—"

"And you're trying to decide about school—"

"And neither of us wants to do a long-distance marriage again."

"Absolutely not."

"But, the reality is, we have five days together—and then the honeymoon is over. You've still got an apartment back in Oklahoma, and I have one in Colorado. And you haven't made a decision about storm chasing."

"I couldn't without talking to you."

The sun's rays broke out golden over the water. "What if I put in my two weeks' notice now and look into subletting my apartment or breaking my lease?"

"You are not upending your life for me. I can move to Denver."

"No, I'll come there."

"No. I've apologized to the team, but that doesn't mean I have to rejoin them."

Vanessa threw her arms around Logan, laughing. "Do you hear us? We're falling all over each other, determined to be so flexible, so willing to make our marriage work this time, we're not talking things out. We're talking over each other."

"You're right."

"We're on our honeymoon."

"Right again."

Vanessa tapped her forefinger against her bottom lip. "How about this?"

"I'm listening."

"We relax. Enjoy being married. We honeymoon."

"Sounds better and better."

"And we talk about our options. Pray. Think about things. We've got time, right?"

"Absolutely. I'm not going anywhere right away, are you?"

"Well, I was thinking about heading back to the bed-and-breakfast."

Logan's grin was slow, the blue of his eyes darkening. "An excellent idea."

"I meant for breakfast, Logan." She tugged at his hand. "I'm hungry."

Logan pulled her up against the length of his body, causing them to stumble backward and the water to splash up onto them.

"So am I, Mrs. Hollister. So am I." He held her so the tide couldn't pull her off balance. "Remember that night when we rescued that boy from drowning?"

"Yes—how could I forget? I'd walked the beach for over an hour, determined to bury all my memories of you in the sand by the time I left."

"Everyone said we were heroes that night—saving his life." He caressed the side of her face with the back of his hand. "But I think . . . I know God used that kid to save us. To bring us back together. I mean, what were the chances?"

"Crazy, right?" Vanessa stood on her tiptoes and kissed her husband, savoring the freedom and safety she found in Logan's arms. "But it's always been like that with you, Logan—and I wouldn't have it any other way."

ACKNOWLEDGMENTS

Not to us, LORD, not to us
but to your name be the glory,
because of your love and faithfulness.
—PSALM 115:1 NIV

My husband, Rob: You've remained true to our wedding vows for thirty-five years—never realizing back then how our lives would be so affected by imaginary characters. Your support is vital to any success I achieve as a novelist.

My children by birth and by marriage: You love me on deadline and off—and lately it's been on . . . on . . . on. Thank you. Thank you. Thank you.

Rachel Hauck: Time to try a series, you said. And then you helped me brainstorm a destination wedding series (three different versions) and the individual books. You. Are. Brilliant.

Susan May Warren: Back in 2010 in the wee small hours of a life-changing morning, you told me I could write fiction. You're still helping me believe and accomplish this dream-come-true.

Rachelle Gardner: My agent and friend—I think I've got it now: *This is publishing, not brain surgery. There's never a reason to panic.* (See, I am listening—because you know your stuff.)

Jessica Wong: Having you as my editor keeps

getting better and better. I am beyond grateful for your expertise and support. And to Katherine Sandell: Thanks for being part of the editing process, too. I appreciated your insights!

Edie Melson: Here's to daily "text prayers"—they made all the difference while I was on deadline.

The My Book Therapy Core Team: Writers who "get" each other. Friends. Prayer warriors. Wise counselors. Yes, that about sums it up.

Randy McDaniel, the Okaloosa County Emergency Management Director: Thank you for fielding my husband's emails and phone calls. (And thank you again to my husband, who also acted as my researcher for this book.) Your information helped me get the details right for when "my" hurricane hit the Panhandle.

Jeni Cherry, the assistant wedding coordinator for the Henderson Park Inn: Thank you for providing so many wonderful details about the location for Vanessa and Logan's destination wedding!

READING GROUP GUIDE

CRAZY LITTLE THING CALLED LOVE
BETH K. VOGT

Paramedic Vanessa Hollister has put her adolescence behind her, including the unwanted label of being the new kid in town over and over again, thanks to her father's military career. She's overcome what her mother called "the biggest mistake of her life" and is planning an elegant destination wedding in Destin, Florida, with her new fiancé. But will the reappearance of her first husband from her *What-were-you-thinking?* teenage elopement disrupt her dream of an idyllic beach wedding?

QUESTIONS FOR DISCUSSION:

1. If you had the chance to plan a destination wedding, what location would you pick? Why?

2. Vanessa starts her senior year of high school at a new school. As part of a military family, Vanessa moved around a lot, perfecting the role of the new girl. What was high school like for you? What were your friendships like during those years?

3. Logan and Vanessa tried to solve a problem by eloping at eighteen. Have you ever made a rash decision—one that looked like a good decision, one that was motivated by good intentions—and then regretted it later?

4. If a friend of yours told you they were planning to elope, what would you say to them?

5. At twenty-eight, Vanessa was still looking for home. How would you define home?

6. Logan and his father were both about providing for and protecting their families—but in two very different ways. How do you look at providing for and protecting your family? How would you help Logan and his dad find common ground?

7. If you could do one thing "for old times' sake," what would you do? Why?

8. Logan, Brady, Max, and Julie were the Stormmeisters—a storm-chasing team. What kind of team have you been part of? What did you learn, being part of a team?

9. To help her grow closer to God, Vanessa started writing her prayers in a journal. What helps you draw closer to God?

10. There are often Voices of Truth in novels: key subcharacters who speak vital truths to the hero and heroine. For Logan, it was Pop Pop, his grandfather—and sometimes his sister, Caron. For Vanessa, it was Mindy and Mrs. Wright. Who is your Voice of Truth?

Center Point Large Print
600 Brooks Road / PO Box 1
Thorndike, ME 04986-0001 USA

(207) 568-3717

US & Canada:
1 800 929-9108
www.centerpointlargeprint.com